Joe Wicklund

THE
LAND
OF
THE
LONG
SHADOW

Books by Oliver Lange

DEFIANCE—AN AMERICAN NOVEL (formerly titled VANDENBERG)
INCIDENT AT LA JUNTA
RED SNOW
NEXT OF KIN
THE LAND OF THE LONG SHADOW

THE LAND OF THE LONG SHADOW

Oliver Lange

Seaview Books
NEW YORK

In Chapter 10, George Gutierrez's notes are drawn, in rearranged form, from the *Encyclopedia Brittanica* (Chicago: Encyclopedia Brittanica, Inc., 1976), and the excerpt from Isaiah is taken from *The Jerusalem Bible* (New York: Doubleday, Reader's Edition, 1971).

Manufactured in the United States of America.

FIRST EDITION

Seaview Books/A Division of PEI Books, Inc.

Library of Congress Cataloging in Publication Data

Lange, Oliver.
      The land of the long shadow.

      I. Title.
PS3562.A485L3   813'.54   80-54523
ISBN 0-87223-683-8   AACR2

Designed by Tere LoPrete

This is for Attila Dogruel
(died 1980)

and some cherished Santa Fe *compadres*:
King Jordan
Dave Neumann
Bill Slenger

. . . our great southwest remains a classic fantasy of the contemporary American psyche. Via tv and the ubiquitous "ranchito"-type of real estate advertising, the west has come to represent one of the last escapes from the sterility of over-crowded suburbia, or, worse, the attrition of inner-city habitation. We must have our dreams . . . and part of the American myth is that no one of us will be denied our own haven or sanctuary, a "little place of our own." Sun Belt Country is the latest sobriquet that has been applied to the southwest. It is an accurate enough term.

But the southwest is being increasingly modified by development. The newcomer or retiree, fresh from California or the eastern seaboard, may wear a Stetson and high-heeled boots but he insists that his house be air-conditioned. If the Rockies or the wide open spaces of the living desert are too lonely, he surrounds himself with sub-communities and even entire towns of fellow escapees, until an environment is created that is at all costs comprehensible: another Westchester, another Thousand Oaks, or an Oak Park.

And again the dream, once captured and held in the hand, vanishes. The west, like any other symbol, must be made livable in jet-age terms, which is to say it must be understandable to the emigré from New York, Chicago, or Los Angeles, or for that matter London, Tokyo, or Teheran. One cannot live with an abstract image. It must be made familiar, even with the help of a microwave oven and cable television piped into the den.

Thus the myth, now vanquished, becomes palatable.

—"Imprints on American Lifestyles,"
A. R. Dornmeyer, M.D., F.A.P.A., in
TRENDS, A Journal of Social
Psychology (Boston: Concord Press, 1980)

THE
LAND
OF
THE
LONG
SHADOW

ONE

In his mind there is a memory, a faded and ancient recollection that is almost like an old dream—something that might never have happened, really—but he knows that this was never a dream, it *did* happen.

The memory goes so:

It is a Saturday. Such a Saturday as happened often enough during that decade, but this particular day takes place sometime during the long hot summer of 1936. They are in a town, one of those many places they came to during their years of endless wandering, to stay a week, a month, three months, rarely longer, before the urge to drift on caught them up, and then they would pack their gear into the truck and begin moving again.

Outside, old wooden buildings front on streets that are baked bone-dry under a sun so fierce that everything looks seared and shimmery. Nor is it much cooler here in the darkness. He is eleven years old.

He is sitting between his father and Uncle Walter, who is not really an uncle, though the boy has always called him this. What the three of them are experiencing is part of a ceremony, an old and established rite. Very often when they are living in a town, such Saturday afternoons are set aside as a special time, of both discomfort and deep pleasure. In the darkness they sit on cramped hardwood seats, staring up with blasted eyes at the flickering white light of the screen, surrounded by noise and a rich assortment of smells. Margarined popcorn, in twisted paper cones. The faintly acrid odor of an assemblage of not very clean bodies crowded together. And, on his left, the funky cayuse rankness of Walter, who is not given to changing his button-front cotton longjohns until the old man himself can't stand them—and that may take months—while on his right there is his father, whose odors are intermixed: tobacco, whiskey, the sharp tang of witch hazel, with maybe a dash of coal oil, all clean smells, the way wet mud caked on boots can somehow smell raw and clayey and good.

Sitting there, the boy feels a marvelous security. Whatever, his father and Walter will take care of him. He knows this. Their presence on either side of him is familiar and dominant, in the way that other aromas—sweet Wrigley's, Milky Ways, jujubes, and licorice—are powerfully overcome by the occasional sharp pungency of the whiskey his father and Uncle Walt tote in pint bottles stashed in hip pockets and which they nip at surreptitiously. For this is a ritual that reads two ways, or so they claim—his father tells him that if they will bring him here on Saturdays, then it is only fair that they bring their own pleasure, too.

But that is a story, and the boy knows it. The teasing about their being so bored they must bring refreshment, and about their spending the afternoon in this way merely to please him, is just another part of the ceremony. He knows that his father, who is the most easygoing and patient man in the world, really likes the movies, but that his way of joking is to pretend disinterest.

Walter, on the other hand, is given to complaining in a low, bitter sotto voce—a sort of ongoing sour commentary—about the hardness of the seats, the goddamned flies that buzz in the dark, and the seemingly endless come-ons that are projected on the enormous screen looming above them . . . all the trivia that precedes the main features. Bingo Nite on Mondays, unaccompanied ladies half price, and Walter, who can barely scrawl his name and cannot read at all, begins muttering about infernal nonsense and why don't they get on with it? There are sing-alongs with a floating pingpong ball on Wednesdays, and on Saturday nights there is the greatest enticement of all: give-aways of precious flatware and dishes, a veritable Comstock lode of "costly additions to the home" that can be gotten for the price of admission, so that, if a family attended for several years straight, it might perhaps end up with a collection of stuff worth, say, in these dustbowl Depression days, in the neighborhood of five dollars.

When all this is finally done with, there are previews of coming attractions. These go on for a long time, too, and like the singalongs and Bingo Nite they are of minor interest to the boy. Eleanor Powell tapdancing in widelegged satin slacks, skipping her way to fame amid the splendor of Busby Berkeley backdrops. Nelson Eddy and Jeannette McDonald, beautifully costumed, bewigged, and powdered, stare with salamander intensity into each other's eyes, and sing . . . and sing. They are America's Favorite Sweethearts—it says so in an announcement that is flashed right on the screen—and the boy wonders about this. Uncle Walter unlimbers his pint. Slouches farther down in the uncomfortable seat. Murmurs to himself, but loudly enough to be heard above the soundtrack, "Is this shit gonna go on *forever* . . . can anybody answer me that?"

But the boy knows a secret about Walter, too, and it is that the old man loves every minute of it. The come-ons, the previews, the serialized episodes of Flash Gordon and Buck Rogers. For it is Walter who, nervously fretful, is most likely to pester them earlier, as they are getting ready to leave, "Come on, can't you folks shake a leg? If we got to waste hard cash on such garbage, we might as well git our money's worth."

They sit in the darkness, to watch the likes of Tom Mix and Bill Boyd and relative newcomers like John Wayne and Gene Autry, who sing and play guitars whenever they are not involved in fistfights. The fights appeal to a dark and powerful side of the boy's nature. He has been raised gently by these two men. Has in fact never been struck, nor has even seen a blow struck in anger. Perhaps understandably then, he is intrigued to discover that a problem can be solved or a solution found in an act of physical violence. He is interested to see that Autry and Wayne hold up so well, and that their splendidly tailored cowboy outfits, rather incredibly, never get mussed even during the most vicious barroom fracas. Moreover, when time is of the essence, they think nothing of leaping from a second-story balcony straight into the saddle of a horse waiting patiently below. The first time Walter sees this he croaks indignantly, "Why, that ain't possible! I never seen no cowboy would dare a fool stunt like that. Git hisself a pair of *heuvos* built like pancakes. Real cowboy might be dumb enough to try that once. But I reckon when he was able to walk again he'd think twice before tryin' it a second time."

From noon until three . . . a whole world of entertainment; adults fifteen cents, kids a dime. The heat and flies and the smell of the audience are free.

Sometimes the fare is varied. Bela Lugosi as a cloaked and loony vampire with a horrific leer and mascaraed eyes that smolder like volcanic pits. Fearful films of zombies in the far-off Caribbean, resurrected from vermin-infested graves to lurch toward a wide-eyed blond heroine whose vocal equipment is, especially in the upper registers, indefatigable. She is caught, trapped, and must choose between being forcibly hauled away (probably to some kind of ghastly sacrifice involving a stone altar and rusty butcher knives, the boy thinks: he has seen similar films and knows that such behavior is commonplace in foreign countries) or else throwing herself from the stony abutment of a grim castle that perches fortresslike above an island cliffside whose base is lashed by a foaming, turbulent surf. Like steadfast mailmen not to be kept from their appointed task, the zombies home in on the cowering blonde, put off neither by her ear-splitting yells nor by six rounds fired at point blank range from the hero's revolver. Uncle Walter whispers admiringly, "Goddamn, looky there! You can see them bullets goin' right *in*, and there ain't even no blood comin' outa that big nigger!"

But the westerns were what the boy loved best. Wherein good triumphed and evil was punished, because that was the way it had to be. Where a hero's Colt Single-Action never emptied, to the consternation of entire populations of Indians, who were shot off the bare backs of galloping mustangs into the dust. Where the usefulness of a white woman counted for so little that the boy could not help but wonder why she was there at *all,* except that in any saga she provided elements of wilting helplessness, an unassailable virtue, and an absolutely incredible talent for getting herself into trouble . . . not necessarily in that order. The boy pondered this. He ended up confounded. It seemed to him that she always twisted or interrupted the main thread of the story. The greatest enigma was that villains—these included bandits, cutthroat Mexicans, drunkards, and reliably treacherous savages—always *wanted* her, who could tell why? It puzzled him even more that they wanted her as badly as they apparently did, to the point of obsession. They thought nothing of resorting to the worst conceivable atrocities, including murder, arson, and kidnapping, in order to get their dirty hands on her, while she, of course, like a lollygagging, simpering ninny (Uncle Walter's words), made everything worse by getting lost, falling off her horse, or locking herself in a ranchhouse at night (anybody *knew* that was asking for it), so that to her list of failures was added the final condemnation: she had to be protected!

A really inept heroine could not leave the side of her bedridden, dying father to go get the mail over at the post office, a walk—for any normal person—of perhaps no more than two minutes at most, without falling down in the street at least once and spraining an ankle, or suffering great hosannahs of derision and lust from a crowd of drunkards loitering on the portal of the local saloon, along with a proposition from the banker that had something to do with his delaying a foreclosure, whatever that was, if she would *do* something for him. Very likely, she might also be splattered by mud from a herd of longhorns some rowdy cowboys had driven through town. To the boy, it seemed that walking over to the post office every day was more trouble than it was worth, and maybe she ought to have sent someone else. Uncle Walter would mutter, "Why buy a cow when buttermilk's cheap?" The boy didn't exactly understand what this meant, but from the scornful tone he sensed that the old man was on his side in the heroine department.

But then the hero appeared, and he looked so decent and fine on his horse compared to all the low, unshaven types that it was obvious he was no one to fool with. He always smiled and was friendly and courteous, even with the worst saloon drunks and gunfighters and gamblers, who teased and mimicked him behind his back, and he never seemed to mind, even when he ordered a sarsaparilla at the bar, and then they'd tease him about this, too. He always acted like he was waiting for a chance to sing a song or play his guitar. Or if the heroine was mudspattered, he would get down from his horse and brush her off, or sometimes even set her up on the back of his big palomino and ride her to the post office for the mail. Then there would be only sullen grumbling from the crowd on the saloon portal.

The boy got the idea that the hero was, like his own father, the most patient man in the world.

But part of it was that he got angry. This always happened sooner or later, and the boy, and Walter, too, waited for this. Anger fascinated the boy, because it was a mystery he had never felt, only suspected. Walter was always angry. His father, never. He himself was mild-natured, yet for him the best part of whatever story they watched had to do with when the hero finally got fed up and lost his temper. Then everybody watched out, especially if some of the cowpokes who were inclined toward malicious mischief had kicked his guitar into kindling. That meant real trouble.

However, it was the heroine who always triggered the worst calamities. If she just sat *still*, she got into a fix. Then she would look around with a kind of vacant, cow-eyed expression, as though she couldn't for the life of her figure out how she'd put her foot in it again. It was her way of asking for protection.

Which the hero provided. But if he had his wits about him, the protection was of a temporary nature and was never meant to be confused with permanent—or, worst of all, romantic—companionship. All that romantic business was usually kept for his horse, and more than one mount had its velvety muzzle bussed by the hero before they rode away into a fading sunset, probably for some richly deserved peace and quiet by themselves out on the solitary plains. It was generally acknowledged that a really efficient heroine—that is to say, a thoroughly dimwitted, *inefficient* one—could create enough problems to keep a hero working overtime seven days out of the week, at the same time causing the death of every wrongdoer for miles around, as well as the expenditure of thousands of rounds of ammunition. The boy figured that even heroes wore out.

When the matinee was over, they emerged into the real world outside, stiffnecked and headachey from sitting so far up front. "That was fun," he said.

"Good," his father said. "Not much on movies myself."

"You laughed," the boy said. "I saw you laughing."

"I did?" His father frowned, then shook his head, pretending puzzlement. "I don't recall laughing."

It was late afternoon but still blistering hot, with a brightness that after the dark of the theater hurt their eyes and made them squint.

In that blinding light his father's pale hair under the Stetson looked even snowier, and as they commenced walking along Main Street the boy reached out and took his hand. A curious trio. The unnaturally tall, strange boy. The father, with his near to albino hair, dragging his crippled leg in the dust, his comfortably baggy trousers held up by both a workbelt and a pair of sturdy galluses—he was never a man to take a needless risk. And Uncle Walter, already old and stooped by then, wearing worn bib overalls, hobbling along beside them, the neck of his bottle protruding from a rear pocket.

THE THING ABOUT holding his father's hand was part of the memory, too. As long as he could remember he had done that. Maybe from the first time he'd been able to get on his feet and walk. The habit lasted.

Now he said, "Pa, what was it really like back then?"

"What was what like, honey?"

"The old-time west. Was it like that movie?"

His father considered this. "Not really."

"It sure looked real to me."

"Roy Aldous Gutierrez, you're a bigger damn fool than your father, and that is goin' some," Walter told him. "All that bullshit was just a lot of actin'."

"Well, then, what *was* it like?" he insisted.

His father looked at him and then smiled. Still holding him by the hand. "The west? Why, Roy, I imagine it must have been kind of like this." He gestured vaguely with his free hand at the hot and broken-down town surrounding them. Weathered buildings of wood or adobe. A few miserable stores, and an old hotel. A spur of railroad siding, and alongside it a small stockyard and some loading pens. Mesquite-covered foothills rising in the near distance. Overhead, the inferno of the sky, with a couple of vultures wheeling in endless circles, their outspread wings motionless as they rode rising thermals. His father said, "Why, sure. We're right here in the middle of it."

"I mean back then."

"Ask Walter," his father said. "He remembers a lot about it. Matter of fact, I remember some myself."

"Well, tell me."

"I guess it was just people living," his father said.

"Could I have been a cowboy?"

"I don't see why not."

"Like one of those gunfighters?"

"There was one gunslinger in the family," Uncle Walter said. "He was enough. Far as I recollect, we never needed another."

The boy's mind was still filled by the movie they had seen that afternoon. "Was he a good or a bad gunfighter?"

Walter said, "That's like askin' if there's a good rattlesnake."

"But did he ever help people?"

"He could never help hisself, so how could he help anybody else? He brought misery to everyone around him."

"Walter," his father said mildly.

"Brought nothin' but trouble on the whole family."

"Walter, let it go," his father said.

But the old man's attention was diverted to a saloon he had been eyeing and which they were approaching. His voice grew wheedling. "Georgie, what d'you say to a couple of cool ones? Git the kid a soda pop."

"Walter, sometimes I believe you can read my mind," his father said. "That's just about the best idea I've heard all day."

"We got any money?"

"Enough," his father said. "Makes a fellow thirsty, watching movies all afternoon."

"You can say that again," Walter agreed.

THE MAN SITS alone in a small apartment drinking wine and smoking a cigarette. When the cigarette is burned to the filter he stares at it, his mind preoccupied, musing, and then, without haste, he lights another. The apartment with its plywood walls and flaked paint is no more than a room really, with a shower stall in the bathroom, a kitchenette that has a two-burner gas jet connected by a rubber tube to an overhead valve, and a sink large enough to contain a frying pan but not much else. Some shelves of books line one wall.

There is in this place the ambience and odor of poverty, of indifferent meals carelessly prepared, the walls filmed with grit, mildew, smogtaste, and oldness, though the building itself is probably not all that old. The windows are grimed and the cotton curtains are sunfaded by years of El Paso's heat and hazy light. Outside, for miles and miles, lies the great border city. It is cheerless enough in the apartment, which seems smaller because of the man—at an emaciated six feet nine inches, he literally verges on giantism—but it provides a certain succor: it is somewhere to hide.

He is mildly drunk by now on the wine, which he pours from a gallon bottle, and is getting there more, thinking his way through to something, a decision, but even now in his drunkenness he understands how his mind is working, and from time to time he smiles to himself as though finding comfort and pleasure in his thoughts. A transistor radio sitting on the open windowsill plays a Beethoven sonata. He puffs at his cigarette and smiles again as he thinks, *it is time to do something.*

Presently he nods in agreement to this, still with that dreamy, wine-laid-back easygoingness. He thinks, *it is time to go,* and then, as though for the first time fully savoring this notion or possibility, he says it out loud: "Roy, you'd best get on back home."

The wine heightens his enjoyment of this concept, and still speaking aloud he explores it further, searching out his feelings about it, weighing it on one side of his mind and then on the other, almost as though it was something he might hold in his hand, turning the thing around this way and that. "Might as well."

He nods again. "You've used up your time here, that's for sure." His mind says, *leastways you got someplace to go back to. That's more than most have these days.*

He helps himself to another glassful of the wine. "Moving. Just moving around, that's all. Always looking to see what's over the next hill, for too many years. And now there is nothing here either. There never was."

He thinks, *after you are done with everything else, I guess home is where you go back to because then that's all there is left. There's nothing here.*

The very idea—going back—begins to sink in. The idea is almost like a dare . . . one of those extemporaneous thoughts that at first seem foolish or even crazy but which, once they take hold, become logical and sensible. Something that in the beginning looks ridiculous but which, as it is turned over inside the mind, attains a purpose . . . such an obvious thing, as though it had been there all the time.

He thinks, *why, sure. Now why didn't I think of it a long time ago?*

He uses the tiny bathroom to urinate, pours another drink, and wanders about the room, still smiling, then finally pauses at the table where he eats his meals, its top covered with cheap imitation-wood-grain plastic that has been chipped and nicked and faded by use. Walks a fore- and middle-finger slowly across its top and speaks again: "You swore you'd never go back there. Not after what happened last time . . . and not alone."

As if that made any difference. How many times have you said that before?

"Nothing there."

There is less here, his mind tells him.

In his drunkenness there is a clarity. Something happens to a man who lives alone too much. He knows he is slowly going crazy with loneliness. Knows that love must exist, but not for him. He smiles to himself somewhat ruefully, and says, "Why, shucks, Roy, if anybody loved you, you wouldn't know it anyway."

And again the question, *but why go back now?*
The answer is simple.
He thinks, *because it is time.*

BENEATH HIS BED there is a battered olive-drab footlocker containing some belongings—odds and ends of clothing designed for a climate colder than that of El Paso, and what he calls his "archives."

Now in the late afternoon the locker is dragged out and its lid raised so that he can sort through the latter—foxed and faded quitclaim deeds, certificates, plats, letters, diaries, maps, photographs, documents tied with bits of ribbon or string, which he lays out with care, in tidy piles, on the bed. There is also a turn-of-the-century gold pocket watch that does not work, and, wrapped in a square of flannel, an oiled and loaded .36-caliber Colt cap-and-ball revolver that does. The watch belonged to his father. The pistol to his grandfather, the gunfighter.

The locker contains not just the past. It holds his identity.

Carefully rooting around, he finally locates what he has been searching for. Holds it up to the light striking in through the windows. An old photograph, a silver-halide dry plate, about five by eight inches, scratched and dimmed, of a man and a woman. An antique studio portrait. Highly improbable painted canvas backdrop: waterfall, Tyrolean mountains, sheep grazing by a serene pond.

He searches further. Finds a powerful magnifying glass, and with this carefully scrutinizes the photograph.

Under the convex lens the couple leap closer in sharp detail.

From the small bouquet she holds in her lap it seems likely that the picture was taken on their wedding day. He is a tall, angular, squareshouldered black man, dressed in boots and the squadron blues and insignia of the 10th United States Cavalry. What scalp-collecting Indians in those days called a buffalo soldier, because the Negroid hair had the feel and texture of that animal's pelt.

He is prognathic-jawed, with a piercing, stupid gaze. Marvelously sensual mouth. She looks equally dullwitted, and stares into the camera with black button-eyes and a terrapin expression.

She is dressed in the formal Mescalero garb of that era. Long
pleated skirt of print calico. Three silver-and-turquoise bracelets
adorn her wrists—perhaps part of her dowry—and from her neck
hangs a superb squash necklace. Leg-of-mutton-sleeved blouse
that under careful inspection with the magnifier appears to be
made of some kind of dark velvet. Raven hair, looking almost
varnished, severely parted and drawn into tight side buns.

His name is Tom. Last name Wardner. That much is noted in
faded calligraphy on the back:

> *Thom. & Cora Wardner*
> *Ft. Stanton, Territory of*
> *New Mexico*
> *July 19, 1894*

Fort Stanton is in the southern part of the state, in Lincoln
County—*mostly Sun Belt Country now*, he muses—where the
most famous outlaw in American history, Billy the Kid, once
wrote letters of entreaty to Governor Lew Wallace, begging in
vain for a pardon. For a psychopathic killer, Billy had a clean,
neat script and a forthright literary style. He knew how to plead
his case, but to no avail. Governor Wallace, something of a writer
himself, produced a long novel that was ultimately made into an
even longer movie called *Ben Hur*, and young Billy Bonney, AKA
the Kid, finally went down under a fusillade delivered by Sheriff
Pat Garrett one night on a ranch where the former was hiding
out. Bonney was twenty-one at the time, a small, slender, buck-
toothed youth who occasionally dressed up as a girl for the fun
of it. Feminine or not, he was supposed to have murdered a
white man for each of his years, Indians and Mexicans not being
tallied in the official score.

Tom Wardner, according to Uncle Walter, was a moody and
dangerous drunk, too handy with his fists ever to make a decent
soldier. He took his Army discharge, moved onto the Mescalero
Reservation with his squaw, raised beans, chili, squash, and children, got fat, and died a drunkard's death.

What made their coupling inevitable is by now too remote to
guess at, just as it cannot be accurately said that they were

the simpletons they looked to be in their formal portrait. Their slightly glazed, almost stunned, expressions may have been due to mere shyness or fear on posing before the hooded rosewood box—he standing, she seated, probably with instruments resembling grappling hooks holding their skulls rigidly. For all anyone knows, these two may have been intuitively noble and full of an engaging winsomeness, but this is doubtful. Those were brutal times for a black man and a reservation woman. There is nothing in the photograph to suggest a GI Othello or cooing Pocahontas.

His grandparents. Maternal side. The last of their issue, born in the year 1900, exact day unknown, was an infant girl who was given the name of Minnie. This was his mother. In later years a holy terror known locally as Mescalero Min. No photograph of her exists. At twenty she was said to have been a ravishing beauty. This may not have been an exaggeration. The intermingling of races frequently produces striking offspring. As Uncle Walter once put it, "Depends on a feller's tastes. You cut into a turkey, some likes the dark, others the white."

Despite Private Wardner's dullard expression, there is a quality about his face that takes the attention. A rather elegant, perhaps even beautiful, bone structure. High cheekbones. The eyes have a marked Mongolian cast, and the nose is not broad and flat but thin, bladelike, with delicately flared nostrils. Perhaps a hint of the Hamitic.

It was this that had first led Gutierrez to libraries in his travels around the country, to seek out detailed descriptions of various African racial types. He had come away reasonably satisfied that that side of his family had originated in Watusiland, maybe from around Burundi.

The natives who made up that ethnic group were tall, haughty types, which might explain his own abnormal height. Flamingo-legged pastoral herdsmen, who mingled not at all with runtier neighboring tribes except for the pastime of warfare. They slew black-maned lions singlehandedly, armed only with knife, spear, and rhinoceros-hide shield—no small feat—and at the same time were so gentle and closely knit in their brotherhood that the warriors, who roamed the veldt beneath the coppery furnace of the African sky, had a custom of holding one another by the hand, an innocent tradition, as if, overwhelmed by the sheer immensity of this land, they found it necessary to maintain intimate contact with another human.

They were said to have been a noble people, but their regal ways would have been of little use when some were ferried across the southern Atlantic on a catch-as-catch-can yachting trip, fourth-class steerage, no outside view. As likely as not, some simply perished of mortification, while those who survived the trip may have wondered with good reason if their stoic determination to stay alive was worth the effort. Whatever, some buck or belle down in the hold, idly whiling away the hours by counting the links in a leg shackle, must have had a special zest for the sweetness of life, else he himself would not be here.

THE QUESTION REMAINS in his mind. Was he, as his father had often claimed, living history . . . a sort of intercultural melting pot that encompassed not centuries but whole epochs? Or was he a walking insult to the finest qualities of the white, black, and red races combined? Uncle Walter had always claimed that the latter was true. He himself could not really disagree.

His father had the ear of a poet, the curiosity of a Copernicus, and the thirst of a camel. People who knew George Gutierrez said he was an impractical dreamer and a failure, but this was mostly because he had his own way of going about life, and a pretty strange way it was, along the lines of a latter-day Herodotus absentmindedly mooning about the American southwest, an amateur scientist who had his own style of listening and watching, and, when he was drinking, an enthralling talker with a weakness for reciting poetry. His oratorical delivery, especially with old favorites like Chaucer, Donne, and Coleridge, was overdramatic, with a heavy reliance on the Delsartian gesture. The brow smote with clenched fist to denote anguish. The horizon indicated by a rigidly extended arm and forefinger. Any reference to God reinforced by a rolling-up of the eyes toward heaven. The technique had its heyday during the era of melodrama, and can still occasionally be seen in early videographs filmed before World War I. Today, it would be considered corny, but back in the thirties the boy was enchanted. His best memories were of the three of them camped out, alone on the plains or in the high mountains, where at night, beside a blazing campfire, his father would drink and recite poetry, or spin wonderfully fanciful tales, and the boy, with a blanket drawn up round his shoulders to ward off the night chill, would sit and listen, raptly attentive. His father filled his mind not only with language but with ideas.

At a time when the Aleutian Land Bridge Theory was still being argued, George Gutierrez accepted the idea and in his talk made it perfectly believable, with stories of nomadic hunters dressed in shaggy skins, who had made that great trek twenty, perhaps thirty thousand years ago. They and the immense migrating herds they lived off stumbled across the frozen tundra together, often—for decades at a time—surviving on the glacial overlap itself, that vast cap of moving ice that elsewhere reached south of where Chicago and New York now stand. In lean times they may have kept body and soul together with a diet of mussels, gull eggs, and lichen that could be harvested along the shoreline bases of grinding ice cliffs, resolutely turning their shaggy backs on blizzards raging out of the polar regions. His father mused, "You have to try to grasp—comprehend—the magnificence of such a journey! Imagine how tired and footsore those poor people must have been when they finally found New Mexico and settled here."

"Maybe that's why injuns to this day would rather fight than walk," Uncle Walter said.

"Oh, but, Walter, what an incredible migration."

"All I can tell you," Walter said, "is that if an injun can't think of anything else to do he'll play it safe and stand still, and I reckon you've noticed that if he is forced to go someplace against his will, he is in no hurry to git the damn job done." Walter thought about this. "And if liquor's handy, four mules and a crowbar ain't goin' to move that injun an inch."

Other genealogical oddities were discussed during those long-ago campfire nights. A part of the boy's heritage included wandering Bavarians, who followed the Scandinavian invasion across the middle west in the latter part of the nineteenth century, stolid and redcheeked *landarbeiters*, who like so many of their type believed implicitly that a little farm somewhere would bring them independence, along with a decent, which is to say a carbohydrate-loaded, standard of living. The little-farm notion may have worked in Wisconsin but in New Mexico it never got anybody anything except death at a premature age, especially for a woman, whose lot in life consisted of overwork, boredom, and the birthing of as many as twenty-four children. In those times it was not at all unusual for a sturdy German farmer to use up four or five wives before settling into drooling senility.

As his father saw it, the link was made. From the Bering Strait, east Africa's hot, dry plains, and northern Europe, to the golden southwest. The migrational lines converged in New Mexico's Lincoln County, a kind of ethnological, not to say anthropological, bull's-eye. The Aleutian tour, a slaver's plying of the Atlantic trade winds, and the Teutonic parabola across the midwest. And, finally, the Spanish side—the at one time modestly successful branch of the family from which Gutierrez took his proper name.

Gutierrezes were in New Mexico ninety years before the first pilgrim debarked at Plymouth Rock, the name goes back that far. The earliest settlers had come from Ciudad Mexico (a former Aztec Eden of mountainous vistas and floating gardens, now unfortunately half-drowned in its own Pemex smog), traveling north to the Pass, or El Paso, and up along the willow-bordered thread of the Rio Grande, wisely bypassing *El Jornado del Muerto*—the Journey of Death—a fabulously hot stretch of roasted sand and blistered lava spill that did in wagon trains right and left. Before that, Gutierrezes had been in Spain for ages, or at least since the time when armorers cast round bullets to shoot Christians with and square slugs to use on Turks and lesser infidels.

His father said, "Migrations and history! Hundreds of generations, from all parts of the world. Roy, do you understand? In a way, you *are* the southwest!"

But Walter carped. "George, whyn't you quit fillin' the boy's ears with all that damned useless nonsense? He ain't historical. He's just ugly, that's all. Shit, I don't know how I ever got myself into this rotten mess, traipsin' all around the country, throwin' in my lot with a born loser and an overgrown half-breed injun brat."

"Living history," his father had insisted. "Walter, you have to take a long view. Look past the end of your nose."

"I don't have to," Walter argued. "How in hell can this son-uvabitchin' kid be historical when we ain't even got a regulation birth certificate on him?" He thought about this as he was rolling a cigarette and then, with natural maliciousness, added, "Georgie, all that bullshit of yours don't amount to nothin'. What counts is somethin' like what happened the other day, when those little kids hangin' around that general store took a look at the boy here and froze paralyzed in their tracks at what was comin' up on 'em."

And that was true. The children had been terrified. Even now, years later. It happened with grown people, too.

GUTIERREZ'S APARTMENT WAS in a *barrio* a few blocks north of the international border . . . a ghettolike warren of narrow, crowded sidestreets in which lived whites, blacks, Mexicans, legal and otherwise, Orientals, and other types, a racially con-glomerated area of small-time crime, prostitution, smuggling, and drugs. It was a noisy enough neighborhood by day, with yelling kids and street venders who peddled everything from *chicherones* to *carne carbón* from their pushcarts, and from the open windows of cheap apartments taco rock and wild *mariachi* music blared. There were lots of barber shops, small grocery stores, tailors, and bars, some of them so tough that the federal narcs and plain-clothes border-patrol agents who hung out in them, trying to judge the pulse of the trade, made a point of displaying the hardware they carried, big Colt automatics and even bigger .44 Magnums. Their theory was that everybody knew who they were anyway, and, too, a man openly packing a small cannon in a clamshell belt holster often has a psychological advantage over a couple of studs who are out to stir up trouble. Even so, the narcs hung out in pairs and trios and never turned their backs on anyone. The corner bar Gutierrez himself sometimes went to for a few beers was an old-time place with a tile floor and a con-crete trough that ran along the base of the bar, so that the cus-tomers could relieve themselves right there without interrupting their conversation to go out in the back alley. It was practical, and not as unsanitary as it sounded, since the trough was fed by a steady stream of fresh water from a faucet, although a patron did have to be careful about dropping a pack of cigarettes or folding money.

The *barrio* was noisy at night, too, with shrieks, gunshots, windows being smashed out, it made no difference. Everybody minded his own business. Nobody cared about anything. Even the starlings roosting on telephone poles looked straight ahead and didn't gossip. In the wee hours, stifflegged alley cats stalked rubbish-filled gutters, alert for love or combat, and by day the fleabitten mongrels who curled up in the afternoon sun in doorways were small, as if they wanted to avoid attracting attention. It was a neighborhood that can be found in any city in the country—Los Angeles, New York, Denver—and was unusual only because of the border that bisected the two countries: the mighty Rio Grande, which at this time of year happened to have as much water in it as Death Valley.

He had stopped here on his way back from a Mexican trip, as he had stopped in other cities in his wanderings, taking the first job that came his way in order to replenish his bankroll, intending to stay on for only a month or two, but often staying longer. This time he had been gone for almost three years, and in that interval had saved more than two thousand dollars; he had learned long ago that a man who lives alone and in a modest fashion does not require much money. Life in the *barrio* suited him well enough. While nobody exactly rolled out the welcome mat, his presence there was at least tolerated. As for El Paso itself, it was hot and ugly and had a smog problem, which is to say it was not much better or worse than any other American city he had seen.

Weekdays, he worked for Acme Novelties, a ceramics factory near the railroad yards, turning out racks of brightly colored bric-a-brac made of silica gel, clay, and glazing slurry that arrived at the back loading dock in fifty-five-gallon drums. Two huge gas-fired kilns, with temperatures that hovered around 2000 degrees Fahrenheit. It was fearfully hot work but it was also a hundred and fifty a week. His labors, while not artistically fulfilling, were at least honest.

Acme's merchandise was timetested, every item a proven seller. Bigbreasted blondes clutching drunken cowboys. Pancho

Villa Frito-*bandito* types, all grin, whiskers, and crossed bando-
leers. The state of Texas made into ashtrays. The jackalope—a
species of fauna unique to the southwest—with the body and
head of a jackrabbit and the curbed horns of an antelope. American Dresden. Glazed oilwells that poured salt right out of the
top. A longhorn steer made into a useful paperweight. Ceramic
outhouses with genuine plastic lift-up seats and a sign on the
door: "Welcome to Amarillo!" Cute kittens with "Want A Little
Pussy?" signs hung around their porcelain necks. Doggy doo-doos
by the thousands, baked in dark brown matte. That was their
trade name. "Doggy Doo's Defy Detection!" It said so right on
the box each was carefully packed in.

He took care of the kilns and the two conveyor belts that led
through holes in the wall to the factory's main room. The incoming belt was staffed by Marcella and Darleen, two black women
who were adroit and fast with brushes, sprayguns and glazes.
Once fired and cooled to a point where they could be handled,
the finished items rolled back out on the other belt to two
Mexican wetback ladies named Esmeralda and Matilda. Esme
and Mattie inspected, wrapped, and boxed each piece.

Acme was owned lock-stock-and-barrel by Ivor Markovich,
pronounced *Mark*ovich, never Mar*kov*ich. Ivor had a sweeping
handlebar moustache, cheerful blue eyes, thinning, shoulder-
length blond hair, a Porsche 927 limited-edition, and a four-
bedroom ranch-style house out past Grandview Park that had a
pretty fine view of the desert, such is the American way of life.
He insisted that his staff call him by his first name—never
Mr. Markovich or even "boss." He had an air of egalitarianism
and friendly goodwill but refused under any circumstances to
discuss the hourly minimum wage rate. In truth, he worked hard
and always took his lunch break with them, and liked to point
out, "I'm just an ordinary workingman myself, so what's the
difference, what we got here is a cottage industry of sorts. Let's
be one big happy family, am I right?"

When Gutierrez gave notice, Ivor acted crushed. "More
money, is that it? Now tell me the truth."

"No. I've been here long enough."

"A couple of years? Is that so long?"

"I'm sorry, Ivor."

Markovich looked sentimental. "It won't be the same without you, Roy."

"You'll find someone else easy."

"Easy? You mean easy for you to say! Roy, you're the best kilnsman Acme's ever had. No butterfingers, that's you. Never breakage. How about twenty a week extra?" Gutierrez shook his head. Ivor had the soul of an artist and a computer mind. As a young man he had studied economics, sculpture, and anatomy at the University of Oregon. It was he who created the master models and latex molds of what was later cast into ceramics, talking all the while of Rodin, Maillol, Lipschitz, and Giacometti: "I've got to kill myself in order to even stay alive, but you take a fellow like that Rodin, he had talent oozing out of his fingertips."

On Gutierrez's last day of work at Acme there was an ill-concealed air of festivity. At ten that morning Esmeralda stole back and left a little something with him, which turned out to be a half-gallon bottle of Chablis, and then she hung around and helped him drink it beside the roaring furnaces. In this way he learned that there was to be a farewell party on his behalf. "At five, when we finish," Esme said. She looked over her shoulder to make sure they were alone, and then hissed, "You ain' supposed to *know!*"

Later in the morning Darleen sneaked back with another little something—port, this time—which the two drank together. So that by noon he was not feeling bad by half. In fact, he was somewhat drunk. He felt a welling of affection and kindness toward these people who, like himself, were locked into a repetitively Sisyphean task. At lunch time—Ivor's daily treat—when the meals came in from a Taco Bell up the street, Gutierrez shared his lettuce-and-cheese enchiladas with Esmeralda. The coffee that came in white plastic cups was ditched, and wine substituted. When sober, he was the quietest of men—perhaps not by nature, but experience had taught him years ago that it was the only way for him to be, keeping a shy distance between himself and others, rarely if ever calling any sort of attention to himself. For certain people, that is the most sensible course in life.

By three in the afternoon, there had been more mischief than in his entire time at Acme, not only at his end of the conveyors but up front where the girls worked. An army of bosomy blondes came down the incoming belt as negresses, and almost two hundred doo-doos had been accidentally dropped. At one point, Esmeralda, feeling devilish, got a scoop, went out to the parking lot, and scraped up a dandy specimen, which she placed on the conveyor among its ceramic doo-doo brethren. Would have suffocated a whale. In back, Roy, speedily transferring items from belt to baking tray, dug right in, was dismayed, knocked over a rack of ashtrays, and had to spend five minutes in the toilet with pumice soap.

Ivor flew around the shop, vexed. "This is work time. Any more, and the party's off!"

"*Patrón, lo siento mucho, pero nada* is off," Esmeralda told him. Meaning that she was sorry but that the party was definitely on. "We got everything, wine and liquor and the potato chips and all the ice out in the cars already."

"Then behave," Ivor said.

"Okay. Just don't tell me my business," Esme said, tapping her fingers on her purse. In that bag, Gutierrez knew, and so did Ivor, Esme carried a seven-inch-long hatpin to ward off dope-crazed rapists. Esme thought of herself as a helpless female, but she was also no one to fool with. A nick with that hatpin could mean a mortal wound.

"Let's just get through the day with a little equanimity," Ivor said placatingly. "And, please, no more breakage."

"Don't worry," Esme told him. "We take care of everything."

"Am I still invited?" Ivor wanted to know.

"*Chico, naturalamente,*" Esme said.

Where else but at Acme could a lowly kilnsman be sent off on the long voyage home by a democratic boss and four lovely ladies?

GUTIERREZ KNEW HE would never see any of them again. Felt sentimental, and for a reason. They had been kind to him. For a long time he had eaten daily with them. Talked, and even kidded around a little, though always with that shyness. And now he was leaving.

The party began with a formal solemnity, but by six o'clock Esmeralda was perched on the end of a conveyor belt with her legs girlishly crossed, displaying her varicose veins in all their awful glory. She was drinking wine and working on a roach affixed to the end of her deadly hatpin. The grass had been supplied by Darleen, and even for El Paso, home of cannabis connoisseurs, it was top grade. Ivor had filled his Kaywoodie with it; he was no longer angry.

Esmeralda was laughing and shaking her head. "You know, when I found that *theeng* in the parking lot and put it on the conveyor for Roy, it remin' me *exactamente* of my first husban', Ignacio. He always like me to hold it in my han'. Roy, you okay. I don't know what got into me this day."

"*De nada, chiquita,*" Gutierrez said.

"You' one good *hombre.*"

Coming from Esme, that was practically a compliment. At five feet two, she looked like a baboon, viewed men with suspicion, and, according to her friend Matilda, was considered one of the toughest ladies in El Paso. Esme lived with a black piano player who was out of work most of the time. They had never gotten married, but this didn't stop them from having nine children. Esme and her tribe of mulatto brats got by on what she earned at Acme Novelties, welfare, *las stampas comidas,* and whatever her old man could hustle at the piano, which wasn't very much. She was into *chicana* lib in a big way, but at the same time was sullenly possessive and jealous about her man, and whenever she suspected he was fooling around—according to her, she couldn't let him out of her sight for five minutes without having some *gringa* wanting to try him on for size—she would unlimber her hatpin and play a xylophone tune on his ribs with it. She claimed she had sensitive feelings just like anybody else, even if she was so used-up and ugly that nobody wanted her anymore, including men in general, and one black dude in particular.

Now, feeling affectionate, she put her arm round Gutierrez's waist—she had to reach up to do it—and said, "Roy, how come you goin' away and leavin' all you fran's here?"

"No reason to stay, Esme."

"*Dondé va, colego?*"

"*Neuvo Mexico.*"

"I think that's a no-good place for someone like you, Roy. 'Most as bad as this Texas. *Y creo*, Texas ain't such a good place."

"I was born there."

"I was born in Bangor, Maine," Darleen said. "But that don't mean I got to go *back* there for any special reason." Darleen was a two-hundred-pound dark brown woman who had formed a spiritual alliance with her pal Marcella after the latter had gotten the bad and the worse together. Marcella, at her best, looked like a crocodile with a grudge, but she and her friend were tender and loving together, the way twelve-year-old girls can be when they get a crush on each other. Marcella said, "I an' my friend Darleen are of one and the same mind . . . ain't New Mexico just another one of them redneck honkey places? You mess around there, you' liable to get into trouble. It's bad enough here, but at least everybody knows who they is and where they's at." She thought about this. "I sure hate prejudice. That is something really pisses me off."

Ivor, seated beside Esmeralda, said, "I know about prejudice."

"It's everywhere," Roy pointed out.

He was feeling marvelously loose and conversational. Maybe it was the liquor and the grass, or maybe it was because he was leaving these people. Whatever, he was by this time filled with a strong urge to talk . . . to show them that he was something more than what they saw. "I lived in Los Angeles once, for nearly two years," he said. "It's as bad there."

Ivor nodded in agreement. "Don't tell me. I spent eleven years there. I know all about *that* place."

Roy said, "Do you know that there are over a hundred thousand Indians in Los Angeles? That's the biggest off-reservation Indian community anywhere in the country."

"So what?"

"They never looked at me," he said.

"Why you pickin' on them for that?" Darleen said. "Why'd they wanta look at someone like you?"

"I'm one-quarter Mescalero Apache, that's why," he pointed out.

Marcella grinned, showing gaps of missing teeth. "Shit! How you talk. Why, Roy, you ain't no more injun than I or Darleen is!"

"I mean it," he insisted. "I can prove it."

"Oh, we heard that before," Marcella said, laughing. "Ain't that right, Darleen?"

"In New Mexico, my grandfather was a famous gunfighter, and I have the newspaper clippings," he said, drinking straight from one of the bottles.

"Roy, I don't mean to act personal or nothin', but if you ask me all you is is a great big funnyspotted nigger what outgrowed himself," Marcella said.

There was a lot of truth in that.

"'Course, you *does* have a sweet nature, honey," Marcella went on sociably. "Can't see a speck of meanness in you. Yes, I will say that much."

He tried to explain. "It's something called vitiligo. Leukodermia. It's not really hereditary. They think it may be caused by a vitamin deficiency."

"You mean you' complexion? Roy, don't talk vitamins at *this* woman," Marcella said. "'Cause back in Alabama, where *I* growed up, all you'd be is a plain ol' liverspotted nigger. Oh, I seen that before. Ain't nothin' to do with no injuns. Liver patches comes from the white and black blood fightin' at each other. Everybody knows that."

"But I really am part Apache," he said.

"Mulatto. That's all you is, honey," Marcella argued. "You take me. I'm three-quarters white, and I happen to know it, but that still makes me a high yellow." She thought about this. "Shit, I could be ninety-five percent white, and you know what? I'd still be black."

"What is all this talk about prejudice?" Ivor interrupted. "What do any of you people know about it?"

They looked at him in astonishment.

"You want prejudice, listen to someone who knows," Ivor said. "You folks think you have a problem? Believe me, I wish I had the same kind of trouble. Why do you think I'm here, after eleven years in Los Angeles, where I killed myself? A town where a Jew is despised by his own kind. Believe me, because you have it from an authority. Do you know how many kinds of Jews there are in Los Angeles? Too many, and they are like barracudas. In that place, a Polish Jew is a dog, a potato-nosed peasant who managed to get out, a good-for-nothing. A French Jew, who can trust that kind of man? A Swiss Jew, who could care less, even if he's a professor at UCLA? But a German Jew, well, they brought in the money, they're the bankers and lawyers up at the top, they have the right connections. A German Jew in Los Angeles is like a god, he can do no wrong. A Polish or a Russian Jew is something he'll use like a doormat to wipe his shoes on. That's prejudice. There is your caste system. And an Alaskan Jew with blue eyes, why at temple I was lucky to sneak in by the back door. My father was a beautiful man, but he had a terrible sense of direction. In the persecutions of the early twenties, nobody knows how many Jews fled Russia . . . a million, two million? They all went west, to France, Germany, England. You think this was good enough for my father? Absolutely not." Ivor shook his head and gazed up at the ceiling in resignation. "That man had to go *east!* Four months on the trans-Siberian railroad, all the way to Vladivostok, where he and my poor mother were finally able to catch a ship across the Bering Straits to Alaska."

"That's very interesting," Roy said, owl-eyed but with genuine curiosity. "Some of my people came that way, too. Only they walked." He had another drink.

"They walked? On water?" Ivor decided to ignore this. "Besides the bad sense of direction, he had no business smarts either. What does he do but open a laundry with two Chinese workers. It was the only business of its kind in Alaska, a Russian-Jewish-Chinese laundry. He didn't exactly make a killing. Up in that part of the world, if you show them a nicely pressed and starched shirt, they think it's something to *eat.* What chance was there for me in California to marry some German-Jewish girl, whose family at least knew how to make a telephone call or two, nothing big, only a step in the right direction, a door knocked on, nothing more, is there harm in that? So I came here. Texas isn't so bad. In Los Angeles, they'll fall down dead for the Muellers, the Hubers, and the Obermeyers, but a young fellow who was born and raised in Anchorage, they'll spit on. I take that as no fault of my own. It's their problem, not mine. Here, my wife, Ethel, is a Baptist—lapsed, thank heaven—and you know what she brings into my life? *Dimension.* Don't talk prejudice, be-

cause I'm someone who knows." Ivor smote his chest in the
vicinity of his heart. "Among your own . . . that's where it always cuts like a knife."

A couple of fresh joints were rolled, lit, and passed. Marcella
opened another half-gallon of wine and said, "Darleen, sugar,
you mayn't know it yet but you's goin' to drive us home."

Darleen said, "How come I never have any fun?"

"I'm savin' some fun for you when we get home," Marcella
said. "That's a promise, honey."

"I am part Indian," Roy said for the third time.

"He flyin' on one wing tonight," Darleen observed.

"Roy's one nigger can sail his boat in any wind," Marcella
said, and she gave him a hug. "You tell it like it is. You so ugly
you's pretty, you know that? Why, if I had a cravin' for men,
which I don't, 'cause I been all through *that,* I might be a little
curious about you. Bet you got a dick on you that's outa sight."

"Marcella, my *glass* is empty," Darleen said, scowling. She
held it out, and Marcella docilely refilled it.

"What's wrong with being part Indian?" he said.

"Must be something in the air these days," Marcella said.
"Seems to me every no-count nigger ain't satisfied less'n he's
part injun. Or else they claim they is *Car*ib with one of them
English accents. I don't understand why they can't just be plain
ol' ordinary U-S-of-A niggers. Why, I an' Darleen here, we happened to be hangin' out in this bar just last week, and this dude,
he come up to us with an act. Claim he was pure Eskimo from
someplace up near the no'th pole where they built that pipeline.
Shoot! Never saw no Eskimo with a black face like *that,* all rollin'
eyeballs and big white teeth! Bet no Eskimo never did neither!
Only ice *that* Eskimo ever saw was what he had in his rum-and-
coke."

"But I'm not lying," he insisted.

"Why, honey, you want to be injun, you go right ahead," Marcella said. "Personally, I an' Darleen couldn't care less. Only
thing I oughta point out to you though is that you don't exactly
resemble any injun I ever seen, and I seen 'em by the jillions on
tv." She considered this. "Come to think of it, you don't look
much like a nigger neither. Actually, now you mention it, you
don't resemble *any*thing I ever seen before. Maybe what you

oughta do is get yourself a feather or something to tie on your head. Sugar, what you need is a dis*guise*."

"I own a whole town in New Mexico," he said.

"Have another drink, Roy."

"It's called Sawmill River Flats. And I own it." He tried to tell them about how the Indians had crossed the Aleutian land bridge during the last ice age. "Can you imagine how cold it was? Just like Ivor's folks. All the way across Siberia. They wandered for thousands of years. Some ended up way down in South America. Land's end. What could have made people do a thing like that?"

"The fuzz was after 'em?" Darleen volunteered.

"Grass in the next pasture always looks greener," Marcella said.

"Could be," he agreed. "Like me. I've been moving around all my life. My father taught me that. He taught me a lot."

"You' daddy was good to you?"

"He was the best man who ever lived."

"How come?"

He thought about this. "He took care of me."

"That is a real sweet thing to say," Marcella said. "My own daddy was the exact same."

"Then you know what I'm talking about," he said, happy at last to have found something they didn't scoff at. "He certainly was a wonderful man."

TWO

HEADING NORTH ACROSS Texas it is hot. Here and there fat thorny cacti poke up like sentinels posed in a sea of faded gramma grass, and from time to time the summer wind bowls clumps of Russian thistle—tumbleweed—across the highway's much-repaired asphalt. Gray, heat-hazed sky. Like radioactive molten lead. Just as weighty. Round the horizon, spinning dustdevils, twisting and funneling helically in the shimmering mirage. Phantasmagorical, he thinks, *rain's long overdue in these parts. A dry summer is hell on a rancher.*

Through the jeep's windshield he sights something hanging way up yonder, a black speck against the ominous sky. Old Mister Hawk, wheeling and dipping on outthrust wings, scarcely ever moving them, regally poised, feathertouching the hot air currents. Mean birds, soaring so slow and easy, as if they were crucified, but always primed for blood and death. "Like most of us," he says aloud.

He remembers going up into the Mescalero Reservation one time on the road out of Cloudcroft, many years ago, and just before the two-lane disappeared into the first tall timber there was this hardbreathing brown-and-white-flecked peregrine with insane eyes that looked like polished amethysts, sitting atop a fencepost beside the road, one scaly foot caught fast in a tricky twist of wire wrapped round the fencepost staple, with a trickle of red blood to mark where the barbs held him. He had stopped the jeep and slipped on the cowhide workgloves he kept under the seat, and had gone over to try and free the bird, though of course he knew better. In a nearby willow a flock of crows were cawing noisily and moving around a lot, waiting to go after that hawk once it gave out. As Roy approached, the crows rose in Van Gogh flight but didn't fly far. He went up to the hawk, moving slowly and making sucking noises with his lips that he hoped a doomed bird might interpret as soothing, and, with a wild, powerful, heartrending flurry, the peregrine tore loose from the barbed loop, leaving the trapped leg in the wire, to rise with wildly beating wings into the bright summer sky, blood spurting freely, then wheeled sharply, glaring back at Roy over one shoulder with a kind of paranoid, fuck-you expression, and headed up the valley with the flock in noisy pursuit, to sink to earth a half-mile or so distant, minus a leg and doubtless drained nearly dry but still a peril to those crows as long as the pronged beak could flex and fasten. "Yes, hawks are all right," he says now. "At a distance, though."

Then, toward sunset, up ahead, there is one of those state highway markers, WELCOME TO THE LAND OF ENCHANTMENT, and he knows he is home, in sunny old New Mexico. Land of the long shadow. Where for no special reason the sky somehow seems brighter, and the air cooler, the highway smoother. Straightaway, the terrain is hillier and the earth colors rawer—powerful ochres, rich umbers, and glaring siennas—and in the unfenced, spooky, deserted wild country pressing in on either side of the highway there is that old, familiar, dry, dead wasteland foliage: blooming yucca, organ pipe, cholla, palo verde, buckthorn, prickly pear.

Off to the left and parallel to the jeep there is a roadrunner—a longtailed, skinnynecked, beaky denizen of the desert whose wings are practically useless but who has overcome this handicap by developing a pair of broomstick legs that can outrace anything around—pounding along with its head down and its ass stuck out, covering ground like the devil was after it. Although

still hung over from yesterday's party, Roy is feeling better by
the minute, and now, for the hell of it, he pops his head out the
open window and lets off a wild "Yahoo!" The roadrunner,
startled by this salutation, stops atop a hillock to look the scene
over with beady eyes.

He pulls the jeep off the road, sets the brake, gets out, and,
euphoric now, starts after the bird, loping through the sagebrush,
waving his arms like a madman and from time to time yelling.
The bird takes off in a skittery run, not in any kind of real hurry
because there is no one in the world who can catch a roadrunner.

Seated on another hillock, a quarter of a mile off, illuminated
by the last red rays of the setting sun, a coyote watches this
weird spectacle—a skinny giant in a cheap straw Stetson, flapping
his arms and shouting as he runs across the desert after a bird
that can never be caught, not ever.

BACK IN THE jeep, he gets a beer out of the cooler, opens it, and
then grins at himself for his foolishness. "You've got parental
love and a pampered childhood to blame for that," he tells himself. "Chasing an old roadrunner. That's not only foolish but impractical as well." But then his father had never been noted for
practicality, else he would never have taken on the job of raising
him. No simple task, yet George Gutierrez and his sidekick,
Walter Kelly, became amateur pediatricians, learning by hit-or-
miss methods the age-old routine of diapers, colic, and teething.

According to Uncle Walter, the maternal side never came to
much. The lady who bore him, that hot-eyed half-breed named
Min, disappeared shortly after he was born. As Walter described
it, the accouchement was done in the traditional Apache
fashion:

". . . she was eighteen hours in labor because you was a
breech brat, but she'd made up her mind not to have any white
doctor or white hospital messin' around her. Come to think of it,
Minnie never cared much for anything white except vanilla
sherbet . . . that, and your pa, although the terrible use she put
him to in the year or so they knew one another aged that poor

man somethin' awful, and at that they wasn't even married. Oh, he was never the same afterward.

"Anyway, when you got stuck, she hauled herself over to a medicine man's lodge. It was just a dirty little shack, not fit for a civilized person, with an open log fire burning right in the middle of the dirt floor and a hole in the roof to let the smoke out. The smoke kept most of the flies calmed down, but it couldn't cover up the natural stink. Injuns got a powerful smell anyway, but it was so strong in that lodge you could've cut it with a knife. I didn't know who was goin' to keel over first, me or your pa. On top of it, Georgie was all nervous and worried because you was so long in comin'. I brung a full jug of *aguardiente* to keep him soothed.

"We seen it ourselves. Lots of times I've gone after a colt or a calf that's troublesome, gone in up to my armpit, but I never experienced anything like that. The medicine man, he built up the fire real hot, to start a sweat, and your daddy and I and two young bucks sat over by one wall taking turns with the *aguardiente* while the medicine man did a little dance and sung some songs—Minnie claimed he could do all kinds of magic an' spells, but he didn't look special to me, just a stragglehaired injun, looked like he was ninety years old if you could've seen under the dirt.

"When he got done singin' and dancin' he tied her hands over her head to a roofbeam, and then he hauled down her skirt and knickers, wrapped an old lariat around her waist above the bulge that was you, cinched it real tight, and then he and the two bucks squatted down around her and hauled away on that lariat for all they was worth until you popped like a watermelon seed. The noise she made was just deafenin' but it was nothin' compared to the yell she let out when she got a look at you and saw what she'd manufactured. Georgie figured it affected her brain. She had a stab at murdering you—injuns are awful superstitious about deformities and such—and then she took off for parts unknown and we never laid eyes on her again, though once we heard talk that someone named Minnie Wardner was doin' business in a Brownsville crib. She passed herself as pure reservation squaw, but nobody 'ceptin' a blind man would've ever bought that story. She had old Tom Wardner's big flappy mouth that no Apache this side of Africa would be caught dead grinnin' through. Yessir, even as an infant, you was pretty remarkable. Them two bucks' eyes popped, and the medicine man hisself, he took a good look at you and then grabbed for the *aguardiente* and practically drained the jug dry."

Walter used to say he favored murder, too. He claimed he said, "Georgie, he's bound to have an interestin' life. Maybe we oughta make things easier on him by holding him by his heels in a barrel of rainwater for a couple of hours." Walter was a pragmatic man, but most of it was just talk.

He said that all of them stood around the medicine man's shack for a while, looking down at the new baby, trying to figure out what it was supposed to be. Minnie decided that a devil had gotten into her, and gave George fishy looks. That was when she reached for a length of firewood and went to brain her son with it, but George wouldn't let her, so she fired off a swing at the medicine man instead and caught him dead between the eyes, and then she went after the two bucks, nothing on but a bloody chemise, chasing them round the open fire. For a while it was pretty lively in that little shack. Uncle Walter and George finally wrapped the baby in a blanket and brought him back to the truck they called home, stopping in Ruidoso for another jug. George insisted that they keep the baby, and they ended up hiring a Spanish *vieja* to feed Roy goat's milk and rub him down with Crisco lard twice a day—her notion was that the Crisco might help the pigmentation problem. Indians came from all over the reservation to see the child, though none dared touch it. They all considered this baby powerful medicine but couldn't seem to make up their minds whether it was the good or the bad kind. Back east, Gershwin's *Rhapsody in Blue* had its first performance.

Both Walter and George were drunkards, and both were cripples. George with most of the muscles of his left calf ripped away—an old sow had nearly chewed the leg off when he was three years old—and Walter with his pelvis and spine ruined from broncbusting when he was young.

All Walter was good for was swamping. That is, swabbing down the latrines and floors of saloons and restaurants in the thousand and one towns they hit in the twenties and thirties. George Gutierrez was a handyman, and could fix anything from a printing press to a tractor. He knew carpentry, plumbing, and even electrical wiring, and could build a fireplace, set a window-pane, repair leather tack, and adjust the sights on a rifle so that it shot straight. He himself must have been an oddity to the ranchers and townspeople who encountered the three of them, a tall, narrowshouldered, gimpy man with blue eyes and that pale albino hair, which he kept combed flat except at the back of his skull, where it stood up in a spiky cowlick. As Walter put it, and none too subtly, the fair complexion and hair belonged on no man with the Spanish name of Gutierrez any more than the Afri-can mouth belonged on Mescalero Min. There was a bar sinister in that part of the family; specifically, incest. Walter said, "You goin' to breed healthy stock, you gotta keep track of who's gettin' into who, else you're liable to end up with a Chinese nightmare." Back then, proper people rarely talked about such matters, but Walter gave out dark hints that Bertha Hoffman Gutierrez and Ephraim Munger, the gunslinger, were more than simple kissing cousins.

Roy himself had no reason to doubt any of this, because in that GI footlocker he had her diary, in which she made sporadic en-tries up until the time she died of cancer, in 1910. That was why he called Ephraim his natural grandfather instead of her hus-band, Herman Gutierrez. He thought this might be a cynical conclusion, but he also believed that there wasn't a reason in the world to think that lust and love didn't make hearts thump as heavily then as now.

His father had educated him from start to finish, and, with Uncle Walter, taught him the pleasures of living the wanderer's life.

Back then, they moseyed from town to town in an old 1918 Mack five-tone delivery van that had solid rubber tires, acetylene headlights, an oversized chain-and-sprocket drive like a bicycle's, and a manually operated horn that, when sharply punched, went *arrooogha*. Lettered across the front bumper was the legend GET THEE BEHIND ME, which was a little arrogant because the big Mack, on a level stretch, was only a shade faster than a horse and wagon: it was not a vehicle designed for someone in a hurry.

In the back, which was roofed and windowed like a gypsy van—
a sort of early-day version of the hippie campers that took to
the highways in the 1960's—there were three bunks, cooking gear,
an iron woodstove, kerosene lamps, a library of books that included a home-correspondence course for the boy to study,
several hundred *National Geographics,* the *Oxford Book of English Verse,* and a 1912 edition of the *Encyclopaedia Britannica,*
which was more or less complete, as well as a tent, tools, spare
engine parts, three rifles, two pistols and a shotgun, a dandy telescope for looking at the stars, food, water, two extra wheels
mounted on their oak rims, and a come-along, which is a kind of
mechanical device useful for winching such a truck out of a
stretch of quicksand. Nothing fancy—no built-in shower or toilet.
When nature beckoned, the boy grabbed the roll of Delsey
sitting up on the dash and beelined for the nearest chamisa.

All things considered, it wasn't a bad life, and often it was fun.
At the height of the Depression, when veterans were trying to
sell apples for a nickel apiece, George Gutierrez could always
earn enough money for food, tobacco, liquor, and gasoline. The
boy was no trouble at all, so Walter grudgingly admitted years
later, a quiet kid, perched on a little wooden box the two men
had set on the front seat between them.

Whenever they hit a new town he stuck close to his father and
Walter. Nobody looked at him, not more than five or six times
anyway, until the adolescent years, and after that things changed.
Around fourteen, his pituitary finally figured out what it was
supposed to be for. In the summer of his fifteenth year he stood
six feet seven, and at that he was slouching. He kept on growing,
but it was all vertical. Walter claimed they nearly went broke
feeding him four times a day, but they could never get his weight
past one fifty. George Gutierrez died shortly after he turned
sixty, but Uncle Walter, with a kind of awesome disregard for
death, was still alive in 1976, when this country celebrated its
Bicentennial . . . he was at that time one hundred and six or so,
give or take a few years either way. No birth records existed, so
there was no way of knowing for sure. This man, who had been
born not many years after George Armstrong Custer made a fool
of himself at the Battle of Little Big Horn, lived well into the
atomic era, and lasted until the fall of 1978.

It was also true that in those early years the boy was never struck nor was a voice raised to him in anger. Not at all a bad record considering that his father and Walter rarely went more than five miles without having a bottle within reach. His father had no kind of violence in him at all. Walter, though, was an irascible terror. That old man was hard to swallow. A cranky little fart, all ugly and gnomelike, stooped, with a wizened face that had a mean, thin mouth and those terrible glittery Irish eyes. His hips and back gave him constant agony, so he was out to get even with the world. He bitched and moaned from dawn to dusk and then into the small hours, when the boy and his father would flop him into his bunk, along with whatever was left of a bottle of rotgut he'd been able to buy. Even drunk, he could hold forth for a surprisingly long time, in a toothless, gummy drawl. In the dark: ". . . I don't know how I ever got myself into this goddamn mess. Traipsin' all over creation. It ain't no fit life."

From his bunk, the boy's father, in calm tones: "Now, Walt. It's late. Go to sleep."

"I ever locate my discharge from the Army I'm goin' up to the VA Hospital in Denver and have me a real rest and some decent food, not this damn Mexican shit you like to brew up. All fulla chilies. Enough to burn the nuts off a brass monkey. No wonder I got to do most of the cookin' around here. I heard that VA Hospital's got *good* conditions."

"That's right, Walt," his father would say.

"You wanta know something, George? You're plumb *loco*. I mean it."

"Sure, Walter."

"All this dragassin' around the country is your doin', Georgie. I don't see why we can't live in a regular house like real folks. Why, any low-life, chickenfuckin', no-good Mexican greaser's got better conditions than us."

"Try and get some sleep, Walter."

"Fuck you, George. Don't you tell me what to do! Nobody pushes me around. All I'm askin' is how I ever got myself into this mess with you and this miserable kid?"

"Why, sure, Walter. We can split up any time you take a mind to."

"That's the first smart thing I heard you say all week. I'm tired of this life."

"That might be the best thing to do, Walt."

"That's for goddamn sure."

"We'll work it out."

"You bet we will."

"First thing tomorrow."

"Goddamn it, Georgie, I *mean* it!"

"We'll talk it over in the morning."

"We sure as shit will!" For a while he'd grumble and swear to himself. Then, in those sneaky, wheedling tones: "George?"

"What is it, Walt?"

"I wanta git laid, George."

"Sure."

"I ain't been laid in so long I plumb forgot what it feels like."

"We'll do that."

"Not one of them Mexican she-gorillas, George. Gettin' at them is worse than drillin' through a mohair sofa. They ain't nothin' but a lot of hairy bush and smell. They open up, it's enough to make a feller's eyes water."

"We'll see what we can do."

"Soak 'em in sheep-dip, they can still stop a clock."

"I know, Walt."

"Want to find me some old gal with a pair of tits on her like demijohns. Plug one in each ear. Somethin' a man can cozy up to. Settle down. I'm fed up with all this."

But Walter never left. There was a reason, of course, though it took the boy a long time to find out. Just as there were reasons why his father put up with the old man's nasty ways.

That was how the early years went. On the surface, it was a scatterbrained, odyssey-like kind of life, but his father, even with the liquor and the poetry, must have had some sort of vision. A stubborn plan. Some kind of crackpot—or maybe loving —scheme only he could decipher.

Because at about the time that Steinbeck's dustbowl Okies were pointing their funky trucks westward along Route 66 under the mistaken impression that life in California would be better, George Gutierrez began buying up bits and pieces of Sawmill River Flats, in Lincoln County. That was where the meager salaries he earned went; that is, whatever was left over after booze, truck repairs, food, books, and stargazing. The deeds to these modest purchases were made out directly in Roy's name.

Sawmill River was already a ghost town. Had been, in fact, since long before the American Expeditionary Force sailed for Le Havre. Nobody cared about a falling-apart abandoned town up in southern New Mexico's Sacramento Mountains. In those days any man with the money could buy such land for a dollar an acre, or even less, if he went to the trouble of checking tax records, which George Gutierrez did from time to time when they were near the county seat in Carrizozo, picking up delinquent parcels that had once been owned by families long since dead or departed.

That, along with the stargazing, was considered a pretty strange hobby for someone in those Depression times, but he paid taxes right up to the year of his death, and Roy had paid them since, $142.85 the year before, for the entire town, fifty-two buildings, and the 640-acre, one-square-mile section they stood on, smack up against the Lincoln National Forest. It was listed on the county records as unimproved land. Unimproved meaning it was uninhabited, unfenced, and unposted except for a few Private Property signs he had nailed up years ago.

His father had given it to him. For more than a century, his family had lived and died there, and been buried one by one in the small cemetery on the slope above the village.

So GEORGE HAD bought the town, but he earned immortality with stargazing. In 1935, he discovered a comet. One of the very few ways left for a common man to go down in the books until they turn to dust.

They had come back from White Sands, which was where the age of nuclear warfare eventually got born when Dr. Oppenheimer set off the biggest firecracker in history. The physicist had chosen that snow-colored, vast desert west of Ruidoso because there was nothing much out there that could be hurt.

Roy's father had quite accidentally met and talked with Robert Goddard, the early-day rocketeer. Two men of science can always find things to talk about, even in a desert. Goddard, as an experimenter, was a kind of American Werner von Braun, and he had chosen the area for the same reason Oppenheimer did years later: he didn't want any of his homemade skyrockets whizzing through the roof of some rancher's house. New Mexican rural people tend to react to an invasion of their privacy with a dead-serious display of firearms, and they are liable to travel a considerable distance to seek out the offender.

After leaving White Sands, they had taken the Mack up into the mountains and camped near Sawmill River. The conversations with Mr. Goddard had been exciting for his father. At that time, the scientific community in that part of the world was, to put it mildly, limited. One evening, his father set up the telescope.

A lot of their nights were spent that way. Walter would hobble around the campfire, working at a bottle and cursing as he put together something for them to eat. The boy would take it easy—his tasks were to haul water and gather enough wood to keep the blaze going. And George would be off at a considerable distance, so as to get out of range of the campfire's brightness, with his telescope mounted and the big volumes of star charts handy, with a flashlight to check the charts and a bottle of his own to hold off the high-altitude chill.

He had fashioned the instrument with his own hands, out of a six-inch-diameter antique Zeiss portrait-camera lens that had a twenty-inch focal length—nowadays, because of its tremendous light-gathering power, it would be known as a rich-field telescope —and had rigged it on an equatorial mounting he had welded from salvaged portions of a Chevrolet rear-axle differential, so that the scope would stay fixed on any star in a constellation he wanted to look at regardless of the earth's rotation.

George Gutierrez was no great mathematician, but he had an insuperable advantage over other amateur stargazers, besides a crude but incredibly lovely piece of optical equipment. The night skies of New Mexico were stunningly clear. So he found this little comet in the upper left quadrant of Taurus, a tiny spark of light that wasn't on the chart—and with the help of the flashlight and some scratch paper he made drawings. The next night the spark had moved. It had to be a planet or an asteroid or a comet. He got so excited he drove into Ruidoso and after much difficulty put a telephone message through to Mr. Goddard, who suggested that he Western Union the Central Bureau for Astronomical Telegrams. He did. The Bureau confirmed the find. Gave him official credit and eventually verified the comet's course . . . a wide oval, almost paraboloid in its approach to our sun—*El Sol*—returning every two hundred and sixty-four years for a peek at what all of us are up to in this little out-of-the-way planetary system. So as long as records were kept, the Comet Gutierrez—"*P-Gutierrez, 1935*"—would keep the name alive. In Anno Domini 2199. In 2463. 2727. And so on, clean down to Armageddon.

George Gutierrez was so thrilled, he went on a week-long toot.

TULAROSA, OSCURA, CARRIZOZO, and on in to Capitan, population 439, one motel, one restaurant, one bar—a town that once had big-time ideas. Around 1890, when coal was still king, Capitan was calling itself the Pittsburgh of the Southwest. Then the mines shut down, and nothing had happened to the place since, except that it took some small pride in having given a home to a badly burned bear cub brought in by a park ranger, who had rescued it in a fire up in Lincoln National Forest. The cub survived, donned a ranger's hat, and went on to become Smokey the Bear, but Capitan itself was on its last legs. The same with Sawmill River Flats, Roy thought. Everybody was going to make millions from all the timber that would be hauled out of the mountains when Colonel Eddy put in the railroad. Only Colonel Eddy put his railroad someplace else. Now rats, centipedes, and bullsnakes had the town all to themselves.

It was almost nine when he drove down Capitan's main street. The place was dark and quiet. The neon sign of the motel had "No Vacancy" showing. Tourist season, such as it was, was at its peak. Capitan does a fair business in summer. Out-of-staters like to visit the town of Lincoln, a few miles down the road, and see where Billy the Kid broke loose and shotgunned Deputy Bob Olinger from the second-story porch of the courthouse. In August, local people stage a sort of pageant, with lots of gunfights to show visitors what the Lincoln County War was supposed to have been like. The war was actually never anything but an extended feud between the Tunstall crowd and J. J. Riley, which got out of hand when Billy, who was a cowboy employed by the former faction, began operating his .41 Colt. Nowadays beer, candy, and souvenirs are sold, and the pageant charges admission. The visibility goes down to zero in the smoke made by blank cartridges, and the tourists blink their eyes and take lots of Kodachromes to prove to everybody back home that the Kid was a real-life person and not a story, and that they had trodden the very same ground used by the young outlaw. Capitan and Lincoln are poor places, but up in the mountains not far away, around Ruidoso and Alto, millionaire Texans and Oklahomans have developed a fancy playground, with a ski resort, private landing strips, and the racetrack at Ruidoso Downs, which offers one of the biggest purses in the country.

From Capitan, Roy headed the jeep southeast, ascending into the foothills until he got to a place called Honcho. Honcho was just a dozen buildings, all old except for a whitepainted house trailer that had a sign out front:

Pearl's Cheese & Wool Goods

Pearl Lowdermilk's lights were still on. He parked out front and went in.

SHE WAS SITTING alone in the living room, watching something on television as she carded wool, which she bought from the Indians up on the reservation. Looked up. Did a double-take, set down her carder, then reached over and lowered the volume on the set. She said, "So!"

And then, as if this wasn't enough: "It's you."

"Hi, Pearl."

"You're back." She was an old friend but would die rather than admit it. Her style was to find fault, so with her he went out of his way to be well-mannered. She hated being teased, and he did this, too.

"Yup."

"In all your glory."

"Sure enough, Pearl."

"Figured you'd drift in one of these days."

"Got lonesome for the old place."

"Staying, or passing through?"

"Staying awhile."

"Well, that'll give folks something to talk about."

"How's everything been, Pearl?"

"Bad, as usual, and going to worse. And now you show up. Funny, Maudie Dalrymple was asking after you just last week, when she came by to take the TB tests on my goats." Maude Dalrymple was the county public health nurse, and had been for almost forty years. "She was wondering if maybe you'd gotten locked away in some mental institution."

"She doesn't mean that."

"Well, that's what she said."

"Maudie's got a heart of gold."

"Billy Maldonado swears he's going to shoot you on sight if he spots you."

"Billy-Evil isn't so bad, Pearl. He's been talking that way for years."

She said ominously, "It wouldn't surprise me if some others felt the same."

"That's their problem."

"Going up to Sawmill?"

"I thought I might."

"People been looking around for you up there."

"You don't say. What kind of people?"

"Money people, I'd guess. They had on suits."

"They wouldn't be locals, then."

"Looked to me like eastern types, Roy."

"You talk to them?"

"Had to. They knew your mail comes care of me."

"What'd they want?"

"Wouldn't say."

"They ask questions about me?"

"Some."

"You tell them anything?"

"They was in too much of a hurry to listen to an old woman."

"Say, Pearl, feel like a six-pack?"

"Sure. You buying?"

"Why not?"

"It's two fifty these days," she said. "You know where the fridge is."

"My treat."

"I'll say it is."

"I'm beat. Been on the road all day."

"Where from?"

"Texas. El Paso."

"El Paso? What were you doing down in a terrible place like that?"

"Nothing much. Before that I was in Mexico."

"I don't know why you've got to go running off to such out-landish places," she said. "What was it like?"

"Just fine. I had a good time."

"I'll bet. Sounds like you were loafing around, as usual."

"Nope. Had a regular job and everything."

She stared at him. "You look awful."

"These are just my traveling clothes."

"I ain't talking about clothes. You lose any more weight you'll have to hold your bones together with chewing gum and hair-pins."

"I'm fit. I'm feeling great, Pearl."

"Couldn't tell by looking."

"I have any mail?"

"You do." She looked at him. "I reckon you want me to fetch it for you."

"I didn't say I wanted it, Pearl. All I asked was if I had any."

"After three years you got a drawerful," she said. "I ought to charge you for being a post office."

"I'll look at it tomorrow."

"I'll get it," she said, a shade too easily.

"Thanks, Pearl."

She stood up. "You just breeze right in, like you own the whole show. I don't know how you figure you rank special treatment."

"You get the mail. I'll get the beer."

He went out to the kitchen and took a cold six-pack from the refrigerator, along with some butter, a loaf of homemade bread, a round of goat cheese, and an onion. She walked past him. "Nice to see you again, Pearl."

She said over her shoulder, "I doubt that. You and your sweet talk."

"You got a way of making a person feel right at home."

"That'll be the day."

"Feel like a sandwich with that beer?"

"Oh, all right," she said, still acting grumpy. "But leave off that onion, else I won't get a minute's sleep. Gets me gassy. Try some of that cheese by itself, if you're hungry. It's something new. I put garlic, pepper, and cilantro in it, and fresh parsley. Some folks say it ain't bad."

He popped open two cans of Coors and followed her back to her bedroom. "How's business been?"

"Gas is up, the dollar is out the window, and the tourist trade is down. I don't like goats, but I've got sixty-seven Nubians, including kids and a new billy, and I got to milk the mammas every day and then pasteurize and process and press it all—I mean, that's work—and I got a hundred and twenty-six chickens, and the garden, and everything else. I wish I was young again and could ride a horse and run a few cows. At my age, I ought to be able to sit back and relax. Now, on top of everything else, I got this sweater sideline. Handmade sweaters bring a good price, but if there is one thing I despise it's knitting. That's what folks want these days, not something nice and neat that you can buy at J. C. Penney's, but a big old hairy wool sweater, with natural dyes and handspun yarn. I just wish I was young again. You know, Roy, when I was eighteen I rode a horse named Whacker all the way from here to Montana by myself with just a dog for company. Twelve hundred miles, and it was the best time I ever had. Took a whole summer, clean up through the middle of the Rockies. I had some real interesting adventures for myself, and pretty near got married. Which is more than what happens around here. But what else can a person do? I have to stay alive, even if it means making cheese from those ugly Satan-eyed Nubians. They got a way of staring at a person that just sets my teeth on edge. I make cheese, and I knit, and live on more fresh chicken than I care to think about, and you want to know how business is. You got no more business sense than a flea."

"Do you know, the church in Rome once made a saint out of

a flea?" he said. "St. Puce he was called, and he was said to have lived in the armpit of Christ."

"You quit that kind of talk. I don't believe a word of it."

"God's truth, Pearl."

"You get crazier every year." She shook her head. "Maudie's right. You ought to be put out of your misery for good."

"No need. I mind my own business and trouble no man."

"Some think different."

"Like who?"

"Bill Maldonado for one."

"He's got a chip on his shoulder is all. Had it all his life."

"And you're the chip."

"I always tried to get along with Bill. Most of the time."

"Sure, like flint and steel," Pearl said. "I don't know why you enjoy aggravating him so. You're smart enough to know better. It ain't entirely his fault he's dumb, without having you point it out to him." She thought about this. "Although, offhand, I don't know of anything dumber than a Spanish ranchhand who's convinced himself he's the All-American Champion Rodeo Cowboy. Only time I ever saw a spark of sense in that man was when I hired him to build a corral for the new breeding billy I bought last spring. This he-goat is as tough as they come, pretty near six feet high at the horns. Three times in a row he tore apart the corral Maldonado had him in, trying to get at the nannies, the nasty thing. So Maldonado went around the corral hammering six-inch common nails through all the planks with the points facing in, figuring no animal would try butting his head through a forest of spikes. He thought he had the situation whipped, but you know what that billygoat did? He went around to each nail and scratched his head on it, and bent every last one flat against the planks, and all the while he was staring Maldonado right in the eye, with one of those think-you-know-it-all? looks. Billy-Evil got so mad he broke a solid oak two-by-four over the he-goat's head, and that goat acted like he thought Billy was maybe getting a mite too friendly so he charged, and Maldonado skipped over the top corral rail like it was nothing. After that, he wouldn't go near that billygoat. So, you see? Billy-Evil ain't quite as dumb as you make out."

They got his mail and went back to the living room. She said she'd make the sandwiches.

Pearl Lowdermilk's trailer was the hub of Honcho. Once a week by telephone she took orders for liquor, meat, and groceries from the outlying ranches in the area and drove her truck to the supermarket in Carrizozo. She also dealt illegally in beer, wine, and cigarettes out of the trailer's kitchen, and when she wasn't doing that she placed her goat cheese and wool goods in shops up in Ruidoso and Alto.

Pearl was a rawboned, lanky old gal, well over six feet tall, whitehaired now, but she was a vivacious brunette as a young woman. She and her first husband had ranched six thousand acres over by Spindle, and Roy had recollections of her clean back to the days of the WPA and the CCC camps. She was pretty salty and hard to get along with even then, and every time she did an act of kindness or generosity she acted surprised. Gruffness came natural to her, and those who knew her made a point of not stepping on her toes.

Roy always suspected that she'd had something of a crush on his father. Pearl was getting long in the tooth now, but there were stories about how she'd had a romantic nature in her day. Once, in 1931, she ran off with a barnstorming aviator all the way to Pensacola, Florida. He was following the crops, dusting. After four months she came back, and her second husband—that was Ben, he was a well-driller—took her to task for her unfaithfulness. "I come back, didn't I?" she told him. "If that ain't being faithful, I don't know what is." So he asked her why she'd done it, and she said, "Well, I'd never been flying, and I was kind of curious about it." So then he had to know how she liked it, and Pearl thought about this for a while and then told him, "About like walking, only faster, Ben." And they left it at that.

She and Roy finished their beers and he opened two more while she made sandwiches. "I got two new cheese lines this year," she said. "One with garlic and wine, the other with green chili and onion."

"They selling okay?" he asked, going through his mail. Most of it was junk stuff.

"Three dollars a pound. That's little enough for the miserable work I put into making it."

"You've got a real eye for business, Pearl."

"I doubt that. There has to be easier ways for a widow to get by." She was eyeing the mail as he went through it. "Roy, is the rest of the country as bad as they say it is on tv?"

"Worse, Pearl. Just awful."

"Lot of them perverts and criminals, I guess."

"Country's just crawling with them."

"What's this world coming to?"

"Pearl, you wouldn't believe it."

Sara Pacheco, the clerk over at the county seat, had written to tell him that his taxes next year would be going up to over four hundred dollars, as part of a county-wide reassessment program. There was an advertisement to buy real estate in southern Colorado: Rustic Ranchettes, $500.00 down, twenty years to pay. An invitation to join a vitamin-of-the-month club. A firm in Joliet, Illinois, was interested in researching and charting his family tree for $8.95, and for a mere twenty-five dollars he could have his coat of arms made up in four colors on "genuine polyurethane plastic," suitable for mounting on a wall or over a fireplace, where it would be a "continuing source of pleasure and admiration for friends and family alike."

But the one letter he was hoping for was not there.

Between sips of beer Pearl went back to carding her wool. She was still keeping an eye on him as he worked through the mail. She said, "Never even a forwarding address out of you this whole time. I don't know why you got to wander around so when you were born right here. I guess Lincoln County ain't good enough for you."

"Sometimes a man gets a craving to see the country."

"I heard that before. Straight out of your late father's mouth." Finally, she lost patience and snapped, "Down near the bottom . . . you got a telegram!"

He found it. The envelope's flap was torn open. Pearl said, "I figured I better look in it, Roy."

"No harm done."

"Thought it was something that could be important."

"You did the right thing."

" 'Course, I would have just sent it along, if I'd known *where* to," she said irritably. "If you had any sense, you'd make provisions for an emergency."

"Emergencies have a way of taking care of themselves, Pearl," he said.

"It must have come at least two months ago."

He looked at the date. "So it did."

"Western Union brought it up from Carrizozo," she said. "You know this fellow Larson?"

"Doesn't ring a bell."

The telegram read:

NO LUCK REPEATED ATTEMPTS CONTACT YOU STOP IMPERATIVE YOU CONTACT ME IMMEDIATELY RE TOP PRIORITY FINANCIAL INVESTMENT OPPORTUNITY STOP REPEAT ONCE IN LIFETIME OPPORTUNITY STOP CALL NEIL LARSON COLLECT 212 435 6607 OR WRITE LARCO 45 EAST 43RD ST NEW YORK NY STOP LARSON

"What do you make of it, Roy?"

"Offhand, nothing."

"You want to call him?"

"Tonight?"

"You don't think it might be important?"

"I'm bushed." No office in New York was open now, but he was enjoying her curiosity.

"I don't think he'd send a telegram like that unless it was important."

"It might be. But I doubt it."

She thought about this. "Well, if you ask me, it sounds like it *might* be important!"

"Not tonight, Pearl. If it came in that long ago, another few days won't make much difference."

She drank some of her beer and then after a minute said, "You know what I think, Roy? I think that telegram has something to do with those other fellows."

"What other fellows?"

"The ones who came snooping around here this spring. They went up to Sawmill two or three times trying to find you."

"Those eastern types you mentioned?"

"Yup. You could spot 'em a mile off just by looking at them."

"You mean they were perverts?"

"Lordy, how would *I* know?" she said grumpily and went back to her wool. "Sometimes you say the craziest things I ever heard of."

There was also a letter from the New Mexico Historical Society up in Santa Fe, signed by someone named Gardiner Potts. Potts wanted to know if he was interested in having all that remained of Sawmill River Flats designated ". . . an official cultural and historical landmark, in accordance with N.M. State Bill 2503, 1960, entitled *An Act to Recognize and Preserve Historical Sites.*"

He showed this letter to Pearl. She read it and said, "Sounds like one of those historical eccentrics. That crowd'll make a state monument out of anything they can lay their hands on, including my billygoat if I let 'em. However, it won't do you any harm to look into it. Find out what this Potts' intentions are."

"A cultural and historical landmark," he said. "Say, after all these years, wouldn't that be something!"

"You fool. I bet you could get yourself one of those property-tax exemptions. These millionaires pull that stunt every day of the week. Look at the Rockefellers, and that old rip, Hearst, who built that big castle—what is it, San Simon's?—out in California."

"Saint Simeon's. But, Pearl, places like that are worth millions."

"Can't you ever be sensible? Nobody's asking you to *sign* anything," she said. "All I was advising is that it won't hurt to check into it."

He thought about this and then started on a fresh beer. "You know something, the idea really appeals to me . . . having one of those bronze markers stuck up on a pedestal at the edge of town. Something for all the world to see: OFFICIAL HISTORICAL SITE."

"Roy, you can't eat a bronze marker," she said. "I ain't your financial advisor. Ain't none of *my* affair. But I'm getting a funny feeling in my bones, and they're telling me that it has to do with that old pile of shacks you got up in the mountains. Somebody's wanting something for nothing. I can smell it in the air. First those eastern types who went up there trying to scout you out. Then that telegram comes in, and now some historical-society idiot is taking an interest."

"Maybe these historical people would let me have the worm concession."

She gave him a hard look. "What're you talking about?"

"There are some pretty fine trout streams around Sawmill."

"Are you teasing me again?"

"Any man who could finagle the worm concession is bound to make money."

"I swear! Talking to you is a waste of my time!"

He made himself another sandwich and got a second six-pack. "Where you fixing to sleep?" she asked.

"Got a goosedown bag out in the jeep," he said. "Had it made special for me. If it's okay, I'll curl up on the back porch."

"Take the extra bedroom," she said. "If I woke up tomorrow and found a frozen cadaver on my porch, this town'd never let me live it down."

"They'll talk anyway, if they hear a man slept in the house with you," he said.

She smiled. "Oh, they'll hear, all right. I may be old, but it don't follow that people can take me for granted. I'd enjoy putting a bee in that Maudie Dalrymple's bonnet. She sure thinks she's the cat's pajamas, coloring her hair and wearing it in those sausage curls like Shirley Temple. Shucks, she went through her first change of life back when Hoover was promising us a chicken in every pot."

AT FIVE THE next morning he heard her get up and go out to the goat pens. Later she banged on his door and yelled through it that breakfast was ready.

"No need to bother, Pearl."

"Who'd bother over you? A person's got to eat, is all."

"I'm not much on breakfast."

"Nor lunch nor supper, from the way you look."

"Okay, I'm coming."

"Nothing fancy, like they serve in them Pancake House places. You don't like it, don't eat it. I don't care."

"Be right there."

He heard her walk away, muttering, "You better be. It ain't going to stay hot all day."

The kitchen was cheerful and tidy. Checkered blue cotton tablecloth. And what they call a ranch breakfast. Hot buttered homemade bread fresh from the oven. Half a dozen sunnyside eggs, more of the goat cheese, and inch-thick patties of pork sausage peppered with red chili. An electric percolator on the counter simmered, giving off a rich smell of coffee. He said, "You expecting company?"

"If you're going to sit, don't be all day doing it."

They sat down and pitched in. Later he said, "Pearl, you've got to be about the best cook in the whole southwest."

"Lot of good it does me," she said. "Three times a day I cook a meal and sit down by myself and eat it, except for Fridays and Sundays, when old lard-bottom Dalrymple looks in for what she calls a snack. You know, she don't hardly fit on a *chair* anymore? Claims she's a dainty eater, but you set a roast chicken in some pan gravy out in front of her and hand her a whole loaf of bread, and then just leap back out of harm's way while she mops up. It's disgusting. The highway department ought to hire her, just to keep the roads clean."

He had another cup of coffee and smoked a cigarette while Pearl operated a toothpick. By the way she went after the bits of her meal that had gotten lodged, she would have made a passable hardrock miner, and the interesting thing was that she carried on a conversation around her leisurely exploration. "Yew grun uph't'a Thawmill thewday?"

"Thought I might. I'm kind of anxious to see the old place."

"Prumb *roco,* yew rask me."

"I want to leave a list of supplies for you to pick up for me. If I stay on, I may fix up that little cabin again."

"I friggered that. Yew gurn call that New Rork ferrer?"

"Maybe in a few days. I want to get up to Sawmill. Listen, thanks for the breakfast."

She removed the toothpick and inspected a pea-sized morsel of sausage stuck on its end. "Kind of nice to have company once in a while. Even if it has to be you."

"Pearl, you ought to get yourself another husband while you're still young enough."

"You're crazy. Why would I want to go do something like that? You're a bigger fool than Maudie, and she's got husbands

on the brain. I been widowed once, and would've been widowed
a second time if I could have gotten my pistol and taken care of
that tricky crosseyed rattlesnake Harold. I was engaged three
other times, once to a fellow almost got himself elected to the
state senate. What do I want with a man? I don't have much, but
I got my goats and I'm independent. No one tells me what to do.
All I ever got from men was misery."

"Sure, Pearl."

"Besides, I'm too old to change."

"You got lots of life left in you."

"Who'd ever want me?"

"Somebody might."

She lit a cigarette of her own. "Fool's talk. I ain't holding my
breath until it happens."

Afterward, he went out back and raked all the goat pens,
wheelbarrowed the droppings and soiled straw over to the com-
post heap, and distributed fresh hay and alfalfa. There were sixteen kids—*cabritos,* or young goats—and they were at the worst
age, tame but full of curiosity and playfulness, making the most
of their gangly, limber legs, bouncing around like pingpong
balls, all frisky and mischievous. Some were atop the pens' little
sheds, and one was up in a tree, proving to himself that young
goats can go anywhere.

He went back into the kitchen, got three gallons of wine and
a carton of cigarettes. She watched him, and then said, "Ain't
you going to take some food with you at least?"

"I've got some leftover stuff in the jeep," he said. "I wouldn't
mind having some of that cheese, though."

"You like it?"

"It's about the best I ever tasted. A little of that cheese and
some bread, and a man has himself a real meal."

"All right," she said. She went to the fridge and got out cheese
and three loaves. "Roy, you ain't changed. You're worse than
your father ever was. If you were going up in the mountains for
six months' prospecting, you'd take a carton of Saltines, two tins
of sardines and pork and beans, and as much of that cheap wine
as you could carry. A man can't hardly live off the land no more.
Things have changed. Those days are gone, when a man could
poach an elk or deer and live on good plain meat."

"I've been taking care of myself. At fifty-two, a man has to."

"Roy Gutierrez, you're fifty-six. Don't trim the edges of the pastry with someone who knows you. And what have you got to show for it? 'Course, you're disadvantaged." She thought about this. "Even so. That's all the more reason for a man to exercise common sense. But you!"

"I'm a free man."

"I don't know what that means. What it looks like to me is that you ain't got a pot to pee in or a grand piano to pour it into."

"I have my health."

"Shucks. I wonder who you think you're talking to? You're getting ready for your dying. I seen it before. I'm sorry you came back. Every time you go up to that old town, you turn strange in the head. That's what comes from not living sensible and taking care of what the Lord gave you. You're on your last legs. Any blind man with two eyes in his head could see that much."

"I'll be okay, Pearl. Really."

"Maybe so. Do me one favor, though, before you go skittering off. Call that man who sent the telegram. I thought about it last night after I went to bed. Find out what's on his mind."

HE SAT WITH her in the kitchen and had another cigarette and a cup of coffee while he made out his shopping list. Took two one-hundred-dollar bills from his money belt. "If there's any change, hang on to it until I need more supplies," he said. She didn't bother to look at the list, but admired the hundreds. "Say, Pearl, while you're in Carrizozo, pick me up a twenty-five-dollar money order at the post office, will you?"

"Want me to get your boots shined and your pants pressed while I'm at it, too?" she said. "You going to make that call or ain't you?"

It was after eleven by then, according to the electric clock on her wall. "Two hours difference in the east," he said. "Can I use your phone? I'll call collect."

"Collect is what it said in that telegram."

She busied herself at the sink with some task or another as he dialed. He knew that nothing short of an earthquake would have gotten her out of the kitchen when he was on long-distance. She dried her hands on a towel, brought over a sheet of scratch paper and a pencil in case he had to take notes, and then went back to the sink.

By now the operator had gotten the New York number. A woman came on the line, some kind of secretary, and said, "Mr. Larson is out of the office right now. Operator, who did you say was calling?"

"Mayor Roy A. Gutierrez," he broke in, "of Sawmill River Flats, New Mexico."

At the sink, he heard Pearl snort, "Mayor!" and then add something like "If you'd just get into the habit of telling the truth once in a blue moon, everybody around you wouldn't get so confused."

"I'll accept the charges, operator," the woman at the other end said. And then, to him, "Good afternoon, Your Honor."

"Afternoon, miss. I have a telegram here . . ."

"I know. He's *terribly* anxious to get in touch with you. May he call you back?"

"Miss, I'm only going to be here in my office for a few minutes."

Pearl glared at him and muttered, "Office!"

The secretary on the line said, "He's placed top priority on getting hold of you."

"Well, I'm sorry I missed him."

"He went out to lunch a while ago," she said. "Mayor Gutierrez, I have the restaurant's number here on my desk. Could you wait for ten minutes while I call there and have him phone you back?"

"I'll wait," he said. "But if you can't reach him, would you call me back and let me know, please?" He gave her Pearl's number and hung up.

Pearl said, "Mayor! I don't know why you have to lie so much."

"I wasn't lying," he said. "Up in Sawmill, I'm a population of one. I can be mayor if I want to, or police chief, or the whole city council."

"Is he going to return the call?"

"He's in a restaurant, having lunch. They're trying to reach him there."

"You mean like they do in the movies, where a waiter just

hauls a phone over to the table on a long cord?" She stared at him. "Oh, Roy, he must be awfully important."

"Not necessarily. Big-city people are like that. They can get by without all kinds of things, but they get nervous if they're more than six feet away from a phone."

In a few minutes the phone rang. Pearl whispered, "You want I should answer it?"

"Go ahead. Maybe it's for you."

"Roy, if it's him, what'll I *say?*"

"Any old thing that comes to mind."

After the fourth ring she lifted the receiver. "Yes. Good afternoon. Only it's morning here. Yes, this here is the mayor's office. Yes, the mayor's still here. I ain't sure if he's busy. Who is this?"

She handed him the receiver with her eyes narrowed into cat slits: "It's *him!*" she hissed.

Neil Larson was not much on social amenities. "Mayor Gutierrez, yes, I'm glad we've finally made contact. I've been trying to get hold of you for months. Listen, I've got a business proposition you can't afford to miss. I'm going to make you rich. You got anything against money?"

"No."

"Good. Very sensible." Larson had a strong, aggressive voice that was like orange marmalade mixed with hickory chips and fine-screened gravel. Plenty of smoothness, but, underneath, a touch of the old rough-and-tumble. "Just a moment." He spoke an aside, apparently to someone sitting at his table: "Ed, flag that waiter and get us more coffee. I'll only be a minute." And, back to Gutierrez: "Roy—you don't mind if I call you Roy?—I'm not talking nickels and dimes. This is *real* money! Listen, I think I can get a representative out there to you before the end of the week. Friday. How's Friday? If I can get away, I'll come out myself."

"Just a second," Gutierrez put in. "What does your company do, Mister Larson?"

"Ever heard of Disneyland?" Larson demanded. "Marineland? Transamerica? Safari West, Club Méditerranée? MCA?"

"Well, yes. Some of them."

"LarCo's done business with all of them. Check Dun and Bradstreet. We have a top rating."

"But what kind of business are you in?"

"We're in conceptual development," Larson said. "We come up with the ideas, and we make them happen." He sounded enthusiastic. "Sometimes negotiated fee, sometimes joint-venture. We have total turnkey capability. We fast-track our projects. Our clients make money. Our emphasis is on re-creational environments. You probably don't know about these things. Actually, I'm sure you've never seen anything like what we do."

"Recreational environments?"

"No, no. Re-*creational*, not *rec*reational! Two entirely different concepts. It'd take too long to explain it right now. Trust me and sit tight. I'll get a man out there double quick."

"But I may not be around."

"For God's sake, stay put until we can get out to your neck of the woods. Is that asking so much? I told you, I'll come myself if I can. Roy, listen. This is millions we're talking about."

"But why me?"

"You own a ghost town?"

"Well, yes. I own some land up in the mountains. There's a town on it."

"D'you still own it outright? You haven't sold any of it?"

"No."

"Don't."

"Mister Larson, how do you know I own it outright?"

"Abstract company ran a title search."

"Listen, Mr. Larson, if this has to do with selling my town, I don't think I'm interested."

"No one has said anything about buying or selling property. Let's talk. That's all I ask. It costs nothing to listen. I guarantee it will be to your advantage. I'll have someone out there in a few days. Good talking with you. You be available."

With that, Larson hung up.

Pearl said, "Well?"

He sat there for a moment, thinking. Then he said, "I think he wants to buy Sawmill River Flats. He wouldn't come right out and say so, but I think that's what it is."

"Real estate man?"

He frowned and shook his head. "No. It didn't sound like that.

He was talking about things like re-creation and fast-tracking and turnkeys."

"You mind telling me what that means in plain English?"

"I don't know."

"Sounds like sweet talk in my opinion."

"He said his company's in conceptual development. Whatever that is."

"Sounds worse than getting pregnant," she said. "What are you going to do about it?"

"Do? Nothing for now, I guess," he said.

"That's smart."

"They're sending someone out to talk to me."

"Just don't sign nothing," Pearl said. She was suspicious, but he could see that she was curious, and more than a little excited, too. Not much happened in or around Honcho. She looked at him. "Might be smart to check out this outfit, so that you know who you're talking to."

"In time, Pearl," he said. "I've been looking forward to getting up to Sawmill."

"Well, if you don't have brains enough to do a little inquiring, then I will," she said, getting angry. "If they're not in real estate, then what in hell *is* their business? Can't ranch up in those mountains. Can't cut but so much timber under the law. Ain't no minerals or mining in that area, that I ever heard of. So, then, who are these people? I got to deliver some cheese up in Ruidoso tomorrow. I think I'll ask around about this Larson. Was he talking money?"

"Big money."

"Talk's cheap."

"He said they'd already run an abstract on the whole six hundred and forty acres."

"Well, you better believe *that* cost him," she said. "He's got something fancy up his sleeve. Mark my words."

SAWMILL RIVER FLATS was four miles from Honcho as the crow flies but more like eleven by the seldom-used logging road that led to it . . . one long series of serpentine switchbacks rising steadily until the town itself was reached at 9,200 feet: in that part of the country, the desert meets the mountains with an abruptness that surprises anyone not used to the geography.

It was no road to fool with in winter, or spring either, when the mud was axle deep. Once the journey was started there was no turning back—no pull-offs, and not a single ranch or cabin anywhere along the route. There was one fork, a mile out of Honcho. The right-hand way led to the Mescalero Reservation and the ski-resort area. A driver had to stay left to reach Sawmill River Flats and not be put off by the "Dead End" and "Road Impassable" signs Roy had posted years ago.

He had the jeep in first gear. Grinding up toward one of those places marked on geodetic maps by crosshatched lines and labeled "Ruins." And, as always in coming back, he felt the old feelings: happiness, and sadness too. Powerful memories—how many times in past years had he and his father and Walter returned here in the old truck? It was their place. Despite the wandering, George had always brought them back, and for a while they would stay there, living half out of the truck and half in a cabin his father and Walter had fixed up, to fish or hunt or just take it easy, and there would be talking, and liquor for the two men. It was home. Even then the place had been long deserted, but it belonged to them.

At the last moment before he topped the switchback that would reveal the town, two does and a half-grown fawn walked out of the scrub oak at the side of the road and gazed at him for a long moment with limpid, troubled eyes. They walked to the other side of the road and then took off, bounding in easy, soaring leaps through the scrub.

Buildings appeared. His first reaction was disappointment, but he had always felt this after being down in civilization. The old place seemed to have become more desolate than he remembered, and he couldn't understand why someone back east—or anywhere else, for that matter—would be interested in what he saw. He drove on.

Along Main Street there were fearful gaps where houses had once stood. A couple of places had caught fire and burned to their foundations. Summer lightning possibly, but more likely someone had set fire to them, out of carelessness or mischief. Other buildings had simply collapsed. The old planked boardwalk along the north side of Main Street was nearly rotted away, and probably not a single unbroken pane of glass existed in the entire settlement.

He parked the jeep and got out. The gaping doorways of the buildings showed interiors filled with a litter of weatherbleached garbage and rusting tin cans. Several more roofs had fallen in. It was a town, he thought, in need of considerable tidying. Yet it was, as he had pointed out to Pearl Lowdermilk, the only place in the world where he was a population of one, and he could, if the mood struck him, take on multitudinous roles: sheriff, postmaster—though no mail came—town drunk.

He walked up the street to what had been the hotel. The only hotel. Former proprietor, Herman Gutierrez, dead now for over seventy years. The rotted clapboard sign above its portal still showed vague traces of white-and-green lettering, done in an ornate style known today as Barnum:

GRE T IMPERI L HO EL
L dgi g   Hostl ry   Me ls

His father had been born here. In a back bedroom, on the ground floor.

His grandmother, Bertha Hoffman Gutierrez, had died here in 1910.

And the grandfather who had been wanted for murder, Ephraim Munger, had been shot to death on the boardwalk right in front of the gaping holes where there had once been polished plate-glass windows.

Over eighty years ago, Walter Kelly, then a cocky young broncbuster, as full of hell as any wrangler in on the town for a Saturday night, had gotten drunk and passed out scores of times. In Rank's Saloon, diagonally across the street . . . up in the hayloft of Jim Montoya's Livery . . . or, when he had money to pay for it, in one of the Imperial Hotel's rooms . . . as much an alcoholic then as he was to be half a century later.

Inside the hotel, there wasn't much left. The floor, of hand-drawn fir tongue-and-groove, was all right to walk on, and the long counter with its racks of wooden mailslots for roomers who had long since turned to dust was still there.

Somebody had dragged a rotten mattress over to one side of the lobby and left it as a fond souvenir of a teenagers' gangfuck weekend. Someone else had shit by the doorway that led to the kitchen. Empty wine bottles and recyclable aluminum beer cans were everywhere. Probably the local kids from around Ruidoso, Alto, and San Patricio had been having summer fun. They couldn't be blamed for visiting the town. Who was there to tell them not to?

He went back to the jeep and drove up past the north end of town, beyond the sawmill. Nothing much left of it anymore, except an immense debris of rusted machinery and fallen sheds, covered with vines, green moss, and ferns . . . more of a mound or heap, really. He could barely make out the last of the enormous old steam engine that had operated the mill. Another few years and it would all go back to nature.

Beyond the mill, where the flat grassy valley that had given the town its name met the first slopes, he put the jeep into four-wheel drive and forded the stream, noting that a sizable pond had developed. Beaver had moved in to make a home, as they will.

He found the cabin he and his father and Uncle Walter had used on the slope behind the pond, hidden in the trees, and was pleased to see that the local kids hadn't rooted it out and destroyed it.

The door was intact, and the padlock he had put on three years ago was still there, though solidly rusted. He got a pry-bar out of the jeep and broke away the entire lock-and-hasp assembly.

Inside, strong memories again. A large, single room with one boarded-up window. The hardpacked dirt floor was unbelievably messed by field mice and rats. Buckshot-sized calling cards everywhere. Sheepherder's stove. Table, and a couple of crude chairs nailed out of scrap wood. Up on a shelf, some old pots and pans. An oversized bunk he had fashioned for himself years ago.

He was home.

He cleaned the place and did chores for the rest of the day.

Weather perfect. Temperatures in the lower nineties . . . that dry, pure, southwest heat. He worked without a shirt, which was something he never did when other people were present—at Acme, even with the heat of the furnaces, he had kept his shirt closed to the collar and the sleeves rolled down and buttoned at the wrists. He chopped deadwood and hauled water from the stream, unpacked his gear, and set up kerosene lanterns and the transistor radio.

Toward sunset he had his first visitor. An elk, almost tame at this season when there were no hunters, just out of velvet. Roy stood still as the bull browsed to within thirty yards before it decided it had gotten close enough, and then it walked off.

At dusk he filled a quart-sized pickle jar with wine and took this and some of the cheese and bread down to the pond to watch the beaver as they got ready to call it a day. He sat on a rotted stump not far from the water's edge, eating and drinking quietly as the animals swam back and forth, rippling the glassy water with their V-wakes.

Then one surfaced in the shallows near him, got scared, and sounded the alarm. The flat tail slapping the water made a report like a .22 going off.

Later, by lantern light in the cabin, he drank more wine. Tomorrow, he would visit the cemetery where his father and Uncle Walter were buried.

That night, in the thick pines and fir that crowded the slopes towering above the cabin, he heard coyotes calling back and forth, as lonesome and beautiful a sound as any human could ever wish for. He figured they were all the company he needed for the time being.

THREE

The next morning, after breakfast, he walked into town and climbed a rocky slope that rose above the west side of Main Street, behind the ruins of Rank's Saloon and Montoya's Livery. Halfway up the slope there was a small field that was more or less level, closed in by the remnants of a crude stone fence.

This was the old cemetery, like everything else abandoned now, and here were buried his grandparents, Ephraim Munger and Bertha Gutierrez, as well as her husband, Herman, and other citizens of the town, all gone back to earth, with only a few gray-weathered scraps of wood markers or exfoliated headstones, eroded by decades of hard winters, to mark their final resting places.

He was still able to locate Bertha's gravesite because he remembered his father and Walter bringing flowers to it—they had buried her themselves, in 1910—but there was nothing to mark where her husband, or the lover, Ephraim, lay.

The most recent graves were on one side of the cemetery near the stone fence—his father's and Uncle Walter's side by side, as they had been for most of their lives. Small concrete slabs marked them:

GEORGE R. GUTIERREZ   WALTER GORDON KELLY
April 4, 1894–August 12, 1956   *1870?–October 18, 1978*
Discoverer—Comet P-1935   *Citizen of This Republic*

Roy had cast the slabs, when the time came for each of these men, using Portland cement and arroyo sand, scratching the inscriptions deeply into the wet concrete so that they would last.

Now he sat down on a flat rock atop the stone fence and lit a cigarette, trying to sort out his feelings and memories. A breeze rippled across a field of yellow mountain daisies in a meadow far below. White fleecy clouds towered in the summer sky overhead.

When his father died there had been no minister or prayers, because George Gutierrez never believed in any of that. Afterward, Roy and Walter had gone back to the cabin.

It was then, over a bottle of wine, on a quiet August afternoon, that he learned some new things about this man who had fathered him. For on that day Walter's mind was clear and, just for once, his sour and bitter disposition had been caged—the old man could for a fact grieve.

As a child, Roy had thought of his father as perfect, someone who had endless love and patience, who had held him by the hand during the long walks they took together. As he grew older, Roy suspected that George Gutierrez was as human as the next man, and, sitting and talking with Walter, he learned that there was some truth in this. He remarked—half to himself, but also to keep the conversation from lagging—"He was really a gentle sort of man, wasn't he?"

"Well, he was," Walter said. "Them's the worst kind."

"What do you mean?"

"George was a good feller, but he wasn't necessarily no saint," the old man replied.

"Shucks, most of his life we just stayed off by ourselves," Roy said. "He was almost like a hermit."

"Oh, he could be solitary, all right," Walter said. "More or less, that is. You know, Roy, a feller can't live off in the mountains all his natural life, staring at stars and messing around rocks and injun ruins. Not when he's young, anyway." Walter drank a little of his wine. "George had his failings. But, you know, he had style, too. A feller with style can always get away with murder."

"You mean he chased around?"

"They all do. I reckon no one can blame him for that, though," Walter said. "When he was on the straight an' narrow, why, butter wouldn't melt in his mouth. He'd stay that way for a while, and then like any other young buck he'd go on the prod. Mind, I'm not sayin' Georgie was ever a gadabout. He couldn't dance, not with that game leg of his, and he couldn't sing or play the guitar or anything like that. Oftentimes he wasn't even much of a talker. Sometimes he'd talk the ear clean off a person, but mostly he was pretty quiet."

"Well, he must have had something," Roy said.

"He surely did."

"But what?"

"Georgie knew how to sit still," the old man said. "You've got a lot of that in you, boy. Just sittin' still."

"I don't know what you mean," Roy said.

"Well, it was like this," Walter said. "When we were in a town —this was way before you was born—I mean, when that mood took hold of him, Georgie was the greatest natural-born sitter I ever laid eyes on. He could outsit the Sphinx. I used to accuse him of bein' a cripple-leg spider, all clutched up in its web, waiting. He wouldn't make a move. But sooner or later something wearing a skirt would come moseying along.

"We'd be in one town or another, see, workin' for wages. And then he'd start gittin' all vacant-eyed an' absentminded, so that you had to ask him five or six times did he want his eggs over easy or straight up, and even then you couldn't git a sensible answer outa him—he'd git so dreamy, you coulda served him hardboiled eggs and said they was scrambled, and he woulda chewed 'em shells an' all. That's how I could tell the mood was on him. He'd git quieter an' quieter. Didn't know nothin' about courtin', or shinin' up to a female. And, worse, he could be so goddamn *particular*. Georgie would sit around and stare down into his drink until all hell froze over, waitin' for one special girl to come walkin' in. He was more like some kinda permanently mounted *fix*ture than a man. Well, after a while, some sweet young filly would finally speak to him. That was the end of her. Then it was like a quail caught in a figure-four trap. He was nothin' to look at, just a skinny young feller with that whitish hair that stuck up in back. But he could talk. And that girl would listen.

"You know, back in those days, he had the most stupendous manners when he took a notion to. Georgie was never pushy. It didn't trouble him if nobody ever spoke to him. He had that knack of just sittin'. Of course, I'd be swampin' out whatever saloon it was we was hangin' around in. I'd keep all the leftovers for him, 'cept what I'd saved for my own use. I've seen that man drink down bourbon slops, wine, and flat beer all flung into one glass and never blink an eye. He'd just gargle it down like it was lemon squash, and then roll hisself a Bull Durham. You know what I think it was? He was different than most of the other fellers around. That's what enticed the females into the web!

"In those days, around this part of the country, most folks was poor ranchers or cowpokes or miners, and that was about it. There were some railroad men, and travelin' salesmen with order books stickin' outa their pockets and a valise. But when he took a mind to, Georgie could quote poetry by the hour, and he knew all about scientific things, and toward the shank of the evenin' when the whiskey an' beer had got him mellowed, he often did. As though romancin' was the very last thing on his mind. Good manners, and polite as can be, just like a bullsnake grinnin' at a gopher.

"I guess young girls in those days were the same as they are now. They were all so goddamn pretty and fired-up to find out what a man was like. Small in the waist and round in the ass, with a full head of steam in their britches an' their chests puffed out like partridge hens, and they had those eyes like a wounded deer. Lookin' around this way and that, you know, just to see what they could see.

"Back then it was ordinary for a ranch family to come into town regular, every couple of months, and after they'd tended to their shoppin' and business, the father would take the whole brood to a saloon. 'Course, a respectable woman wasn't allowed in no saloon by herself, but often there was a family section in the back where people could sit. So there would be a few beers for the grownups, and soda pops and pretzels for the kids.

"It was a chance for folks to git together and talk. That's how lots of people got to know each other, who ended up marryin' and raisin' families. There is nothing better on a Saturday afternoon when it's blisterin' outside and real cool and shadowy in a barroom than to have a few drinks and carry on a little. Give the older girls in the family a chance to show off what nature gave 'em, and at the same time, look over the year's prospects, such as they were.

"And there would be Georgie an' me, with him sittin' in his web, waitin'. He wouldn't go after just *any* ol' gal, you understand. It wasn't just prettiness either. Some of them young heifers was simply ravishin', all big brown flashin' eyes, and so clean 'an wholesome, you know, with freckles and teeth whiter'n snow, oh, they was full of mischief, so that a feller couldn't make up his mind which end to take a bite outa first. And don't you think these country girls was stupid, 'cause they weren't. Some was real smart. Those was the ones Georgie went for. I don't mean education—most of 'em had never got past grade school—but you kin always spot brains in a girl by the way she moves her eyes while she's natterin' away.

"For instance, she might be talkin' a mile a minute with some other lady about a recipe for sourdough pan biscuits, as if her only ambition in life was to fill a Denver & Rio Grande boxcar with 'em, and all the while those eyes of hers are measurin' the worth of every man within rifle range. You ever happen to notice how a female can just sense it clean down to her toenails when a feller comes within a thousand yards? They kinda come alive.

"I will say that about Georgie. He didn't seem to mind women, and could take his ease with 'em, an' be comfortable. Women grate my nerves. They never stop talkin'. But he'd listen to everything they had to say, though most of it was gabble to me. In that way, he was a very easygoin' feller to be around. I never could figger why, but women seemed partial to him. I've seen females married twenty years, who oughta known better, git restless with George. They'd sit there, yappin' away, an' their legs would cross, an' then uncross, and then cross again, an' one foot would be tap-tappin' on the floor nervous like, and all the while ol' Georgie would just sit there, smilin' and lookin' absentminded, and listenin' politely. But it was the young, pretty ones he got a cravin' for most. You might even say he had a weakness in that direction. He told me one time, 'They got all the evil in 'em they'll ever need, only they ain't quite figgered out how to put it to use yet.'

"The thing was, bein' so absentminded, it never showed on him that he was interested in romancin'. That set their teeth on edge. So he'd just sit and wait, an' by and by some young lalapalooza would come along, and nothin' would satisfy her but that she had to try her luck in that web. I think Georgie just loved all those big, pretty, strapping girls that used to come into town. And in some way, he'd romance 'em. Don't ask me how, but he did it, and right under the noses of their fathers and uncles. More'n once we cleared outa some town before dawn, and we stayed on back roads an' didn't stop until we'd put considerable distance between ourselves and what we'd left behind—in certain instances, a preacher, a father, and a shotgun."

"Is that how he met my mother?" Roy asked.

"That common trash?" Walter said, snorting. "Nope. We stole her."

"He told me a little about that," Roy said.

"He did? When?"

"Back last week. A couple of days before he died."

"Well, if he told you, what are you askin' me for?"

"I was curious to hear your side of it, Walter."

"There ain't nothin' to tell," Walter said. "We was just foolin' around, down on the reservation. We'd cashed in some gold dust we'd panned, and were taking it easy. I ain't exactly partial to injuns, y'know, but I will say that sometimes their company ain't bad. We was someplace south of here, like I said, on the reservation, north of Cloudcroft, where there was this general store that had a one-pump gas station out in front. We always used to stop there and buy our gas.

"This store had a long portal in front where it was shady, so this time we were sittin' around and passin' the time of day with some Apaches who were hangin' around, too. Musta been seven or eight of 'em. There was always a stack of Apaches laid out along that portal during the hot time of day. That was years ago. Well, we had plenty of beer in the back of the truck, and we gave 'em some. Georgie, y'know, was just fascinated by injuns.

He couldn't git enough of 'em. I couldn't see why. Some of 'em was young bucks, but some were ugly ol' geezers, too. Y'know how an injun can be, if he's feelin' sociable. He'll siphon off every drop of rotgut you have, and then he'll trot out his own, and share it. When our beer was gone, whiskey started appearin'. Why, they had bottles hid all over the place! Their stuff was awful, but we got used to it after a while.

"I reckon that started it. You know, an Apache will smoke up your cigarette makings, and when it's gone he'll just go git some more, and if he has to sell or pawn a solid silver bracelet or belt buckle, why, he never gives it a second thought. It ain't generosity, 'cause injuns are naturally tightfisted, it's just how they are. They don't like white men, but they didn't seem to mind Georgie. He knew how to be as easy as they were.

"We sat there drinkin' and smokin' and swappin' stories, and presently the afternoon drifted by that way into sunset, and we were talkin' and havin' fun. George would tell some funny story, and then some buck would tell one, too, in that singsong way they talk that you can't hardly understand.

"Don't you think that an Apache won't talk. Give him decent conditions and you can't stop him. And don't think he won't laugh either. They got a sense of humor just like anybody else, only nobody can understand it. I will say this. An Apache, if you cut close to the bone, is probably more peaceful than most white men, despite what everybody claims. That's 'cause he's learned how to do with less. He'd rather lay around on his ass and sleep and drink an' smoke, and maybe gamble, than go to war. He don't mind givin' his money to his womenfolk, that is, when he's got any, which is seldom, though it is true that he'll whip 'em something awful from time to time. That's something the women git used to. But he ain't got the kind of meanness some white people seem born with. An Apache, he'll run a good horse to death for the fun of it, and he'll bury his women and children, but he knows how to live his own life, such as it may be, and doesn't let nothin' faze him. The only thing an Apache is scared shitless of is a tub of hot water.

"We ended up spendin' the whole weekend parked right there by that general store. When things got boring we pitched pennies against the side of the building, and then they taught us how to play one of their gamblin' games with little sticks. In the morning, we set on one side of the store where it was shady. When it come afternoon, we'd all move over to the other side, and the liquor just kept croppin' up like it was growin' outa the ground. 'Course, by then we'd tossed in what we had in the truck, most of a case of Juarez tequila.

"You might think that bein' on injun territory, where alcohol was against the law, it wouldn't be that easy to put your hand on, but there it was. In this country, if you want something, just go where it's illegal, and you'll always get more'n you can handle. Come evening, this ol' Apache grandpa with snow-white hair hangin' clean down to his waist, he snuck off for a bit and when he come back he had a burlap feed bag filled with nine or ten fresh-killed chickens and some fresh corn, so we cleaned the chickens and built us a fire beside the store and roasted everything. I showed 'em how to make a genuine dangle-spit with wire, and they were real interested in that. Before that store closed, we all chipped in and bought some loaves of bread and chili. Then we sat around all night, eatin' chicken and corn and partyin'.

"They started singin' songs. Then they danced around the fire for quite a while. We was right by the highway, and sometimes a truck passin' would light us up in its headlights, and then the injun drivin' the truck would stop, and he'd join in.

"Your father tried to dance with 'em, only he wasn't any good with that bad leg of his. Then he convinced himself that the songs they were singin' were some ancient tribal chants an' stuff like that. Only the real old geezer, the one with the filthy white hair, who'd stole the chickens, he explained them for us. Roy, they were the dirtiest songs you ever heard of, and had to do with certain young Apache females they knew about. That's why the bucks and old-timers alike would laugh and carry on so when a song got goin'.

"I'll tell you something, when injuns start having a party, it just goes from bad to worse. Nothin's sacred to an Apache. That weekend we learned more about how injun women are built, and what they will do, and how one buck who was sittin' right there had a terrible curve in his hinkus-dinkus, like the end of a walkin' cane, so that to git it in he had to back up to a female, and he just sat there and laughed with us, didn't mind a bit, even offered to show it to all of us if we'd pay him fifty cents. 'Course nobody'd pay two cents to see something like that.

"We had us a fine time. Just men, no womenfolk. I like that. When they git in a mood, Apache men will go off and stay by themselves for a spell and git drunk or whatever. And the women, they will do the same. There are times when a man and a woman ain't got no business talkin' to one another or even bein' in the same house together. A woman don't want to listen to her man. She just wants the money in her hand. And the man, sometimes he just has to git off alone. Well, we sure had fun that weekend."

"But when did you meet my mother?" Roy said.

"I was just gittin' to it," Walter said irritably, "and if you'd pass that bottle and not interrupt all the time, it wouldn't take so long to tell." He poured drinks for the two of them. "I don't know why you're so goddamn curious to hear about her. She was never more'n a half-wild animal. Your grandma, Bertha, was the most beautiful and gracious lady in the whole New Mexico Territory, but Minnie Wardner was something that belonged out back with the rest of the livestock. Her brain wasn't quite right, if you sense my meanin'. What she did, she vamped your pa. She worked a spell on him. How else can you explain it? Bertha gave him the finest kinda upbringin', and some of that lays over onto you, though it don't often show. If Georgie'd wanted to settle down, there was a whole country full of decent young white gals dyin' to git at him. He didn't need no half-breed to light his candle. Roy, as you know, I ain't no one to speak out against any person, but that Minnie wasn't even human. If I live to be a hundred, I'll never know what he saw in her. She did something to him. I know it! The spider got caught in his own trap. It's a mystery to me. You know what I always suspected? I think that idiot had a notion to reform her! Make somethin' different out of what she naturally was. A fool's task. Ain't no man can make a silk purse outa a sow's ear that's been spat into by every man in the Territory."

"But she wasn't at that party you had," Roy said.

"No, she wasn't," Walter said. "But those Apaches put us onto her. I hate to say it, but even they didn't have no respect for her. 'Course, an Apache hasn't got any respect for any female to start with. Anyway, what they told Georgie was that if he wanted to know about injun females, he oughta go down by a place in Tularosa, some bar, where the disgrace of the Mescalero Reservation was doin' business at a buck a throw.

"I used to think that as much by accident as anything else we eventually headed in that direction. But later I thought about it some. And I wondered if that crowd we'd partied with all weekend had put an idea in his head that led him straight into depravity. Later, when I give it some thought, it was like he was lookin' for it. That fool. Oh, I saw enough, Roy. No disrespect to you, but Minnie got sold twenty, thirty times a night, and it never troubled her a bit. Nothin' fazed that woman. And the thing is, she was so homely. Just a skinny bag of bones, and those wild eyes."

"How old was she?" he asked.

"With that kind of woman, who could tell?" Walter said. "Squaws age fast. She looked in her thirties somewhere. There was no way of knowin' with the use she'd been put to. It don't take much to ruin a woman permanently, and if there's mixed blood, it happens faster. When we buried your grandma, she'd lost most of sixty pounds, and yet Bertha had smooth, clear skin, all clean. That was what I could never tolerate about Minnie— she always looked so dark and dirty, with that stringy black hair, and her fingers always movin' nervous." Walter thought about this for a while and then scowled. "Shit! I don't even want to think about that awful female. Why can't we talk about something else? She was your father's ruination, and he never had the sense to see it. She was the worst kind of no-good, half-breed trash you could imagine. Thank God you got some of your grandma's good breeding runnin' in your veins. You ain't no prize package, but compared to Minnie Wardner you're plumb respectable. In this world, you got just two sorts of women— there's the respectable ones, and then there's the ones who're loose with no sense of moral turpitude. Well, if you could round up the worst ones in the lot and roll 'em up into one female, why, hell, she'd come out lookin' like Joan of Arc compared to Minnie."

BUT TWO DAYS before George Gutierrez died, Roy had heard a different version.

By then his father was conscious for only four or five hours a day and in a coma the rest of the time under the ravaging onslaught of a liver that had first turned cirrhotic and then cancerous. He suffered terrible pain all through the illness but the end, when it finally came, was quick. He was never a man to carry much weight on his frame, and in those final months, as both diseases ate at him, he wasted away to a skeleton.

When Roy and Uncle Walter realized how ill he was, they brought him back to Sawmill River Flats and set up housekeeping in the cabin. That was where George wanted to be. They lived half out of the cabin and half out of the big Dodge truck they had at the time—the old Mack, with nobody knew how many hundreds of thousands of miles on it, had simply fallen apart.

A doctor at the hospital in Roswell had prescribed medicine. They doubled up on the Rx's with whiskey, which seemed to help as much as the drugs.

They put all their cash together, and then Roy sold three good lever-action Winchester rifles they had, and with this money they were all right for a while.

On the way up to the old town, they stopped at a ranch they knew of and bought a yearling calf, and Walter slaughtered it and hung the meat in the back of the truck to age, wrapped in cheesecloth so blowflies could not infest it with eggs. When they were set up at the cabin, the old man used a lot of the meat to make gallons of beef broth. "It's the best thing in the world to keep a dyin' man's strength goin'," Walter said.

He cut the meat into very small chunks and let them simmer for a good part of the day in a covered pot, and then he would strain all of it through a square of the cheesecloth several times so that the broth was clear and rich and brown, and he would feed this to George, a tablespoon at a time, sitting beside the bed, blowing on the spoonful to cool it, and saying, "Just quit givin' me those dirty looks, Georgie, I know it's hot but it's good for you, goddamn it." The dying man would smile and try to drink a little.

Sometimes Roy drove down to Pearl Lowdermilk's for fresh goat milk. He never told her how ill his father was. George said he did not want old friends to see him like this. Uncle Walter used the goat milk to make *requesón,* a kind of mild Mexican cream cheese. He used two gallons of milk and a rennet tablet, and without any kind of thermometer, knew somehow where to store it so that it stayed at sixty-eight degrees, and when the curd and whey had separated, he pressed the curd for twenty-four hours. The two gallons made about a quart and a half of fine, delicate cheese. The cheese and the broth and the liquor kept George alive.

They took care of him like that, as he gradually weakened. By then the sphincter muscles were useless and he had to be washed. Outside, summer flowers bloomed everywhere on the grassy slopes: mountain lupine, purple columbine, larkspur, calypso, forget-me-nots, and tall chiming bells.

When he was conscious, George talked a lot during the last week. At times his mind rambled terribly, but he seemed to enjoy conversation. Roy sat beside him, and once he said, "Pa, what are you thinking of?"

"Roy, I'm trying to get it all in focus," George said.

"Get what in focus?"

"You know, son . . . all of it."

Walter hobbled in and sat down with them. "You been tryin' to do that all your asshole life, Georgie, and if you ain't done it by now, you never will. You never had any trouble focusing that crazy telescope of yours. I recollect you made me look through that thing one time at a place called Mars, with them old moons like little white buckshot floatin' around. What I could never figger is, what's the sense in zeroin' in sharper'n a tack on somethin' way the fuck and gone out there, where there clearly ain't *nothin',* when what counts is goin' on right down here?"

"I think there has to be a rhythm to all this," George said.

"George, rhythm is dancin' and you got about as much talent for dancin' as a cowchip!" Walter said. "A rhythm to *what?*"

"To the universe."

"I'm goin' to git you more broth. You ain't makin' sense." Walter rose and limped over to the sheepherder stove and filled a bowl.

"The problem is, we're handicapped . . . we don't have adequate equipment," George said. A spasm of pain took him. He tried to hide it, but in a moment tears trickled from his inflamed lids.

Walter returned and sat down. "Equipment for what? What in the goddamn hell are you jabberin' about?"

"The equipment to measure, and see, and feel, and sense," George said.

"I got five good senses, an' that's plenty for me," Walter told him. "How much more does a normal man need?"

"Lots," George said. "What we need is about twenty or thirty extra senses. That might help." His breathing was bad, and he paused. "Or even just a few more. Yes, I'd settle for that. So that we might get a hint. You see, there has to be something else to this universe. I don't care whether it's exploding or contracting, or just standing still. There is some grand design."

"Shut your mouth and eat some of this broth."

"Walt, I can't."

Walter stared down at him. Then, after a while, he said, "You want a little whiskey, George? Would that be better?"

"Yes. I wouldn't mind going for that, Walt. Give me a cigarette too, while you're at it, will you?"

"Dumb shit. You wanta kill yourself, go right ahead. That's all right by me. I don't give a hoot." He poured a double hooker into a tin coffee cup and lit a Sir Walter Raleigh, which had been George's favorite cigarette in recent years, and placed it between the man's lips.

George coughed and then stared up at his friend. "Shucks, Walt."

"How you feelin'?"

"Not too good."

"Is it hurtin' again?"

"Feels like a stomachful of rats gnawing at that part of me, Walt. Otherwise, it isn't so bad."

"Have a little broth."

"It won't blunt their teeth."

"You'll be feelin' better tomorrow, Georgie."

"No, I won't. I'm feeling tired, Walt."

"Why'n hell don't you quit that talk. Pretty soon you'll perk up and be your old self."

"I never would have believed I'd get this tired," George said. He smiled. "I guess that's when your age starts catching up with you . . . when you feel tired."

"You ain't scarcely past sixty yet," Walter said.

"I used to be curious about everything under the sun. Now I feel like I could sleep for a month." For a while the dying man rested. Then he stared up at the two of them and said, "It's like I've found out everything I really feel I need to know. Not everything. But enough of what I have to know in order to get on. That surprises me. I didn't ever think I'd be filled up with learning about things."

Walter said, "Just take it easy, Georgie. You'll be all right."

"I know," George said. Later he drifted into a sleep, eased a little by liquor and drugs. He breathed in long, slow, heavy breaths. Beneath the quilt his abdomen was extended with edema and the disease, and his skin was jaundiced to a brownish-yellow. Walter went out, saying he was going to collect firewood.

Presently, the man in the bed wakened. His mind seemed refreshed and cleared by even a half-hour's rest. It was then that he and Roy talked.

"I BELIEVE THAT we will go forward in spite of ourselves."

"Who?" Roy said.

"All of us. The brotherhood of man," his father said. "The trouble is, men cannot live together. That's why I spent my life off with you and Walter, by ourselves, having fun. Life is too short. Yes, I think that was the best course of action. With your background . . . we would have always had difficulty fitting into normal society."

"You mean, the way I look?" Roy said. "Are you saying we lived like this all these years because you knew people wouldn't want to have anything to do with someone like me?"

His father smiled. "Well, perhaps that was part of it. But not all of it. We lived this way because it was the only way open to us. Walter certainly never had any kind of place in this modern world. Neither did I, really. The three of us are misfits. Anomalies, actually. Today's world doesn't need people like us. Once I understood that, it never bothered me again . . . we've had fun and lots of exciting times . . . good food, plenty to drink, and . . . freedom. What more could a man want? Roy, do you know how a man can tell if he's had a good life? It's when he can look back on it, at the very end, and not regret a single minute of it, or want to do any of it differently."

"Pa, you've got plenty of years left."

"Maybe. You know, when the pain lets up I start wishing I could live for a long time. I'd like to see how it turns out."

"How what turns outs?"

"Us. What Malraux used to call *la condition humaine*." His voice was erratic and forced. "Man's capacity for self-deception is endless. Now we have the H-bomb, and the fools are saying that it is the ultimate weapon. But in 1918 they were saying the same thing about World War I, that it was the war to end all wars. The ultimate weapons back then were the tank, the machine gun, and mustard gas. What naiveté. And now, science is married to politics and the military, and, worst of all, it's become a kind of religion. You know something I always regretted, Roy? That I never had a really sound education. I always wished I'd had the proper training that would enable me to think and analyze and define. 'Science' is a sham word, but it will produce things in the next hundred years that I wouldn't mind living to see. There are weapons still to be created that will make trench warfare and nuclear devices look like peanuts. It's true . . . to believe in science these days, you need a lot of faith."

Roy listened, marveling at this extraordinary man who, although dying, could ramble on about things no dying man ought to be interested in. But, then, it *was* like his father to discourse on any subject that caught his interest . . . to the everlasting irritation of someone like Uncle Walter, who had always said he'd teamed up with the "most exasperatin' idiot west of the Mississippi." There was silence, and Roy said, "Do you want anything?"

"Whiskey, please."

Roy poured some.

His father said, "Do you happen to know why the Emperor Charlemagne was universally acclaimed as the humanitarian of his day? I'll bet you don't. That merciless old fraud! What a schemer that one was. It was all politics. What he did, he outlawed the crossbow, and everybody loved him for it. You see, that was the ultimate weapon of *his* time. It was regarded as too horrible a device for dignified warfare. Some of those medieval crossbows, you know, had a drawweight on the string of fifteen hundred pounds, tremendously heavy weapons that were mounted on a tripod and that needed a crank-and-lever mechanism called a goat's-foot to even get them cocked. A very lethal instrument. That kind of weapon could fire a half-pound iron bolt clean through ten or twelve lined-up ranks of foot soldiers. They inflicted horrible damage. But the worst part was that the mounted knight was just as helpless. How can you be a splendid hero and lead a charge against something that from a considerable distance can shoot you out of the saddle? The heaviest armor a knight's horse could transport was simply no match at all for the crossbow. There was no glamour to this awesome device. No jousting with lances, no pretty swordwork, not even the heavyhanded application of mace or morning-star. So Charlemagne formally outlawed the crossbow, and all Europe cheered him. You know, I've always thought that professional warrior-knights in those days must have built up incredible accumulations of scar tissue, just from being knocked about inside those iron suits. And they were such tiny men, too, compared to us . . . I once saw a real Japanese samurai antique suit of armor, and a contemporary boy of twelve would have had difficulty getting into it. Imagine Sir Lancelot standing all of five feet, or Sir Gawain at maybe a towering four feet eleven . . . to think that such as they inspired our greatest romantic legend! Yes, I have a hunch that there are inventions on the drawing boards right now that will make all of it look silly. Roy, you'll live to see some interesting times." He thought for a while, resting, and then went on, "I wish now I'd taught you differently, and given you more."

"Pa, you've given me everything."

"The only obligation any generation has is to try and arm the succeeding one," his father told him. "And the only ultimate

weapons that count a darn are intelligence . . . and curiosity."
Roy helped him drink some of the whiskey. Then his mind
drifted again. "Do you know a place I always dreamed of visiting? Tierra del Fuego, right down at the southernmost tip of the
South American continent. By golly. Just to stand there, at the
end of the western hemisphere! You could get a real feeling of
the inconsequentiality of the human race, I think, if you spent
some time down there. They say that whatever natives who still
survive are lacking in any kind of real culture or skills. Well, that
doesn't surprise me. It's a harsh place in which to exist. But I
also wonder if they lost their spirit because they'd reached a cul-
de-sac. It was the end of the trail for that last magnificent migration. People on their long journey. Think of that walk! Clean
across Asia, Alaska, North America, South America, what a time
that must have been. I've always wondered why some of them
simply did not stop dead in their tracks and turn around and go
back. Some settled down, but others went on, yet none, so far as
we know, turned around or gave up. Tierra del Fuego is only one
example, Roy. Baja California is another. At some point in pre-
history, someplace over by what is now the Arizona-California
border, by the delta of the Colorado River, the migrating tribes
split. One branch stayed on the mainland and traveled south to
create the Mayan and Incan civilizations. But the western branch
took a wrong turn down the Baja Peninsula, and at the southern
end of that tip of land nearly died out. Just think, on the Mexican
mainland there were great cities flourishing. But down at the end
of the Baja region there was nothing. You know, when Spanish
missionary priests first came ashore in the Baja they discovered
that the aboriginals were of such a lowly species that the natives,
existing as humbly as they did, on the verge of starvation,
would pass around a chunk of raw meat that was tied to a rawhide thong, swallow it, and then yank it back up so that it could
be passed on to a neighbor. So that everybody could at least taste
that piece of raw gristle and fat. And on the mainland, not many
leagues away, this same ethnic group of people had, all by themselves, created lavish pyramids and figured out an astonishingly
accurate calendar."

For a few minutes, he dozed. Then he wakened again, and said,
"Roy, I hope in time you'll find a decent woman. I don't know if

it's possible, but I hope so. That's important. A woman can bring
a lot into a man's life."

"Don't worry about that for now."

"They can be difficult to live with. But all things considered,
they are wonderful."

There was that terrible, wrenching cough. Particular only to
someone who is dying and who knows that the end is at hand but
who still struggles, because that is the way of life, to stay alive,
that's all . . . no grace, no dignity, nothing but that fading, human personality that fights against extinguishment there in the
bed, the eyes agonized, the mouth drawn cruelly back . . . and
all Roy could do was sit there and gently touch the shriveled
thigh, and then bow his head and weep.

He felt guilt. He did not know why. Above and beyond the
grief. There was no reason. But at that moment he felt he was
dying with his father. He wept again.

To see the hands. Folded on the quilt. Moving aimlessly, picking at the fabric. That practically killed him. There was a frail-
ness. This man, who was almost dead. So gentle. Yet in his own
way so terrifyingly strong.

What was his father? A monster, or a child of nature?

Was he magic, or was he farce?

Looking at the man in the bed, Roy felt an awful moment of
doubt and uncertainty.

Did he love his father or hate him? Or was it a mixture?

He knew that this man had raised him, taught him, loved and
disciplined him. But to what end? What did it mean? Who was
he, and *what* was he without this dying man?

How could he ever prove himself to someone who was not
there to approve? How could he ever escape his father's love?

He had never asked for that love. And at times he wished it
had never come to him, for this man, who was everything to him,
had also contributed to a curse Roy knew he could never escape.
He was a pariah, a true outcast.

What it all came down to was right here: sitting in a primitive
cabin on a grassy slope alongside a forgotten town, high in the
mountains.

Paying his last dues.

He would have wept, had there been more tears.

Would have wept not just for his father but for himself as well. He would have wept for the loss of love. When a person dies, what is there left to love? A memory, that was all. And that was not very much.

In the back of his mind was anger. It said, *who will love me now? How will I keep on with no one to love?* He felt resentment that this man he needed was leaving him. It was a selfish feeling but inevitable. Something that had its roots in love and hate, in fear and despair for the future, and, worst of all, the awful prospect of loneliness.

The man in bed said, "Roy?"

"Yes, Pa."

"If it's possible, I'd like you to keep an eye on Walt."

"I will."

"I mean that. He needs someone to look after him."

"I swear I will, Pa."

"Walter doesn't really know how to take care of himself."

"I'll watch out for him."

"Promise?"

"Yes."

"He's too old to make it on his own anymore," his father said, and then he smiled again. "It's funny, you know . . . the way certain things repeat. Your grandmother—Bertha—made me swear to take care of Walter, just before she died. I was only fifteen years old. And now, almost half a century later, I'm asking you to do the same."

"I'll do like you say, Pa."

"Do you want to know something even stranger than that? I found out, quite some time after she was buried and gone, that she had talked to Walt alone and had made him swear the same thing about me. He told me that himself. I guess it was her way of looking after the two of us. Also, she considered Walt to be in her debt for something wrong he once did. She was a strong woman that way, and hard. She was gentle and patient, but she was very formidable. She knew how to fight for what she wanted." He sighed. "Walt's not easy, you know."

"Don't worry."

"He's my friend. Do you know what a friend is?"

"I think so."

"It's someone who just sticks by you. That's all. I've given him some terrible times. And he's done the same to me."

"It averages out, Pa."

"But you will look after him? He can't have many more years left."

"Yes."

"That's good." The man in bed sighed again. "I feel a lot better about that now. Would you let me have a little more of that whiskey?"

Roy did this. Presently his father said, "I hope you find a woman to love. Your mother, you know, had a fine quality of spirit. She was a very impressive woman."

"Uncle Walt has never thought so."

"Pay no mind. He has his way of looking at life. He's harsh, but it isn't his fault. He can't help himself."

"He's always said she was no good."

"Well, Walt isn't always too generous when it comes to giving somebody the benefit of a doubt," his father said. "You know, she was only twenty-three when we found her." He thought for a moment. "It was on July twenty-ninth, 1923."

"How did you find her?" Roy asked.

"It so happened Walt and I were having a drink in a bar. We'd just spent three days up in the hills camping with some Mescaleros who were having a sort of social gathering."

"Pa? Can I ask you something?"

"Sure."

"What did you see in her?"

"Why, everything, son."

"But what sort of got you together?"

The man in bed smiled. "Well, what gets any man and woman together?"

"I don't know."

"She was the most beautiful woman I'd ever set eyes on."

"Walt always claimed she was ugly."

His father said, "No . . . she was beautiful."

"He's said some pretty awful things about her."

"I know. But I loved her, and I believe she loved me. You should know that."

"Was she really all that pretty?"

"I always thought so, Roy. Her complexion, of course, was much darker than any Mescalero woman, with none of the reddish tint an Indian usually has. She had a wide mouth, like yours, and the longest, straightest black hair in the world. Usually she wore it in braids, but when she let it out at night it hung to her haunches. She had dark brown eyes. She was not a small woman, you know. Many Indian women tend toward squatness, but not your mother. She was close to six feet tall. And she was remarkably graceful in her movements. Straightbacked, with a fine posture. She was terribly thin, though. I learned much later that she was given little to eat."

"Was she really as bad as Walter claims?"

"Yes. But it was not her fault."

"What happened?"

"Nothing, son." The man in bed took more whiskey. He was having pain, but his mind seemed sharp now. "I fell in love with her. That's all. You might say she was the love of my life. That sounds exaggerated. But I suspect there's considerable truth in it."

"I've heard Walt say she was a whore."

"Well, I'd have to admit that he's not far off the mark," his father said. "She was for a fact."

"But what happened, Pa?"

"She was with some old Apache who claimed he was related to her," his father said. "That was just a story . . . he wasn't related to her any more than I'm related to the Pope. He was using her for licentious purposes, if you follow. He would ply her with liquor and then take her off the reservation, around the state from place to place, where there were bars frequented by the worst kind of white men. She would earn money for this old Indian. She was a beautiful girl, you see, but, really, she was like a slave."

"Did he sell her to you?"

"Not exactly," his father said. "She was worth a good deal of money to the old demon . . . she supported the two of them. No. What we did was to sort of invite her to take a trip with us. Walt, I think, was very worried that we might be accused of kidnapping, because at various times we took her out of the state and even out of the country. It's hard to know how a court of law might interpret what we did. She came with us of her own free will, but at the same time that old Indian claimed he really owned her, whatever that meant. What happened was that we stayed around this bar. That's how we became friendly with him. One night, we bought him fourteen or fifteen whiskies, and he got pretty mellow. Ordinarily, he kept her locked in a shed behind the saloon, and whenever he let her out to eat he watched her like a hawk. He wore the key to the shed's padlock around his neck. So, after he'd had a bellyful of the whiskey we were buying him, he fell asleep for a while. We went out in back and hacksawed the padlock, and after talking to her we put her in the back of the Mack and cleared out of that place as fast as we could."

"She just went along?"

"When we first got the door to the shed open, she thought we'd come to abuse her, like the others. But then I talked to her for a bit, and she saw that we meant her no harm, so she decided to throw in her lot with us," his father explained. "I suspect she figured she had nothing to lose. She was an emotional girl, you see, and ordinarily the only way she knew how to express her feelings was through violence, but she listened to me there in the shed, and finally understood that we wouldn't use her. Her English was fair, and she was intelligent, but she had no education at all. There were schools on the Mescalero Reservation, but she'd never gone to any. She had a deadly temper, and believed that she was cursed . . . she was very superstitious. She owned little except the clothes on her back, and that old photograph of her parents, Tom and Cora Wardner, that I keep with my private papers. You've seen it. The little farm they had was passed on to an older sister, so Minnie literally had nothing. She suffered greatly from what the Bureau of Indian Affairs nowadays is calling cultural deprivation. That's just a two-dollar name for a condition that has plagued mankind throughout history. I told her we'd help her get away from reservation life forever, and that made an impression on her. You should understand that in those years life for an Indian on a reservation was pretty bad, and for a woman it could be a living hell . . . I can't even begin to imagine what it was like for a child who was half Negro. I don't doubt that Mescalero men treated her worse than any white man. She was bought and traded like an animal, from the age of fourteen on. Things had been done to her that affected her mind. Walter always thought she was half mad. There may have been something to that. I don't think there was ever a possibility she could have lived what most people call a normal life. Being with the two of us was something new for her. The men she'd known had used her body to vent their blackest instincts. She knew what it was like to be horsewhipped. I myself saw the scars across her breasts. She'd been forced to undergo unspeakable acts of degradation. She was already an alcoholic, you know. She was very slender . . . skinny would be more like it. Roy, she had the most perfect teeth I have ever seen on any human being. So white and uniform, whiter than the finest porcelain."

"It's a wonder that old Apache didn't follow you and hunt you down."

"I'm sure he tried, when he sobered up. But we knew all about hiding out in the mountains," his father said, smiling again. "One time, after we'd been together for a month or two, I left Walter down in Carrizozo, and your mother and I went camping by ourselves up on Sierra Blanca, for a week. We took a tent and some steaks and salt pork and beans and chili, and at night we sat under the stars by the campfire. She was not a talkative person. But on this evening we were sitting there and she looked at me in a funny way, and then said, 'This is our moment. Any person who lives should have the right to one good moment.' A tall, thin girl in a long pleated skirt that came to the ground. You know, your great-grandfather, Tom Wardner, who was a soldier, was said to be a huge man . . . there was a rumor that he once killed a man with a single punch during some kind of dispute. His side showed in her high cheekbones and mouth. She had a wretched, miserable life. During that week we camped, at night she would wash my feet, and then dry them with her hair. I always liked to see it hanging loose. She washed her hair once every three months, and it took her most of a day to do it. Her skin was like caramel, and she rarely laughed. She didn't really know how to. When she did, her face looked almost strange or unnatural, the way a monkey will grimace at you across the bars in a zoo. But on those few times when she did smile or laugh, you saw those marvelously white teeth."

"Walt always said she was as hard as nails."

"Well, there wasn't much in the way of gentleness to her nature," his father said. "You see, she'd never been educated along those lines. The Mescaleros, of course, have their own caste system. Because of her mixed blood they judged her to have a low status, which, of course, was just an excuse for the men to take advantage of her in any way they wanted. Yes, she was pretty tough, all things considered. She was very strong for such a thin girl. If something went wrong, that temper of hers could explode. She told me once that she would die fighting. I imagine something like that may have happened. Roy, do you know we searched for her for nearly five years, after she ran away? I always admired the passion and anger she had in her. In her fashion, I think, she was proud to have me as her man. To have a white man, even a cripple like me, was something. To me, she was beautiful, but I suppose that by the standards of the nineteen twenties, she would have been plain, or perhaps even unattractive. She was too tall and dark-complexioned and thin. You see, in those days, girls like Mary Pickford and Clara Bow were all the rage. Little cupid's-bow mouths, sad, wilting eyes, and alabaster-white skin. Minnie wasn't exactly the dainty type. She had that wide mouth, and a thin, straight nose, not one of those pert, tilted jobs. She had extraordinarily thick black eyebrows, and the lashes were thick and black, too, almost furry. She always wore a full-length squaw skirt, and she walked like a man. Oh, she was impressive, all right."

"She doesn't sound all that tough," Roy said.

"You're wrong there. Even Walter and I were surprised," his father said. "One time that year the three of us went down to old Mexico on a trip, and we stopped at a little town called Benjamin Hill, south of Magdalena. Just fooling around, you know. Benjamin Hill was out in the middle of the great Sonoran Desert. Back then it was a drop-off place for gun smugglers. So we did some drinking, and in a cantina that night there was a dance, and we went. Toward midnight, things got ugly . . . a group of Mexican men got belligerent and refused to let us leave. You know, I never liked to carry a pistol on me in Mexico, and I wouldn't let Walter carry one either, so we were unarmed. These men were talking hard, and they had us backed up against a wall to one side of the dance floor. Someone shoved me, and with this bad leg I lost my balance and fell. Minnie said to them in Spanish, 'Enough. Get away, we are going now.' She spoke reservation Spanish but they understood her well enough. She had on a bright red Navajo blouse and a full skirt, and, underneath that, knee-high deerskin moccasins. Inside one of those mocs, she had Tom Wardner's razor. It had a white whalebone handle. One of those old-fashioned razors, you know, with the blade sharp and bright and oiled. She took it out. They made way for us, and in fact got very polite. I was astounded. An ordinary woman would have been terrified. But she gave the impression that she'd been in a few arguments with that razor, and that she knew how to use it. As a matter of fact, she seemed quite comfortable with it, cocked open in her hand. She certainly didn't look like one of those timid Mary Pickford types in the movies, let me tell you. Those Mexican men took one look at her, and then they got out of the way. We left that cantina, and it was she who led the way out the door, with her shoulders flung back and murder glaring out of her eyes. We had our pistols hidden in the truck. Walter was for going back in there and teaching them a lesson. She said, 'Go by yourself, old man. Those people are ready to make real trouble for us.' Son, pour me more of that whiskey, will you? It's starting."

Roy did, and the man in bed said, "I think I'm leaking again."

Months earlier, at the hospital in Roswell, a surgeon had done a quick exploratory. Had flapped open the abdominal wall, taken one look, assessed the hopelessness of the situation, and then closed the incision. There was seepage everywhere through the lower abdomen, and the foot-long incision had never healed. He said, "I don't reckon I smell so good."

Roy said, "That's all right." He put on a fresh dressing, wrapping the old soaked one in newspaper; feminine napkins were the most absorbent.

Except for the swollen stomach, there was little left of his father by now. The poor penis, from which Roy had sprung, was shriveled and naked, surrounded by a white stubble where they had shaved him, and the scrotum was drawn up small and tight, the way it will with pure fear and pain. The incision gave off a foul odor, and the row of crude black sutures was ugly. Roy sponged the thighs with alcohol and water, and asked his father if he wanted some hot broth. What they were feeding with Walter's broth and the cheese and the whiskey was the cancer, not George. It raged everywhere through him. Above the pubis there were great dark-purple blotches where the skin was deteriorating and the cancer was ready to burst through.

George drank some more of the whiskey, and when the attack had passed, he essayed a smile. "Well. I must say. It's a hell of a fix to be in, isn't it?"

Roy said, "Oh, Pa."

"You know I love you," the man in bed said. "I've always loved you."

"I love you, Pa."

"Ah, Roy."

"What can I do?"

"Kiss me. Just give me a hug and a kiss. Like you used to when you were a little boy."

And Roy did. They locked arms round each other, and he kissed his father's feverish, chapped lips. He wept and said again, "Oh, Pa. Oh, Pa."

And that was how his father had died. Two days later. In his arms.

Walter never shed a tear, but his face got more bitter and stony than ever. After the grave was heaped, the two of them talked for hours. As if Walter, in the telling of it, could somehow hold on to the friendship, and all the years.

But when there was no more to talk about, the old man took a bottle of whiskey and hobbled off by himself. Roy went to follow but he said, "Leave me be for a while, son. Just leave me be, now."

FOUR

Sitting there on the stone fence in the warm sunlight he thought, *Pearl Lowdermilk is right. Every time you come here your head gets mixed up, and then you start thinking too much. Other people know how to put things out of their minds, and that's what you ought to do, too. You ought to get away from this place and never come back again.*

He knew what was going on inside him. It had happened plenty of times before.

Everything was starting to pile up again.

It always began with old memories. Places, people, long-ago conversations. At first that was good but then came depression. He would start feeling low and lost and sad. And then it would get worse until, eventually, the drinking caught him up. The liquor at least made the loneliness endurable.

The strangest part of it was that this place, Sawmill River Flats, was so real to him. But almost no one else knew it existed, and those who did could not have cared less, one way or the other.

Back at the Acme Novelty Co. in El Paso, everybody had

laughed at him and said right out that he was crazy when he told them he owned an entire town and that his grandfather had figured in the last real gun battle in New Mexico. He'd gotten that kind of response before. That was why he almost never discussed his background with others.

The thing was, down in civilization, nobody ever believed him. To the rest of the world, Sawmill River was some kind of forgotten, unreal dream.

What the contemporary world understood was the ceramic bric-a-brac he'd fired in those gas kilns. That stuff was real. So was El Paso and other cities he'd been to—New York, Los Angeles.

And now, suddenly, people were interested in this dead, forgotten town. Some businessman named Larson, all the way up in New York City, and somebody else named Gardiner Potts, who was involved with a historical society. Why this sudden interest in a town that had been abandoned for decades . . . a place that even on a detailed geodetic map was identified by one word: *Ruins?* Pearl Lowdermilk didn't understand it. Neither did he.

He felt a familiar, frightening mood that had come to him before . . . a weird feeling of disassociation. He sat looking across the valley at spruce-covered slopes. Finally, he said to himself, "Things change too fast these days to suit me. Nothing makes sense anymore."

He knew what was wrong with him, and thought, *only two days up here, and you're ready for a psychiatrist. It's gotten so that you can't tell anymore what is real and what is make-believe.*

He stood up, and stared at his father's and Walter's graves for a while. Then he walked back down the slope to town and spent the rest of the morning cleaning the main lobby of the hotel, carrying the rotted mattress that had been left by kids, cans, and garbage out to the back, where the pigpens had once stood, burning what was flammable and heaping the metal and glass junk into a tidy pile.

By early afternoon he was tired, and he returned to the cabin and had a glass of wine and a sandwich. He could feel that his mood was getting worse, and, restless now, he got out a portable typewriter from the jeep and wrote a letter to the New Mexico Historical Society.

He could not take such correspondence seriously, any more than he could appreciate Larson thousands of miles away.

There was a side of his mind that had a certain weakness for the printed word. Perhaps a direct link with his impractical father. George Gutierrez, who had surely been one of the most honest men who ever lived, always said of himself that when it came to telling the truth about his private affairs, he was "susceptible to a vile and crooked Byzantine embellishment." By this he meant that he was not so much an outright liar as a storyteller who was convinced that any tale could be enriched by a touch of embroidery. Walter put it more succinctly when he said that it was easier to get a whore in a silvermining town to stay home crocheting on a Saturday night than to get a simple yes or no out of George.

Now an eagle cried once for its mate in the forested slopes above the cabin as he typed to Gardiner Potts:

. . . I apologize for not replying earlier but I have been traveling about the country for the past year or two.

I might conceivably be interested in having the unincorporated township of Sawmill River Flats designated as an official historical site. Would this be possible in view of the fact that the entire village is on private land owned by me?

For many years I have acted as caretaker of the place, as did my father before me. I would describe the present condition of the town as excellent; fifty-two of the original buildings remain standing, no doubt largely due to the preservative qualities of our high, dry atmosphere. Due to an exceedingly difficult primitive road, originally used by ox teams to haul timber, vandalism has been kept to a minimum.

Personally, I am of the opinion that Sawmill River Flats, situated as it is in a high, alpinelike valley, is one of the loveliest ghost towns to be found in the entire southwest. I speak from a certain experience since, over the years, either alone or with my father, I have visited most of these forgotten testaments to a bygone era.

Thank you for your interest.

Sincerely,
Roy A. Gutierrez
Mayor, pro tem
Sawmill River Flats
c/o Lowdermilk
Honcho, NM 88341

The letter took a while to compose. Then he retyped it neatly, with a carbon for the footlocker that contained his archives.

He reread it, and then, for good measure, got out an old notary of the public seal he had bought for two dollars in a junk shop in Cerrillos years ago, and laid an official stamp in the lower left-hand corner, thinking to himself, *the letter hasn't yet been written that can't be improved by a bit of embossment.*

Then, still restless, he put some wine and crackers in the jeep, and drove off, in search of whatever the rest of the day might offer.

THAT TOO WAS part of his coming back to this place, having a look around the countryside and seeing the towns again—old settlements that would never change, and the newer ones, which were changing all the time—and maybe running into people he'd known for years.

He drove first to Ruidoso, where the rich hung out—a half-hour trip east.

In a way, Ruidoso and its environs typified the contemporary American southwest—the last great frontier in this country to be discovered and exploited.

Money counted around here, not tradition.

Sun Belt Country. The term had been familiar to him for years, but now he realized how important it had become.

Down on the plains around Carrizozo and Capitan ranching folk drank their Coors straight out of the can, but here in Ruidoso the cocktail lounges served martinis mixed with genuine Tanqueray.

Down there, the talk was of cow-units and the high cost of supplementary feed, but up in these cool, high altitudes Ruidoso and Alto matrons flew their personal Cessnas all the way to Dallas when Neiman-Marcus threw a clearance sale.

In Carrizozo in winter, windburned, leathery-faced ranchwomen wore wool mackinaws and drove battered trucks. But in Ruidoso mink coats were in evidence, and when a housewife tooled off to the big downtown shopping center, she often drove a Mercedes or, at the lowliest, a BMW. Roy said to himself, "Why, Ruidoso is where the beautiful people don't wash their blue jeans . . . they send 'em out to be Martinized!"

All through the Ruidoso-Alto area he saw new hotels and highrise condominium complexes. There were restaurants, boutiques, and all kinds of fancy shops. This was the White Mountain ski area, and that meant money, and there was the big racetrack, and that meant more money. Roy thought, *it's a playland. I remember when it was nothing at all.*

He'd seen it before in his wanderings around the country. It was happening everywhere. Taos, New Mexico. Scottsdale, Tubac, and Tucson, in Arizona. Steamboat Springs, in Colorado. Jackson Hole, Wyoming . . . that picturesque hideaway for the rich and truly ultra-rich, nestled at the base of the incredibly beautiful Grand Tetons Range, which translates into nothing fancier than the Big Tits Mountains . . . the old mountain men and trappers who first saw those towering snowcovered peaks were not without a certain dry, laconic sense of humor.

He thought, *by God, it isn't the distribution of wealth! No sir . . . it's the uses wealth is being put to these days!*

He was so intrigued by this notion that he pulled off the road by a large highway sign and had a cupful of wine and a cigarette. The sign read:

WELCOME TO RUIDOSO
FASTEST GROWING TOWN IN THE
SOUTHWEST!

"Fastest growing, and doubtless the most expensive, too," he said, and had another drink on it.

It was a wonderfully hot, dry afternoon, and, feeling better now, he drove down to the village of Lincoln, where he paid fifty cents to the little old lady who for years had acted as a kind of curator for the former courthouse building that was now a ramshackle museum.

Inside, he spent some time looking over the glass cases filled with western memorabilia and junk commemorating the Lincoln County War . . . letters written by the Kid himself, and Governor Wallace's replies, and the execution order issued to Sheriff Garrett on Billy.

In the adobe wall of the stairwell leading to the upstairs courtroom, there were Billy's bullet holes, made when he broke loose and carried off his famous escape. The holes were covered now with a large sheet of glass to keep tourists from gouging into the adobe with penknives in their frantic search for an actual souvenir fired from the Kid's pistol. Outside, the town itself was only a cut above Sawmill River Flats. About all that saved it from becoming a ruin was the macadam highway that bisected it.

From there he drove to Capitan. Cruising slowly down the dusty main street he spotted a tall, skinny cowboy in a black felt Stetson who was giving him a dirty look.

This was Guillermo Maldonado—known locally as Billy-Evil. Roy had know him from childhood.

Without thinking, he gave Maldonado a friendly wave and called out the window, "*Qué tal*, Billy-Evil, how's it going?" He stopped the jeep for a moment.

The greeting was not returned. There was just that hostile, angry look that seemed to say that Roy's appearance on the scene had spoiled what had been, up to then, a perfectly fine day.

After a moment, without speaking, Maldonado flipped the stub of a cigarette he had been smoking into the gutter beside the pump of the Conoco station, where a sign said NO SMOKING, and then, using two canes, hobbled over to a nearby pickup truck. The back window of the pickup had a rifle rack bolted to it. Billy-Evil placed his canes on the rack, and got in.

Seeing the canes and the crippled gait, Roy grinned and called, "You been rodeoing again, Billy?" Maldonado gave him another hard look, and drove off.

In lots of ways Billy was a living, breathing, genuine professional cowboy. Tourists thought so anyway. Even Pearl Lowdermilk, who ought to have known better, said of him, "You know, he actually *looks* the way I always imagined a cowboy ought to." Billy was bone-thin slim. Iron-jawed, with a narrow, fleshless face burned nut-brown by the sun and the wind, and an elegant, clipped moustache that had been black once but which now was gray-fading-to-white. Though several years older than Roy, he was still a rather incredibly handsome man. Faded, hiphugging jeans and big, rawboned shoulders. Billy-Evil was one of those sort who regularly drank four six-packs a day, never worked a lick unless they had to, and never gained an ounce.

He looked at home on a horse, although he had not been an actual working ranchhand in years. Whenever a Hollywood movie outfit came to New Mexico to film location shots for a western, Billy was sure of employment, as an extra, or a bit player. When he wasn't working, he had a tendency to get into trouble. Roy remembered the time when Billy had gotten drunk and ridden a big Apaloosa named Chaco right into the warm-up paddock at the Ruidoso Downs track just before a race was about to start, and not even the security guards dared fool with him or try to move him out. Billy was not the brightest person but he made up for it by being fairly handy with his fists.

Billy had a few specialties. One was rodeoing. He was quick with a lariat and usually placed in the money in calf-roping, and he was almost as good with broncs and steer-wrestling.

The only thing that did him in was Brahmas. Brahma bulls, of course, are about the biggest, meanest animals left on the American continent, and since they have a remarkably nasty temperament it is considered either a mark of stupidity or gutsy manhood even to mount one. A Brahma is one of the few beasts that will run a man down and kill him just for the fun of it. Billy regularly entered the Brahma lists, and just as regularly got bucked, stomped, broken-up, and hospitalized. Whenever Billy was seen on canes or crutches, or trundling himself up Capitan's main street in his wheelchair, it was safe to assume he'd been Brahma-ing.

Another specialty of his was women from California or back east. Preferably young, pretty, and loaded with money, out touring the great Wild West, and mortally convinced that the trip would be a tragic waste unless they locked in at least once with a handsome rodeo-cowboy stud.

With them, Billy had developed a sure-fire act. He was polite and courteous, but at the same time shy and almost aloof . . . then those sad, gray eyes of his seemed fixed on distant, heat-hazed mountains. He looked just like someone out of a Marlboro advertisement, and ladies liked this very much. When he was ambulatory, they took him to the most expensive Ruidoso steak-houses and cocktail lounges and got writer's cramp from endorsing travelers' checks, while they waited for a kind word from him.

Whenever their attentions got to be more than a patient man could tolerate, Billy had another routine he liked to work (still gazing off at those distant, smoky mountains, his eyes moody, sad, weary, gentle): "You wanna know what matters the most to me? Well, ma'am, I don' mind showin' you." He would take out his snakeskin wallet, while the young lady with him waited in anticipation. The wallet was opened. A cascade of accordion-pleated plexiglass folders. Guess what? No harem of sexual conquests; not even·a snapshot of his loving mother. Just horses. Every single horse Billy-Evil had owned since he learned to ride at the age of seven. How could a cultured, sophisticated girl from Stanford or Bryn Mawr compete against something like that?

The thing was, he was really a beautiful man. That long, angular Castilian face. There was probably a small army of young ladies around the country who, if they had wished to make such a disclosure, could say, "You know, one time I nearly got it on with this simply divine bullrider." That was Billy-Evil.

Trouble was, Billy had another side. A part of that sad, brooding expression was genuine, and from time to time, when life weighed too heavily on him, he and the roughneck pals he hung out with got a yen for lipstick and mascara and pancake makeup.

Roy had once made the mistake of kidding him about this.

Billy had not taken kindly to such teasing, low-pressure though it was. His sense of humor had never gotten past the Sunday comics.

That was one reason he had given Roy a hard look at the Conoco station. There were other reasons, so awful that Roy preferred not to think about them, first of all because he had never been able to discover if Billy even *knew*, and second, because if Billy did know, it could mean real trouble.

Maldonado was always a fellow to hold a grudge.

FARTHER UP THE street, parked among some tourists' cars outside the Smokey Bear Saloon, Roy spotted a familiar three-ton stake-bed truck loaded with cedar fenceposts, and a battered Dodge pickup. He pulled over, parked, and went in.

The barroom was dark and dusty but not without a certain charm. Eulalio Mondragon, who owned the place, had put up all sorts of bygone western stuff on the walls, and even the ceiling was festooned with old cowboy hats, boots, horseshoes, rotted saddles, antique newspaper headlines, crosstrees for ox teams, and rusted-out rifles and handguns. The bar was old, and made of solid walnut carved in baroque floral designs. Behind it there was a wall-length tarnished mirror. Down at the far end of the bar some tourist people were drinking while their kids worked on Cokes and played the pinball machines.

Up front, not far from the swinging bat-wing doors he had just entered, Lloyd Parmalee and Rowdy Roth were having a serious discussion about pistols.

Lloyd was saying, "I'll take all the .44 Magnums you can lay your hands on."

"Well, I only got one right now, a Western Arms, imitation stag grips, four-inch barrel, just like new," Rowdy said. "I retouched the blueing a little, where she was holster worn, but that's all."

"How much?"

"I'd consider seventy-five, Lloyd."

"I'd consider fifty," Lloyd said. "Sight unseen."

"Done, *amigo*. Buy you a brew on that."

Roy leaned closer and said into Rowdy's ear, "Treasury De-

98 *Oliver Lange*

partment . . . Bureau of Alcohol, Tobacco, and Firearms. You
are both under arrest for dealing in firearms without a license.
Anything you say will be held against you."

It didn't bother Rowdy. He tipped his big Stetson back, looked
around, and then grinned. "Well! Goddamn! Howdy, Roy! Pull
yourself up a beer and set a spell."

Lloyd Parmalee stood up and shook hands with Roy. "Where
you been? We heard rumors you were back."

The barkeep was a new young fellow. Roy motioned for three
beers and dropped money on the bar. Then he sat down and
chatted for a while.

He'd known Lloyd Parmalee as a friend for years. A wiry, griz-
zled cuss, now in his middle sixties. Lloyd worked as a roofer,
and on the side he ran a small gunshop out of his garage. At one
time or another he had probably put a roof on every house between Carrizozo and San Patricio. Lloyd was married but had
never had children, and his wife, Alma, taught home ec at the
Carrizozo High School. Lloyd was famous for his work habits.
Despite his skinniness and age, he could put in a ten-hour day in
the middle of July, mopping hot tar onto a ninety-pound-weight
asphalt roof, and come off it feeling refreshed and ready to party,
while the helpers he'd hired, maybe half his age or even less,
limped home and went to bed for two weeks. Also, despite his
being softspoken and easygoing, he was known to have a temper
that occasionally went off like a case of dynamite. He was an old-
time, hardbitten, blue-collar workingman who took pride in any
task he set himself, from surveying to gunsmithing, and he knew
more ways to turn a dollar than any man in this part of the state:
the big truck outside, loaded with cedar posts, was his.

Lloyd also happened to be the director of the Billy the Kid
Pageant that was held every August over in Lincoln. He played
the part of Sheriff Pat Garrett, and it made no difference that the
real-life Garrett had been miles away when the Kid got loose, or
that the whole town had literally held its breath until the outlaw
rode off. The staged Pageant had to have box-office appeal, so
there was a grand-slam shoot-'em-up, with posses and a stagecoach and fast-draw gunslinging. That was when all the blank
cartridges went off, and that was why Lloyd was interested in
buying heavy-caliber pistols.

Actually, Roy thought that the true-to-life story had been more interesting. Billy, having mysteriously broken loose and having in some way gotten those small, girlish, deadly hands of his on a pistol, gunned down Deputy J. W. Bell (the slugs in the adobe wall of the courthouse stairwell were from two quick snap-shots, but on the third try Billy caught Bell neatly between the shoulderblades).

After that the Kid broke open the gun cabinet and then leisurely waited up in the open second-story window of the Lincoln County Courthouse with a double-barreled scattergun . . . in no kind of hurry at all, just sitting with one leg propped on the sill of that open window, waiting for his arch enemy, Deputy Bob Olinger, to come dashing across the deserted street from the restaurant where he'd been having lunch.

Bob, of course, was the kind of not-very-bright law officer who was just stupid enough to come galloping out into the middle of the street at the first sound of gunfire. Bob also was a big loutish fellow who didn't mind having some fun by slapping hell out of a prisoner when Sheriff Garrett wasn't around, especially one in waist and ankle manacles, like the Kid, who was pretty puny anyway, so maybe it is understandable why young Billy Bonney happened to hate Bob with a passion.

Anyway, Olinger came hoofing it across that dusty street at a little after high noon on the eighteenth day of April, 1881. A bad *hombre,* just itching for a chance to show how he could keep law and order.

Then, suddenly, he pulled up short, put on the brakes, sensing that something was wrong. It was too quiet, too ominous, something wasn't right. There wasn't another soul out there in the street except him. And he had this intuition, just a feeling, that the Kid had somehow managed to get loose from the hand-forged, six-inch ringbolt Garrett kept him chained to (that heavy ring is still on exhibit, bolted solidly into the floor upstairs).

And just then, young Mister William Bonney, still twenty-one years of age and sitting in the open window, called down in the most pleasant sort of way, "Hello, Bob. Here's something for you."

Olinger stared up for one awful moment to see Billy sitting there on the windowsill with that 12-gauge double-barrel cradled easily across one thigh. One version reports that Bob just stood there alone in the middle of the hot and deserted street, sensing in that split second that he was already a dead man, that he had lost, been fooled, and with the realization of this had muttered weakly, "Oh, shit!" Another version has it that he actually went for the revolver strapped to his thigh. Whatever, Billy cut loose. First one barrel, and then the other. *Adios*, Bob.

Billy walked out on the upstairs porch and scornfully broke the shotgun on the railing and threw the smashed pieces down at Olinger's buckshot-torn corpse. After that he calmly armed himself with another pistol, a rifle, and plenty of ammunition from the same gun cabinet, walked downstairs, and mounted the nearest saddled horse. The only one who could have stopped him, or who would have had the courage to try, was Pat Garrett, who had been a kind of friend to Billy and who had tried to steer him straight, and Garrett was up in White Oaks serving a tax notice. On that day no man showed his face in Lincoln. William Antrim Bonney had killed twice again, and was armed and loose. It really happened that way.

AND HERE WAS an atomic-age Pat Garrett—Lloyd Parmalee himself—buying pistols from none other than Billy Bonney . . . in the reincarnated form of Rowdy!

Roy felt that sensation of disassociation again, that inability to keep track of what was real and what was make-believe.

Because Rowdy Roth *was* Billy the Kid . . . or at least what passed for young Bonney in these modern times. Rowdy had only been in Lincoln County for a dozen or so years, and was considered a newcomer, but for most of that time, when the annual Billy the Kid Pageant came around, he had acted out the part of ". . . the fearless and ruthless young outlaw."

As director of the show, Parmalee had given Rowdy the part because he looked quite a lot like the young fellow in the only photograph taken of Billy, when he was working for the Tunstall spread on the nearby Rio Feliz. That photograph showed a short, slender, somewhat retarded-looking cowhand dressed in the heavy wool clothing favored by ranchhands in winter, a floppy broadbrimmed hat, and a bandanna-kerchief knotted about the

neck. The face is high-cheekboned, with a long lantern jaw, mo-
ronic eyes, and a set of crooked buck teeth revealed in what was
perhaps intended to be an engaging grin. A revolver is stuck in
the belt, and held in one hand, with its butt resting on the
ground, is a big lever-action Winchester repeating rifle. It is
precisely the kind of posed photograph that was made by the
tens of thousands during the last half of the nineteenth century
by itinerant photographers, when a working cowboy, in off the
range and desirous of something to send back home to family or
sweetheart, could, for the sum of a dollar, have his full-length
portrait taken—the rifle, the pistol, even the kerchief and som-
brero were part of a lensman's studio props.

The modest height and the face with its evil expression fit
Rowdy well enough except for the teeth. While he was rodeoing
one afternoon, a sidewinding broomtail bronc had taken out
most of Rowdy's eating equipment with a fast-flying hoof. The
toothless smile made him look older than his thirty-five years.

The strange thing was that, just like William A. Bonney,
Rowdy had been born in New York City. He spoke in a heavy,
twangy drawl that was as authentic as Texas, except for an occasional lapse into street talk. Quite a few professional cowboys
had come out of the east. The name Rowdy Roth was a picturesque pseudonym—he had been born Abraham Rothstein, a name
which he figured might carry little charisma in the rodeo circuit.

Between rodeos—that is, between hospitalizations, because he
spent almost as much time mending as Billy-Evil Maldonado
—Rowdy hung out in Capitan, San Patricio, or Lincoln, cadging
drinks. He also worked at odd jobs with Lloyd Parmalee, and
sometimes when he was really hard up for cash he'd get on a
roof with the old man and feed him buckets of molten tar, but
the most important job he had was in the Billy the Kid Pageant.
Rowdy admitted he had a wife and children in Peekskill, New
York, but was quick to add, with some pride, that she loathed the
west, horses, rodeoing, and Rowdy's drunken ways. When he
wasn't handymanning around with his friend Lloyd, Rowdy was
an affable hustler and a part-time gun smuggler.

The first thing he said when Roy sat down with them was,
"Say, *amigo,* can you spring for a hundred? I got to get entry
money together for the big stomp down at 'Cruces next month."

Roy knew there was no putdown or unfriendliness in Rowdy's attempt to hustle money—the little cowboy just naturally tried to put the touch on anybody he talked to. Roy also knew that if he gave Rowdy easy cash most of it would go over the bar before sundown. He said, "I'm watching my nickels and dimes these days, Rowdy."

"How about getting laid, then?" Rowdy said. "It so happens I got an inside connection with this big old squaw down on the reservation, name of Ophelia Boggs, only everybody calls her Fat Peggy for some reason. She ain't much to look at, but I gave her a hundred-pound sack of pinto beans I took in a gun trade last week, and she said she'd do right by me for a month along with any friends I cared to bring so long as they had their own drinking liquor."

"No thanks, Rowdy."

"What's the matter, old sport, you got something against having your ashes hauled once in a while?"

"No. It's just that that Indian princess of yours sounds a little awesome."

"Fat Peggy ain't so bad, Roy. At least she's got a sense of humor. For a squaw, anyway. Hell, when she giggles, a man can feel the earth tremors half a mile off."

Lloyd said, "Roy, Billy-Evil was in for a beer a while ago."

"Is that where you heard I was back?"

Lloyd nodded. "He had his usual kind remarks about you to pass along."

"Wonder how he found out."

"He said Pearl Lowdermilk told him. Half the county probably knows you're back up at Sawmill."

"I spotted him just now as I was driving into town," Roy said. "Bill is something else."

"I wouldn't recommend turning your back on him, Roy," Parmalee said. "How come he's got it in for you so?"

"Lloyd, it's a long story . . . about something that happened years ago. It's not worth telling."

"Only trouble with Bill Maldonado, he's full of prejudice," Rowdy said. "You combine that with ignorance, it can be a heavy scene. Say, Roy, you can't lend me anything, how about buying a gun?"

"I don't have any use for a gun," Roy said.

"It never hurts to keep a piece handy. What d'you say—I got over twenty out in the truck."

"One of these days you're liable to get into real trouble, hauling all that iron around."

"Fellow's got to eat, Roy."

"You still peddling them down in old Mexico?"

"Hey, man! Not on your life." Rowdy grinned toothlessly and rubbed one hand over a quarter-inch of stubble on his jaw. He signaled for three more beers. "I mean to tell you, it's gotten heavy down there. The heroin and maryjane trade has ruined everything. Those *federales* got roadblocks from one end of the country to the other. This spring, they nearly caught me outside Chihuahua. I was only delivering a small consignment, too, about a dozen pistols to this old black-market revolutionary I happen to know down in Ciudad Obregon. 'Course I got places in that truck where I could stash fifty handguns but even so I just about shit little green apples when those Mexican feds yanked me over to the side of the highway. Why, I was only taking a vacation. I was selling that consignment merely to cover travel expenses. But after that I quit. Life in a Mexican slammer ain't so mellow from what I hear."

Roy looked at him. "Rowdy, if you quit, how come you have a truckload outside right now?"

"Oh, I quit hauling into Mexico is all, Roy. I'm delivering now up in Spanish Harlem. Hell, those Puerto Rican suckers'll pay five hundred for an ol' busted-down Army Colt .45 auto, they don't even check to see if it's in operating condition. Not like Parmalee here. He ain't happy unless he pisses in a beer can and sells it back to the saloon he bought it from."

Their fresh beers came, and Roy said, "You mean to tell me you actually fill up the back of that pickup with pistols and then drive them twenty-five hundred miles across the country to New York?"

"Only once or twice a year, no more."

"That's not only illegal—it's scary."

"So's income taxes," Rowdy pointed out. He drank half his beer.

Roy said, "The man ever check you?"

"Once, outside Pittsburgh, on the 'pike. They didn't look hard."

"And you actually make money on that kind of operation?"

"Not as much as you might think," Rowdy said. "After gas and oil and depreciation an' all that, plus what I got to set aside to reinvest in new iron . . . well, the overhead mounts up, you know."

Lloyd said, "Let's have a look at that .44."

They took their beers and started out the bat-wing doors. The young barkeep said, "Sorry, gents, it's against the rules to take drinks off the premises."

"That's okay, Timmie, these boys are with me," Lloyd said. The barkeep stared at him for a moment and then shrugged as if it was none of his business. Lloyd Parmalee was not only Sheriff Pat Garrett in the annual pageant. In real life, aside from handy-manning, he was a county underdeputy with the sheriff's department.

In the pickup outside there was a sheet-metal toolbox bolted to the bed. Rowdy unlocked it. Spread out on a blanket was a small arsenal. Three Winchester rifles, four shotguns, a Ruger .44 carbine and some .22 rifles, plus a dozen or so pistols—two 9-millimeter Lugers, a Walther P-38, some Smith & Wessons and Hi-Standard automatics, a snubnosed, hammerless detective special, as well as the big Western Arms magnum which he and Lloyd had been discussing when Roy first came in. Lloyd immediately reached for the .44. After checking it over, he handed Rowdy two twenties and a ten. Rowdy put the money into a shirt pocket and said, "I'll jump for a fresh round."

On their way back to the bar, Roy saw that Lloyd had a chain-saw sitting atop the stacks of freshly cut posts. He said, "What are you cutting cedar posts for, Lloyd?"

"Me and Rowdy contracted to build a fence down by San Patricio," Lloyd said.

"Hard work."

"Easy money at two fifty a post." Lloyd nodded toward the back of the loaded stake-bed. "There's pretty near fifteen hundred bucks' worth of cedar right there."

"Any chance I could borrow your saw when you're done?"

"For how long?"

"Couple of weeks."

"Take it now. We'll be that long digging and setting these poles we cut."

"Thanks, Lloyd." He got the chainsaw, a two-gallon gas can, and some cans of oil out of the truck's cab and put them in the jeep.

"I'll be needing it around September," Lloyd said. "The chain's dull, though."

"I'll file it for you."

"What you want to cut?"

"I'm thinking of laying in a supply of wood for the winter."

"Up at Sawmill?" Lloyd said. "That's a mess of wood, Roy. You're way up past nine thousand. You ever winter there before?"

"Not really," Roy admitted. "I've lived up there through summer and fall is all."

"*Amigo,* come January you're liable to start feeling mighty high, lonesome, and cold," Rowdy said.

"I don't know if I'll really do it," Roy said. "I've just been thinking about it. I might change my mind. The thing is, I've got some time loose right now, so I thought I might as well buck out a little ponderosa in case I do decide to stay on."

"Shucks, Roy, if I was you, I wouldn't sweat out no winter up in *those* mountains," Rowdy said. "I bet it gets down to thirty below when a storm comes in. Funny . . . you know, when I was a kid back east, I thought all this country was sun and desert. The books I read never told nothing about blizzards that can rip the top of a feller's head clean off. No, sir! I'm a snowbird. If it was me, I'd point my nose south come first freeze, and I wouldn't stop until I saw Acapulco Bay staring me straight in the eye. That's the only place to be, come winter, Roy. That's when all them New York and Chicago secretaries take their winter vacations. Man, I bet there must be five hundred excursion flights a day leaving O'Hare and Kennedy, all bound for old 'Pulco and Porty Vallarty! Suntanning, and romancing, that's all *those* ladies got on the brain. Why, Roy, you can't even see the sand on the beaches for all the pussy. A feller's got to crawl over it, for mile after mile. Couple of winters back, I made it down that way. I had me a *fine* time!"

"I was thinking of something more restful," Roy said.

"Roy here happens to be one of those recluses," Lloyd said. "He only works at it part-time, though."

"Oh, you don't have to tell me about *that,*" Rowdy said. "Why, I'm a recluse myself when I ain't drinking. Sure. Sometimes I'll just pack up a carton full of groceries and beer and drive out twenty or thirty miles on the plains up past Capitan Gap and camp by myself for a couple of days. Maybe shoot up a few boxes of shells in whatever pistol I happen to have along. Go where there ain't no fences and where you can still see antelope come dawn. They look so pretty in that first light . . . you can spot 'em three, four miles off. They're so shy, you know. And there's just you, all by your lonesome, and maybe a campfire and a pot of coffee bubbling and a drop of bourbon to get your eyeballs unglued. Just miles and miles of nothing. Offhand, I don't know what's better than that. That's what counts about this country. A feller can still get off by himself when he feels the need to, without half the world peeking over his shoulder every two seconds to see what he's up to. Shit, I don't fault a man *that.*"

BACK IN THE bar, Lloyd said, "You need some help bucking out that ponderosa, maybe Rowdy and me will come up for a day."

"Thanks. Like I said, I haven't made up my mind. I'll take care of that chainsaw for you."

"You hear me worrying? Better break out that plug and scrape the gap, though. It soots up every few hours."

They ordered another round of beers and Roy said, "Lloyd, exactly what did Bill Maldonado have to say about me?"

"Well, I don't remember his exact words, but it had something to do with a day of reckoning, and how it was long overdue—he also said something about seeing to it personally that you were run out of Lincoln County for keeps," Lloyd said.

"I think he slipped in a remark too about how some folks ain't fit to walk around on the face of the earth," Rowdy added. "I wouldn't count on him fallin' in love with you, Roy."

"Bill doesn't care for Anglos," Roy said. "Moreover, he can't stand Indians, and of course he hates blacks even worse. I can't even imagine how he'd feel about a half-breed. No . . . come to think of it, I can. Bill doesn't like anything that isn't Spanish. I've got a Spanish name but that doesn't make me Spanish."

"Ain't he a pisser, though?" Rowdy mused. "A man his age. Still unmarried and living at home with his momma. I heard she does all his cooking and washing and sewing."

"That's not uncommon with the Spanish," Roy pointed out.

"Well, about the only ones he fools anymore are college snatch," Rowdy said. He giggled and shook his head. "You know, I once saw him ride a big chestnut Morgan right up the main drag of Ruidoso. Oh, he looked grand! He was dressed in solid black. Black silk shirt that his momma had made for him, black jeans and Stetson, and a turquoise-and-silver concho belt that must have weighed sixteen pounds. Had him a gallon jug of muscatel riding on the pommel. He swigged at it as he moseyed along. Drunk and feeling mean, you know. Out for trouble. Had on a pair of those sunglasses where the lenses look chrome-plated, so you couldn't see his nasty snake-eyes. Well, shit. Right there, a New Hampshire girl fell down in the street foaming at the mouth, and three of those female flower children from Malibu got fits and fainting spells and had to be taken by Blue Cross ambulance to Intensive Care. I ain't exaggerating. I saw it personally. I wonder if there's any truth in the rumor that he's got a real French lace peg-noir and a collection of fancy perfume?"

"You might ask him, Rowdy," Roy said. "Only I don't think that'd be smart."

A voice said, "It's true . . . like attracts like." They looked around. It was Pearl Lowdermilk. "Is that all you broken-down has-beens have to do, sit around swilling beer and gossiping?"

"Howdy, Pearl," Lloyd Parmalee said, getting up.

"Afternoon, Miz Lowdermilk," Rowdy said, putting on his best manners. Pearl wasn't exactly fond of him, and he knew it. "You care to join us in a cold one?"

"I saw your jeep outside, Roy," she said. "Then I seen Parmalee's stake-bed, and Roth's heap of junk. Ain't no problem locating the men of this territory . . . just check the bars. Hello, Lloyd." She turned to Roy. "I'll have a beer. I got your money order and your booze and groceries. Must be nice to be retired and rich and just sit back and relax when I got to run my tail off in Ruidoso and half the rest of the county, doing your errands."

They ordered more beers. Rowdy said politely, "You care to sit at a table, Miz Lowdermilk?"

"I ain't planning on being here all week," Pearl said. "I don't mind standing at the bar. Roth, don't you *ever* take a bath or shave? My billygoat smells better. And how come you were bad-mouthing Bill Maldonado? I heard what you was saying. If Maldonado hears, he'll come around and stomp you into the mud."

"Billy don't scare me none," Rowdy said. "He tries to hassle me, he'll spend the next two years in that wheelchair of his."

"You ain't nothing but a big-mouthed, sawed-off midget," Pearl said. "Why, if I was young again, I'd wrap you around my little finger."

"I bet you was a fine specimen of womanhood," Rowdy said, grinning.

"You better believe it," she agreed. "At twenty-two I stood six feet three inches in a pair of lumberjack socks, and I weighed a hundred and eighty-five, and that, in case you don't know it, was Dempsey's exact fighting weight when he made mincemeat out of old Jess Willard, back in 1919. I heard he broke that poor man's jaw in fourteen different places. Oh, I was something, all right."

"You still are, Pearl," Roy said.

"Don't hand me that slop. I'm just a broken-down old wreck." She took a wallet out of her hip pocket and gave him the twenty-five-dollar money order he had asked for. "Your groceries came to a hundred and thirty-five plus change. I got the receipt. Also, when I was up in Ruidoso today I did some asking around at real estate offices for you. None of them shysters ever heard of that Larson outfit. What d'you think of that?"

"I haven't decided what to think, Pearl," he said.

Frowning, she drank some of her beer. "For someone who claims he has brains, it sure doesn't show. I bet it's a dummy company with a phony name. Some bird-doggin' outfit looking to rustle land."

"Who is?" Lloyd asked.

"Some crook named Larson back east," she said.

Lloyd looked interested. He glanced at Roy. "Say, did you

happen to want a survey done this spring on that section you got up there?"

"No."

"Well, a survey was done on it, Roy."

"How do you know?"

"Me and Rowdy did it. Some Albuquerque abstract company hired us."

"Lloyd, that land is posted for no trespassing."

"Didn't actually go on it, Roy. Not much, anyway. Went along the perimeter. The old cut lines are still there, more or less, except that most of them are straight up and down. I had my measuring wheel. I didn't want to fool with the surveying chain. Those Albuquerque people paid me and Rowdy five hundred."

Pearl glared at Parmalee. "How come you're just mentioning it now, you fool?"

Lloyd shrugged. "You know how it is, Pearl . . . it's best not to talk around about certain things. A man has his property surveyed, there's a reason. Maybe he's going to sell it, maybe he's going to do something else with it. I figure that's his personal business, not mine. I'll just do the job and charge a fair rate. Sometimes people around here get strong feelings about their land. Anyway, I never gave this job a second thought . . . I figured Roy here had requested it. I couldn't see nobody else asking for that kind of survey. Hell, there ain't no contiguous owners around that square mile except the federal government and the reservation." He looked at Roy again. "You didn't pay for that survey?"

"No."

Lloyd thought. "A bunch of old shacks sitting up in the middle of nowhere. This Albuquerque dude who paid us seemed to know all about the place, though. Had plat records and the whole description, copied out of county tax books. I just figured it was you paying for it, Roy."

"Did you talk to him?" Pearl demanded.

"Not any more than I had to," Lloyd said. Pearl got out a cigarette and Rowdy made a fuss over lighting it for her. "This fellow didn't actually go up there with us. Didn't want to get his shoes muddy," Lloyd went on. He looked a little troubled. "Roy, it ain't none of my affair, but have you had an offer to sell? If I'm out of line, just say so."

Land in these parts was a touchy subject. Old-timers could remember when hundreds of square miles were bought and sold for incredibly small sums. Nowadays it wasn't tens of thousands of acres; it had boiled down to five- and ten-acre parcels, or even less, bought by "outside" people. The old families did not like this. Births and deaths were a matter of course, but a land transaction always generated talk . . . how much money had been involved, why the land was sold, and, most of all, the use "outsiders" would put it to. An outsider was anyone who had not lived in the county for fifty years, and all outsiders, regardless of whether they came from Texas or California or New England, were considered filthy rich, and corrupt to boot. Ruidoso was a case in point. A skilled ranch cowboy could make five times more a month grooming a stable of polo ponies than he could working out on the range, and the owner might even invite him up to the main house for a real cocktail when the day was done. What sense was there in teaching a youngster to rope and brand when, at nineteen, he could find easy winter work up at the ski lift, where there were ski bunnies to flirt with, and the pleasant attentions of older ladies who knew what they wanted and could pay for it? Yes, small-time ranching was gone. It was a lost cause. And people were bitter. Not just over the loss of an old and established way of life . . . they were angry for a less complex reason: they had never had the brains or sophistication to understand the value of land, and so they had sold it for next to nothing. An illness, or age, or plain weariness with struggling, could do it. So it just might be that Lloyd Parmalee, by unwittingly allying himself with "outside folks," felt himself in the wrong. Now he looked almost a touch embarrassed. "Roy, me and Rowdy didn't know. We figured it was you asked for it."

"Somebody want to buy you out?" Rowdy asked.

"Sort of. I can't really tell yet."

"Never was a gun made or a woman laid that didn't have a price tag," Rowdy said cheerfully.

"Roth, that mouth of yours is as filthy as the rest of you," Pearl said.

"Roy, that was your dad's place," Lloyd said.

"I know," Roy said.

"I remember your dad real well," Lloyd went on. "He thought the world of Sawmill. I don't think he'd want you to sell out."

"He's been dead a long time, Lloyd."

"Maybe so," the old roofer said. "I still don't think he'd like the idea."

"You might have something there."

"Money talks, *amigo*," Rowdy said. He chuckled, and signaled for another round of beers.

"So do you, Roth," Pearl said angrily. "Too much, if you ask me. I don't know why squinchy little roosters have to make so much noise. Whyn't you just sit back and behave inferior like you ought to? Rooster? Capon is more like it!"

"I've fathered four children," Rowdy told her proudly.

"Pardon me while I applaud," she said. "You must've climbed on a table, you sneaky worm." She shuddered. "Little men give me goose pimples. I don't know why they have to act so confident all the time."

" 'Cause we *know*, Miz Lowdermilk."

"You sound like my first husband, Harold," Pearl said. "He was five foot four and all mouth." She stared somberly down at her beer. "Well, not exactly. I reckon he had considerable enthusiasm, too." She frowned, and shook her head. "The first six months we was married, I lost forty-three pounds, and I never gained 'em back. Who wants a woman my height that's built like a piece of clothesline? I even went to a doctor. He thought I'd come down with tuberculosis, with those big black circles I had under my eyes. He wanted to take tests, but I didn't bother, 'cause I knew better. There was no test that had ever been invented for Harold."

ROY DROVE BACK up to Honcho with Pearl, and there they transferred his groceries from her truck to the jeep. She said, "It just kills me to go into a supermarket these days. I can remember when a whole family could eat on a ten-dollar bill a week. You want to stay for dinner?"

"Thanks, Pearl." He helped her carry her own packages into the kitchen and then sat down at the table while she put things away and talked: "What puzzles me is how poor people even manage to stay alive anymore. Up in Ruidoso, they got millions to play around with—dude ranches, and skiing, and horse racing, and I don't know what all else."

Roy nodded, and uncapped a bottle of wine he'd brought in. "I think that a lot of people have gotten confused about the difference between the pursuit of happiness and the pursuit of pleasure."

"But, damn it, Roy, where do they get the *money?*" she said angrily. "I'm poor. Everybody I know is poor. All I hear on tv or read in magazines is the recession, high unemployment, inflation, and petrodollars . . . and on top of it, that rotten Chase Bank in New York juggles the prime interest rate so fast you can't tell if you're watching a financial institution or Salami dancing with her seven veils! I ain't stupid, you know. I watch the *MacNeil-Lehrer Report*, and *Wall Street Week.*" She shook her head. "It ain't fair."

"You can say that again," he agreed. "Feel like a glass of wine?"

"I don't like wine," she said. "What kind is it?"

"Rosé. It's mild."

"Well, just a little." She brought over a twelve-ounce glass.

He filled it and said, "What're you going to cook?"

"It's one of them Italian catchachickie recipes I cut out of *Woman's Day.*"

"You mean cacciatore."

"Tastes like plain old baked chicken with a mess of ketchup tossed in. I been saving the recipe to try on you. You got strange tastes."

"You know, Pearl, they say if a man eats too much chicken it will grow bosoms on him."

"Roy Aldous, you are the most disgusting man!" She thought about this. "Why do they say that?"

"It's something to do with all those female hormones they shoot into the birds . . . on those chicken ranches."

"I don't believe that. Really?"

"So I hear."

"That's just another of those crazy stories of yours," she said. "Chicken never did a thing for me."

"You have a fine figure, Pearl."

"Bee stings. That's what my Harold called 'em."

"You're kind of willowy."

"Willowy is just a high-class way of saying a woman's built like a plank," she said. "Well, it's lucky I never heard about those hormones when I was young. I'd'a plowed through chicken until it come outa my ears, if it would've done some good." She smiled without humor. "When a girl gets stuck with bee stings, she's plumb outa luck."

"Some men like narrow-built women, Pearl."

"My Harold didn't."

"Say, what was your maiden name?"

"What business is it of yours?"

"Just curious."

"Grüber."

"German?"

"No. It's Ethiopian, you idiot. 'Course it's German. Get over here and peel these potatoes for me instead of asking stupid questions. Say, that wine ain't bad, is it?"

"Have some more." She did. He said, "I'll get to those potatoes in a minute." From his shirt pocket he took out the order blank from the genealogical heraldic arms outfit whose advertisement had been in with his mail. On the line for the applicant's name he printed PEARL GRÜBER, along with the address, put in the money order she had purchased for him, and sealed everything in a return envelope. He had an idea that something like that might please her.

She looked at him with a frown. "What's that?"

"Nothing, Pearl."

"You got more secrets than a senator. I don't know why men have to be so naturally devious all the time."

"Where'd you ever get that idea?"

"Via matrimony."

He went over to the kitchen counter and sat on the far side of it, working on the spuds. "Say, Pearl, aren't you supposed to have noodles with cacciatore?"

"I'm doing it German-style. You sound worse'n that Julia Child. Got to have everything authentic and la-de-dah, don't you? That woman doesn't know the value of money. One time I saw her do a leg of lamb for what she called a Sunday brunch—I reckon that's something for them who're too hung over to get up for breakfast and too weak to wait until noon—and the price tag on that joint of meat, which she said was for *snacks,* would have looked more appropriate on a new car. She is a passable cook, though, as long as somebody else is footing the bill."

When it came to doing a dinner, Pearl moved slowly, and there was no way in the world to hurry her. She liked to smoke and have a few drinks and talk as she prepared things, with a cigarette dangling from one corner of her mouth and a butcher knife and chopping block at hand. Onions, green peppers, fresh tomatoes and zucchini, as well as celery and a quarter-cup of fresh garlic cloves, were leisurely washed, inspected from all angles, and then cut to precise configurations on the oak block. The choice of herbs from the spice rack—parsley, oregano, basil, marjoram, thyme, bay leaves, and cilantro—took additional time. It didn't pay to arrive at her house with a raging appetite, because hours were sure to pass before anything actually got to the table. The rest of the world could hurry but Pearl knew her pace and was not about to change. Although she claimed to do only "plain and simple ranch cooking," this was a lie; she was a fabulous cook.

Now, as she went about her work, she said, "Well, I'd say you've got yourself in a real predicament, Roy."

"How's that?"

"To be land-rich and purse-poor. I've seen it before. Folks sitting on thousands of acres, and no money to buy shoes for kids going to school."

"You mean Sawmill River Flats?"

She nodded. "Don't it make you boil to see the way these pushy easterners come crowding in?"

"Not exactly. I guess they have the same rights as everyone else. If somebody sells them property, they ought to be able to do what they want with it."

"But don't it make you *sad?*"

She got to him with that. He thought for a while and then drank some wine and said, "As a matter of fact, Pearl, yes. I do get kind of sad sometimes."

"Why, I can remember when it might take a stranger four or

five days to even *find* Ruidoso," she went on. "Now they got a highway and real streets and electricity and everything. How does something like that start, Roy?"

"Times are changing," he said. "I drove around up there today, before I ran into Lloyd and Rowdy. I hardly recognized the place."

"You get the picture, then. With that land your father left you, you're sitting on a fortune."

"I wouldn't go that far, Pearl," he said. "Of course it's worth something. It's worth a lot more than what he paid for it. But exactly how much . . . that's hard to say."

"No, it ain't," she snapped. "Just ask old lard-bottom Maudie Dalrymple. Not two months ago she come through here on her rounds, and she sat there in the exact same place you're sitting, and bragged her fool head off about those four acres she owns for her retirement—which should've come fifteen years ago—not far from them condominiums they put up a few years back . . . you know, on that branch road about a mile south of Alto, just before you hit Ruidoso? What she said tied in pretty close with some remarks I heard this morning from this realtor I was checking with. You ought to go up there and have a look at those shacks. They're kind of like teepees."

"You mean A-frames?" he said. "I saw them today."

"That's what Maudie called 'em," Pearl went on. "Little A-frame teepees, knocked together out of pine siding and plaster-board and gussied up with some chrome and fresh paint. Each on two acres. They got a little two-bit stream moseying through that development that a coyote could spit across, they call it a *rio*, shoot! I can get twenty times more *rio* out of my kitchen faucet! But they call it *Rio Vista Estates*. Would you believe it, they're peddling those teepees that ain't held together with any-thing more'n carpet tacks and glue right and left to rich Texas sodbusters from Dallas and Midland, for two hundred and fifty thousand apiece! I swear! And, Roy, that development ain't more than three walking miles from Sawmill River Flats."

"Pearl, I'm not saying my land doesn't have some value these days."

"The only thing you know is sentimental value," she pointed out. "Your father was no different . . . he was a good man but he had no sense. There's another kind of value, and it's the kind you can stick in a bank and draw interest on. You just try and deposit sentimental value and see what it gets you. Do you know what that land of yours may be worth? I mean, if they did the very same thing on it that they've done with that Rio Vista Estates eyesore? I did a little figuring . . ." She got out a scrap of envelope from her jeans. "Roy, they could stick three hundred and twenty of those A-frame teepees on a six-hundred-forty-acre section. Do you understand how much something like that is worth in real estate these days? At the prices they're asking—and getting?"

He couldn't figure it in his mind that fast, and without waiting she went on, scowling, staring down at the piece of paper she'd smoothed out on the chopping block. "Unless my multiplication and long division is off, and it ain't, that comes out to over eighty million dollars."

"Pearl, that doesn't make sense."

" 'Course it doesn't, but figures don't lie," she said. "I'll tell you something else. This spring I was talking to Sara Pacheco over at the courthouse when I went to pay my taxes. She told me herself that just about every scrap of land in sight around there has been snapped up by developers. Every speck of Sierra Blanca that ain't actually in the National Forest or on Indian land. Roy, I suspect you may own the last big chunk of land up there. One square mile of free-and-clear property, with a ski resort on one side, National Forest on the other, the Mescaleros on the third, and quarter-million-dollar teepees jammed full of millionaires as far as the eye can see on the fourth? I'm telling you, I wouldn't waste my time setting a match to Sawmill River, but the land that old town sits on, well . . . that might be something else again."

"Eighty million sounds like a real piece of money," he said. The figure did not really register in his mind. It was too much . . . like the national debt, or the way his father had explained the distance involved in a light-year: there were too many zeroes to absorb.

"Roy, it's no money at all if this Larson Corporation you talked to already has its hand in your pocket."

"Pearl, you're talking about developed land," he argued. "That means roads, and power and water. Improvements like that are awfully expensive. The raw land itself isn't worth anywhere near that."

"It's worth *something*," she said, giving him a hard look. "You know how I can tell?"

"How?"

"'Cause somebody *wants* it! Some fancy outfit back east that probably couldn't even find the state of New Mexico on the map. And you can bet your bottom dollar, they don't want it for sentimental reasons. Maybe you love that place, but it don't follow they do, too. People like that run their accounting ledgers in just two columns, black and red. I don't know exactly what they want your land for, but I'll bet you one thing . . . they ain't fixing to *lose* money. Roy, you're like the lamb before the slaughter that didn't know enough to come in out of the rain."

"I'll be careful, Pearl."

"You better be," she said. "'Cause if you let them take that land away, you ain't got nothing. Just look at you! Old cambray workshirt, must be seven years old, both sleeves worn out with your bony elbows sticking through. Levi's held together with patches like a cross-quilt. You look like some kind of scarecrow. I'm embarrassed to have you inside my house. Roy, for a rich man, you sure hide it well. And take off that beat-up old Stetson in my kitchen . . . you ain't no cowboy, and never was. I swear, if I hadn't known you for over fifty years, I'd take one look and it'd be a tossup whether I'd shoot first or faint."

FIVE

A WEEK LATER, Neil Larson showed up in person as he had promised.

By then Roy had cut several tons of spruce and ponderosa billets with the borrowed chain saw. The pile they made was higher than the roof of the cabin. The wood was too green and wet to split yet but he knew that even with the showers that had begun, it would cure out. By October he would be able to break it into stove-sized chunks with only a tap of the axe.

Larson and an associate of his, a legal advisor named Bingham Hunt, arrived in a brand-new Hertz station wagon. Roy heard the car down in the forest for at least a mile before it came into view. It sounded like whoever was driving was going to a lot of trouble to iron out chuckholes and ruts in the primitive logging road, and every so often there was a louder noise when the underbody was used to smooth away a few hundred-pound boulders. He had been sitting on a stump in the sun, sharpening the Homelite's teeth, and now he put down his rattail file and said, "Somebody's grading the road . . . or else they're building a new one."

From the slope by the cabin he watched the station wagon drive up and down the town's main street while the driver blew the horn constantly to attract attention. Eventually, the horn got on his nerves and Roy said, "I can hear you. Just take it easy." He put on his Stetson, climbed into the jeep, forded the stream, and drove down to where the station wagon was parked, out in front of what had been Rank's Saloon.

Even before introductions, Roy was pretty sure who it was. Larson was a tall, barrelchested man of about sixty with the huge shoulders of an ex-football linesman. He wore a turtleneck jersey in white knit, an expensive-looking tweed jacket, gray slacks, oxblood loafers, and Ray-Ban sunglasses. He had curly gray hair, full, white sideburns, and an honest, open expression. As Roy got out of the jeep, Larson, regarding the view with admiration, announced to no one in particular, "God, what potential!"

The associate, Mr. Hunt, was limping around after him, holding an attaché case. His dark-gray, three-piece suit and hairstyle were in disarray. He looked like he'd traveled more distance vertically than horizontally. Steam was hissing from a leak in the station wagon's radiator, and a couple of hubcaps were missing from the wheels.

Roy walked up and said, "Good morning." The two men stared at him. Then they glanced at each other with expressions of astonishment.

"I'm looking for somebody who calls himself Mayor Gutierrez," Larson said. His diction and voice were distinctive—cultured, but with that gravelly smoothness Roy remembered from the telephone conversation. Then Larson blinked. "Are *you* Gutierrez?"

"That's right. The mayor part is more or less an honorary title," Roy said.

"Bing, we *are* in the right place then," Larson said to his companion. And then, to Roy, "That's the damnedest road I ever saw in my life! You ought to put up some signs or directions. A man could drive around up in these mountains forever. I'm Larson."

"I figured."

They shook hands. Bingham Hunt was introduced. He said, "How do you do?" Then he looked around. "So this is Sawmill River Flats."

"That's right."

"And you actually live here?"

"Yes."

Mr. Hunt looked around at the town and murmured, "Incredible. Literally incredible." Roy wasn't sure if this remark had to do with the town or the fact that he lived in it.

Larson was staring at him. "Well, I got to say, you're not what I expected."

"I suppose not."

"Oh, you know. Way the hell out west here . . . a name like Gutierrez, I figured maybe a Caesar Romero or a Montalban type."

"Like one of those late-show movies?" Roy observed.

"Precisely, now that you mention it," Larson said. "Do you actually have tv up here?"

"No," Roy said. "How did you figure out where the road was?"

"Some old woman named Lowdermilk, down at a place called Honcho," Larson replied. "God, I thought *that* place was out of the way."

"Might as well get in the jeep. I have a cabin up on the slope above town. That car can't ford the stream."

On the way, Larson said, "Marvelous place you have here. You know, I had two men out here this spring, looking for you. They took color slides. Beautiful, just terrific. It's got what you might call high-class schmaltz."

"The town? Or the land?" Roy asked.

"Both."

"Mister Larson, was it you who had the land surveyed?"

"We had to make sure that a place called Sawmill River Flats actually existed. Mind if I call you Roy?"

"Go ahead. How did you find out about Sawmill?"

"Research. You know, if we hadn't checked the abstract I would have thought that old lady owned a piece of this property."

"Pearl's just a friend."

"Not much on conversation, is she? You know what we had to do? Stand around and wait for almost half an hour while she milked a herd of goats. I never saw a goat milked before. She talked to them more than she did to us."

"What brings you out to this part of the country?"

"I'm here to see you, Roy," Larson said. He was looking out

the window on his side. "Bing and I have five other potential sites to visit this week. This is my first time in New Mexico. Wish I could delegate this sort of junket to a dependable subordinate —I hate to travel—but, hell, I suppose it's invaluable for me to actually see something like this for myself. God, look at these mountains, Bing. Picture-postcard stuff. Almost scary. You know, Roy, coming into Albuquerque we flew over plains so goddamned big you could've dropped half a dozen New Yorks on them and they wouldn't even have been noticed. Desolate." At the cabin, they got out. Larson said, "Stunning views. Quiet, though. Doesn't all this silence get on your nerves?"

"No."

"Not a city person, eh? Thought so. You look like a loner." Roy did not comment on this.

At the cabin he offered them coffee or vodka. Larson chose liquor; Bingham Hunt, politely protesting that the drive back down to civilization would not be any pleasanter than the one on the way up, elected to stay with coffee. He was a rather serious and silent young man, almost colorless or even invisible in comparison to Neil Larson, who in his brash and straightforward manner seemed to feel obligated to fill every moment with words. Yet Hunt's presence—for most of the visit he sat straightbacked on a stool, with the attaché case placed primly across his knees, using its top as a table for the steaming cup of coffee he had been given—was strongly felt by Roy. Hunt reminded him a little of an electronic computer that can be programmed to absorb and analyze complex inventories of information . . . a sort of humanized storage-and-retrieval system, humorless, lacking in personality, seldom intruding but always primed to offer up a fact or statistic when needed, and capable only of a detached, pure objectivity. With Larson, Roy felt wariness; with Hunt, there was no kind of rapport at all . . . in comparison, the young lawyer's ebullient and talkative boss was almost appealing.

Larson was saying now, "I wanted to meet you face to face. That's the way I like to do business. Before we leave, I'm going to give you a copy of the Larson Corporation's prospectus to look over. Better yet, take it to your lawyer, if you have one—and if you don't, you ought to retain a good man—and have him go over it."

"You want to buy my land?"

"We can go any of several different routes," Larson explained. "Of course, an outright sale would be the most beneficial to you."

"This place is pretty special to me, Mister Larson," Roy said.

Larson apparently interpreted this remark as a cautious but clever invitation to dicker. "Of course it is! As an investment property, with enormous growth potential? You're sitting on top of something very nice. But the kind of money I'm talking about is very special, too. Big money is always special."

Roy said, "To tell the truth, I kind of like this town the way it is. My father thought a lot of it, too . . . that's why he bought it. I'd hate to see it bulldozed."

Larson astonished him then. He gave Roy a cool look. "Who said anything about bulldozing?" He turned to Bingham Hunt. "Did I say anything about bulldozing?"

"No. You didn't say anything like that," Hunt murmured.

Roy couldn't think of anything to say. Larson leaned closer and said forcefully, "No bulldozing! What ever gave you that idea? The town as it stands is the most important part of any agreement we work out."

"It is?"

Larson removed his sunglasses and smiled, giving Roy a look of open, disarming candor. "You don't have to tell me. You think LarCo is another one of those cheap-assed land development outfits. I know . . . I've had it said to me before." He nodded and drank off his vodka. "Pour me another." Roy handed him the bottle, and he helped himself. "Gutierrez, listen to me. Any business relationship has to be based on mutual trust. Without that, you have nothing, right?"

"I suppose so," Roy said.

"Goddamned right. Well, what I am going to talk to you about now, while it is not exactly confidential—who in hell can keep a secret these days?—is a new, a *daring*, and, if I may say so, a brilliant business concept. I'm telling you all this because I trust you, and if we are ever going to work out anything between us, you are going to have to do the same with me, right?"

"Sure."

"LarCo, friend, is in the business of buying history. Conceptualizing the past. And making it pay."

"I don't understand."

"Ah, Roy, come off it. You sound like an intelligent person. The writing's on the wall for anybody to see. What this country is going out of its mind for these days is *history*. Nostalgia . . . remembrance of things past." Larson let this weighty announcement sink in, and then he gave Roy another look. "In the next decade, friend, there'll be a coast-to-coast explosion of old-time Americana. And we are going to bring all this about. 'The Past Recaptured,' that's LarCo's motto. We have nearly twenty potential sites already picked out. And one of them happens to be Sawmill River Flats . . . yes, right *here!* History! Everybody's wild for it."

"That's really interesting," Roy said, frowning.

"You think it's crazy, don't you?" Larson said, smiling again.

"I don't know."

"Well, it is crazy! And you know something? The Wright brothers were crazy, and so was Henry Ford with his assembly line." Larson was a little excited.

"When we talked on the phone, you said something about conceptual development."

"Precisely."

"What does that mean?"

"In simple terms . . . filling the gap," Larson explained.

"What gap?"

"Look at it this way. On the one hand, you've got operations like Disneyland. Strictly cornball, but money, hand over fist, slanted for an age level of about six . . . I'm being generous. At the other end of the spectrum, you've got a lot of professional historians who spend their lives in university libraries . . . I've got a master's in history from Columbia, so I know what I'm talking about. Now, about all you've got in that gap between Disneyland and the career scholar are a couple of outfits like Williamsburg, or Mystic, Connecticut, and *they're* slanted toward the types who like to sit down for a really exciting evening with a copy of *American Heritage*. What you have left, friend, is a literally incredible, untapped potential audience! Huge! Not just the average American family. Tell me, what's the first thing these Jap, Italian, German, and Arab tourists want to see after they've taken a couple of snapshots of the Statue of Liberty? They want to see *America!* Mention the antebellum south and they start drooling. Mention Indians, mesas, deserts, cowboys, cattle, and they go crazy."

"Really?"

"It's a fact," Larson said coolly. "I majored in American . . . almost ended up teaching it but there was no future in it. A historian is useless except to teach history to other historians. My graduate thesis was entitled 'Practical Applications of History.' History is something that's *alive*, or it should be. It can be successfully married to business enterprise. It's a merchantable item! It can be developed, exploited . . . it has *value!* I say take history out of the classroom!"

"You want to make Sawmill River Flats into some kind of tourist attraction?" Roy asked.

Larson sat back and smiled. Roy said, "Like Tombstone, or Virginia City, or some of those other old-time towns?"

"Nickel-and-dime operations," Larson said scornfully, and poured himself another drink. "I'm talking about something big. A nationwide, multi-billion-dollar *chain* that will make Disneyland look like peanuts. Roy, we are going to be the Holiday Inn of Historical America!"

"Sounds pretty ambitious," Roy said.

"Ambitious, but feasible," Larson said. "This isn't something that's merely on the drawing board. We're almost ready to start construction at six sites. But, hell, why am I talking? Look for yourself. Bing?"

The young lawyer set his coffee cup on the floor beside him and opened the attaché case. He handed over a large, thick album bound in black leather. On its front was an ornate logo in gilt: LarCo. Larson opened the album. Mounted under protective acetate sheets were ten-by-fourteen Kodacolor glossies of the most elaborate models Roy had ever seen—diaramas, really. Larson explained: "Here's our Indian village—we've already leased a thousand acres from some Cherokees up in Oklahoma. We'll have wigwams with real Indians living in them. Bone and flint-tipped tools, all that ethnic stuff. Look here! Pilgrim settlement. Not far from Cape Cod. Stockade with hand-hewn timbers, a gristmill, the works. Can you imagine it? Instead of staring at the tube, you're right there in the middle of it! All five senses operational. A true re-created environment." Larson paused, and then went on. "We'll have organized tours. Charter buses, chartered flights. Trains." He flipped a page. "Here. We're working out a nice arrangement with some Mennonites down in Pennsylvania, black hats, garters on the sleeves, buckboards. These folks make their own furniture out of walnut—early American—right by Reading."

For the first time, Bingham Hunt interjected a low-keyed remark: "Vermont's my favorite." Larson flipped pages, and then stopped at one:

"Maple-syrup farm, Cape Cod house, roof angled thirty degrees toward the sun and fifteen degrees on the cold side to hold in heat," he said. "We've got special trees developed that give out pure syrup all year long, with tubes inside hooked up to pressurized tanks. No need to boil that stuff down, the way they used to. Just plug into a cut and in five minutes you've got a pint of the finest grade-A maple, better than anything you can buy at Gristede's. We have a five-thousand-acre plantation down near Biloxi. Twenty-four-room mansion, white columns out in front. Blacks out in the fields working the cotton, all year long."

"Cotton doesn't grow that way," Roy objected.

"We'll use plastic cotton balls, recyclable, clip them back on at the end of the day. Keep those darkies busy around the clock."

"Imitation slaves? People won't go for that these days, Mister Larson."

"That's where you're wrong. We'll pay our people better than minimum wage." Larson stared at Roy. "Well, you'd know about the color problem. Our employees will be getting more than most black people in Mississippi. We'll have them on four-hour-long shifts, no longer. From what I understand, the heat and humidity are tough."

Roy said, "It sounds like an enterprising program."

Larson smiled. "You know how I think of it?" He paused for effect. *"Instant history!"*

"What does that mean?"

"Neatly processed and neatly packaged . . . instant coffee, instant foods, everything we have is instant these days," Larson replied. "Why not history? A safari into the *past!* We'll have conducted tours, guides, indigenous regional cuisine in our res-

taurants and cafeterias. Authentic music piped in through hidden
speakers . . . banjos in that Biloxi mansion, guitars and cowboy
laments on the great annual LarCo Roundup and Cattle Drive.
All LarCo staff members will wear costumes particular to the
locale and time period!" He stared at Roy. "You're skeptical?"

"Yes."

"Why?"

Roy sought for the right word. "You were talking about
schmaltz before. That sort of means corny, doesn't it?"

Larson frowned for a moment. Then he said coldly, "Bing?"

"Yes?"

"Is LarCo schmaltzy?"

Hunt thought this over and then drank the last of his coffee.
"Yes, it certainly is."

"Of *course* it's schmaltzy," Larson cried. "What you're ignor-
ing, Roy, is that schmaltz works! Schmaltz is a salable item these
days. The world is up to its ears in it! Where would we be today
without schmaltz? Look at Disneyland, or Knotts Berry Farm.
The Sound of Music, Mary Poppins, that stuff goes on forever.
In Vienna, what's the first thing a tourist buys: *strudel!* Look at
foxy Kissinger, wheeling and dealing in that voice that would
sound better on a Bavarian butcher! London Bridge, now over
Lake Havasu, who in hell needs a bridge out there in the middle
of noplace? Princess Grace and Jackie Onassis, what in the world
are they but schmaltz with a capital S? The Queen Mary, stuck
out in Long Beach, California. Dick Nixon crying real tears for
the whole country to see. All those athletes who never got to the
summer Olympics. Willie Stargell and Terry Bradshaw. Raising
Old Glory at Iwo Jima. Did you ever see such schmaltz in your
entire life? I ask you!"

"Yes. Of course," Roy said. The strange thing was that he could
see a kind of weird sanity in what Larson was explaining. It was
a completely mad idea, except for one thing: it was a vision. Neil
Larson obviously believed in that vision, body and soul. It was
the same kind of impractical, crazy concept that must have at
one time or another come to a Hitler, a Stalin, or a John Jacob
Astor, or one that, more lately, might have occurred to a moder-
ately wealthy peanut farmer from Georgia. De Gaulle had had
such a vision, and so had a man named Land, who had been

convinced that the Kodak and Agfa monopolies would go down in defeat before a cheap camera that was capable of developing the photograph it had taken only a minute earlier. Such visions usually die; but not always. Roy said now, "Exactly how does all this apply to Sawmill River Flats?"

Larson paused for a moment. "We'd restore it . . . to what it once was. An exquisitely re-created western town, circa 1885. You'd like that, wouldn't you? Right down to the last authentic detail. Of course, it would be a major investment on our part. The market for such an attraction exists, we're sure of it."

Roy's feelings were confused. "Really authentic?"

"Every building authentically rebuilt and refurbished," Larson said. "Right now, all you have here is the raw material . . . the land and what's left of the town. Cowboys, cattle, dancehalls, honkeytonks."

"Rank's Saloon was the only bar in town," Roy said. "It was a conservatively run place, just a bar for men to drink in. There were gambling tables and pool, but I don't think dancing was allowed. I doubt if the ladies or wives of the town would have put up with that."

"A daily stagecoach run," Larson went on.

"There was never a stagecoach line," Roy said. "I'm sure of that."

"Part of the concept is a modern hotel," Larson said. "Eighty units to start with. In winter we'd shunt visitors over to the ski area and Ruidoso."

"From here you can't get near the ski area in winter," Roy objected. "There's no real road. For that matter, the road you drove up today is impassable for months at a time."

"We'll build our own roads . . . wherever we have to," Larson said quietly. "Roy, you're thinking small. This is not small-time. I tried to explain that to you. We'll bring in our own power lines, and there'll be telephones and running water. We'll have our own restaurants and snack bars, and gift shops, as well as a gay-nineties melodrama theater. There'll be a dude ranch where you can rent horses for overnight pack trips. There'll be all kinds of organized activities and historical lectures . . . an adult or a kid will be able to spend a week up here and never be bored for a minute. We'll even have our own film-developing service.

I mean, friend, we are going to lock up the whole goddamned ball of wax! And you—sitting right here—have an opportunity to become a part of the world of LarCo."

"In other words, you want to buy me out," Roy said.

"Three hundred thousand is the figure," Larson said easily. "That's a firm offer, by the way. I'm not a man to bargain back and forth. That's almost five hundred dollars an acre for your square-mile section. That's an excellent price for raw, undeveloped timber and mountain land with no improvements whatsoever. Like I said, check with a lawyer. I think he'll agree. Of course, we can prorate the money over a period of years, so Internal Revenue won't snap it up. Bing, let me have one of those prospectuses." Hunt handed over a large, colorful booklet printed on expensive coated paper. Roy glanced at it and saw that it contained a more elaborate and formal description of what Larson had been talking about. He said, "Well, I'll think about your offer, Mister Larson."

"See your lawyer, that's my advice," Larson said again. "Give me a couple of those aerials, Bing." Hunt brought some eight-by-ten black-and-white glossies forth from the attaché case. "Here's some souvenirs for you, Roy. Tack them up on the wall where you can see them every day. I had them shot this spring, when my men were looking the place over. I always like aerials. They give a man a sense of perspective . . . of what he's really dealing with. Don't think of these as merely aerial photographs . . . what you're looking at is three hundred thousand dollars. Sitting in your pocket."

The photographs were of Sawmill River Flats, taken from an altitude of eight or nine hundred feet above Main Street. The place did not look like much. A collection of weathered buildings, or what was left of them. He could make out the sawmill and the beaver pond, but not his cabin. That was hidden in the trees. The cemetery with its rectangular stone fence was visible. There was no sign of life anywhere; what the photographs showed was a deserted place.

Larson said, "Take a good look. What do you see? Nothing! It's just a pile of shit, Roy. But with some imagination and capital investment, what you're looking at could become a viable entity again, the way it once was. Listen, friend—if you want to keep history alive, you've got to give it a *future!* Tens of thousands will be able to say, 'Sawmill River Flats? Yes . . . I was *there*.'"

"I kind of like it the way it is," Roy said.

And without realizing it, Larson said something that struck through to Roy like a blow to the stomach. "What are you talking about? It's disappearing, right in front of your eyes! My men wrote a complete report, and I saw for myself today. It's falling apart, friend. It isn't dying . . . it's already dead and in the last stages of decay. In another ten years, there'll be nothing left at all unless we take immediate steps to do something about it."

Feeling miserable, Roy thought, *and in another ten years there won't be anything left of me either.*

OUTSIDE THE CABIN, as they were getting ready to climb into the jeep, Larson said, "Listen, I need a way to keep in touch with you."

"Pearl Lowdermilk's the best contact. I check with her once a week or so, for mail," Roy said. "You see how I live up here."

Larson stood there for a minute, thinking about something. He said, "Well, maybe we could do something about that. It could be—if we work out an agreement—that LarCo might set aside a few acres for you. Maybe even build a nice little modern house on it, all the conveniences. How'd you like something like that, Roy? I mean, after all, we understand. People can get attached to a place. Wouldn't you like that? Seeing the old joint alive and bustling? Main Street all lit up at night?"

"There were never any street lights or anything like that," Roy said. "It was just an out-of-the-way mountain town."

"Say—I bet you know a *hell* of a lot about Sawmill," Larson said.

"Yes, I guess I do."

"We come to terms, maybe we can get you on the payroll. Sort of a technical advisor. How'd you like that? Make yourself rich and at the same time be a real help to us."

"You mean like a manager?" Roy asked.

"Not exactly," Bingham Hunt said. "You wouldn't have to take part in anything directly."

"Oh," Roy said. "More like a behind-the-scenes type person."

"Something along those lines, yes," Hunt said.

Roy thought about this, and he began to feel anger building up in him. He knew what Hunt was saying, and it hurt. The young lawyer was just doing the job he was being paid to do—but even so. Roy stared at him for a long moment, and then nodded. "Once before—years ago—I heard something similar, Mister Hunt. I was younger then, and I still believed in all kinds of things. The details aren't important. Let's just say that I was traveling in Texas, and there were some serious problems, so I talked to some people in the NAACP. I asked if there was anything that I could do. The marches and the demonstrations seemed important to me—so important that I believed everybody ought to do his part." He smiled at Hunt. "The fellow I talked to was a lawyer—a black man, well educated, and very intelligent. That's what reminded me—because you're a lawyer too. Well, I don't want to make a big story out of it. What happened, he took one look at me and said that if I really wanted to help, the best thing I could do was disappear. He was a forthright man. I respected him for that. All he was saying is that the black man's cause would not be helped if somebody like me was 'visible'. He said I could donate some money if I wanted to, but that I wasn't personally needed. At first I was angry, but then I saw that it wasn't racial discrimination. It was just personal rejection. I know how I affect people. Well, I won't take up any more of your time. There are some stories I could tell you—about blacks, and whites. And Indians, too. After that, I gave up working for good causes." He paused, and then continued, "No, I can see why, if you fixed up Sawmill River, you wouldn't want me up front giving the tourists illustrated lectures. Even though I am the town's last surviving citizen. I don't look the part."

Larson had been watching him through all this. He said now, "You like honesty? Well, I'm being honest. Three hundred thousand is a hell of a lot of money."

"I'll think about it."

"Don't think about it for too long."

"What's the rush?"

"Did anybody say there's a rush? On the other hand, if you sit around for a month, the deal may be off. We have other sites under consideration." Larson glanced down the slope and frowned. "What in hell is that?" Three beaver were leaving V-wakes on the surface of the pond.

"Beaver," Roy explained. "They're building a den."

"You just let them run around wild like that?" Larson demanded. "I hear they can give you a wicked bite."

"Wild animals seldom bother humans," Roy said. "Mostly they just want to be left alone."

He brought them back down to where the station wagon was parked, and waved a farewell as they took off, with Hunt behind the wheel. The car disappeared from view and once again there was the sound of distant and gradually diminishing noises as the lawyer, whose driving skills were apparently slanted toward interstate freeways, attacked the rutted switchback road.

Afterward, Roy went back to the cabin and had a drink. He felt depressed, and when that happened his mind began wandering and at the same time working overtime. Desultorily, he flipped through the prospectus and thought about Larson.

A businessman, out to make money. That was comprehensible to everybody these days. This was a man who ate in restaurants, took taxis and jet planes. Every day of his life he went out to face the world. Other people worked out business deals with him. To some at least, he might even be an important person.

Larson was a functioning part of the everyday world.

Roy wished he could say the same of himself. It was not Larson who was crazy. He was.

Larson wanted to do something practical with the old town. He'd make of it a "re-creation." The sagging, decaying old structures would be redone. New paint, new windows, modern plastics. Main Street paved, a fancy new hotel, and even a paved road over to the ski area. Money no object. To the tourists who came to enjoy it, there would be nothing strange about such a place.

It would be alien only to Roy.

The only town he'd ever known was what it was now—a derelict ghost. Feeling more disturbed, he had another drink.

He could no longer figure out what kind of world he was living in, where artificial maple trees gave refined syrup, and where

imitation darkies harvested plastic cotton bolls in make-believe
fields. Would the plants themselves be plastic, too? If that was
the case, then the fields would be entirely free of drought or
blight, and would be as lushly verdant in January as real fields
were in August. He was reminded of the rumor that the Apollo
moon landing had never really happened, and that what the
world had seen on television was only an elaborate movie set
constructed by NASA to one-up the Russians.

Larson's concept of history was dramatic enough. If Sawmill
River had seen actual gunfights, then gunfights there would be,
once again, with paid actors to play out the roles of the good and
the bad.

But what could have been more dramatic than the tragedy that
Roy knew had taken place? How did Larson intend reproducing
facsimiles of Ephraim Munger's murderous jealousy, or Bertha's
resigned patience? What of Uncle Walter's Judas-betrayal?
What of the terror young George Gutierrez had experienced?
Was it atonement or guilt that had made Herman Gutierrez at
last move into action?

These people. Caught in such a whirlwind of self-destruction.
How was Larson going to catch that in his "re-created" environment?

Would a staged gunfight using blank cartridges be more impressive than the actual confrontation, when Roy's grandfather,
on a July evening in the year 1907, had stepped out on the
wooden boardwalk fronting the Imperial Hotel and taken a .44
slug in the stomach and a broadside shotgun blast in the shoulder? Dying, Ephraim had, with cool deliberation, aimed and
killed two of the three men who had sworn to take his life, while,
from an upstairs hotel window, Herman Gutierrez, drunk, had
murdered the third man. Uncle Walter had witnessed all this, as
well as the phenomenon Bertha for the rest of her life referred to
simply as "the miracle."

All this had actually happened, but it existed now only in Roy's
memory, and with his own passing to the grave, would be gone
forever.

Larson, however, would salvage such a spectacle. Such a confrontation had currency today. Crowds of gaping tourists would
pay to see mock combat, providing it was done in good taste and

did not offend the senses. Everything had to be authentic without being shocking.

In a sense, then, Karo syrup dyed red was more believable than actual blood.

Roy took a taste of his drink, and said aloud, "People today don't love the west. They love the *idea* of it." He thought, *somehow, in some way, everything now has to do with make-believe.*

Back when the real Pat Garrett and Billy Bonney were doing their thing, this had been true ranching country. Lincoln had been the largest county in the United States. Over 27,000 square miles, taking in an area bigger than Connecticut, Massachusetts, Delaware, and Rhode Island combined. More than 300,000 cattle had roamed that vast, magnificent, open range.

All that was gone. His father, George, would not have understood anything of this contemporary life. He had been an intelligent man but he was not complicated.

George Gutierrez would have been confounded—as was Roy— by an aggressive businessman who had come all the way from New York City to explain where the money really was: leisure . . . recreation . . . make-believe.

THE REST OF that day was spoiled. He tried to read through the prospectus, but the facts and figures and goals of the Larson Corporation seemed out of place up here, and his attention kept wandering until finally he put the thing away on a bookshelf above his bunk. He could have bucked out more wood with the chainsaw, but after Larson's visit the noisy racket of its engine had no appeal.

Instead, he went on drinking, finishing off what was left in the bottle of vodka he had brought out for his guests and then, when that was gone, breaking open a fresh quart. He had not been drunk since the going-away party in El Paso, and now, gauging his mood, he knew what would happen. That was something else he had inherited from his father besides the town . . . a weakness for alcohol. He wasn't really sure what it was that the liquor provided but whatever it was helped. It seemed that liquor made life easier to take. Not just the present but the past, and maybe even the future.

By midafternoon the weather was building toward a cloud-
burst. For a while it was hot and sunny. Then heavy black thun-
derheads massed over the whole mountain range, bringing with
them a chill, wet breeze that sighed through the tall pines. He
made up a mix in a quart Mason jar of half vodka and half powdered orange drink and went outside to watch the storm.

At first a few fat drops here and there . . . spatting down
through the foliage, maculating the delicate lime-green aspens
and bending the slender branches. Then it began sheeting down
in buckets, and, soaked now, he walked back to the cabin to hide
out. Tried changing clothes. Sprawled on the bunk with a book
to read—by then the tumult of the storm had made everything
so dark and forlorn and gloomy that he had to light one of the
kerosene lamps to see by. He added wood to the sheepherder to
drive off the damp, but it was no good: outside, the rain was
sleeting down and finally he gave up, put on a slicker and his
Stetson, and went out to walk.

In the rain there was no visibility to speak of. Serpentine gray
mists and thick fogbanks slid along the heavily wooded slopes,
and the trunks of the trees were black and wet, so that everything seemed antediluvian, like the forgotten dawn of some ancient time, a dark and brooding Beethoven mood, all somber and
frightening, with the thunder rumbling and reverberating higher
up on the mountain somewhere, and there was the rain lashing
down, starting up thousands of small freshets and waterfalls, a
noisy fall of water everywhere. And then just before sunset it
stopped, and the sky cleared, the low western sun spearing
through the last of the cloudbanks overhead, lighting them all
red and gold, illuminating in a splendid outburst their dark wet
grayness, and by evening it was perfectly clear and cool. Later, a
million stars glittered above him, and with still another jar of
vodka, he went out of the cabin once again to sit on a billet of
firewood he had cut, to stare up at the constellations wheeling
ponderously in their great orbits, talking to himself as he drank
and smoked, naming them aloud as his father used to, like old
and valued friends . . . Orion, Pegasus, Ursa Majoris, Cygnus
the Swan, Ursa Minoris, old Cassiopeia shaped like a lopsided
W drawn by a little kid, and the Seven Sisters, the Pleiades . . .
all of them up there, looking down on him the same as they had

nearly fifty years ago when he had huddled beside his father wrapped in a blanket and listened as George Gutierrez had recited their myths and legends. And then, everywhere in the darkness, he heard them—the frogs!—they came out by the thousands when it rained, croaking back and forth to one another in the darkness of the forest; the nighttime was just filled with the sound of them declaring to all the world—to whoever wanted to *listen*—that they too exulted in this, their brief sweet season of life!

It was lonely. For a while he wept and wished he was dead. He lit a cigarette, pissed slowly and leisurely on the already soaked ground, went back in the cabin, and tried to sleep; but all that night he was restless and moody, and every hour or so he was up and wandering again with a fresh drink, though toward dawn, he finally did drift off into a troubled, nightmare-filled slumber.

When he woke the sun was well up in the sky. He turned on the transistor radio and set the volume low. Then he stepped outside the mud-chinked cabin and breathed deeply, taking in the cool clear morning air, which smelled sweetly of honeysuckle and clover. Yawned, scratched himself, looked around, and listened. Still drunk, but feeling good now, with all his senses working.

The air was magically still. Birds singing. A hum of midges— a busy cloud of them suspended above a glassy puddle. A dazzlingly blue sky and white clouds overhead, and, perched at the top of his pile of firewood, a beautiful pileated woodpecker with an ivory bill, angry eyes, and crimson head markings. Roy said to the bird, "Don't be giving me that dirty look—I haven't done anything to you."

In that moment he felt so good that he wished he could live for another fifty years, a hundred. He wanted to live on and on forever. He went back into the cabin and poured a glass of vodka, knowing that he would keep on drinking this way for another three or four days or until the liquor was gone.

Something Larson had said yesterday, as a kind of parting shot, stayed in his mind. Larson was a good salesman. He knew how to use money as an enticement but he also knew how to twist that enticement into a personal thing. Today, Roy could feel a mild, tolerant amusement over Larson's relentless probing.

But yesterday it had not been funny at all.

As he was getting into the rented station wagon, Larson had said, "Have you ever been broke?"

"Yes."

"Then you know the value of money. I know it too, because I've been flat broke that way myself, more than once," Larson said, staring up at him. "Once you've really been down and out, well, you never forget that feeling, do you?"

"I suppose not."

"Let me ask you something personal. What's your background . . . I mean, besides Negro?"

"Apache. And white."

"And none of these people are crazy about you, am I right?" Larson said bluntly. "That story you were telling Bing about screwing around with the NAACP tipped me. No . . . don't tell me. I know! I understand. At first I couldn't figure you, but now it's clear. That's why you're up here. Alone. Living like this. Now, be honest, isn't that the real reason? Well, friend, let me tell you something—I can understand very well how you must feel. It's a hell of a lousy feeling when everybody looks the other way . . . when there isn't a single person you can call friend. It's tough."

Roy frowned and thought, *you're wrong! I have friends. Some people around here like me. That's not true! There are people who know me and they like me.*

Before he could say these words, Larson went on, "Well, Roy, now you have an opportunity to fix that for the rest of your life. Money won't buy everything. But you might be amazed by what it *will* buy. LarCo is offering you financial security! *Ciao,* Roy."

But here again Larson was wrong. As a businessman-entrepreneur, his natural style was to probe for the psychological jugular, searching for the weakness or vulnerability that in one way or another every man is heir to. He had touched it with the racial business, and he should have stayed on that subject. Instead he had veered off on another tack—money—and in doing so widened the gulf between himself and the man he was trying to do business with.

It was true—Roy had never once in his life been rich.

But then neither had he been poor.

His father had seen to that. George Gutierrez, that mild-mannered and eccentric man, had given him something else besides a forgotten ghost town. He had shown Roy the secret of Sawmill River Flats.

THAT WAS IN 1937, when he was twelve years old.

They had come up there in the late spring of that year, still driving the rattletrap Mack truck. His father had a great affection for that vehicle, and he managed to keep it going almost up to the time he died.

So this turned out to be a kind of extended picnic and camping trip of the sort the two men and the boy frequently enjoyed.

The country was said to be in lots better shape now that F.D.R. was in office. The New Deal was going great guns and there were so many different government programs, like the NRA, PWA, WPA, and TVA, that people called it the Alphabet Administration. Several million uneducated and unskilled city-bred boys enlisted in the CCC, and they toiled everywhere at makework, fix-up jobs, improving the nation, building roads, planting trees, and creating soil-erosion dams. In Germany, Mr. Hitler had set in motion a virtually identical program for the unemployed—the great Autobahns were built, and it was not until years later that this superb network of highways was looked at a second time: lo and behold, every Autobahn, like spokes of a wagonwheel, led out of the country on an invasion route into other territories.

All kinds of wonderful and exciting things were happening. Shirley Temple was the top box-office draw. Haile Selassie complained to the League of Nations about the Italians, who were using gas against his troops, and got nowhere. A few weeks earlier, Edward of England had married Wally Simpson, giving up his throne for the woman he loved, making an honest woman out of her and proving to the world that an Englishman is as good as his word. All over the country there were sit-down strikes as labor and management fought it out in one bloody confrontation after another. W. C. Fields said that any man who despised dogs and children couldn't be all bad, and gangster folk-heroes like Dillinger and Baby-Face Nelson learned that crime did not pay. It was a time of great tension and romance.

His father and Walter had quit their jobs up in Durango, Colorado, and headed south into New Mexico.

That was their way. They would work for a couple of months, and then get restless. It didn't take much to get them into a traveling mood. One morning, his father might say, "Walter? How long have we been here in this town?"

"Too damn long to suit me," Walter would reply.

"You know, I heard about a place the other day . . ."

And so it would go.

On this trip, besides everything else in the back of the truck, there were two cases of bourbon and four Smithfield hams, which at that time could be bought for three dollars apiece. Walter knew of a place that sold them. A Smithfield is a dark brown, crusted club of meat that has been cured into something that looks like leather, only it isn't. Cut into paper-thin slices, it is a little like Italian prosciutto, only far better, with a smoky taste that lingers on the tongue. Walter liked to make it up into sandwiches, using homemade sourdough loaves, thickly buttered and laced with wild parsley, tomatoes, and sliced Bermuda onion, with the meat sliced that way, very thin, so that it almost dissolved in the mouth. "Sandwiches ain't really a meal," Walter would say. And Roy would stick in close, his mouth filled with saliva, watching as the old man slowly and meticulously sliced the ham.

They had also packed the back of the truck with other things: plenty of beer, piccalilli relish and jars of hot mustard, two full sacks of fresh blue-corn tortillas, chili, both *rojo* and *verde*, almost two hundred eggs, and a *cabrito*—a live young goat they had bought on the spur of the moment for a dollar from a Spanish lady in Corrales they had stopped by to say hello to. They kept the *cabrito* double-tethered between two of the bunks, and Roy cleaned up its droppings when they stopped and then took it for a walk. His father called the goat Pan, after the Greek god.

Besides everything else, they had one of the very first battery-powered portable radios in that part of the southwest, a Zenith. The battery pack must have weighed fifteen pounds. In the evenings as the long twilight slowly turned dark they would sit by the campfire and listen to Guy Lombardo and his Royal Canadians. Gabriel Heatter, who never had anything good to say about anyone. *I Love a Mystery* with Doc and Reggie, and *Amos 'n' Andy*. Jack Benny and his "Jello again." Fred Allen and Portland Hoffa, and Fibber McGee and Molly.

Back then it was a big thing merely to be able to hear the sound of voices that did not belong to one's own family. They would build up the fire for warmth and listen to the Zenith and have a good time. His father, quiet as always, almost shy, but glancing at the boy or Walter to see if they'd caught him grinning when Digger O'Dell the Friendly Undertaker got off a really fast one.

On this evening, Walter bent the neck of the little *cabrito* across one knee and gently slit its throat, his crippled legs grasping the thrashing body, collecting the blood in a pot for the awful pancakes he liked to fry up for breakfast. Neither George nor the boy could eat these without feeling queasy. In two minutes he had the goat skinned, gutted, and trussed on his dangle-spit. This was something he claimed to have invented, a length of steel piano wire suspended from three saplings tied together over the fire. He sat there and drank bourbon, talking to himself as he dangle-barbecued the little goat, twirling it first one way and then the other—a piece of meat would rotate for a long time that way. Every so often Walter basted the carcass with Heinz ketchup, buttermilk, and hot red chili. He complained about chili but couldn't live without it. By the time the *cabrito* was done, to a crisp and flaky-skinned golden brown, he was too drunk to serve it, so the three of them pitched in with their pocket knives, slicing off what they wanted. Later, George set up his telescope, but with all that liquor and goat he was in too good a mood for stargazing and he fell asleep beside the heavy equatorial mounting. Roy tried to wake him but couldn't, so he folded his jacket into a pillow and slipped it under his father's head, kissed him, and then covered him with two blankets and a rubber poncho. George mumbled something about "waiting for Orion's belt and sword to rise above the summit," and commenced snoring.

Next day, the men were hung over and for most of the morning they didn't stir far from the campfire. They drank coffee and beer and smoked cigarettes, and George, who could do anything with his hands even when he wasn't feeling well, got out a heavy-duty needle and some sailmaker's thread and repaired a long tear in the leather upholstery on the driver's side of the truck's front seat, while Walter cleaned up around camp.

They had a late lunch of tortillas and goat and drank bourbon thinned with spring water. That made them feel better—a little better, anyway—and George started talking about what might be fun to do next. "Say, Walt, I've got a notion to drive down to Mexico and explore that *barranca* country south of Casas Grandes."

"What in Christ's name for?" Walter said. "Goddamn it, Georgie, we ain't hardly just got *here*. Can't you sit still for two seconds?"

"I want to see those Tarahumara Indians."

"That *barranca* country is a bad place. We don't have to go that far to look at injuns," Walter complained. "There's more redskins than a civilized person knows what to do with right here in New Mexico . . . you can't throw a rock ten feet without knocking one over."

"These Tarahumaras are champion runners," George said. "I was reading about them in *National Geographic*."

"Sometimes you sound like a complete asshole," Walter said. His hangover was apparently hurting more than George's, and he was in a rotten mood. Even when he was feeling all right, Walter played devil's advocate to George's schemes. He'd always go along, but from start to finish all he talked about was death and destruction for the three of them. "I swear, livin' with you is enough to drive a sane person crazy," he said, and shook his head. "It's true what they say . . . walk a mile with a cripple, you'll go lame."

"The men in that tribe can run thirty, forty miles a day," Roy's father explained. "It's something about their lung development. I guess their hearts and circulatory systems must be overdeveloped, too. They can run down deer."

"I don't see what's so special about that," Walter said.

"Well, *I* can't run down a deer. You can't either."

"Considerin' the shape we're in, we'd be lucky to run down a turtle," Walter snorted. "Besides which, I never in my life *cared* to chase after a deer. No man in his right senses'd wanta do something like that."

"I'd kind of like to see them."

"You wanta see injuns, let's go over to Gallup, where ten thousand of 'em get drunk every weekend. Or we could go up to Cochiti. They oughta be having some of their dances. They always got some kind of dancing organized for the tourists. Every time you spit, those pueblo idiots are thinking of new things to dance up a storm about."

"I want to see Tarahumaras," George said. By now he was having fun teasing Walter, who was looking madder by the minute.

"George, if we go to Cochiti at least *part* of the fuckin' trip would be on a paved highway," the old man argued. "I swear, you must be allergic or something to a paved road! We can't drive two miles down a highway without you have to git off it and go explorin'. You know how bad my back and hips are. No wonder they're all ruined. And now you're talking about traipsin' all the way to old Mexico to look at some crazy injuns who ain't got nothin' better to do than run their asses off. That's the stupidest goddamned thing I ever heard of, George, and you know I'm right."

"We could be down there in five or six days."

"You sound like a fool with two left balls . . . five or six days! I *been* to that place. Them Chihuahua *barrancas* is what they call *malpais* . . . bad country. There ain't even no roads. Just big-assed old canyons and ravines thousands of feet deep that you could drop the Mack into and it'd take twelve minutes before you'd hear it hit bottom. That's no place for a white man. You go there, you better buy plenty of extra shells for the pistols. There's gangs of real Mexican bandits roaming through those hills. They wouldn't think nothing of sticking us up and maybe killin' us and taking the truck and all our gear."

"How do you know, Walt?" Roy's father said. He liked to listen to Walter's stories.

"Goddamn it, I told you, I was *there,*" Walter said. "Back in '92, or mebbe it was '91. I hired out as a driver with a wagon train, down in Nogales. We had more'n two hundred and twenty mules and ox. Had us a contract to haul in mining equipment someplace near Casas Grandes. In them *barrancas*. It was less than two hundred miles but it took us nine weeks to get in and back out. Most of the mules were dead by then. We had a squad of greaser cavalry to guard us against bandits, but they weren't worth shit. We had something like eighty tons of mining equipment, all of it dismantled and loaded onto the wagons. That whole caravan was over half a mile long. We got up into that *malpais* country in some of those little villages, and the natives made your hair stand on end! They were *bad*. They had nothin' to do to pass the time except whack arms and legs off one another with machetes. Why, George, they had no kind of regard for human life at all! I never thought I'd see Nogales again. The other drovers all felt the same. At night we slept with six-shooters and rifles by our bedrolls. And you want to go down there? Christ almighty, they got cockroaches so big that when they stand up on their hind legs, waitin' like pet dogs for you to toss 'em a scrap, their front paws rest against your knees."

"If we make a trip like that, it'll be a regular expedition," Roy's father said. "We'll need money for expenses."

"George, talkin' to you is like talkin' to a *tree*," Walter said. "About the third week out I ate some enchiladas that the greaser cooks in the chuckwagons had brewed up, and I got the Aztec Two-Step something awful. Durned near shit myself inside out."

"Yes sir, that kind of trip takes money," the boy's father said. "Maybe we ought to show Roy how to make a withdrawal from the bank."

The bank was what they called the gold mine they had found.

It was above the cabin they used, not much more than a quarter of a mile. This was where the stream that passed through Sawmill River Flats originated. The three of them climbed up there, until they were maybe two hundred feet higher than the cabin on the slope below them. They stopped in a little glade where it was gloomy. The big pines towered overhead, shutting out almost all of the sky. The banks on either side of the stream were covered with green moss and ferns, and up at the far end of this glade there were some rock outcroppings, so that there was a small waterfall, no more than two or three feet. It was a pretty place. The stream itself was perhaps five or six feet wide here. George Gutierrez said, "Son, tell me . . . what do you see?"

So the boy described it as best he could, and was even able to name a species of *malaxis* fern growing out of the side of a spruce, what they call adder's mouth. His father said, "That's wonderful, Roy. I swear, you ought to be a naturalist. You've got an eye like a camera. But what I want to teach you today is that different people see the same thing in different ways. Come over here by me. Take a good look at the outcroppings by this waterfall."

Roy studied the scene. Walter sat down and had a swig out of a pint he'd slipped into the pocket of his overalls. George said, "Roy, you see anything that maybe piques your curiosity just a little?"

He said, "There might be a couple of good-sized trout in this pool under the waterfall, if winterkill hasn't taken them off, Pa."

"There could be that," his father said. "But let me tell you what I first saw when I found this place, must have been in '14 or '15. I was walking around up here one day and I came upon these outcroppings and this little teacup of a waterfall. Black granite, as you can see—igneous, formed by volcanic action. That means it's real old. I could see that it was a curious kind of formation. And then I got to wondering if the rock formation extended right under the streambed, you know, sort of like a shelf. So I stripped off my pants and boots and got in and rooted around with my toes . . . or at least the toes on my good foot. Mountain spring water is the coldest thing there is. Inside of ten seconds I was just blue. But in that time I'd gotten a feel of what was underneath, and by golly I was right! There was a sort of saucer-shaped depression, Roy, under the sand and gravel and silt. Maybe five feet across at most. Next day, I could hardly wait. I hotfooted it back up here with a shovel and a bucket and a skillet that I could use as a pan."

"You mean there's gold down there?"

"Is there ever! Why, Roy Aldous, you are looking at the finest gold pan ever devised by Mother Nature," his father said.

The boy got excited. He stared down at the pool in front of them. "You mean we're rich?"

"No," his father said. "But my guess is that as long as this little stream keeps flowing, we'll be in pocket money. Don't get ideas that we have a bona-fide gold mine on our hands. It's just that somewhere, way up on the watershed of this mountain, there is a vein of low-grade ore exposed. And whenever it rains, why, some dust gets washed loose and is carried down to this waterfall. You can wash out color upstream from under most any boulder. Not much, not even paying wages, but some. The biggest concentration is right here in this natural pool. Look."

He took off his boots and socks and waded into the pool with a shovel, while Walter held a bucket they had brought along. George scooped up four or five shovelfuls, digging deep into the sand at the bottom. Walter put some of this into a tin pie-plate and hunkered down by the water's edge, rocking the plate with a swirling motion. George and the boy stood by, watching. Roy saw some bright yellow specks on top of the mud and sand, and he got excited again. Walter said, "That ain't gold, you overgrown idiot! Them's pyrites—fool's gold. Pyrites float on top. The stuff we're after sinks to the bottom." He swirled the plate some more, slowly washing out the sand and pyrites. Finally, he was left with a spoonful of dirty brown granules.

"Is that it?" the boy asked, disappointed.

Walter peered closely at the stuff, and then touched it with the tip of a finger. "Yup. That's it."

They got almost an ounce from that single bucketful. His father said, "This stuff would probably assay out over a hundred thousand dollars a ton, Roy. And if we could get a ton of it, we'd be rich for a fact. The trouble is, the rock depression underwater doesn't hold more than a wheelbarrowful at most. There may be a thousand dollars' worth of gold down there. But if we take it all out, we might have to wait a year or two for it to fill up again. It comes down awfully slow. I've measured the rate of accumulation."

"Nobody knows about it?"

"Not a soul in the world, Roy, except the three of us."

"Why don't we go farther upstream and try to track down that exposed vein?" the boy asked. "Heck, we could blast it wide open. We could divert the stream if we had to. We could be rich."

"Why bother?" his father said. "We have a perfectly balanced little placer operation right here that nature has provided us. Why spoil it? The Indians believe it's not good to take more than you need."

"I wish they'd remember that when it comes to liquor," Walter said.

"Sometimes I wish this whole country would remember it," George said. Even then he was interested in what today is known as ecology: he disliked cutting a live tree, and would go out of his way to collect deadwood for their cooking fires, and when they fished for trout he would keep just enough for their immediate needs although at that time there were no catch limits or wardens to enforce them. Before breaking camp, George would make Walter help him tidy up the place, and he would even bury their garbage. Walter would have fits. "Son of a bitch, what do we have to bury it for? It'll all go back to earth by itself, George. In time, it'll go back to nature, like everything does."

"Including tin cans and bottles?" the boy's father asked.

"In time, Georgie, in *time.*"

They'd wrangle on and on like that, yet nothing could have parted them. Both men were terribly set in their ways—Walter with his poisonous view of life, matched against George's vague but cheerful optimism—a person would be hard put to find two more disparate temperaments but in endless ways each man balanced out the other, and when George Gutierrez died, Walter went numb with grief. He had followed George from cradle to grave, never very far away, a complaining, bitter man, but in his way devoted. When he and Roy finally buried George, they had talked, and then the old man had taken a bottle and limped off by himself. "Leave me be for a while, son," he said. "Just leave me be now." He was never the same afterward.

ON THAT AFTERNOON in 1937 they panned six ounces out of the little pool. That gave them around two hundred dollars for George's "expedition" after they had made out the federal mining statement at the assayer's office in Las Cruces. They never did make that trip to Chihuahua's wild *barrancas*. The front axle of the Mack snapped, and they spent most of the rest of that summer fooling around Alamogordo searching for parts in junkyards.

The strangest thing was that no one else had ever stumbled across the little waterfall. Some very odd types wandered around this part of the southwest—sheepherders, cowhands, farmers, and miners—and, turned loose on the countryside, they had a tendency to become a little crazy in the head, so consuming was the curiosity that gnawed at them. They were all amateur geological sleuths, forever picking and poking at everything in sight: rocks, streambeds, gravel slides, caves, gulches, ravines, and arroyos, searching with magnifying glasses, vials of acids, and even Geiger counters, for anything that would make them rich—gold, silver, lead, copper, molybdenum, perlite, agate . . . the fabled Mother Lode that in one way or another we all pursue through life.

And on this day after Larson's visit he went to the pool again, still drunk, and, almost ceremoniously, went through the procedure Walter had painstakingly taught him, gently rocking the sand back and forth in a large metal dish until he had almost four ounces. At current prices, now that gold had gone sky-high, that was enough to see him comfortably through the winter. He didn't really need the money, but he felt a need to prove to himself that the "bank," as his father had called it, was still in business. It helped take the edge off Larson's talk of security and the comforts that money could buy.

For Roy, that natural rock formation under the fall of water was a little like the discovery his father had made back in 1935, the comet, *P-Gutierrez*. It was comforting to have a little ready cash, in the form of dust, on hand—one never knew when an emergency would arise—just as it was nice to know that that comet was out there, whizzing around the galaxy somewhere, keeping an eye on him.

SIX

A WEEK AND a half later, he was sitting in Pearl's trailer, un-shaven, seedy, and horribly hung over.

The drunk had lasted that long. He had cruised bars in places like Glencoe and San Patricio and other villages where he was not known, drinking alone and, from time to time, replenishing the liquor supply at the cabin.

When he finally snapped out of it, feeling sick and wretched and at the same time unrepentant, he had stopped at Pearl's trailer for a meal and a hot shower. She'd been more furious with him than usual: "Where've you been? No, don't tell me! All any-one has to do is look at you. You and your disappearing acts! I figured you'd gone up in a puff of smoke again. Run off for an-other couple of years. Roy Gutierrez, you want to know some-thing? You're no damned good, that's what!"

"Have a heart, Pearl," Roy said.

"Like hell I will," she snapped.

"Once in a while a man just has to get it out of his system. A little alcohol purifies the liver."

"Oh, why don't you blow it out your you-know-what?" Pearl snapped. But she fed him eggs and sausage, coffee and aspirin, and after he had a shower, he felt somewhat better. She was dying to know about Larson's visit, so he told her. She said, "Imagine that! He came all the way from New York City just to talk to you. And he offered three hundred thousand?"

"Yes."

"You think he really means it?"

"I don't know, Pearl."

"He's a pushy son of a gun," she said. "I didn't think much of him when he and his flunky stopped by to ask directions. I can't stand easterners. They think the rest of the country owes 'em a living or something. But, you know how I see it, Roy?" She smiled humorlessly. "By God, I think you got them by the short hairs."

He shook his head. "Who's got who where? Nobody's got anybody as far as I can see, Pearl."

She stared at him. "You're stupid." She got up. "Let me fetch your mail." In a moment she returned with three letters.

One was from the New Mexico Historical Society. The second was from Neil Larson. The third had no return address—just his own name, with the in-care-of-Lowdermilk address typed on the envelope.

The letter from the historical society was wildly earnest:

. . . I am driving down to talk personally with you in the next few days.

Until then, I implore you not to make any firm decision or commitment concerning the future of Sawmill River Flats.

The New Mexico Historical Society is a modest endeavor. Yet in our fashion we keep a pulse on what is happening.

It has come to our attention that an organization calling itself the Larson Corporation is interested in buying the town. Let me assure you that this is a highly dubious firm to attempt to do business with.

Need I say more?

At all costs, hold fast, until we can talk.

                                        Sincerely,
                                        Gardiner Potts, NMHS

Roy said, "I think they're all crazy."

Pearl grinned mischievously. "I think it's exciting."

The communiqué from Larson was terse:

> . . . Decision needed immediately. The offer still stands. It is not a bargaining price. Please let me know as quickly as possible. . . .

Pearl read this and said, "Play both of them against the other. That's the trick."

"No. I'm going to weigh it."

"Weigh what? What in hell are you talking about?"

"That's what I remember my father saying. 'An important decision ought to be judiciously weighed.' "

"Oh, for God's *sake!*" Pearl said, looking sour again. "That was just Georgie Gutierrez listening to the sound of his own music. He never gave careful consideration to nothing that didn't suit his fancy at the moment. For the first damned time in your whole life you're calling the shots, and you get a chance to set yourself up with some real security for your old age, but no . . . you got to sit on it, like a hen trying to hatch a billiard ball. Well, I'm just warning you, don't sit too long."

"I know, Pearl," he said, nodding. "What it is, I guess, is that I get edgy if too many pressures come at me too quickly. Larson . . . and now this historical society."

"Oh, you know how to cope with *that*," she said. "You just plug your nose into a gallon of booze and leave it there until the contents are drained dry!"

He opened the third letter, thinking that she was not far off the mark.

HIS HEART TURNED over in his chest. That was a bad way of describing it, but it was strangely accurate. Quite literally, that organ seemed to experience a fearful spasm, a violent wrenching so acute that for a moment he could not breathe.

The handwritten note was brief:

2183 Floral Hill Dr.
Shrevesport, LA

Dear Roy: I will be leaving here on July 27th, en route to California. I would very much like to see you—I hope you are not angry with me. If you like, I'll be on the Capitan bus, July 28th. Please let me know. I've missed you.

As ever,
Rae

With just those few words everything changed.

How many times in the past three years had he told himself, *don't think about her. Put her and that whole summer out of your mind for good. She's gone. Living her own life. You'll never hear from her again. Let it go.*

In time, he had come to believe this. Yet a part of him kept alive the hope that it was not true.

PEARL SAID, "WHAT in hell are you grinning at?"

"It's from Rae Ehrenson," he said. "Remember her?"

"Who could forget her?"

He got up and went to the refrigerator. "I need a beer."

"You starting up again?"

Roy was still grinning, and now he began shaking his head wonderingly. "I really need a beer, Pearl. In fact, I may need a couple. I'll be darned! She's written."

Pearl stared at him suspiciously. "You all right, Roy? You look kind of shook up."

"I'm all right," he said. He was almost in a state of shock. He got a beer and came back over to the table and sat down. "I'm fine, Pearl." He shook his head again. "I'll be damned. How about that!"

Pearl took the note and read it. Then she lit one of Roy's cigarettes, puffed at it several times, and, in a haze of smoke, with narrowed eyes, slowly reread the note. Roy sat there, drinking the beer and smiling. Finally, she put the letter down and sighed: "A man is the biggest fool there is."

"How so, Pearl?"

"He'll pay money for a doughnut without ever realizing that all he's interested in is the hole that goes with it." She shook her head. "Honest to God . . . it beats me."

Roy, though, was in too good a mood to be put down by her. Still smiling, he said. "You sure have a way of saying exactly what's on your mind, don't you?"

"At my age, there ain't no future in beating about the bush. I never was one of those Miss Goodie-Two-Shoes to start with, like old Dalrymple thinks she is. Mention a man in her presence, she starts blushing and getting twiddlepated, and rolling her eyes around like a cow mired in quicksand. It's enough to make a person throw up." She stared at Roy angrily. "And you ain't a bit better!"

"Pearl, Rae's coming back!"

"So she indicated."

"Wasn't she something?"

"Trouble on two legs."

"Rae's not such a bad gal."

"I reckon you're going to meet that bus."

"Well . . . yes, I suppose I will. Of course, with her, you know, she might not even show up."

Pearl's naturally baleful expression got grimmer. "You'd never make a gambler. Your mouth says one thing but the rest of you is saying what's on your mind. Roy Aldous, that woman will take advantage of you and use you. Same as she did last time."

"She didn't use me, Pearl."

But the old woman wasn't listening. "And when she's tired of leading you around by the nose, she'll run off again, same as she did before. You skinny fathead! Ain't you ever going to learn your lesson?"

"I think she's had a hard life."

Pearl snorted again. "*That* one? No girl that pretty, and who makes a point of showing every blessed asset she was born with, ever gets to have a hard life! The hardest part of *her* life is trying to make up her scatterbrained mind as to which man to make a fool out of next! I wish I'd had that kind of hard life. Get that smirk off your face and quit looking so pleased with yourself." She shook her head. "The only difference between a man and a boy is the size of the toy he plays with."

"A man can get lonesome."

"Lonesome ain't exactly the word I had in mind," she said. She got up and took one of the beers, opened it, and then wandered about. "If there is one thing I can't stand it's someone who's so stupid he can't learn from his own mistakes. A person like that, there's no showing him *any*thing, 'cause he knows it all." She lit another cigarette. "Sure, I remember her, all right. Big eyes and long blond hair, looking like a lost orphan, and about as helpless as that shark in that movie. You found her hitchhiking along the road and took pity on her, and what happened? She moved in with you, and then left when it suited her. Throw a woman like that into a pit of acid and she'll land on her feet and jump out smiling and looking better than ever." She thought for a moment. "I didn't like her back then, and I ain't impressed by her now, and I suspect I ain't going to change my feelings in the future. Oh, Roy! You poor fool. Can't you see?"

"I think I'm sorry I let you read her letter," Roy said.

"No, you ain't. You couldn't wait! Had to show it off, like a twelve-year-old with his first valentine. You remind me of a Cheshire cat."

"Rae and I are just friends, Pearl."

"Oh, I heard that before," she said glumly. "More'n once. You couldn't pick yourself out someone who'd look after you in your old age and keep house decent. No, you got to mess with some wildhaired woman out wandering the highways by herself, just wants to lie around in the sun all day, drinking liquor and smoking drugs, and, worse, she's from California! I don't know where your mind is supposed to be."

"Pearl, you think she'll really show up?"

"Sure she will, if you answer that letter. More'n likely pretending she's on vacation, though why she has to pretend, I don't know. Her type is on perpetual vacation, from the cradle to the grave. I bet the law is after her. That's why she wrote."

"I don't think so."

"You're stupid, is all. You think she wrote that letter for the fun of it? In a pig's left ear she did. She had a purpose, and she's apt to do anything. That kind of girl gets pure enjoyment outa taking a man's precious jewels and tyin' 'em in knots. You better watch out. She's one of those liberated women. Roy, they are apt to do *anything*."

"She's a decent sort."

"Decent?"

"I'd say so, Pearl."

"Tell me another."

"She means well."

"Oh, God. Them's the worst!"

"I like her."

"Sounds like love."

"No. I know better."

"I heard that before too," she said. "Why don't you come to your senses?"

"I'm trying to."

"Roy, you ain't! Here you have an important business deal that you ought to be turning over in your mind, but instead some female snaps her fingers and your brains go flying out the window. I never seen anything like men for continuous stupidity. I used to think women were dumb because they got such a talent for getting into a predicament, especially when it's wearing trousers. But a woman ain't bad at all compared to men. The only thing I know is, if there is a mountain and a man is on one side of it and a female in a predicament is on the other, why that man will bore right through that mountain with his teeth for a chance to get at her. I never saw anything like it. It's no damned wonder women don't respect men! Shoot! A woman has got her own miserable problems. But men are no different than moths around a back-porch light on a summer's night. They got a craving for women that's downright unnatural. And the only thing that ruins it is the predicament a woman gets into. Roy, ten to one says this girl is in some kind of predicament."

"She's probably taking a vacation, like you said, Pearl."

"Sounds like a predicament to me."

"She's a person who enjoys life is all."

"Oh, I been in a predicament and found it enjoyable," Pearl said. She thought about this, and then added sourly, "Quite a few times, I reckon."

"Pearl, you ever been happy?"

"Once or twice."

"What was it like?"

"Well, I reckon it felt so good I knew it couldn't last, so I just kept my mouth shut and made the most of what I had at hand," she said.

"Would you have traded it?"

"Not on your life."

"Why?"

"I was in love, that's why," she said. "A female in love is worse than a sick cat with a fatal disease that is habit-forming."

"But how did you know you were in love?"

"You feel it all over you, like a case of shingles. Take Harold, my first husband. Why, he wasn't nothing at all to look at, only five feet four, with teeth like a picket fence. When he got tired and stared too hard at something, his eyes got incompatible and had a habit of wandering. Up in Watrous at the high school, everybody called him Cock-eye Harold. During a math or English test he could look the teacher straight in the eye and copy answers off a girl's paper who was sitting two rows off. He had the most beautiful eyes I ever saw, if you could've ever gotten 'em lined up. Hell, when he started courting me serious, it took me three months before I figured out he wasn't staring out the window half the time. But in spite of his runty size and them eyes like loose marbles, he was a loving man. Harold didn't fool around. He specialized in predicaments, just like this Ehrenson snip. I wouldn't give five cents for love or marriage."

"Why not, Pearl?"

"There ain't no future in it. People get divorced the way they change their socks, practically twice a month. Roy, you be careful. If that girl finds out you're sitting on a piece of big money, she'll get ideas. I'm only looking at things sensible. You're fifty-six, and you got no heirs, and you ain't got much mileage left in your engine. She wouldn't be above marrying you if she saw a little gravy in it for herself. That's the trouble with the world today . . . everybody wants to be as free as the air, less'n there's some reason for 'em not to be. Everybody wants to do their *thing*. Well, we all know what *that* means!" She puffed at her cigarette and then stared at its tip. "All you got to do is look in one of those slick ladies'-fashion magazines that Maude Dalrymple brings me. Every single one of those skinny brats who pose for them awful photographs got their legs spread so wide apart you could drive a backhoe between their knees at full speed. What're they trying to do, air themselves out? It's gotten so that the only way a girl knows how to sit in a chair is with one foot aimed at Los Angeles and the other at New York. What do they think they got, something unique? You ask me, they'd do better to take every one of them snouzely-haired young rips and wrap 'em in logging chains from the waist down. That'd at least slow 'em down to a full gallop when it came to doing their *thing*, the nasty critters."

"Pearl, people are carefree and loose these days."

"Loose ain't the word for it," she said. "All I know is, that ain't what life's about. Life is hard work. I know. You take the whole business of living seventy years or so, why, that takes work, and it's tiring. But you wouldn't know about that. A piece of trouble snaps her fingers, and you sit up to attention."

In honesty, he could not say she was entirely wrong.

That brief note of Rae's had affected him. There was no helping it.

A flood of memories and feelings came back, despite the fact that she had drifted into his life for only a short time and had then, when the time came, drifted out of it.

Not a word, in almost three years.

What Pearl did not understand was that Rae, besides being pretty, was a very special person.

In an odd way, she was a connection with the past.

It might even be that of everyone alive she was the only person who understood how he really felt about Sawmill River Flats.

He asked Pearl for some stationery. With a look of disgust, she got it, and he wrote a single line: *"I'll be waiting in Capitan, July 28th. I've missed you, too!"*

A TALL, LANKY young woman, say, thirty or thirty-one, wearing sneakers, faded hiphugging jeans, and a cotton workshirt. Tanned by the summer sun. Long blond hair, tied at the nape of her neck with a scrap of red wool bunting. Good teeth, and a wide mouth capable of a friendly smile. Enormous brown eyes that stared coolly and appraisingly at a person.

The face, though thin, was simply beautiful. You saw faces like that in movies or *Mademoiselle*. Not in Radium Springs, New Mexico.

That was where he had found her, and that was how he still remembered her. A rangy, lovely, sunbrowned girl with a dusting of freckles across her cheeks and the bridge of her nose . . . loose on her own in the great southwest, stranded in a little nowhere town just off the big interstate four-lane.

Radium Springs, at one hundred and five in the shade, was not the best place in the world for an independent woman and a kind of female jack-of-all-trades to be. Her last job had been in a vet's large-animal clinic.

Actually, she had not been hitchhiking. Roy had pulled into Radium to fuel the jeep, and there on the concrete apron to one side of the gas station was her car, an old Kharman-Ghia in royal blue, not bad-looking even under a coat of road grime, its engine-compartment hood propped open.

She was sitting in the gas station's office beside a large floor fan, with an expression that could have been angry or despondent, or perhaps merely disgusted. Roy came in with the attendant to pay the bill and get a cold drink. He put a quarter into the soft-drink machine, got a Fresca from the slot, and stood there, enjoying the bit of breeze being pushed around by the floor fan. The back of his shirt was wet with perspiration. He said, "Looks like you have car trouble."

The attendant, a middle-aged man, was getting Roy's change from a twenty. He grinned and shook his head. "Disaster is more like it. Somebody adjusted them valves and then didn't torque the heads down proper. She barely got in off the highway. There wasn't a cup of oil left. That adds up to about seven hundred bucks' worth of new engine."

"The whole car isn't worth that much," she said.

"You might have something there, miss," the attendant agreed. "This is no place to break down. Tow it back to 'Cruces, that's expensive, before you even get it into a shop. Junkyard price, as it sits out there, is twenty-five bucks."

"Does a bus go through here?" she asked. Her expression was bitter.

"Not until seven this evening."

Roy thought about this as he stood there sipping at the cold drink. Finally, he said, "Miss, I'm going as far as Truth or Consequences. If you're heading that way, I can give you a lift."

She turned in her chair and looked up at him. Gave him that cool, direct stare for a long moment. Her eyes seemed to be examining not just him but various doubts and questions in her own mind as well. After what seemed a terribly long time, she nodded slightly: "Yes, I was headed that way."

AND THAT WAS how it started. She walked away from the ruined Kharman: took the twenty-five dollars and handed over the registration. In the back seat were two small suitcases and a large one, but that was no problem—Roy strapped them to the heavy-duty luggage carrier atop the jeep, along with his camping gear. She told him she was going to Albuquerque.

Driving north on the interstate, they exchanged names perfunctorily. He said, "I think an express bus stops at T or C. That ought to get you to Albuquerque pretty quick."

"Great." She lit a cigarette and for a while they drove on in silence. Then she said, "Do you always offer people a lift?"

"No, as a matter of fact I don't."

"It was nice of you."

"Good to have company sometimes, on a long drive."

They were silent again, and he felt her staring at him. She said, "How come you don't offer hitchhikers a ride? Scared of them?"

He smiled and shook his head. "Other way around is more like it."

She nodded. "You're big, all right."

He glanced at her. "You don't have to be worried, miss."

"I'm not," she said, and, seeing his surprise, smiled dryly. "At that gas station, I decided that someone with your appearance and height would have to be pretty straight. You stand out. If you did anything wrong, they could spot you ten miles off."

He in turn looked at her. He liked her directness. Most strangers went out of their way to avoid referring to how he looked.

"Well, I try to stay out of trouble, if that's what you mean," he said.

"I bet you make a point of it."

"I suppose I do."

"You have business in Truth or Consequences?"

"I'm going up there to get an old man," he said. "He's sort of an adopted uncle. He's in El Mirador. That's a home for the elderly."

"What are you going to do with him?"

"I want to bring him home." He explained a little about his father and Walter, and how the three of them had lived together. "I had to put him in El Mirador nine years ago, when he got pneumonia. Everybody was sure he'd die, but he's really a tough old man. Then, when he recovered, he said he liked it there and didn't want to leave, so I made out the application for long-term admission. Up until then, he'd never been away from me for a day. We traveled all over together. So, for a long time he was happy, and I'd stop by whenever I was in the area and visit with him. But now the people who operate the facility have been writing and saying how he's complaining about going home. They don't think he has much longer to live." Roy shook his head and smiled again. "They may be wrong there. If Uncle Walt is griping, he's a long way from dying."

She looked thoughtful. Finally, she mused, "Tying yourself down to someone you're not even related to . . ."

"I owe it to him—he helped raise me."

"Is he terribly senile?"

"Well, at one hundred and six or so you can't expect too much," Roy explained. "But, you know, he's always interesting. He swears he knew Billy the Kid—the outlaw. At times, he can talk your ear off. His mind jumps around a lot—by now, of course, his notions of time and history are all mixed up. Like, one minute he'll be reminiscing about the opening of the Panama Canal, and the next he'll be talking about Lindbergh's flight. Can you imagine somebody living that long! Sure, he's difficult. He can be like a three-year-old, but at other times he's really amazing."

"And you're taking him home with you?"

Roy thought about this and said, "Yes, I'm going to do whatever he wants, Miss Ehrenson. It might not work out. I really have to keep an eye on him. But we'll try it."

"Are you married? I mean, do you have someone who can help you with him?"

"No."

She was looking at him again. "No woman?"

"Not right now,'" he said. And then, hearing the lameness in this remark, he went on, in a casual way, "Looking the way I do . . . well, it's something that just doesn't work out."

"You mean women are scared of you?"

He thought this over. Then he said, "Maybe by now I'm scared of them."

By which he meant a number of things. Like his father he had, over the course of his years, known women. Not many, but enough. The experiences were not gratifying. He was left with the feeling that something had been taken from him, and that nothing, or very little, had been given in return. That was bad enough. The loneliness—the awareness of being isolated—made it worse.

For a moment, he wondered why he was talking about this—he never had before—and at that he was talking about it pretty easily. But that was an odd quality about this young woman sitting beside him. Her questions and comments were forthright . . . even blunt. She glanced at him now, and put her finger on it: "They take you for some kind of freak?"

"Something like that."

She nodded. "This world's full of kinky people," she said. "It can happen to a woman, too. It's happened to me. Being pretty can be as much of a handicap as anything else."

"It can?"

"Sure. A man looks at a woman, he sees a body, a face. So he starts getting some feelings inside, and that's all he's interested in. He doesn't care about the woman. It's his feelings that count. When a woman finally understands that, she can start having some very negative reactions about men."

"Suspiciousness?"

"Yes," she said. "Not hostility . . . but not friendliness or trust, either."

He thought she was confused on this point, but he said nothing. What he had known was rejection. She was talking about attraction, or being attractive. Two different things entirely. He said, "What are you doing here in New Mexico?"

She shrugged. "Traveling."

"Just traveling?"

"That's right." Then, as if some further comment was required, she mentioned some of the places she'd seen in the past year or two: Denver, Flagstaff, Tucson, Durango, San Antonio, Las Cruces most recently—that was the town she'd just left. "I'm from California originally," she added.

"What kind of work do you do?"

"Lab technician—hospital. Vet's assistant. Plant nursery—gardener," she said. "These days there are all kinds of jobs for women. I can hit any town you care to name, and find a job inside of two days."

"How about Radium Springs?"

She laughed, and then rolled her eyes upward in mock exasperation. "A whore just might starve to death in a place like that."

AT ONE O'CLOCK, when the heat was almost unbearable, Roy pulled into a rest area off the four-lane, and they took a lunch break. He got the big Coleman cooler out, and they ate leisurely beneath a roofed concrete picnic table. There was cheese, salami, ham, Vienna sausage, a cold roast chicken, crackers, sweet pickles, fresh tomatoes, onions, and a loaf of heavy, dark, homemade pumpernickel bread, as well as beer and wine.

It turned into a lazy picnic lunch that lasted almost two hours, and it was here that they talked more and became friendlier. She was relaxed, and so was he. Cars and trucks sped by on the highway. It was cool under the shade of the roof. He said, "Do you always travel alone?"

"Yes. I'm my own person."

"I can see that. Never any problem?"

"Not really. I know how to take care of myself," she said. "The only trouble I've ever gotten into is the kind I wanted to get into. If what you're asking about has to do with men or drugs or some

other things I can think of, well, I know about that end of life.
I spent most of my early teens in a commune in northern California, near Redding. There was more to that life than just the
back-to-nature garbage everybody preached. A kid growing up
in that lifestyle acquires some useful survival techniques, and
she learns about the tools she has to work with." She paused, and
then glanced at him. "Listen, I'd just as soon not get personal.
Let's just say that being alone doesn't bother me. Being in the
middle of Los Angeles doesn't bother me, either." She thought
about this. "A person's always alone anyway."

"What made you start traveling?"

"Various things." She grinned that wide smile, and then
shrugged. "You either move, or you sit still. It's that simple, isn't
it? I decided I wanted to see the country."

"I've moved around most of my life, too," he said.

She nodded in agreement. "Everything I own is in those three
suitcases. I get uneasy with people who have to surround themselves with houses, and swimming pools, and clothes—it's a way
of getting into a rut, and a rut is just an identity that has nothing
to do with the person who's stuck in it. I don't like contracts.
That doesn't necessarily mean there can't be a person in my life.
Maybe I'll be with somebody, and that can be nice, but when
the time comes . . . well, you know, I just have to be able to
walk away. I don't want to think about the past . . . there's the
present, and, with luck, the future. That's a great feeling, knowing there is that door, and when your time comes, all you have to
do is open it and walk out. I wouldn't trade it for anything. To
me, it's the closest thing to freedom there is."

"What are you going to do up in Albuquerque?"

"I know some people there I can stay with for a few days, and
that'll give me time to get something going . . . which means
pulling together enough money for another car. After that, I'll
look around. See what comes next."

"Sounds like you're running away from something."

"Aren't we all?" She shrugged, and began making another
sandwich for herself. "Don't look back. There's nothing back
there you really want to see. Pass me that mayonnaise, please."
He did, and she added, somewhat enigmatically, "Roy, all things
considered, the less you have the better off you are."

"You might have something there," he said. "I've got a whole town. Sometimes I wish I'd never seen it."

"You've got a what?"

"I own a little town up in the mountains. It's a ghost town."

"Come off it," she said, smiling at him. "Nobody owns a town."

"I do."

"Who lives there?"

"Just me. When I'm there, that is. And now Uncle Walter."

"Is that where you're taking that poor old geriatric man?"

"It's where he wants to go. He spent most of his first forty years around there. Back then it was populated, of course."

"That's the craziest thing I ever heard of," she said.

"Could be."

She shook her head. "There are some weird people in this part of the southwest, and I thought I'd seen them all . . . but you're something new. A ghost town!"

"I'm telling the truth."

She glanced at him. "You know, I think you are. That's what I meant before, when I said you were straight. I don't mean square-straight. I read you as an on-the-level type of person. God! You certainly don't see much of *that* these days." She bit into her sandwich and began chewing slowly. She swallowed, and then looked around. "This is really fun. I mean, having a picnic out here like this. Just imagine, a couple of hours ago I was so disgusted I was ready to cry. That's what I like about waiting for what's up ahead. Very often it's bad news, but you'd be surprised . . . sometimes it really turns into something neat."

By the time the picnic was over, a good deal of the food had disappeared. For a thin woman, she had a fine appetite. She helped him repack the Coleman, and then the two of them tidied up around the camp table.

Back on the highway, she glanced at him. There was a look of mild amusement on her face. She said, "I thought you didn't have a woman."

"I don't."

"No man puts together a picnic like that."

"Pearl Lowdermilk's to blame. She's a friend of mine. We've sort of kept an eye on each other for years. She's a rare old lady."

"How far is Truth or Consequences from where you live?"

"Oh, maybe a half-day's drive. Taking it easy."

"She must have thought you were going by way of Quebec," she said.

PEARL HAD BEEN vehemently against his bringing Walter home. Two days earlier, she and Roy had been sitting in the living room of her trailer watching television and talking about Sawmill. She said, "One of these days I've got to drive up and see what the old town looks like. I guess there can't be much left of it."

"Well, you know . . . every year a little bit more goes."

"Just like my teeth," she agreed.

"It's still an awfully pretty place, though."

"Must be almost forty years since I last saw it," Pearl said. "One time your father invited me to spend the day there. You were just a youngster. I remember it, because I hardly ever managed to get a word in edgewise. That old sidekick of your father's grouched the whole time."

"That was Uncle Walter."

"Sure. Walter Kelly was his name. You finally put him in a rest home, didn't you? Whatever happened to him?"

"He's still alive."

"He *is?*"

"That letter I got yesterday was from the home. They want me to come get him."

She frowned. "Good heavens, Roy, he must be near petrified by now. He was decrepit forty years ago."

"I'm not so sure of that."

"I imagine he's failed terribly."

"That might be."

"Oh, that's *sad,*" she said.

"What is?"

"To fail . . . *that* way, you know." She thought about this. "I couldn't stand having somebody that old around me."

"He's all I have left, Pearl."

"Oh, but to be that age, Roy!" She lit a cigarette and said, half to herself, "Why, it's just amazing. It goes to show you the natural injustice of life . . . the way some go, while others just seem to drag on forever. That Walter Kelly was the worst old drunk I ever saw. He guzzled enough red-eye in his day to float an air-craft carrier, and here you are telling me he's still going strong. You want my opinion, it's criminal. You take my Ben. He was the finest husband a woman could ask for. He never drunk a drop in his entire life, or smoked or cussed or even lost his temper, and at fifty-four he had his one and only major heart attack, right there in church on Sunday morning. It plumb ruined the service. The doctor said later that he'd never in all his years of medical practice seen such a first-rate heart attack. He said poor Ben's heart just sort of exploded. Well, of course, you could tell from the way his eyes bulged that *some*thing inside him had blown up. We were right in the middle of 'Jesus Is My Shepherd,' singing away, when it happened. Afterward, Reverend Beaner did his best to get things going again, but he didn't have much luck. So he just tried to smooth things over and finish up with a commentary about how the Lord giveth and the Lord taketh away . . . oh, it was sad. The giveth part was okay but the taketh-away business got everybody in the congregation edgy . . . folks started lookin' around at one another . . . you know, like if they had to be taken they didn't 'specially want it to happen the way it did with poor Ben, because the screech he let out when his heart blew up was just bloodcurdling. He was sitting right there beside me, too. If you think my hair didn't stand straight on end, you better think again. No, Roy, I don't know why you'd want anybody that far gone around you."

"I've got to look after him, Pearl. If I left him there, knowing he wanted to come back to Sawmill, I'd feel awful."

"One time I went to one of those rest homes with Maudie Dalrymple," she said. "I couldn't sleep for two weeks afterward. There's something about those senile people that gives me goose-flesh all over."

"How come? They's just old."

"It's the way they *look*, Roy."

"Well, what do you expect them to look like?"

"Not *that* awful," she said. "No sir, if that's what old age is like, just count me out. Gives me the heebie-jeebies to even think about it. All wrinkled like prunes, and those *beady* eyes, and not a tooth in the whole crowd. They just sat there drooling, and, *oh,* the smell they had . . . 'most as bad as swamp mushrooms. I was reminded of something that was dug up a million years ago, like those dinosaurs or reptiles, or those awful seagoing turtles that that Frenchie, Cousteau, is always showing on television, and, you know, he ain't exactly any prime specimen either. No, Roy, I ain't one to criticize, but those old people ain't actually human anymore. You mark my word, you'll be sorry if you bring that terrible old man back up to Sawmill."

Roy had smiled and shaken his head. "You know what, Pearl, I think you're wrong. I'm starting to feel excited about going to get him. I'm going to fuss over him."

"You'll be nothing but a wet nurse," she said. "It'll be like taking care of a baby."

"You might have something there."

"You don't know doodleydick about looking after a kid, Roy."

"That's true," he'd said. "Only what I learned from my father . . . and from Walter. It'll be fun." He had reflected on this, and then smiled again. "It fascinates me. Just think, Walter was born only seventy-odd years after George Washington finished out his second term as president."

"I got enough depressing things to think about," Pearl told him. "Trouble with you, you were born with a morbid imagination. Not only that, you're *loco*."

HE HAD BEEN telling the truth. Once on the road he felt a tremendous excitement over the prospect of bringing the old man home. Not even the leisurely and enjoyable roadside picnic with Miss Ehrenson had quelled this good feeling; moreover, they would be parting company soon.

But just before they got to Truth or Consequences, she expressed an interest in going with him to the convalescent home. He looked at her and then said, "Why would you want to do that?"

"I've never met anyone over a hundred years old."

"Don't you have to get on up to Albuquerque?"

"I don't *have* to get anywhere; I was on my way there, that's all. If I get there tomorrow, or next week, or next year, what's the difference?" She thought for a moment. "Besides, I've enjoyed being with you." Then she laughed. "The food was great, but the conversation was just as good."

He said, "Hanging around with someone like me . . . well, people might get ideas."

At that, she frowned; finally, she nodded and said, "I know. But you can't always let other people's stupidity make your decisions for you."

He felt two ways about this, and it left him confused and upset. She was for a fact just about the most beautiful woman he'd ever seen—she almost took his breath away.

But, on the other hand, who was she? *What* was she?

He sensed that, though much younger, she had acquired a world of wisdom and experience alien to most of what he had known, and that this world had a great deal to do with her beauty, and with men. When she said that she had worked at regular jobs, he did not exactly doubt her. Yet, this was not all of the story.

He knew, too, that it would be unwise to ask. Intuited that direct questions would only turn her aloof and distant. For a while, they drove on in silence.

Actually, his choice was simple. He could either drop her at the bus depot in town, or invite her.

Truth or Consequences came into view. He said, "I'd enjoy having you along for company, for as long as you like, Miss Ehrenson."

"You might as well start calling me Rae," she replied.

THE EL MIRADOR Home for the Elderly was in Alcalde, a little village outside T or C. Roy explained, "Alcalde means a public official. Like, local people will say, '*Quien padre tiene alcalde, seguro va a juicio*'—'He whose father is mayor goes to court with a light heart.'"

"Are you excited about seeing your uncle?" she asked.

"Yes. Nervous, too. I hope he's all right." As they drove through the rest home's gateway, he went on, "Don't expect too much. It's been two years since I saw him. I mean, he's terribly old."

"Roy, calm down."

"He's the only family I have."

"He'll be tickled to see you."

"He may not even recognize me."

"Sure he will."

"I hope so."

They parked at the administration building and she said, "Should I wait out here?"

"Do you want to come?"

"Yes." They got out. "Say . . . this place is terrific."

"It's a hacienda," he explained. "An old-time Spanish ranching family willed the place to the state. It's not a warehouse for the senile, or anything like that. The residents have cottages, with five or six people in each one. There's a big cafeteria where the ones who can still walk go to eat."

It was quiet and sunny and pleasant, and spotted here and there around the grassy lawns were old-timers enjoying the sun. Wrinkled and bent men and women, some in wheelchairs, others on benches, just sitting or dozing.

They began walking toward the administration building's entrance but some little grandma, a *vieja*, who must have been in her nineties, came tottering up on a cane and grabbed Roy's arm. She was mumbling in Spanish, "Ai-*eeee*, Josephito, you've come to take me home, take me away from here, I want to go home now . . ."

Roy said, "*Mamacita, lo siento mucho, pero no soy Jose. Quien Jose?*"

She said in Spanish, "He is my son. You look like him. You are him, oh, yes, my little Jose."

But her pupils behind the thick spectacles were clouded over with cataracts to a pearly translucence. He doubted if she could have seen any more of him then a vague silhouette, even in the bright sunlight. And her mind was clouded in another way. Roy said, "Mama, I'm sorry, I have to go. Jose will come to see you soon."

"He hasn't come in a long time," she said, still in Spanish. Then she let go of Roy's hand and stood there on the sidewalk, staring off . . . lost in some reverie of her own.

They stepped around her and went on, and he said in a low

voice, "She thought I was her son. They get like that sometimes. The mind sees what they wish was there."

Rae did not reply, but he could see that she had been shaken by that small encounter. There was fear in her eyes. He could understand how she was too young to comprehend ancient decrepitude and blindness and a brain that no longer worked, or how such things might some day come to her. The wreckage of a human mentality is always ugly and sad. To have a rounded life and, then, to lose it all. And, at the end, be left alone. He said, "Are you sure you wouldn't rather wait in the jeep?"

"No. I want to stay with you."

"It's not that bad a place," he said again. They walked on. "The staff is wonderful. Some of these people need lots of special care."

Inside, they talked to a young social worker named Ortega, who got out Walter's records, and the forms that would discharge him. Roy said, "Is he all right? That's what I really want to know."

"Difficult to say," Ortega told him. "Some days he's fine. He's relevant. His hearing, sight, and speech are excellent, and his appetite's about what you'd expect. But he's got rheumatism, and arthritis, low blood pressure, and arteriosclerosis. His body's about worn out. We keep him in a wheelchair most of the day now, but that's just a precaution. He's perfectly capable of walking."

"Toilet functions?"

"Fine, when he remembers," Ortega said. "He's like some of our other residents—an occasional tendency toward exhibitionism in front of the ladies. For that matter, some of the women are a problem, too."

"It sounds like he's aged a lot," Roy said.

"Don't sell him short. He can get around in the wheelchair. You know, at ten every morning we have sick call . . . or what we call sick call. Actually, it's cough-syrup time. We buy it in five-gallon bottles, prescription stuff, codeine and alcohol. It's the closest thing to a real drink we can legally let them have. Anybody who says he has a cough can go down to the infirmary and get a one-ounce paper cupful. Well, we have fifty-six walking and wheelchair residents, plus some on crutches. By nine forty-five, you can see them beelining for the infirmary, every one of them hacking away like they were in the terminal stages of tuberculosis. And Walter is right up front. Maybe not the first, but he usually places around second or third."

"Has he been causing any trouble?" Roy asked.

"Nothing serious," Ortega replied. "Last month he stole some money from a nurse's purse. There's a bar and package store up on the highway a few miles from here. A state trooper stopped him and another wheelchair resident out in the middle of the road. They'd made it to the bar in their chairs, bought themselves a gallon of wine, and were drinking it on the way back. And last week he got into a cane fight with Jake Barnes. They all want canes, you know, even if they have a chair. The social room, where we keep the big tv, is where most of them spend the day. They're like kids—each has his or her favorite spot, and they treat it like personal territory. They get pretty mad if somebody tries to steal it. Sometimes, half a dozen will get into it with canes. Anyway, last week, your uncle let off a swing and really laid poor Jake out. Jake's ninety-seven himself. It took twelve stitches to close up the gash behind his ear."

"Well, at least he's not a vegetable," Roy said. "Sounds like they keep you hopping."

"They don't mean harm, but you have to keep an eye on them," Ortega said.

AT FIRST, WALTER pretended not to know him. Roy said, "Uncle Walt, it's me, Roy Aldous."

"You ain't Roy."

"Sure I am."

"You don't look right." His querulous voice was thin and sere, like an autumn wind stirring fallen leaves. He spoke very slowly, but his speech was clear.

"It's me, all right," Roy said.

"Roy's just a kid. You're a big, ugly ol' man."

"Time passes, Uncle Walter."

"You're tall like him," Walter said. "And you got the skin taint, but you're not him. Roy Aldous was the nicest little half-breed kid you ever saw. You look big and mean." He turned to one of the other old-timers. "Ain't he ugly?"

"I've come back, Uncle Walt."

"Well, what for!" Walter snapped angrily. "Got nothin' else to do?"

"I missed you."

"I reckon you come by to have yourself a good *laugh*."

"No."

"How'd you like to be locked away in this goddamn place?"

"You're looking fine, Uncle Walt."

"You're blind. Lookit me!"

"I love you."

"You never loved me."

"That's not true."

"No one ever loved me," he said. "You no-good nigger-injun son of a bitch. The only thing you ever loved was yourself." He turned and glared at Rae, taking his time about it—the glittering eyes gave her a good going-over. Finally, he said, "Who in hell are you?"

"I'm Rae."

"You his squaw?"

"No."

"How old are you?"

"Thirty-one."

"How about that." He was still regarding her. "You a virgin?"

"No."

"How *'bout* that!"

The odd thing was that they knew how to relate to each other. Rae gave the old man a long, level look, and then she smiled and said, "You're a regular pisser, aren't you?"

"Damn right," Walter said. He was silent for a moment, studying her, and presently he said, "Say . . . would you object if I took a personal liberty with you?"

"That depends."

She wasn't wearing a bra under her thin cotton workshirt. That was what he'd been studying. Suddenly, he reached out quickly and fondled her left breast. Hand like a shriveled monkey's paw, all covered with wrinkles and brown age-spots. She flinched sharply, and then let him do it. He withdrew his hand and shook his head, grinning toothlessly: "Wanta know somethin'? I ain't felt a real tit in twenty years."

"How'd it feel, Uncle Walter?" she said.

"Mite small," he said. "It'll do, though. Yessir." He was staring at her again. "I bet you're some hot number."

"Not really."

"You look like you could go," he said. "Skinny. They say them's the best kind. All gristle, and as limber as a bullwhip."

Then he leaned closer, still staring at her, with a sly, crazy glare in his eyes. Voice sotto voce. A sibilant whisper, hoarsely croaked, but loud enough to be clearly heard. A confidence exchanged: "You wanta know the only two things someone *my* age thinks about, girl?"

"What?" she said.

The whisper got fainter: "Death and *pussy!*" He threw back his head and cackled. "How 'bout *them* beans!"

A group of other old-timers, men in their eighties and nineties, were sitting around admiring Walter's scandalous behavior. He was the only one with visitors, and Roy could see that he wasn't about to give up the spotlight.

He was not as bad as Roy had feared, although he'd aged terribly. No skin on his face at all, just a kind of crinkled parchment stretched over the skull. Mostly bald, with ears that stuck out and a nose that looked like a potato. But he was alert, and surprisingly aware of the situation. He said, "Roy Aldous, did you bring me something to drink?"

"There's wine out in the jeep."

"Well, damn you, fetch it."

"I'm afraid to leave this young woman alone with you."

"You *better* be 'fraid!" And, a moment later, the voice, sly and wheedling: "Roy, come on—I ain't had a drink in a coon's age."

"I heard a different version," Roy said. But he went out and got the wine from the cooler and some cups, and put everything into a paper bag.

When he got back, Walter was telling Rae, "He ain't a bad boy, actually. I love him. I gave him the best years of my life— him and his no-count father. I coulda had opportunities 'cept for them. He abandoned me here. He shouldn't have done that. I'm

on my last legs. We're all waitin' to die here. He don't give a
shit." He began weeping a little. "This place is awful."

Rae poured wine for him and his cronies. An old fellow in an
armchair said, "Somebody keep watch at the window. If they
catch us drinking, they'll yell at us."

"I'll take the responsibility," Roy said. He opened a couple of
packages of cigarettes and passed them around.

"You're a visitor. You don't have to worry," the old fellow said.
"You can just get in your car and drive away."

The wine seemed at least as popular as the cough syrup Ortega
had described. There was a gallon of it, and for about ten minutes it went pretty fast. Then they slowed down.

Walter was still coming on like a bantam rooster in front of his
friends. He said, "You see this boy here? Well, I want to tell all of
you, I raised him from a little baby. I taught him everything he
knows. He wouldn't be here if it wasn't for me. And now he's
come back. He's goin' to take me outa here. He ain't much, but
I made him what he is." And, then, that wheedling voice again:
"You ain't goin' to leave me here, are you, son?"

"No," Roy said. "I'm taking you home."

Walter looked at his *compadres* and let off his wheezing
capon's cackle: "Didn't I tell you? *Didn't I?*"

SEVEN

In the Jeep, Rae shared the back seat with the cooler. Walter sat up front. He said, pausing sometimes between words, in the way of the very old, "You got nice taste in women. I always liked small tits better'n big ones. Who needs fried eggs hangin' on a nail?"

He was still in pajamas, bedroom slippers, and a tattered bathrobe. His clothes had disappeared years ago. In Truth or Consequences they stopped at a mercantile store and Roy bought him a new outfit: denim jacket, jogging sneakers, a blue workshirt, Levi's, and a Stetson. He wanted a fancy red kerchief to tie round his neck, so Roy got him that, too, as well as a cowboy belt with an enormous engraved buckle.

When he was all dressed up, Rae said, "Walter, you look like a different man."

"Clothes don't make a person," he said. "They just cover up the wreckage is all."

"You look great," Rae insisted.

He wriggled uncomfortably. "New denims are hell. Stiff. Let's go find us a Mexican washerwoman who can scrub 'em and soften 'em a little."

"There are no more washerwomen, Walter," Roy said. "We'll find a laundromat when we get a chance."

Next they shopped at a supermarket and replenished the wine and food. Walter saw some sunglasses he liked, so Roy bought them, and then got a pair for Rae, too.

Back in the jeep, he said to her, "It's getting late. Would you like me to take you to the bus station?"

She hesitated. "I'd just as soon hang in with you and Walter, if it's all right. I don't want to be an inconvenience, though."

"You won't be."

"What bus station?" Walter said. "You goin' someplace, girl? You stay with us, if you know what's good for you."

Roy thought for a minute. Finally, he said, "Listen. I spotted a nice-looking motel when we were coming into town. I was planning on getting a room for tonight—I've about had enough of this heat. Suppose I get a room with two beds? Walt and I could take one, and you could have the other. Would that be all right?"

Rae nodded. "That sounds fine. I'm kind of washed out, too." She looked it. The temperature was still in the upper nineties, even though the sun was low in the west.

"We'll have us a party," Walter said.

At the desk, the bill was forty-eight dollars, including tax. Rae tried to chip in with twenty dollars, but Roy said, "No, I was planning on finding a good place anyway. You know, to celebrate his first night out."

Their room was upstairs, and it had air conditioning and a large color tv. Roy brought up the Coleman and they sat around watching the evening news, eating cold cuts and enjoying the beer and wine. Walter went around touching the walls, and saying, "It looks like adobe, but it ain't. It's just ol' chickenshit plasterboard painted brown to look like 'dobe. Why, there ain't a real 'dobe in this whole place."

They left Walter with the tv and went down to the jeep. She got one of her small suitcases and Roy fished a change of clothing and his toilet kit out of his travel bag.

Back in the room, she took a shower, and came out looking clean and refreshed, in a white terrycloth bathrobe that came to her knees. She had her long hair tied up in a towel. Roy used the shower and put on a fresh shirt and jeans. When he was finished, he asked Walter if he wanted to wash up. The old man wasn't interested. He was watching Rae.

She was sitting on her bed, brushing her wet hair. Tanned, bare legs crossed. Head tilted to one side as she worked with the brush. An expression on her face that was almost dreamy. Serenely absorbed. Her skin was moist and fresh-looking, and at that moment she seemed young and vulnerable, scarcely out of her teens.

Walter looked on. The hooded eyes blinked from time to time, as quick as a camera's shutter. He said, "Roy, I ain't seen nothin' like that in years. Real pretty, ain't she?"

Roy did not reply, and the old man went on, "By jingo! Girl, you sure are an eyeful."

"Thank you," Rae said.

"You're better'n watchin' television," Walter said. He grinned and bobbed his bald head up and down like a gobbler, glancing slyly at Roy. "I thought all my feelin's were gone. But I was wrong! Ain't that somethin'? For a man of my years? I mean, I ain't no youngster anymore."

"I'm beginning to wonder," Roy said.

DOWN IN THE motel's cocktail lounge, he was no better. If his old, failing body was tired, it was not getting the message across to his brain. He moved very slowly and with care, but he seldom stopped talking. Rae was fascinated. She said in a low voice, "I swear, he's got to be on an adrenaline-and-wine high. I keep waiting for him to fold up. He acts like a kid in a toy store."

Roy nodded. "Maybe he'll sleep late tomorrow."

They were sitting at a table near the bar. A young cocktail waitress in a brief ruffled skirt that showed her underpants took their order. That got Walter started again, the ruffles and the panties. Rae wanted a Chablis, and so did Roy. He looked at Walter. "What would you like?"

Walter thought this over. Finally, he said, "A double brandy Alexander."

"Where'd you learn about brandy Alexanders?" Roy said.

"*The Edge of Night*," Walter replied. The waitress left, and he went on, "How come it's so dark in here? They too cheap to turn on the lights? Did you see how that little floozie was dressed? Are all bloomers like that these days? She gets in a draft, she'll sneeze where it matters. Roy, give me a custom-made." Rae gave him one of hers. He broke the filter off and then put what was left of the cigarette in his mouth. "Why don't you buy real cigarettes, girl? These filter things look like a toothpick with an eraser stuck on."

Their drinks came, and the waitress made a fuss over asking Walter if his was all right. She seemed as fascinated by Walter as Rae was. He tasted some of it and said, "Lemonade." He was eyeing her. "How old are you, girl?"

"Twenty-three."

"You interested in makin' a little extra money?"

For a second, she didn't get it. Then she looked surprised. She grinned and shook her head. "No, thanks." As she left, Walter called after her, "You change your mind, we're up on the second floor. We're havin' us a real party up there."

He drank some more and sat there, puffing at the cigarette and staring around, acting pleased with his new outfit, the stiff Levi's and shirt, the red kerchief, and the jogging sneakers. He was in a mood to talk to the world if it would listen, and more than one table of drinkers were interested in him.

It seemed to be a young people's hangout, for both locals and tourists in off I-25, and they dressed in accordance with their tastes, which ranged from far-out disco to western, and a noticeably elegant western at that—expensive boots and pants, and shirts that could not be found in a Sears catalog—costumes, really. At the nearest table were two girls and a young man. One of the girls had on a floor-length calico dress straight out of the 1880's —all it lacked to make it complete was a Mother Hubbard. Her friend liked Indian: red velvet squaw blouse, and lots of turquoise bracelets and rings. The young man squiring them seemed to have a yearning for the gunfighter image. He was tall and very thin and handsome, with long, blond, wavy hair and a marvelous, drooping handlebar moustache. He was dressed in black pipestem jeans and a black nineteenth-century placket shirt that buttoned at the side of one breast. Highheeled boots and an expensive flat-brimmed Stetson with a porkpie crown and a simple silver band set off the outfit. He smoked a long, slender cheroot.

All he lacked was a gunbelt. He lounged back in his chair watching Walter with an expression that was mildly amused, or perhaps bored, it was hard to tell. Legs crossed, all bony indolence. The two girls with him were very pretty. They were talking, but they too kept an eye on Walter, who finally said to Roy, "That boy sittin' there looks like he'd be real fast with a gun, don't he?"

Rae said, "Walter, the fastest thing that turkey's ever reached for is a joint."

"He's mean. I seen his kind before," Walter said. "I wanta talk to him." Before they could stop him he'd gotten up, brandy Alexander in one hand, and hobbled over to their table. "I'm Walter Kelly, and I'm pleased to meet you. You as mean as you look? I'm over a hundred. That takes some doin'."

There was more than a three-quarter-century generation gap. They didn't know how to respond. With care, as though afraid it might be broken, Walter offered his hand to the boy, who reluctantly shook it. At the same time Walter was inspecting the fronts of the girls' blouses. They and the young man exchanged glances, but they were superficially polite. That was all Walter needed. "I'm goin' to sit with you. That is my nephew and his female over there. Roy, you-all shag your asses over here."

Rae smiled and murmured between her teeth, "Something tells me we're going to do a little socializing."

"I think he really believes he's found a gunfighter," Roy said. He thought for a moment and then shook his head a little. "That makes me sad. He's been watching too much television."

"Who? Walter . . . or the boy?"

"Maybe both of them," Roy said. "We might as well go over."

They joined the other table. Introductions were exchanged. One of the girls said to Roy, "My God, you're the tallest man I've ever seen." The gunless young gunfighter didn't seem to care for that. He stared down at his cheroot introspectively, and then puffed at it.

Walter wouldn't let the young man alone. He said, "We're passin' through. What'd you say your name was again? You sure look mean. You from around here?"

"Fred Leopopoulis. Denver," the young man said without enthusiasm.

"Shoot! With a name like that you got to be a local feller,"

Walter said. He turned to Roy. "That's somethin' you wouldn't recollect. Back in the eighteen nineties, there was all sorts of Jews and Armenians and Greeks an' Syrians hangin' out in these parts. They was all peddlers. They sold sundries, like needles an' thread, an' sewing patterns an' fabrics that they lugged around on their backs. They'd wander right through the worst injun country with those backpacks. They didn't care. To this day I bet you can look in places like Encino and Ancho and find stores where they settled. By God, they went everywhere. And you know something, they was always welcome. Some of them ranch folks didn't see a strange face for a year at a shot. So when some ol' Jew or Armenian peddler would come hoofin' by, why, he was company. It was a real occasion. The injuns loved 'em, too. You see, they was tradin' folks, and the injuns could understand that. An injun will sit down and trade with you just to keep his hand in. He mayn't have nothin' *to* trade, and the other feller mayn't have nothin' *worth* tradin', but he'll sit and trade till the sun goes down. Why, I recollect seeing Jew peddlers get off the train at 'Cruces, dressed in them black suits and haulin' an ol' backpack, and they'd build a fire right by the train depot and boil up five or six dozen eggs to take along with them into injun country because their religion said they couldn't eat pemmican or jerky. Roy, most of this country was opened up by folks like that. Can you imagine? Some ol' peddler amblin' right into an injun camp an' showin' a profit after they'd powwowed. Say, son, you a gambler?"

"I play a little poker sometimes," Leopopoulis said.

"What's your trade?"

"I'm an accountant."

One of the girls, whose name was Betsy, said to Roy, "What do you do?"

Roy, who was feeling loose from the wine they'd drunk all afternoon, said, "Gold miner."

"Really? Far out? You sure are tall."

"Roy here is part Apache," Walter said. "The only reason he looks the way he does is 'cause there was a nigger in the woodpile."

Betsy said, "I majored in anthropology. One summer when I

was doing field work I lived with this Hopi man over in Arizona, up by Shongopovi."

"Why aren't you with him now?" Rae asked.

"He went off with some woman."

The gunfighter, Leopopoulis, was growing restive. "Why don't we cruise?"

"You *sit* there," Walter said. "I want to tell you something. You ever been in a gunfight?"

"No, have you?"

" 'Deed, yes."

The young man gave him a dry look. "Just like in the movies, eh?"

"It was awful."

Betsy and her girlfriend were more interested. "You actually were?"

"I was smack in the middle of it," Walter said. He drank some of his brandy Alexander and stared down at the glass.

Then Roy heard him say something he'd suspected for years but had always put out of his mind. "Why, it was me *started* it." For a moment Walter was silent. Finally he said, half to himself, "Poor Bertha. How we all loved that girl."

"Who was she?" Betsy asked.

"He's talking about my grandmother," Roy said.

"I think we ought to cruise," Leopopoulis said.

Walter stared at him. "You think you're somethin' really special, don't you? Think you'll never get old. But it'll happen." He paused. "Didn't you ever know a girl so pretty an' wholesome that men just wanted to die for her? That was Bertha. She was a true beauty."

"I'm not following you," Leopopoulis said, stroking his handlebar. "A minute ago you were talking about a gunfight."

"Bertha was so sweet and decent," Walter said. "Her family made her marry Herman—he loved her, an' so did Ephraim, an' I reckon I did, too. So did every young feller in Lincoln County. They'd ride in for two days just to get a look at her an' say hello."

"Was the gunfight over her?" Betsy asked.

"No," Walter said, but his mind had veered off on some tangent of its own. He said, "Decent or not, one time I saw her ready to commit murder. That was when little Georgie got hurt."

"Who was Georgie?"

"He was my father," Roy said.

"What about the gunfight?" Leopopoulis insisted.

But he would never hear about that. Roy sensed that Walter's mind had gone back into the past, when he was young. For him, the cocktail lounge had vanished, and the people in it as well, like wraiths. The old man drank his brandy Alexander, and began talking, more to himself than to the others: "Sawmill was a bustlin' town then. We didn't have no coal or gold but there was timber. Folks needed timber. Back then, the town had 'most a thousand people. There was a newspaper an' just about everything. Rank's Saloon had a forty-foot bar of handcarved oak, all leaves and flowers, an' a checkerboard terrazzo floor made of white and black marble shipped all the way from Vermont. The windows of that place were frosted glass with pictures on 'em, and there were tables for poker an' euchre. The whole ceiling was stamped outa tin. It was a goin' town. Bertha married Herman along about then. Everybody admired Herman. He was a go-getter. He fooled with real estate an' anything else that would turn two bucks into three, and then he built the Imperial Hotel. He run it himself. Eighteen rooms, a dollar a night with bath privileges."

"What got her murderous?" Betsy asked.

Walter was silent for a moment. Then he said, "Something happened."

"What?"

"It was one of them marriages that're arranged," Walter went on. "Ephraim was the only man she ever loved. But they was first-blood cousins. So her folks hammered at her to marry Herman. He was simply dyin' for her. She did, only it was a mismatch. The two of 'em ran the Imperial. Herman worked the desk, an' she cooked for the lodgers. They had two Mexican gals who cleaned the upstairs rooms. By then I was livin' there with 'em. Had me a room in back. I'd lend a hand whenever it was needed, sweepin' out the lobby, an' tendin' the pigs an' chickens Herman kept."

Walter paused for a moment, thinking about this. Then he continued slowly, "Ephraim was still hangin' around. By then he was hidin' from the law. There was a murder warrant on him. Even so, he'd sneak into town sometimes and spend time with Herman and Bertha in their own rooms downstairs. We was all good friends. Eph an' Herman an' Bertha had gone to school together as kids. Only Herman was scared of him. Not that Herman was a coward. It's just that anyone woulda felt a mite edgy about havin' a murderer sittin' there in his kitchen with a Colt strapped to his hip, eatin' an' drinkin' an' makin' eyes at Bertha. Anyway, a year or so afterward, Georgie come along. Bertha thought the world of that baby, only it caused a rift twixt her an' Herman. Georgie was fair, with hair like snow. So was Bertha, and Ephraim, he was sorta light-complexioned. But Herman was dark-skinned and had hair as black as coal. 'Course, *that* didn't signify nothin'. Kids turn out every which way. But it didn't sit right with Herman. He wasn't a talker, though. He never mentioned it, an' neither did Bertha, leastways not in my presence, not in all the years they was married. They just put in year after year together and run the hotel. By then Eph had run off and disappeared for good. Or so everybody thought."

"What a deadly life for her," Betsy said. "No wonder she got murderous. That'd be enough to drive anybody crazy."

"That wasn't what did it. She just got old before her time was all," Walter said. "She was still a beauty and she could still smile, but anyone could see that she'd made up her mind to make the best of a rotten deal. Little Georgie was about two or three by then. She doted on that kid. Herman liked him, too. Even I did. You couldn't get mad at him. So, as a family, they was all gettin' along okay, more or less, 'cept that Herman turned to drink. He was always quiet, an' now he got quieter, an' he put on lots of weight. He never got piss-assed drunk, but it was no secret that he put down more'n a quart a day. Bertha never chided him about it, though. The only thing she picked on him about was the chickens and the pigs he kept out back of the hotel by the stable. She said they stank up the place. I reckon they did some. But that was Herman's way. If he was servin' bacon and eggs an' pork chops to lodgers, he'd make money both ways by bein' his own butcher. He didn't mind the stink or the flies."

The waitress came by, and Roy ordered a round of drinks. Walter went on, "Herman had this enormous ol' brood sow out

back. She was a bad pig. She'd farrow a mess of piglets an' if
you didn't drive her off she'd eat half of 'em and then crush the
rest in the mud by rollin' on 'em. That sow musta weighed over
four hundred pounds. She had tushes almost two inches long.
With that tough hide, you couldn't hurt her. She was a mean
animal, all right. Well, one summer day—that woulda been '96,
I reckon, around August or September—that sow busted outa her
pen. Herman was in his office, workin' on a quart. Bertha an' me
happened to be out in the lobby. Runnin' the hotel wasn't such
hard work, and the afternoons was mostly always slow. Then her
an' me would sit down and play cards or talk. So this bad sow
was messin' around out back. Somehow it got in through the
kitchen screen door. There was little Georgie, all by himself,
playin' on the floor in the kitchen, with a toy. I always figgered
he was just too petrified to yell when that big bitch-sow come
moseyin' in. He musta just sat there.

"Well, by an' by, Bertha and me heard the noises that sow was
makin' back in the kitchen. At first it didn't register on us, and
then it did. I mean, you don't expect to hear pig noises comin'
from your livin' quarters like that.

"All of a sudden, Bertha, she leaped up. So did I. I swear, her
face had gone snow-white. She never looked at me or spoke.
Neither did I, but we was both thinkin' the same thing. We
dashed for the kitchen. It seemed to me later that she just kinda
made one long leap all the way to the back, with me limpin'
along in the rear. My hips had been crushed by then, so I couldn't
move fast. I got there just as she let out the most awful scream I
ever heard. That sow, all covered with mud an' filth, had little
Georgie pinned to the floor, an' was eatin' his leg. The only part
of him we could see was his poor little face stickin' out from
underneath her, with his eyes bugged out an' his mouth gapped
open, but makin' no sound, while that sow ate on his leg. He
couldn't have made any outcry, 'cause she'd squeezed all the air
outa him."

Their drinks came, and Roy paid for them. The girl named
Betsy pushed hers away. She was beginning to look a little sick.
Walter went on:

"There was blood spurtin' everywhere. The sow looked up at

us. Its ugly snout an' tushes was all over blood. Bertha let off another screech.

"I never seen a woman move so fast. She grabbed up the first thing handy. It was a big cast-iron frying pan that musta weighed fifteen pounds. It was sittin' on the woodstove. She brained that sow with it. Knocked that awful critter clean across the kitchen with one swipe. Broke the iron handle clean off. You can imagine the strength that was in her to be able to do that. Then she snatched up a butcher knife, musta been as long as my forearm, and sank it into the sow's back three or four times.

"That pig took the hint and cleared out fast. 'Course, Bertha hadn't hurt the sow much. A pig that size can't hardly be killed. The two of us run to Georgie. We made a tourniquet. He was just lyin' there, starin' up at us. Herman, he was in the kitchen doorway, lookin' like he was ready to pass out. He'd heard her screams and come runnin'.

"We tied up the leg an' put Georgie in a buckboard and galloped down to Fort Stanton, where there was an Army surgeon. He patched up the leg as best he could.

"But from that day on, Georgie never spoke a word. Bertha took him all the way to specialists in Albuquerque. None of 'em could find anything wrong with his throat. It was just that he couldn't talk. An' he stayed that way for the next eleven years. Until July seventh, nineteen-ought-seven.

"That was the day Ephraim and the Tidwell brothers and their foreman, Bonafacio Sanchez, had it out, right in front of the Imperial. I saw it all. Men, dead or dyin' in their own blood, and that boy screamin', 'Momma, come quick.' Bertha swore to her dyin' day it was a miracle."

"That's nonsense," young Leopopoulis said. "If there's any truth in the story at all, it was just a speech block caused by trauma . . . and erased by another trauma."

"Whatever, he never spoke," Walter said. "After that business with the sow, things were never the same. They kept Georgie almost a month at the infirmary at Fort Stanton. He'd lost a horrible amount of blood. For a while the surgeon was sayin' it'd be better to cut the leg off and be done with it. Bertha stayed with Georgie all that time. Herman and I would go a lot, too. She told

Herman, 'When I bring him home, I want those pigs gone. I don't wanta ever lay eyes on 'em again.'

"But Herman didn't do it. He'd gone to a lot of trouble and expense buildin' those sheds and pens. I took him aside and told him the same thing, that he oughta get rid of 'em, but he kept puttin' it off.

"When Bertha finally brought the boy home, she made him nice and comfortable, in the big bed she an' Herman slept in. Then she went into the kitchen and looked out back. 'Course, the pigs was still there, includin' that sow. Bertha kept starin' out the window, and, presently, she turned around and stared first at Herman and then at me. She had a funny look in her eyes that I didn't like. She didn't look crazy or anything. She looked real calm. Finally, she said to me, 'I married a fool.'

"Then she went into the hallway. We heard her rummagin' in the closet. When she come back into the kitchen, she had Herman's twelve-gauge double-barreled Ithaca in one hand and a box of shells in the other.

"Herman said, 'Damn it, woman, just a minute.' But she strode right past him, out the back door. We stood at the window watchin'.

"She shot every pig. Took her time about it. She knew how to handle that shotgun. She'd let off one barrel, and then the other, and then reload, in no hurry. Between the pigs squealin' and the Ithaca blastin' away, it sounded like a war out there. Herman started to go out and stop her. I said, 'Herman, if you value your life, stay in here with me.'

"When she was done, she come back inside and leaned the shotgun in a corner. Walked over to the stove an' put on a kettle for tea—just like nothin' at all had happened. She never said a single word to either of us. I felt so bad I went to my room and stayed in it with a bottle.

"On that day, Herman moved outa their bedroom for good. Even after Georgie was well enough to go back to his own room, Herman left her alone. He took one of the upstairs rooms. Drank his liquor there, did his bookkeepin', an' ate his meals alone. They never talked much after that. I mean, they was civil together, but he never moved back in with her."

"What about the gunfight?" Leopopoulis demanded.

But Walter was fading into sleep. Too much excitement, too much drink. Just like that, he slumped in his chair. Roy said, "He's had an awfully long day."

The girl sitting beside Betsy said to Roy, "Do you think any of that really happened?"

"Yes," he said.

"I mean, do you think it happened *that* way?"

"What's the difference?" Leopopoulis said.

"Well, I don't know about you, but I'd rather hear a pleasant kind of story," the girl said. "What he was talking about was horrible."

"He probably made up most of it," Leopopoulis said. "Some of these old dudes will talk your ear off."

Roy could have told him that he was wrong. But then he thought to himself, *what's the use? He won't listen. They wouldn't understand.*

He gave Rae a look. They finished their drinks and said good night. Walter was snoring gently. Roy lifted the old man in his arms and carried him out of the cocktail lounge. Walter couldn't have weighed eighty-five pounds.

UPSTAIRS, THEY UNDRESSED him and got him under the covers. Roy pushed the bed over so that one side was up against the wall. "He's better like that—on the inside," he said. "Sometimes at night he gets up and wanders. A couple of times he's fallen out of bed."

They sat down on her bed, turned on a tv movie, poured wine, and shared a little marijuana Rae had in a plastic 35-mm film container. She said, "You know, those kids didn't believe a word he said."

"I know. He was telling the truth, though," Roy said. "I never heard him explain it that well . . . about how my father was crippled, and how he never spoke for so many years. Actually, you know, my father was a wonderful talker. When I was small I used to sit and listen to him by the hour."

"How can you be so sure he was on track?" she asked. "I mean, that was an unbelievably long time ago."

Roy said, "I have her diary."

"Whose?"

"My grandmother's."

"My God, really? Where?"

"Back at the cabin."

"What finally happened to her?"

"Herman died of a heart attack, in 1909. She followed in 1910, with a cancer. Walter and my father nursed her in the back rooms of the hotel. By then, the town was deserted. They fed her opium, which was easy to buy in those days. Walter once told me she died screaming."

"Do you have a photograph of her?"

"None exists," Roy said. "Walter described her, though. He had a terrible crush on her. She had green eyes, and was slim but with a good figure. Tonight, he was saying she was beautiful. I think she probably was. My guess is that maybe she was a lot of woman, with strong emotions and needs. She was only forty when she died. Everything had gone wrong for her. The men in her life all seemed weak somehow. Ephraim and Herman. They loved her but they must have lacked a certain strength. Walter, too—a busted-up drunk, good for nothing but sweeping and doing little chores around the hotel. I think in the end it got to her." Roy paused. "She died hard. From what Walter once described, below the navel she was one wide-open wound."

They looked over at him lying in his bed. Chin ceilingward, snoring softly, the toothless gums revealed by a slack mouth. Perhaps dreaming. For all Roy knew, he was back in his twenties again, fit and able to walk as well as the next man, a wiry little cowpoke, kidding around in a high mountain village and doing a bit of shy flirting with a long-skirted, green-eyed young woman.

They had another drink. Rae said, "I wouldn't mind seeing this town."

"There's not much left of it."

"I'd like to judge for myself." She thought about this, and then frowned. "There's something bothering me, though."

"What's that?"

She looked at him. "I'd want to keep it casual. That's all. Do you know what I mean?"

"Yes, I think so."

"I mean, I'd really love to go up there with you and Walter, but I don't want it to turn into some kind of big thing. I don't like strings. I want to be friends with you and Walter. I really do. You understand?"

"Yes," Roy said. And it was his turn to think. Finally, he said, "Well, you're welcome to come with us for as long as you want."

"Thank you. That makes me feel good. I really enjoyed today. I've enjoyed today more than anything I've done in the past year. You feel like another joint?"

"No," he said. "A little goes a long way with me."

"Well . . . is that all right with you? I mean, if we just leave it loose?"

"Sure."

She was staring at him. "Listen, don't be angry. I just want to be straight with you. That's all. I don't want a confusion later on. Okay?"

"There won't be any confusion," he said, and then: "We better get to bed. We have some driving to do tomorrow. I want to take him home by way of Elephant Butte Lake. See if he remembers any of it."

"That sounds like fun," she said, but her expression was still serious. "I think we could really have a good time. And I want you to let me chip in. I'm not penniless, you know."

"Let's worry about that later."

"All right. We'd better hit the sack then."

"Fine." He brushed his teeth, and then put out the lights and went over to the bed he would share with Walter, took off his jeans and boots, and got under the covers. She went into the bathroom. He heard the sound of a toothbrush, and then, later, the toilet flushed. She came out and got into her own bed. Time passed. Then she said in the dark, "Roy?"

"Yes."

"I don't think you understand what I meant."

"No. I understood."

She was silent for a while. "When I said we should be friends, I meant it."

There was another long silence that in some way seemed edged by an irritation in her. Finally, she said, "It seems to me

you have a choice, but you're going to have to make it, not me.
There are two beds in this room. I'm in one, and you and a hun-
dred-year-old man are in the other."

"You said you didn't want anything to get confused."

"I meant that we shouldn't take each other for granted, or use
each other badly, that's all. I didn't say we couldn't give to each
other."

"You've thought about this?"

"Yes," she said in the darkness. "As a matter of fact, all day."

He heard her move, as though she was trying to find a comfortable position in which to doze off. He got up and went to her
bed, and under the covers discovered that she was not sleepy at
all.

In his arms, she was as supple and quick as a mink, breathless
and alive with her own powerful desires. He could not guide her;
she led the way, and when he hesitated she murmured, beneath
the cool, clean sheets and blankets, "Now. Oh, please!" Her mouth
was heaven, and the rest of her was a hot, wet tactile blessing.
The magic of a woman's skin, that certain fragrance and texture.
Her breasts were firm, with pointed nipples. The cavity between
her restive thighs smelled rich and faintly rancid, devoid of
unguents or lotions, simply *her,* all curly hair and slick lubricos-
ity, a powerful female odor and taste, the mound swollen now
with heat and desire, a fountain to drink at, and, yes, he would
slake a lifetime's thirst there. Until, finally, he could wait no
more, and mounted her. A beast unleashed, in her as well as him
. . . knees drawn almost up to her shoulders, face pressed
against the crook of his neck. She moaned, and, out of control,
murmured, when she could catch her breath, "Go deep, oh, yes, I
like it deep, my God!" Quite artfully, she pressed the palm of each
hand against his thrusting buttocks, and thus timed the pace and
rhythm, forcing him to go slower, and at the same time deeper,
and then slower still, and then the hands, pressing downward to
gather all his strength in still another thrust, and then another,
and a pause, and then still another, until something deep inside
her began to swell and open; all of her unfolded; finally, the
fierce spasms and contractions came, the core of her collapsing
in a powerful convulsion, a pulsing that went on and on. Later,
they nestled, and she said lazily, "Good. Good."

"For me, too."

"How long has it been for you?"

"A while."

"Quite a while?"

"Yes. Quite a while."

"Matter of fact, now that I think of it, it's been a while for me, too."

He wanted to reply but was already beginning to doze off, his arm flung out and around her as she lay close. Outside the motel, somebody was honking the horn of a car. The air conditioner hummed, and Walter, in the nearby bed, snored. There were voices in the corridor outside, and then, somewhere, a door slammed.

Through the imitation plaster-adobe walls, they could hear a woman's voice saying bitterly, "I've been looking forward to this all year. Why do you have to be this way?"

More clearly, a man's voice said, "It's my holiday too, you rotten bitch."

Something was knocked about. There was a sound of scuffling, or struggling, and then the woman's voice wailed, "I love you. I always have, Bobby."

"Go fuck yourself," the man's voice said. "That's what you like best."

There was another outcry from her. "Can't you see that all I want is for us to be happy!"

And then, the man's voice again: "Why did I have to marry a shallow woman? I keep asking myself that. Why in the world, of all the women, did I have to pick out a shallow imbecile? I'm going for a walk."

A door slammed. In the corridor: footsteps that finally faded.

Rae got up, half asleep, and went to the window to look out into the vast motel parking lot, packed with cars and illuminated by ghostly blue-green mercury lights. Roy joined her.

She said, "Look."

Down there, a young man strode among the car lanes, his head bowed. He was small and wiry, and looked no more than twenty-two or twenty-three. A slender, bitter youth. Disillusioned by shallowness. Rae said, "That's what I mean."

"No strings?"

She turned. In the glare of the mercury lights that came in from the curtains she had parted, she had the body of a girl. But her face was older, and sad. Crow's-feet round the eyes. Lines at the neck. She left the window and said unhappily, "Would you just hold me? In bed? That's all I want."

They went back to bed, and under the covers she said, "Roy, don't count on me."

"I understand."

She wept for a moment. "Please don't ever do that."

"Don't worry. I'm taking Walter home. You're welcome to come along. I'd like that."

"Well, then, that's okay. I mean, that's really *okay*."

He covered her bare shoulders. She turned on her side and began to drift off to sleep. Murmured drowsily, "It's been a wonderful day."

In the dark he could not see her face, but from the way she said those words, she sounded like she was content. She moved again, taking one of his hands and making it into a pillow. Her entire face fitted into his large, open palm. "Roy?"

"Umn?"

"Ask you something?"

"What?"

"You have those discolorations all over you?"

"Yes. Why?"

She hesitated, and then said, "Will you show them to me? I mean, sometime?"

"I don't know." Only a few times in his life had he ever removed his shirt in front of others.

She said, "I want to see all of you. We're friends. That's great."

He wanted to respond, but could not, and they finally slept, staying close all through the night. Toward five, they woke and after using the bathroom made love again, and then dozed. The next thing Roy knew, it was past seven. Walter, in new skivvies and t-shirt, was sitting in an armchair before the television, munching salami and crackers with his toothless gums and watching *Captain Kangaroo*. He said, "A man could starve to death 'fore you two got around to fixin' breakfast." Rae sat up in bed, yawned, and slipped into her shirt, but not before Walter got a look. She went into the bathroom. Walter stared after her and said, "Don't take care of herself. Skinny as a broom."

Roy pulled on his jeans, grinning at the old man. "How can you find fault on a grand summer day like this?"

Walter glared at him and then bit into a chunk of salami. "What in hell would *you* know 'bout what kinda day this is? Curtains all pulled shut tight . . . no lights on. It's dark as sin in here. An' how come you're so goddamn cheerful? As if I didn't know." He chewed slowly, watching the tv program. "Man drops a pebble in a woman's well, right away the whole rotten world's a better place to live in."

THE REST OF the trip back had gone that way. They'd had fun. The Coleman cooler was reloaded with fresh ice and beer and wine. The temperature stayed in the upper nineties. Roy drove slowly. They stopped when they felt like it, ate and drank when the mood took them, and talked. Walter chose the back seat because the breeze coming in the opened windows was stronger. Roy folded some blankets into a thick pillow so that the old man sat higher and could see out, and told Rae, smiling bemusedly, "My mind's back almost forty-five years . . . then it was me who used to sit between Walt and my father. They had a little box for me to sit on. We had this big old Mack truck. We went all over the country, and at night we'd camp. They'd take it easy and listen to me recite my home-study lessons. My father had a regular library in back of the truck. That was my whole life, traveling around with them. I felt really secure and safe, sitting on that little box."

Only now it was Walter who was propped up, looking this way and that, his bald head twisting in a serpentine fashion. He seemed to be tickled by all of it . . . just being out on the road again, and he divided his attention between the splendid countryside and Rae's traveling costume.

Because of the heat, she had on white nylon gym shorts and a t-shirt. No bra, and no shoes. The long blond hair set in two thick braids at each side of her skull. Suntanned legs smoothly muscled. Walter, admiring all this, was transported. Fierce eyes blinking, a watery agate blue, the whites rheumy and bloodshot. And, outside, that beautiful, endless southwestern landscape. Gentle foothills, like giant, swollen waves, tinted in a thousand shades of green and ochre and dusty rust red. And, above, the dazzling New Mexican sky, a bright, blinding blue.

"You all right, girl?"

"Just fine."

"Can I have a smoke?"

"Here, Uncle Walt." She broke the filter off one of her cigarettes, lit it, and passed it back to him. He said, "Thanks. How'd you know I can't abide them filter things?"

"You told me so last night."

"That's mighty considerate," Walter said, puffing. "Roy, he can't remember shit from one minute to the next."

She saw Roy shaking his head a little, and she said, "What are you smiling about now?"

"I'm not sure," Roy said. "I may be wrong . . . but I don't think I am . . . I think it's the first time in my life I ever heard him thank anybody."

They stopped at a tourist trap off I-25 for more beer, potato chips, and gas. The place was done up like an old-time Indian trading post, only all the souvenirs—cheap jewelry, beaded Indian moccasins, and the like—had been manufactured in Korea. Rae picked out a straw Stetson like Walter's and put it on at a rakish angle. The trading post was packed with out-of-staters, and they were giving the three of them a lot of interested looks. In truth they made an odd sort of trio . . . a stunning, tanned young woman, the lanky giant of a man who towered above everybody, and a shriveled old-timer, who stood perhaps five feet, no more. Rae, ambling through the gift section barefoot, in her big new hat, a can of beer in one hand. The looks became mildly disapproving. Outside, on the apron, a tourist tried to take a surreptitious snapshot with his Instamatic and grew embarrassed when Rae caught him at it and posed prettily with one arm about Roy's waist and the other embracing Walter. An entire family by a large RV with Kentucky plates got stonyfaced and turned coldly away, and the head of a household of Californians stood petrified beside an Airstream trailer in openmouthed shock. Roy gently urged her to move on, and, still with that bright, sassy smile, she murmured, "Some goddamned people have a way of really getting on my nerves."

Walter gimped after her, acting fussy and decorous. As if he'd elected himself to the role of chaperone. She was something to see, all right. Youth and beauty captured in an outfit he could have rolled up and stuck into his shirt pocket. But the acne-ridden pump boy who filled the tank and did their windows got Walter mad. Roy could see those insane Irish eyes, behind the sunglasses, glittering with hate. The young man, working slowly with a paper towel and Windex, and masticating a grenade-sized lump of Wrigley's, was voyeuristically wiped out by the vision of Rae in those abbreviated shorts, propped over the front seat as she knelt facing backward, rearranging the cooler on the rear seat. Walter, with a furious expression, his Adam's apple bobbing: "Listen, boy, if'n I want this whole damn vehicle inspected, I'll *ask* for it. Now git about your business!" The boy did just that, although reluctantly.

Northward, they stopped to camp for the night at a recreational area at the top end of Elephant Butte Lake. It was neat and tidy and organized. The garbage cans had a special designation: *"Litter Control Station,"* and there were signs that read, *"Discarding Burning Materials Unlawful,"* which Roy translated as "Don't chuck your cigarette on the ground."

They paid the three-dollar registration fee, and told the ranger in charge that they wanted to camp off by themselves as much as possible. He showed them a place nobody used, off on a knoll away from the main camp complex. Actually, it had the finest view of the lake but there were no electrical hookups, and it was some distance to the showers and toilets. Most of the main area was filled with travel homes and trailers and RV's, cheek-by-jowl, with out-of-state plates. There were lots of kids, either making friends or fighting, or else taking leashed pets for a stroll, and the hibachis and rotisseries were already being stoked with charcoal briquets and hickory chips in preparation for the evening steaks. Tape decks and television sets played, and every so often a distraught parent yelled at a youngster, "For God's sake, can't you turn it down a *little?*" Walter said, "Who are all these people? Some kinda gypsy caravan?"

"These are just tourists, Walt," Roy said.

"How come they're all squashed together?"

"People tend to cluster."

"But, Roy, what're they *doin'* here?"

"Camping, Walter. Having fun. It's a big pastime."

"There ain't no fun in campin'," Walter said. "For years I told Georgie that nobody but a lunatic would do it. Roy, you mean to say these people got regular houses to live in an' they come fuckin' around out here?"

"Something like that."

"I don't understand no more," Walter said. "Folks hangin' in clusters from the cradle to the grave. Well, when my time comes, I wanta be buried by myself." He stared at Roy. "That's how come you're bringin' me back to Sawmill, ain't it? To *die!* Well, you just remember, I wanta be buried in peace. Don't go stickin' me in no goddamn amusement park of a cemetery with folks I never even heard of pissin' on top of my grave an' using my head-stone to strike matches for their cigarettes on."

"You're a long way from that, Uncle Walter. I wouldn't worry about it."

"I ain't worried," the old man said dourly. "But that don't mean I'm lookin' forward to it either."

Rae excused herself and took a short trip into some nearby bushes. When she returned, Walter looked her over and said, "You sure didn't take long, girl."

"Beer comes and goes fast."

"Sometimes it takes me most of an hour," Walter said. "As for the rest of it, why, sometimes I spend half the day thinkin' about it and the other half gettin' around to accomplishin' it." Presently, he grinned toothlessly. Rae, watching him, smiled too, and said, "What are you thinking about, Walter?"

"I fooled Georgie one time. That's all," Walter said. And then, still grinning: "Yessir. I sure fooled him good that time. Thought he was so smart."

"What happened?" Roy said.

"It was way before you was born, Roy," Walter said. "But even then he was so clean and finicky an' girlish, you know, sorta delicate in his ways. One time he was natterin' at me about actin' civilized. That was a word he always used a lot. So I got fed up. There ain't no way you can act civilized, livin' the way he chose.

I put him in his place, once an' for all. And he never did figure it out. I played a trick on him."

"How?"

"We was camped in some asshole canyon over in the Gila Wilderness," Walter said. "It'd snowed a little, maybe a two-inch dustin', and it was nice to sit by that campfire, believe me. We'd been doin' our drinkin', an' he was gabbin' about how we had to keep this stinkin' country clean an' beautiful, and all. Come dark, he had to take a crap for himself, so he took some newspaper and went behind the Mack. He just couldn't go any-place, y'know, he had to get off in private, like a nun sayin' her prayers. Well, I was feelin' pretty good. So I got a long-handled shovel and then I crawled under the truck. The wind was howlin', that kept him from hearin'. I slid that shovel underneath him to catch his droppage, an' when he was done I snaked it back real quiet-like, an' then skedaddled out from under the truck, got rid of what I'd collected. Pretty soon I heard him walkin' around. I put on a straight face, and said, 'Something wrong, Georgie?' He was frowning. Looked real troubled. He said, 'Nothin', Walter.' 'What's the matter?' I asked him. 'I know I did,' he said. Then he fired up a kerosene lantern and went walkin' around behind the Mack. I went with him. The snow was nice and clean there, 'cept for his tracks, and a scrap or two of paper. He said, 'I'm dead sure I did.' I said, 'Did what, Georgie?' 'Nothin', Walt,' he said. So we walked around there for quite a while, with him frownin' and shakin' his head. Later that night when we'd gotten into our bedrolls, he got up twice, lit the lantern, and went outside, wanderin'. He come back in, and I'd say, 'What's the matter, George?' 'Nothin', Walter,' he said. In the mornin', he paced all over that area behind the truck, and then he spent half that day readin' through those scientific books of his, tryin' to learn what happened. That just goes to show you, all that science stuff don't amount to nothin', if some-one has to be taught a lesson about behavin' natural." Walter grinned again. "That Georgie. He was smart, but he was a fool, too."

Later, when they had put him to bed under blankets, Roy said to her, "I'm seeing something I never saw before."

"What's that?"

"He really likes to talk to you. Now that I think about it, it's odd . . . I've known him all my life . . . but never around a woman."

"Men like to talk around women, Roy."

"He sure does." Roy thought about this, and then said, "He's trying to impress you."

THEY HAD DRIVEN into Honcho the following afternoon and parked in front of Pearl Lowdermilk's trailer. She'd invited them into the kitchen and put on coffee while Roy got some wine and beer. It was hard to tell who she was more wary of, Rae or Walter. After the introductions were over, Roy said, "Uncle Walter, do you remember Mrs. Lowdermilk?"

"Should I?" was all Walter said.

"Walter, I can't believe you're still alive and kicking," Pearl said. She and the old man were looking each other over. "Lord, you weren't any spring chicken back when the stock market crashed. How do you manage to go on?"

"I live right," Walter said, "and I don't let women push me around. I don't recall you. No man'd ever forget a face like yours."

"You look like some kind of ancient hippie in that get-up," she said. "Where'd you ever find those stupid sunglasses and those sneakers?"

"Roy bought 'em for me. He takes good care of me."

"I'll just bet," she said, getting out cups and glasses. She managed to check Rae's shorts and t-shirt two or three times while she was pouring the wine, as if she couldn't make up her mind whether they were some kind of athletic costume or regular everyday underwear, but she didn't say anything, except to Roy: "All of you fixing to live up at Sawmill?"

"For the time being, Pearl."

Walter shoved his cup away and said, "I want wine."

"A man your age oughtn't be drinking," Pearl told him.

"Mind your damn business," Walter said. "Roy, give me a little of that wine. Come'n, son." Roy did, and the old man stared at Pearl with his mean, hating eyes. "See? This boy takes care of me. He does just like I tell him."

Pearl gave him a disgusted look and then decided to ignore

him. She said, "You and Roy been acquainted long, Miss Ehrenson?"

"Call me Rae. No, not long."

"I was just wondering. I ain't never heard him mention your name. What nationality might that be?"

"Swedish."

"Oh? Swedes come from good stock," Pearl said. "We had Swedes in this part of the country years ago. They were hardworking folks, only real clannish. Stayed to themselves mostly. Maybe that was 'cause none of them could speak English. You married?"

"No."

"Well, that's nice. Where'd you say you and Roy met up?"

"I had some trouble. He helped me out."

"Is that so?" Pearl said. "You don't look much like a girl who'd need help. Roy's like that, though. He's real decent about helping somebody. It don't matter who it is. So. You're heading up to Sawmill?"

"Roy invited me."

"Ain't nothing up there."

"He and Walter have told me a lot about what it's like. I want to see it."

"You'll get bored," Pearl said grumpily. "Ain't nothing up there to excite a young girl's fancy." She considered this. "Then again, maybe there is."

"That was a wonderful picnic lunch you fixed," Rae said, trying to change the subject.

"That? Oh, *that* wasn't nothing," Pearl said. "Sounds like the two of you had yourselves a regular party." She stared at Rae and then said, "I reckon you're on the pill they talk about."

"More or less."

Pearl nodded. "That's how come there ain't any heirs no more, everybody flighty and skipping around like no-see-ums, looking for a place to light and bite." She sat there with them, staring down at her glass of wine. Big, rawboned, hulking shoulders. A little gray left in the hair, but most of it was snow-white. Face like a mule. Only sometime, someplace, in the way of years long vanished, Roy had another recollection. Of a far younger woman, with beautifully marcelled dark hair and mischievous eyes that searched and gauged what they saw. Even then she had that sly, sour smile when she checked a man over, and there was that set to her shoulders, so full of get-up-and-go. Whatever else she had been many years ago, she had expressed one thing: a latency for pleasure. It might not have come her way often, but Roy suspected that when it did she was primed. She said now, "Sounds like all three of you are out for fun and frolics. Never a thought for the morrow." She shook her head and concluded bitterly, "Well then, go play the fool. It'll all come back to you. Wait and see."

There was doom written in her voice. Sullen prophecies and dark portents. She had little more to say, and after a while they left.

ON THE WAY up to Sawmill, Roy said, "I'm sorry if she got a little rough with you."

"That's all right."

"It's just that she's blunt . . . and she has her own way of looking at life. Pearl's been a friend for a long time."

Rae glanced over at him. "You know, she thinks the world of you."

"I wouldn't go that far."

"You're wrong. In that lady's book, you're special."

"Here's Sawmill." They topped the last rise, and then drove down into the town. In the back seat, Walter said, "Shit, this here place ain't changed a bit." They went up Main Street in low gear, with Roy pointing out things he knew, and then they were past the sawmill and fording the stream and driving up to the cabin in the trees. He said, "Rae, this is where I live."

She was quiet. Finally, she said, "We're in a valley. This whole place is surrounded by forests. God, Roy, how high are we?"

"Over nine thousand."

At the cabin, they unloaded the jeep. Carried in suitcases, sleeping bags, the cooler, food. It was quiet except for songbirds singing, a diminished twittering of minor communication on the heavily timbered slopes. At this altitude, the sun felt hot and good.

She seemed to be in a strange mood. When everything was put away, she said, "Roy, could I have something to drink? A bottle of wine? I mean, I want to walk by myself for a while. Is that all right?"

"You go ahead," Roy said. "I'm going to make up cold cuts for dinner. Walter could use a nap. I'll tend to him. Take your time."

She left with a half-gallon of rosé and was gone for over an hour. By then, the sun was setting over the western slopes. She came back dreamy, half drunk, and in an oddly fragile and gentle mood. She said, "Roy—" The name dwindled off.

"You okay?"

"Yes."

"What's wrong?"

"Nothing." She thought for a while and then smiled distantly, and said, "Oh, hell. I mean, really. I walked all over the place. The whole town."

"Good."

"I mean, it's all *there*," she insisted. "Just like you said!"

"Well, sure."

"You don't understand," she went on. "I thought you were at least exaggerating when you described it before. Most men do that, you know." She mused over this, drinking a little wine, and then pursing her lips. "But this—" She mused again.

"It's just a place to be," Roy said.

"Yes." She nodded and smiled, a little drunkenly, "*Yes!*"

And later that night. Walter tucked away, on a thick pallet before the sheepherder, snoring peacefully. The two of them, in that oversized bunk. A glitter through the mica panes of the stove. Golden flicker of light. The walls of the cabin shadowy. A fearsome intimacy. All is well. Outside, the primeval night, dark and foreboding. But here, a quiet sort of life.

"Roy?"

"Yes?"

"It's so beautiful up here."

"I know."

"Can I stay here with you for a while?"

"Yes."

She was silent for a moment and then said sleepily, "This

should be called *Roy's Place*. Not Sawmill River Flats. That's the name of the town, but it doesn't tell anything about your feelings. It's your place. It's you."

He said nothing.

Presently, she said, "You want to fool around?"

"It's been a long day. I could use some sleep."

"You sure? We can if you want to."

"How about later?"

"When?"

"Morning?"

"You like it then, don't you?"

"Yes."

"Okay." She moved closer to him and then became quiet. Before she fell off to sleep she said, "This is just about the best place I've ever seen. Roy, it's like a sanctuary."

EIGHT

THAT SUMMER WITH Rae and Uncle Walter had been the best of his life. What a golden time!

In the three years that had passed, he had thought of those months with pain. Something had gone from him, never to be recaptured. He had told himself, again and again, *nothing lasts forever.*

But now she was returning.

In just a few days.

A brief, handwritten note. It had turned his world inside out.

To STAY CALM, he kept busy, inventing makework projects around the place. Early one afternoon he was in the cabin when he heard the sound of a vehicle coming up the slope. For a moment, he thought, *it's her! She's come early and has gotten somebody to give her a lift.*

And with that he ran outside.

It was Lloyd Parmalee's flatbed. As it pulled up, Roy saw Rowdy sandwiched in between Lloyd and Pearl Lowdermilk.

They got out, and Roy said, "'Afternoon. What are you doing up here? Come on in."

"You're going to have company anyway," Pearl said, "so we figured we might as well come calling, too." She got an enormous old-fashioned wicker picnic hamper from the back of the flatbed. Roy could see that, although it was still early, she'd had a few drinks.

Rowdy beamed at Roy and said, "Howdy, Roy! Golly, it's a fine day, ain't it?" He was dressed in wrangling clothes and had a bottle of bourbon in one hand and two six-packs of beer under his other arm. They all went into the cabin. Lloyd said, "They're in a partyin' mood, Roy. I don't know what got into them."

Pearl was looking around the cabin. "I ain't been here since we had the funeral for that old rip, Walter Kelly, and now I know why. That road rearranged my bones six different ways. We ain't intruding, are we?"

"No, I was ready for a break anyway," Roy told her. "What's all this about company?"

"It's Gardiner *Potts,* you fool," she said. "He and Maudie Dalrymple are down below in the village right this minute. He's taking photographs right and left. We drove on up to warn you they were coming. You better fix yourself a drink. Some company drops by, you act like a hermit in shock."

Roy did, at the same time trying to get the story straight.

It seemed that the N.M. Historical Society's director had appeared this morning at the county seat to ask directions to Sawmill River Flats. Maudie Dalrymple had her office there. She had offered to guide Mr. Potts. They had stopped by Pearl's trailer to say hello. Pearl decided to go along with them, only Potts' car was too small and her own ancient truck could not make it up to Sawmill. Lloyd and Rowdy happened to be fixing the gaskets on a shallow-well pump next door to Pearl, so she had enlisted them.

Now Rowdy was making drinks. He said, "Miz Lowdermilk, you want your bourbon and beer together or separate?"

"Throw 'em in one glass and let them fight it out," she told him. "What's the difference? When it hits bottom it all gets mixed up anyway."

When he got a chance, Lloyd whispered to Roy, "I swear, I don't know how this got started. Rowdy's been hinting about having a party, but, then, he's always talking about that. Then

Pearl got in on it. Roy, coming up in the truck, she musta drunk half a quart. She oughtn't be doing that at her age."

Pearl said from across the room, "I heard that, you lickspittle runt. Parmalee, you keep it up, I'll stomp you! If you got to talk behind my back, look me in the eye when you do it."

"No offense, Pearl."

"Some men!" she said, and then, to Roy, "How come you're too lazy to get your mail anymore?" She reached into the hamper and gave him a large, thick brown envelope bearing the Larson Corporation's return address. "Those people called me twice in the past two days. I swear, I wish you'd hurry up and leave Lincoln County again so's civilized folks could have a moment's peace. Roth, go get that beer cooler off the back of the truck."

Rowdy did so, and by the time he had returned, Roy had opened the envelope. It contained a letter and a legal contract. Pearl eyed the contract and said, "They're putting the screws on you all right."

Before Roy could answer, there was the sound of another car outside. Pearl jumped up. "By God, here they are!" For a moment, she tried fixing her hair a little but it was too windblown from the ride in the flatbed. She and Roy went to the door.

Outside, by the pile of firewood, Maude Dalrymple and a man were getting out of a vintage 1952 Jaguar XK-150, a dark green, powerful-looking, low-slung roadster that was really more of a racing car. Pearl whispered to Roy, "Ain't she scandalous! Why, when she stopped by my place she was just busting her straps to let me know she'd lassoed a pair of pants." And then, cheerfully and in a loud voice, " 'Lo, Maudie, we thought you'd *never* get here. Howdy, Mister Potts." And then again, that hissed sotto voce: "Ain't that just like that big old cow?"

Maude Dalrymple had gained some weight since Roy had seen her last, which was kind of like piling insult upon injury. She had been the county public-health nurse for decades. Agewise, she had been firmly anchored somewhere in her late forties since the Korean conflict. Maude had violet eyes and a round, unwrinkled, smiling face; her hair was dyed a Jean Harlow blond and was worn in spring-coil ringlets; she had on rouge and mascara, and her nails were painted a bright red. Maude was one of those women who just love being female. She refused to wear a white RN's uniform because she said white didn't suit her complexion. Today she had on a cheery blue-and-yellow billowy chiffon dress that didn't quite match the knee-high, lace-up lumberjack boots she wore on rural visits. She came toward Roy and Pearl, giving off an aura of eternal girlishness and several different types of perfume: "Roy Aldous Gutierrez, so this is where you been hiding!"

The fellow who owned the Jaguar, who was now walking up the slope with her, was about sixty-five, and he resembled an ambulatory camera store. He had three cameras slung from his neck, and hanging from one shoulder was a leather accessory bag big enough to hold a week's groceries. He was dressed oddly, in fawn-colored riding britches that were tucked into English equestrian boots, a Harris tweed jacket, and a Tattersall shirt and tie. He was tall and very slim, and to top off his outfit he had on a black crash helmet, which he removed now, to reveal a thick mane of wavy gray-white hair. The final touches were horn-rimmed eyeglasses and a small, square moustache that looked like it had been pasted on his upper lip. The overall effect was decidedly elegant except that he had the biggest nose Roy had ever seen on a human—a huge, curved, pink honker that took up half his face. The nose, moustache, and spectacles made him look like a mild, inquisitive merino sheep. He stared at Roy and the others, who were standing outside the cabin by now, and finally, as if almost overcome by a fit of embarrassment, murmured to Roy, "Potts."

"Yes, of course. The Historical Society," Roy said. "My name's Gutierrez."

"Delighted," Potts said. After that, he seemed at a loss for words, and looked more embarrassed and ill at ease than ever. Finally, as though feeling compelled to say something, he gazed around at Sawmill River Flats and the splendid mountains surrounding it: "Pristine! A hidden jewel. It's everything I thought it would be!"

POTTS HAD AN old-fashioned courtliness that was almost Victorian. He had dashed around to Maude's side of the Jaguar to help her out and then offered her an arm to lean on as they came up the slope. She took advantage of it and hung on, teetering as though she was in high-heeled pumps.

Everybody went into the cabin, and Roy poured drinks for the new guests. The single, large room was starting to look a little crowded considering the space Maudie displaced, and with her perfume it was smelling crowded, too. She explained, "I was just getting ready to leave the courthouse and go over to the high school to give everybody eye tests when Gardiner here stuck his nose in my office and asked how to find you, so I figured I'd help."

"What about those eye tests?" Pearl asked.

"School'll keep," Maudie said airily.

"That's an awful pretty car you have, Mister Potts," Pearl told him.

"I restored it myself," Potts said proudly. "It's considered an antique classic."

"Oh, I adore antiques. Ain't they got style?"

Potts went over to Roy and with his shy smile said, "Would you have any objections to my recording this?"

"It's all right with me," Roy said. Potts began snapping up roll after roll of available-light pictures. Pearl said, "If you're going to take a snapshot, you might at least let me comb my hair."

Roy said, "Why pictures, Mister Potts? Are you writing a book?"

"Posterity, Mister Gutierrez . . . may I call you Roy? We have to preserve all this. Everything is vanishing. This kind of life. All these incredibly beautiful old towns. I'm trying to record them before they go. I've been at it for years."

And, without waiting for Roy to respond, he reeled off a list of names that sounded like a gazetteer of the forgotten west. All of them in New Mexico.

Towns like *Dolores, Elizabethtown*—known simply as *E-town* —*Baldy, Loma Parda, Trementina, Hagan.*

A litany . . . of old historic names.

Valverde, Kelly, Rosedale.

Chloride, Roundyville, and *Fleurine.*

Palomas Camp, Cooks, Tyrone, and *Nutt. Jose, Clairmont, Cooney,* and *Alma.*

Shakespeare, Pyramid, and *Leopold. Claunch, Dawson, Winston, Hillsboro, Cabezon, Kingston, Pinos Altos,* and *Mogollon.*

Roy listened, smiling and nodding. He said, "Some of those places I've been to, you know. My father . . . well, he had a curiosity for old towns. When I was young we went all over."

"Sawmill River is very possibly the finest," Potts said. "You know, this is my third attempt to find the place in the past ten years. I never knew anyone lived here part of the time. I was quite surprised when the county clerk wrote this year saying that I might be able to get in touch with you. And then, of course, Miss Dalrymple's help has been invaluable. Meeting her was a stroke of luck."

"Wait'll you get to know her better," Pearl said, coming over to join them. Maude followed.

Potts took a sizable swallow of his bourbon-and-water. He looked excited and pleased and happy, as he explained, "Roy, for the society to find a resource like you . . . someone who remembers the way it was. Inestimable value! Miss Dalrymple, too. We had a lovely chat driving up. She's a veritable mine of historical information."

Maude said, "Well, if you want to know really old-time history, you'd better check with Pearl."

"But of course," Potts said, beaming. "Actually, I'd love to tape yours and Roy's and Mrs. Lowdermilk's reminiscences."

"You mean in one of those recording things?" Pearl said.

"I have one here in my bag," Potts said, and got it out.

Pearl said, "You mean to tell me you just speak your thoughts into that gadget?"

"It's sort of fun," Potts said.

She seemed intrigued by the tape recorder. Finally, she said, "Mister Potts, why don't I freshen that drink of yours a bit? Let me get you a sandwich while I'm at it. A man has to eat."

Roy said, "Can you tell me more about this society?"

"Well, I more or less do just what I've been telling you," Potts said.

It took a moment for this to register. Then Roy stared at him. "You mean, you're *it*?"

"No. A printer does the mailing literature," Potts said. "And I have a secretarial service for the correspondence."

"Is this a sort of hobby?" Roy said, frowning.

"But, Roy, I can't begin to list the organizations that began modestly," Potts said. "Look at the Sierra Club."

"I've had a good offer to sell this town, you know."

"Yes, of course. That's one reason I'm here—to urge you not to consider such a course of action."

"I might need the money."

"Isn't it always that," Potts said sadly. "Money talks."

"What about your society?"

"Limited funds, I'm afraid."

"I see."

"Non-profit, you know."

"Do you lobby?"

"Oh, endlessly, Roy. Thorn in the side of the state legislature." He smiled sheepishly. "The society's name is rather notorious when the state house is in session."

"Then I couldn't count on any real help from the society?"

"Not in a dollar-value sense, I'm afraid. We could do this, however." Potts rummaged in the accessory bag and brought out an eight-by-ten glossy of an official state marker. He said, "This is at White Oaks."

White Oaks was a semi-ghost-town, thirty miles north of Carrizozo. The sign read:

REGISTERED PROPERTY—STATE OF NEW MEXICO

THIS AREA IS A REGISTERED HISTORICAL DISTRICT AND IS UNDER THE PROTECTION OF THE STATE OF NEW MEXICO. ANY DESTRUCTION, COLLECTION, OR EXCAVATION IS EXPRESSLY PROHIBITED UNDER PROVISIONS OF THE CULTURAL PROPERTY ACT (Chap. 222, Laws of 1969). VIOLATORS ARE SUBJECT TO A FINE OF $500.00 OR 90 DAYS IMPRISONMENT, OR BOTH.

Pearl returned with a plate of food and a fresh drink for Potts. Lloyd was standing beside Roy, staring down at the black-and-white enlargement. He said, "Roy, something like that might come in handy."

"It doesn't really solve anything for me," Roy said.

"I'm not so sure," Lloyd said. "Can I talk to you alone, outside for a minute? Could you folks excuse us?"

THEY TOOK THEIR drinks outside the cabin and stood by the flatbed.

What Parmalee had to say was simple: "Pearl asked us to bring her up here, but I wanted to see you anyhow. Roy, Bill Maldonado's been making big noises in the bars around Carrizozo and Capitan. He claims he and his buddies are either going to tear this town to pieces or burn it. I figured you ought to know."

"Billy-Evil's a lot of talk," Roy said.

"Sure, I know . . . but this time I'd swear there's more to it than talk, Roy. I haven't been able to find out what's going on, but it's something serious. It ain't just brag. He means it."

"Lloyd, I think your imagination's running away with you."

"Maybe," Lloyd said, but then he stared at Roy, and his expression became serious. "You're a hard man to talk to . . . always did have a mind of your own. So, this is all I'm going to say to you. Any sign of trouble up here, you get hold of me *pronto.* Billy by himself don't worry me worth shit. But, Roy, him and his pals, that's something different. You understand? I don't want you taking on a deal like that by your lonesome."

"I appreciate your concern, Lloyd."

"I just hope you're hearing what I'm telling you, *amigo.*"

The two men stood there a while, and finally Lloyd went back into the cabin for a fresh drink. Roy leaned against the flatbed's fender, thinking. He lit another cigarette, inhaled deeply, and let the smoke out leisurely into the clear mountain air. He didn't notice Pearl standing by him until she spoke: "Roy, if that Larson calls again, what do you want me to tell him?"

"Don't tell him anything."

"Did Lloyd talk to you about Billy-Evil?"

"Yes."

"Lloyd's worried, Roy."

"I know he is." Roy thought for a moment and then said, "Pearl, I'm not a man to provoke a fight. You know that. But if it comes to one, I won't let somebody else stand up for me. Not Lloyd or anyone else." He shook his head. "No way."

"What d'you think of this Potts?"

"Real nice, isn't he?"

"Oh, he *is*," Pearl agreed. "But can he help you?"

"No. He means well, but he's just a rich easterner who fell in love with the west," Roy said.

And that's what Pottsy was. Sweet and decent and sheepy . . . and he had money written all over him. He looked the sort who'd come out of New England forty years ago with an inheritance and a king-sized crush on the wild west, all excited about the great deserts and high mountain ranges he'd read about as a boy. Potts was ready to immortalize Sawmill River Flats in photographs and by tape-recorded cassettes, and Roy loved him for it.

But what counted just as much as Potts' veneration for bygone days was the fact that Roy had exactly fourteen hundred and twenty dollars buried in a thermos jug outside the cabin beside the geraniums. Plus what he could "withdraw" from the bank— the old gold mine. That didn't look like much compared to Neil Larson's offer of three hundred thousand dollars. Roy said, "Potts would like me to donate everything to the state. Donations are for rich people."

Pearl was staring at him. She said, "You're thinking about that girl coming back, ain't you, Roy?"

After a while he nodded. Pearl said, "She that all-fired important?"

"Yes."

"I reckon she's everything?"

"Yes."

She thought this over. "Well, that's understandable . . . you wouldn't be the first man in this world to get into a predicament." And, for the first time that he could recall, she made an overt physical gesture . . . put an arm around his waist and hugged him a little. She said, "I know how it is, honey. But you listen to me. Everything'll work out. Now, whyn't the two of us just go

back inside and keep everybody company? Let's have a little fun
before the day is done."

SEVERAL HOURS LATER, he was feeling better. In fact, he was feeling fine. A good deal of wine and beer and whiskey had disappeared by then. Somebody had turned up the volume on the
radio, and Rowdy had danced three times with Maudie. He
fancied himself a killer when the right music was available. His
style was half disco, half country-western, with a lot of elbow
flapping and wild gyrations of the pelvis, and what he lacked in
skill he made up for with indefatigable gusto.

The others were sitting at the table. Potts, with an expression
of utmost seriousness, was trying to talk Pearl into joining his
society, and the Sierra Club, too. He said, "The Club has been
incredibly instrumental in saving the natural splendors of this
great country."

"I ain't got time for nature-loving," Pearl said. "It's all I can
do to keep body and soul together, what with my goats and the
cheese and knitting. All this ecology racket ain't up my alley,
Pottsy."

"They do all kinds of wonderful things," Potts insisted. "Why,
not too long ago they discovered a brand-new species of field
mouse that has been living in the big dunes down at White Sands
for thousands of years . . . this little mouse is almost albino
when its burrows are in the dunes, but it turns brown if it nests
in darker terrain. Isn't that remarkable! They've got it on the
endangered list."

"I *hate* mice," Pearl said. "If there's one thing that'll make my
hair stand on end and send chills racing all through me, it's one
of those danged little beady-eyed boogers skittering around the
floor under my bedroom slippers . . . *Arr-gh!*" She shook her
head. "Did you know a mouse'll scare a full-growed elephant
clean out of its wits? That's the truth! And you know why? 'Cause
the mouse'll run up the elephant's nostril. Thinks it's a hideaway,
ten feet long! And then the poor elephant suffocates. No, thanks.
Elephants ain't stupid, and neither am I." She took a ladylike sip
of her drink, and then made up a snack for herself out of crackers
and anchovy fillets that she had set on the table—an hors d'oeuvre,

only she called it horses' ovaries—and then she went on, "God, these fish ain't fit for human consumption. The things they pass off on the public as food these days! Give me a good hunk of beef any time. That's what we lived on mostly when I was young, 'cause it was so cheap. Back then, if you had a piece of land that cows could graze on, you could raise a whole family of kids on nothing."

Roy asked, "Pearl, were people in the old days as land-crazy as they are now?"

"They was lots looser," she said. "You see, there was so much more of it. I remember my daddy talking once about selling some land we owned down around the west side of Albuquerque, to pay taxes. Must've been around 1920. We had our own spread up by Watrous, and this land in Albuquerque wasn't worth anything, so he sold it for twelve cents an acre for tax money. A thousand acres, right there at the edge of that city, fetched him a hundred and twenty dollars. And he was glad to get it! Don't I wish I had that land today! Roy, that's what I been telling you all along. Just don't give your land away."

"I won't."

Over by the stove, Rowdy was showing Maude Dalrymple his version of a Saturday-night-fever waltz. Pearl watched for a moment and then said glumly, "How come a little man ain't happy unless he's aggravating the whole population?"

"Pearl, what've you got against little men?" Roy asked.

"'Cause a runty man always looks ready to play, that's why," she said. "Usually, that means he's getting itchy pants and is thinking about the grass in the next pasture. My first, Harold, was that way. The one with the cock-eye. We'd be off eating dinner in a restaurant someplace, and he'd be staring me straight in the face, all smiles and sweet talk . . . with me carrying on like a young fool . . . and all the time he was looking up the skirt of some floozie halfway across the room." She took another sip of her drink and said, "It got so bad, the only time I could relax around that man was when I could see he *wasn't* looking at me."

"Whatever happened to him?" Roy said.

"Oh, he finally run off with some girl from Gallaudet College," Pearl said. "That's that college they have for deaf-and-dumb people, y'know. Her name was Agnes. She could tapdance and at the same time sing 'She's Only a Bird in a Gilded Cage.' Only she had to do it in sign language. She could also whistle 'Let's All Sing Like the Birdies Sing' very nicely. I saw her one time. Only girl I ever knew who could whistle between her fingers like a man."

"Harold fell for her?"

"She sort of stole him with her whistling," Pearl said. "It was the only time I ever saw his eyes working halfway together. She knew how to make her arms go like regular wings, and she'd hop around on the stage in those patent leather tapdancing pumps, which was pretty impressive, 'cause she was awful busty, like all those deaf girls are." Pearl considered this for a moment. "She and Harold finally got married and settled over in Show Low, Arizona, running a Texaco station. Last I heard, they had five children, all with straight eyes and ears sharper than bats, only every single one of those kids had six fingers on each hand, which must have been a help when it came to washing windshields and the like."

"Don't you ever wish you had children, Pearl?" Roy asked.

"I got sixty-seven goats. Who needs kids?" she replied. "Anyway, I checked all that out one time, when I was young. What with Harold being in the condition he usually was, I got to wondering. So I went to a doctor, and after looking me over he said that in his opinion I was about as fertile as a chocolate Easter egg."

"That's too bad."

"Why?"

"Life must go on," Potts interjected. "We're part of an evolutionary lifestream that dates back to the primeval oceans."

"I don't know about you, but I was evolved by a midwife right in the kitchen of my folks' place outside Watrous," Pearl said. "Besides which, I despise oceans. One time, Harold took me all the way to Galveston to see one."

"What'd you think of it?" Roy asked.

"It was just a lot of water. Harold liked wading in the waves. All that splashing got on my nerves. I want to see where I'm putting my feet. You never knew from one second to the next when some critter down there was going to reach up and snatch at you. I'd get edgy if I went past knee-depth. One time, smart-aleck Harold pulled a trick. I was out there wading—had a brand-new swimsuit, the latest style, made out of rubber—and he was on the shore. He started jumping up and down and yelling, '*Shark, shark!*' So I yelled back, 'Where?' He had a voice on him like a bull. He said, 'Right behind you!' My heart stopped dead in my chest. I should have known he was joshing, 'cause one eye was pointed at the sky and the other was aimed at a lighthouse. He rolled around in the sand and laughed himself sick. He said I looked like a speedboat coming out of that water." She shook her head and put an arm around Gardiner Potts' shoulders. "Pottsy, how about a freshener?"

Maudie came over and said, "He likes to be called Gardiner, Pearl. He's a gentleman, but he don't mind at all being called by his first name."

"Oh, I know refinement when I see it," Pearl told her. "It just sticks out on a man. Gardiner, you married?"

"Widowed, I'm afraid. Twelve years now."

"You don't say. I beat you by six years—I been widowed for eighteen." She paused, and then went on, "Did you really drive that great big racing car clean across the state to see us?"

"It's a Jaguar," Potts said with a modest grin. "Would you like a ride in it?"

"Oh, I'd be scared."

"I wouldn't go fast. I'm really quite conservative."

"Have some more bourbon," she said. "When you get done with your tape-recording, we'll talk about it."

"Oh . . . but the tape recorder's been going all this time," Potts said.

"It *has?* Why didn't you tell me, so's I could have at least combed my hair."

Maudie said, "It doesn't record how you *look*, Pearl."

"Lucky for both of us, I reckon," Pearl said. "In your case we'd need Vistavision."

"What do you know about the Larson Corporation, Mister Potts?" Roy asked.

"It advertises in the *New York Times* and the *Wall Street Journal*," Potts said. "Retirement condominiums and 'ranchettes,' in a restored historical environment. Larson is nothing more than a land developer with a new angle. We've been keeping an eye on him. The historical-restorations angle is merely a ruse . . . a way to make money. It's a shady business."

"Business is just a way to make money," Pearl pointed out. "That's what made this rotten country what it is today."

"If you sell Sawmill River, it will vanish," Potts told Roy. "I can guarantee it." He looked to Pearl for help. Roy could have sworn there were tears in his eyes. "Simply vanish!"

"Oh, that's sad," Pearl said. "Say, you got the loveliest hair, do you know that? How come the men always get hair that looks like it's been permed, while the women end up with a mopful of boiled noodles? It ain't fair."

"Pearl, a woman has to take care of herself if she's going to be attractive," Maude told her.

"You sure been doing that," Pearl said, eyeing the nurse as she reached for another slice of ham. Maude sat down and said, "There's nothing wrong with being presentable."

"Do you buy that awful perfume by the gallon, or do they ship it to you by truck?" Pearl said.

Maude got huffy and said, "I do my best. Of course, I'm not a youngster anymore, but that's no crime."

"You ain't blond either," Pearl said.

"Men appreciate comeliness in a woman," Maude insisted.

"What they appreciate is some twitty young snip in a short skirt twitching her butt and walking down the street in a hurricane," Pearl said. "That's 'cause a man can't see past the end of his big, stupid nose except when a female floats past." She still had her arm around Potts' shoulder. "Nothing personal, Gardiner."

Potts was drunk by now. He smiled and shook his head, and then said, to no one in particular, "Money always talks, doesn't it? Well, I can understand that. There's an old saying, *the wise man kisses the hand he cannot sever*. It's a Tuareg proverb . . . you know, those Berber people who live like nomads in the Algerian desert."

"Those A-rabs are crookeder than snakes," Pearl told him. "Why, look at all we went and done for them. Educated them to the hilt, taught 'em English, built oil fields all over creation, and how do they show their appreciation? Why, they just stole every-thing that wasn't nailed down. Every time I fill up my gas tank, I get so mad thinking about those filthy Iranians and their petro-dollars that I see red. What we ought to do is have a little private talk with the Russians, and then have both of us just walk in there and squish 'em flat! Divvy up *all* those oil fields between us and the Commies, and tell the rest of the world where to shove it! Maybe *that'd* teach 'em for a change."

Roy said, "Well, they seem to be getting by pretty well."

"Getting rich is more like it," Pearl said grumpily. "And at our expense."

"That's more than I've ever been able to do," Roy said.

"You got yourself a chance now to make a real piece of money," Pearl pointed out.

"I don't know if I want to do that," Roy said. He shook his head. "Sometimes I wish my father had never bought this old town."

Pearl shook her head in disgust. "Ain't that you all over! You'd stand in the sun and complain about the heat. For your whole life, this old town wasn't worth five cents. And you *loved* it! Now, all of a sudden, it's worth money, and what do you do? Twiddle your thumbs and moon and sigh like a lovestruck bull when the first clover sprouts. If you don't take the cake!"

WHAT PEARL DESCRIBED as a "friendly get-together" went on un-til sunset, and it might have lasted longer except that the beer and liquor were gone, and most of the food, too. Outside the cabin, the farewells were loud and affectionate.

Pottsy was not navigating at all well, and Pearl insisted that he ride with her on the back of the big flatbed. "The fresh air will do him a world of good."

"But he may fall off," Maude said.

"Not with me hanging on to him he won't," Pearl told her.

"Well, I'm going to ride with the two of you then," Maude said.

"Suit yourself. Rowdy, can you drive that fancy racing car of Gardiner's?"

"Can I ever!" Rowdy said. "You-all just watch my smoke."

Pearl glowered at him. "You so much as put a scratch on that car, I'll tear you in half. We'll meet at my trailer for a nightcap."

"Why don't we go to my house?" Maude asked.

"'Cause I got an extra bedroom, and you don't," Pearl said. "Gardiner's in no condition to drive tonight."

Maude didn't like this. "If you're going to put him up, then I'm going to stay too."

"Stickier than a postage stamp, ain't you?"

They finally managed to help Potts onto the flatbed. Neither woman was particularly steady, but he was almost helpless, a gangly, loosejointed rag doll. He kept insisting to Roy that he would return as quickly as possible, to begin a "definitive photographic and oral history of Sawmill River."

They finally departed. Roy stood by the cabin and watched as the big truck and the sports car successfully forded the little stream—he had filled it in somewhat with rocks so that it could be crossed without four-wheel drive.

Later, as the twilight deepened, he lit the lamps in the cabin, enjoying the silence. He had enjoyed the company, too, and it had been a fine afternoon, but years ago he had learned to make the best of living alone—or at least he had learned to endure it. Loneliness was what ultimately got to him, and he made a sharp distinction between that and the business of merely being by himself.

Now he put some music on the radio, and turned the lamps up brighter. Although he had drunk a lot, he was in an odd fashion virtually sober.

He was disappointed over what Gardiner Potts had revealed. Potts' historical society would never really be of any help. True, the society was clearly Gardiner's passion, but it seemed to Roy that it had only a limited usefulness.

On the table beside the kerosene lamp were the Larson Corporation's letter and contract. Roy glanced through both. The letter was an echo of what Larson himself had said: it recommended that Roy seek legal assistance in analyzing the many merits of the attached contract.

None of it interested him much, and finally he got Rae's letter from its niche—he kept it on the shelf by the radio. He had probably reread it twenty times, but now he took it from its envelope and smoothed it out on the table and stared at it again:

"*I will be leaving here on July 27th, en route to California. I would very much like to see you. . . .*"

He thought again of the summer they'd had together. It had seemed to go on forever, and at the same time it had sped by so quickly. He thought, *maybe that's what love is . . . when a person takes the place of time passing.*

NINE

In a way, Rae herself had said it: "Roy, you've shown me a side of living I never knew about. I'm grateful to you for that."

They had explored the surrounding country and met different people. The old man spun out endless stories in his dry, rasping voice, and she listened. Roy listened, too. At night he and Rae drank wine and beer together, and later, after Walter had been put to bed, made love. Roy would watch her wash in the soft, golden light of the lamp, and then her expression became inward and languorous. Serene, and at the same time lazily mischievous. Arch of back and delicious curve of flank and smooth haunch, breasts swinging a little as she bent, the nipples pointing and hardening in response to a splash of cold, sudsy water. The ridged spine, showing like a small mountain range arcing down to pale goosefleshed buttocks. Her face half hidden in that full cascade of hair. A thin layer of smoke from his cigarette floating in the air, as he lay waiting. The big sponge, loaded with Ivory as she scrubbed her soapy loins. Wet, dripping curls disappearing into a secret shadow, and the stomach, flat and smoothly muscled. Once, noting his obvious enjoyment of the scene, she whacked him square in the face with the sponge.

Lloyd Parmalee and Rowdy Roth not unnaturally thought the world of her. Rowdy especially developed a fearful crush, and made no secret of it. Not five minutes after being introduced, he was trying to convince her that he could teach her to be a champion lady broncbuster. "It sure beats working for a living," he said. "You get to travel all over creation, and after a while you know *everybody.* I don't mind telling you, rodeo folks has tons of fun."

Rae grinned and said, "It sounds like a great life."

"You got the frame for it," Rowdy insisted. "You're kinda nice and wiry. A bronc wouldn't scarcely notice you was in the saddle. Put you in a big cowgirl's hat and one of those fancy shirts with all that nice rhinestone embroidery, why, you'd paralyze 'em."

"I'll keep it in mind," she had said.

Lloyd was quiet with her and seemed suddenly taken by a severe case of shyness. There are still men like that left in the southwest, who in the presence of womanly beauty function as if they had two left feet and ten thumbs instead of fingers. She had shaken hands with him and then said to Roy, "This man has got the most gorgeous blue eyes in the world." Lloyd had come as close to blushing as a man his age could, and looked as though he wished the earth would swallow him up.

"Roy, you better take care. I'm goin' to steal her away from you, first time you turn your back," Rowdy said. "She's the coolest lady this ol' county's seen in a long time." Parmalee seemed more and more embarrassed by Rowdy's open admiration. Rowdy grinned and said, "Lloyd, all you got to do is talk to 'em. I mean, if you don't *talk* to 'em, how else can they figure out that you *like* 'em? Hell, you can't expect a woman to be a mindreader."

Only Pearl continued to act reserved toward Rae. Perhaps it had something to do with the disapproval the old lady had registered over Rae's brief hot-weather costume on that first day they'd met. Or maybe it was only protectiveness toward Roy. Once, when she did have him alone for a moment, she said, "I don't think Rae's a bad gal. Just make sure you ain't heading for a fall."

"Let's see what happens," Roy had told her. "Pearl, right now I'm feeling pretty good."

"I hope it lasts," she said.

A WEEK LATER, Roy almost got into it with Bill Maldonado.

He and Rae were in Carrizozo to shop at the market; Walter had been left with Pearl. They had parked the jeep and were walking down the street when Billy-Evil spotted them. He pulled his pickup truck over to the curb beside them, got out, and leaned indolently against a fender. He stared directly at Rae, and then smiled and said, "Howdy, ma'am."

For a moment she looked at him uncomprehendingly. He went on easily, "You oughtn't be walking on a hot day like this. Want a lift?"

It was Billy-Evil's version of the blunt *macho* approach—a style predicated on the notion that every woman—and particularly a beautiful woman—is simply dying to be picked up, is aching for it. Every female seen as fair game . . . a vulnerable target.

And what better candidate could there be to demonstrate the *machismo* method than a lanky, handsome cowboy-stud wearing an elegant Stetson cocked to one side?

Billy-Evil. With his gentle smile, and those sad Spanish eyes that seemed perpetually fixed on distant, smoky mountains. Unlike Rowdy Roth, whose flirtatiousness was easygoing and up-front, there was a certain seriousness behind Maldonado's laconic approach.

His invitation to Rae was a sort of test, too. Not only of Billy's irresistible charm, but of Roy. Maldonado had pointedly ignored him and stared intently at Rae. In this part of the country it was a way for one man to say to another, "I'm ready for a little fun or trouble. I'll take your woman, just to keep in practice, and to hell with you." It was a challenge that happened all the time.

She handled it coolly. "Thanks, but no thanks."

"This is Billy-Evil Maldonado," Roy said to her. And then: "She's busy, Billy."

"She can speak for herself."

"I'm busy, Billy-Evil," Rae said.

Billy looked her up and down. Finally, he said, with a humorless smile, "Well, I reckon that tells me all I'll ever need to know about you, ma'am." Then, for the first time, he turned to Roy, and said in a flat voice, "There oughta be a law against your kind."

"Don't push it too far, Bill," Roy said.

"Let's go," Rae said; she turned away.

"I heard a rumor that you finally got yourself a woman," Billy-Evil said. "And a white woman, at that. That's what people've been saying. 'Course, I didn't believe it, but now that I've seen it, well . . . now ain't that something?"

Roy moved toward him. "Let's go," Rae said again, grabbing his arm. She was surprisingly strong. They walked off.

But later, on the way back to Honcho, she said, "Roy, for God's sake, what was all that crap about?"

"Bill Maldonado's kind of old-fashioned, that's all," he said.

"Old-fashioned, my ass! And it wasn't just prejudice either," she said. "That man's really got a case against you. I mean, when he looked at you, all I saw was murder." She thought for a moment. "That kind of hatred scares me."

"He's one of those types who brood a lot," Roy told her.

"You can say that again. I mean, Roy, what did you ever *do* to him?"

"I never did anything to him," Roy said. For a while they drove on in silence. Then he said, "Do you really want to know? It didn't exactly have to do with me . . . but in a way it does. It's the kind of thing you shouldn't talk to anybody else about. I've never told anyone."

"I can understand about not talking," Rae said.

"In the early twenties, before I was born, my father and Walter wintered in Capitan," Roy explained. "When I went through my father's papers after Walter and I buried him, I came across a bundle of old letters. Some of them dated back around then, and they were from a girl my father knew, named Cynthia Bachicha. She and my father apparently saw a good deal of each other. He was a quiet man, you know, but Walter always claimed he made out all right. Anyway, in one of the letters, she hinted about being in a family way. Nothing definite, just that she was worried. Well, for years I never gave it a second thought—the name Cynthia Bachicha meant nothing. But then, one time, I happened to be going through the county clerk's books down at the courthouse, looking over marriage licenses—actually, I thought I might come across a license for my father and Minnie Wardner, my mother, though Walter was positive they'd never married—and I came across an entry for a Cynthia Bachicha and Tomaso Maldonado. Rae, she's Billy-Evil's mother. She's still alive, and Billy lives with her."

Rae said, "God, you mean you two are related?"

"It's possible," he said. "Of course, she could have had half a dozen other boyfriends back then. Even so, my father was in the picture." He thought about this. "When my father and mother started going together, Walter said they were the flaming romance of that part of New Mexico, but that isn't important here. What counts is whether Bill Maldonado knows, or suspects, that we might be half-brothers. I've always wondered if his mother or somebody else in the family might have told him something. I don't know of any other reason for him to hate me so. If he *does* know, well, I'd be scared. Around here, something like that's a big taboo."

"Because you're interracial?" she asked.

"Partially that," he said. "But with the Spanish, you leave their women alone. An insult to a wife or a sister can lead to a shooting. I mean that. And an insult to someone's mother, or a question about her morality . . . that could be the last straw for a man like Bill."

"But, Roy, if he's your half-brother, mightn't he have some kind of claim to Sawmill River Flats?"

"I don't see how," Roy said. "My father had all the deeds made out in my name, right from the start. Legally, Bill Maldonado doesn't have a leg to stand on." Roy smiled and shook his head. "Besides, I think he'd rather be shot than actually come out and admit that he might be related to me. To his way of thinking, having Roy Gutierrez for a brother would make him the laughingstock of the county."

"If he had any brains, he'd simply forget the whole thing," Rae pointed out.

"You're wrong. If he suspects, or knows anything, it'd eat at him," Roy said. "That's another part of the Spanish mentality. Property goes to the oldest son. If we both had the same father, and if I own all that land up there, while Billy-Evil's got noth-

ing, not even the Gutierrez name . . . well, he'd be someone to
watch out for."

BY SEPTEMBER OF that year he had begun hoping that she would
stay. The feeling was natural and inevitable. He was happy, and
she acted as though she was, too. They lived lazily, did as they
pleased, and often went a week or more without going down to
civilization. She gained some weight. The hollows in her cheeks
filled out, and, if it was possible, she became more tanned than
ever. Her blond hair bleached in the sun, and at one temple there
was a thick streak of gray.

With Walter, she had a remarkably adept talent for listening
and at the same time a caringness. She was patient, and drew
him out. He liked this. He kept close to her, gimping along in her
steps. Often they sat together in the sun outside the cabin, and
he told his stories, as if secure in some private knowledge that
all this young woman needed in life was the sound of his voice.
If she felt otherwise, it never showed. She seemed drawn to the
old man, and he to her. Toward the end, he permitted her the
worst indignity of all—she would give him an occasional sponge
bath, and Walter would stand there, childlike and grinning owl-
ishly, as she soaped and rinsed his loins and then dried them.
Afterward, she pulled up his jeans and belted them tightly about
his skinny waist. It was also true that by now she knew as much
about the hidden valley and the old town as Roy.

He was never able to decide if their life in the ghost town was
a powerfully engrossing but only temporary experience for her,
or if there was a deeper significance. On one hand, she seemed
to thrive on this outcast, isolated life. Yet he couldn't help asking
himself: how long could a young woman survive this primitive
and lonely existence? Even he could not take it indefinitely.

Roy knew he was in love by then, and there was absolutely
nothing he could do about it. He was a cynic trapped by reality.
Such a condition can be the most blissful of states. Once again,
he was caught in a terrible conflict. The practical side of him
knew it could not last. Yet his romantic nature dreaded the
moment it would all end. There was no answer, of course, and
so he did what experience had taught him was the safest course:

he did not ask or demand anything of her. He seemed willing to leave things as they were, and might be. That was an old expression of his: "Leave it be." And yet, he could not help hoping.

The nights were cold now. The leaves of the aspens had turned red, and then yellow, and had fallen.

Even so, the winter seemed a hundred years off. Together, they enjoyed the last of those long, hot autumn days that are found only in the great southwest. The sky was of such a bright, blinding blue that it hurt the eyes, and the ground seemed so wonderfully solid under Roy's feet that he felt in tune with the entire planet and with life. Once, noting his contented mood, she had said, "You look like you have the whole world in your hip pocket."

He smiled and tried to explain. "The Indians call it 'life feeling.' A kind of pleasure in the awareness of simply being alive . . . sort of like experiencing the universe through all your senses."

She smiled too, and nodded. "I know what you mean."

He went on. "It's as though there's some splendid and majestic scheme to everything, and, somehow, you're in on it. The Navajos and Hopis know a lot about this feeling. They have sacred places where they go to meditate . . . where they can 'feel' the land. That's something almost every white person misses, you know, the absolute beauty of the countryside out here. Really, it can stun the mind." He wanted to explain it better, and shook his head: "You take some tourist. He's driving down I-40, with his mind set on making Flagstaff or Needles before sunset. Well, he wouldn't feel a thing. His wife or kids might say something like 'Hey, look at that big old mesa over there.' In three minutes, it would be out of sight behind them. Gone forever. But sometimes, when a Navajo or a Hopi or an Apache finds a special spot like that, well, he might sit around for a week staring at it and letting all kinds of feelings soak into his mind. This land can just crush the mind. It makes you feel the insignificance of man. There are lots of these sacred places around. They're easy to find, if you aren't in a hurry. A person can't push something like that. I mean, if you start looking at your wristwatch, you might as well forget it."

But just as important was the information Rae was able to extract from Walter. Through her, the old man rounded out the last details of the story . . . of himself, the gunfight, and Sawmill River as it had once been. Some of it Roy had heard, but much of it was new even to him.

This happened one evening in late September. The three of them had taken a walk and were returning to the cabin. Halfway up Main Street they had stopped to rest, sitting on the rotting boardwalk outside the Imperial Hotel, enjoying the last of the twilight. The days were growing short now. They sat with their feet on the boardwalk steps, smoking and talking. Across the way the weathered remains of Rank's Saloon and Montoya's Livery were highlighted by the fading sunset, and farther down the street Schmidt's Mercantile was already in shadow. Behind them gaped the windows and entrance of the hotel. Walter looked around, and then, after a while, said, "It's all gone now, ain't it? Dead and gone."

Before either of them could comment, he went on, almost to himself, "By God, didn't I ever have fun then! On Saturday night I used to run around this here town from one end to the other, drinkin' with the fellers and raisin' sixty different kinds of hell. Sunday was church, but we set Saturday nights aside for the devil. I'd dress up in a clean shirt and trousers an' grease my boots . . . shit, I was ready for anything that come along. Back then there was lights in all the stores an' houses along this street. Rank's had a player piano an' a quartet of four mechanical violins in a glass case—they'd play fancy music if you put in a nickel. At the bar, men were lined up three deep. Cowboys from the ranches, and loggers, and sawmill workers. In the evening, families would promenade up and down the boardwalk in their best clothes. There was talk of puttin' in a gaslight system with regular street lamps. The Masonic Lodge had organized a fire brigade. This hotel would be booked full, and there would be so many carriages and horses over at Jim Montoya's that he had to stake 'em out on the slopes. On Saturday afternoons there'd be a line of fifty or more fellers waiting outside the German's barber shop for a shave and a bath. He had hot towels and real eau de cologne. They'd come outa his place with faces like scalded beets, all shiny an' clean. In the evenings, there was dances up by the sawmill. There was a big platform for folks to dance on, and a six-piece brass band that wasn't much on style, but let me tell you,

when those players swung into a good waltz you could hear
music from one end of this valley to the other. We lived a good
life. Three or four times every summer the whole town'd throw
a picnic, an' there was all kinds of races and games for the kids
to play. Oh, it was fine."

"Were you cowboying back then, Uncle Walter?" Rae asked.

"I broke horses," Walter said. "Then I went in the Army for
a couple of years. I wanted to see the world, an' I was tired of
cowpunchin', an' ridin' fence in the dead of winter, an' blizzards,
an' starvation wages, so I joined up. They sent me to a remount
outfit at Fort Sill, Oklahoma. We was breakin' horses for cavalry
outfits. There was about twenty of us in this remount outfit, all
young fellers like me, who'd growed up in the saddle. That's
where I got hurt. I was workin' this big chestnut gelding in the
corral. He got me up against the side of a shed an' pinned me
there for quite a spell. They thought I'd never walk again, 'cause
my hip was broke, an' part of my backbone, too. I wore a corset
for years. It was made outa canvas, with buckles an' leather
straps. That goddamned corset hurt worse'n not wearin' anything
at all. They gave me a medical discharge, only I lost it. Else I'd'a
had myself an Army pension. So, I come back here, an' ended
up workin' for Herman an' Bertha. I couldn't ride no more or
even walk much, but I was okay, except when it rained or
snowed . . . then the damp gave me hell. I lived on patent medicine and aspirin for years. That's what ruined my guts."

He paused for a moment. Rae said, "What about the gunfight?
What started it?"

The old man's expression changed as he considered this—grief,
anger, and, finally, a bitter disgust. He said, "Jealousy . . . ain't
that always the way it is?"

"Ephraim?"

"Who else? He shot Perry Tidwell. The Tidwell boys' spread
was right alongside Ephraim's ranch."

"Was it over Bertha?" Rae asked.

Walter's expression grew bitterer. "Everybody had his own
story. The way Ephraim told it, Perry made a bad remark about
Bertha. Both men were drinking, right over there in Rank's, and
Perry said something, and Eph took out his pistol and shot him.
He oughtn't have done that. Tidwell was unarmed. That made it

murder. Worse, Perry's two brothers were known to be bad-tempered."

"Then Ephraim really had a violent side?" Rae asked.

"No. I wouldn't say that. He was actually kinda mild-natured. In those days no man drew a weapon less'n he was sure he could get away with it . . . or unless he didn't give a rat's ass. I'd judge the latter applied to Eph."

"In what way?"

"He just got so jealous-sick when Bertha married Herman. It's a wonder he never fired a slug into Herman, who was his best friend. Herman meant no harm . . . he was as wild about Bertha as Eph was."

"What happened after Tidwell was shot?"

"Oh, Ephraim walked out of the bar and got on his horse an' rode off. No one wanted to trifle with him. It was then that everybody started callin' him a gunslinger."

"But he wasn't, not really, from the way you tell it."

Walter looked disgusted. " 'Course not! He was just an ol' ranch boy. I could make a pig dance faster'n Eph Munger could draw an' shoot! He had to hold that pistol out at arm's length an' aim. That made it deliberate murder, with a dozen witnesses."

"What happened then?"

"He went into hidin'," Walter said. "The Tidwell boys swore they'd get him, and, of course, he was what lawmen in those times called bounty meat—there was a hundred-dollar reward on him. Bounty meat was someone a deputy might bushwhack. Easier, y'know, to bring in a body than to have a trial. Eph hid out with the Mescaleros, but from time to time he would sneak back to see us. He told Bertha, 'I ain't goin' to be hung, an' I ain't goin' to jail.' He was real good at evadin' the law, 'cause he knew how to stay off by himself for long spells. The only dangerous thing he did was come in to the Imperial. Then he disappeared for years, and he didn't come back till nineteen-ought-seven." The old man considered this, and then asked Rae for a smoke. She gave him one, and he went on, with growing emotion, "That was when I informed on him. My own friend."

"You didn't really do that, Walter," Rae said.

"It's true," he said. For a moment, he seemed unable to talk anymore. Then he went on, "The town was dead an' gone by

then. He was hidin' out in an abandoned cabin south of here a
few miles, but he'd come up most every night to take supper with
us in back of the hotel. That was queer, y'know . . . it was like
he'd never gone away at all. It was like old times, only none of
us was young anymore. We'd all sit at the kitchen table with a
bottle of rye, and Eph would tell us about his adventures an'
where he'd been. He went all the way to the Klondike, but he
never had no kind of luck. He looked like a worn-out ol' man.
Years had passed, but even so he was takin' an awful chance
comin' back like that. That's why he hid out in the cabin. The
Tidwell brothers—Ben an' Harry—they was well up in years, too,
but they'd always swore they'd do for Eph."

Roy interrupted: "Walter, how did Ephraim and Pa get along?"

"Just fine," the old man said. "Georgie was about thirteen then,
all crippled up. He was fascinated by Eph. It ain't every day
you git an ol'-time outlaw sittin' down to dinner with you. Nobody carried a gun anymore, but there was Eph with that long-
barreled Colt strapped to his hip under his coat. He'd make small
talk with Georgie and Georgie'd answer back with a little note-
pad and pencil . . . that was the only way he could talk. 'Course,
he could talk with Bertha—they'd worked out a kinda sign language that nobody but them could savvy."

The old man paused again. He seemed torn by a need to tell
more and at the same time avoid a hated subject. He continued,
"It was me who talked . . . and it wasn't that I did it once. I
talked twice. One day I was havin' a few over at Rank's—the
saloon an' the hotel was the only two businesses still open—an'
somehow, I can't even remember it, I musta let slip that Eph
was back. Word got to the Tidwells. Until then all that was
known was that some saddle-tramp was squattin' in that abandoned cabin. Nobody knew it was Eph. They got their ranch
foreman, Bonafacio Sanchez, an' went to the cabin, armed, only
by coincidence Eph had been stayin' here at the hotel for the
past two days, in an upstairs room. So, when they didn't find him
they come into town. It was evenin' by then, and they found me
at Rank's. They wasn't about to be put off. They dragged me out
the back door, the three of 'em, and held me down on the
ground an' demanded Eph's whereabouts. I was mad by then, an'
I cussed 'em out good, 'cause they was treatin' me hard. Then

Bonafacio hauled down my britches and got out his clasp knife an' said he'd geld me if I didn't tell. An' he started to do just that."

Rae said, "Oh, my God."

"He grabbed holt of my balls, an' I felt the edge of that knife cuttin' into the sack. Well, I'd gelded a thousand colts in my time. I knew what a terrible mess it was, rootin' around inside the sack wrist-deep, lookin' for the cord, y'know, 'cause if you don't get the cord the animal has trouble an' can git infected. I reckon something inside me just died. I couldn't take it. I said, 'God Almighty, fellers, don't do it . . . he's over at the hotel.' One of 'em hit me on the jaw, and they left me lyin' in the mud of that alleyway. I found out later that they'd gone back into the bar and had seven or eight whiskies apiece to fortify themselves. They knew Eph was no one to go up against. Say, girl, can I have another cigarette?"

Rae gave him one, and he went on, "I musta laid out there pretty near half an hour before I come to, with my britches around my ankles. I hurt something awful down there, an' for a minute I thought they'd done for me . . . but I felt myself, an' everything was still there, just sore. I pulled my britches up an' went into the bar, holdin' 'em with both hands. They'd just walked out the front door. It'd started to rain."

Walter paused, and then went on haltingly. "They was walkin' across the street, headin' right here, where we're sittin'. I run after 'em, only I slipped an' fell in a pool of muddy water. The big glass windows of the hotel was all lit up. You could see into the lobby. I was yellin', to warn Eph. The Tidwells an' Sanchez turned an' looked at me. Then all three of 'em grinned at one another. I musta looked a sight, all covered with mud an' holdin' my britches up. Bonafacio had a double-barrel shotgun under his rain slicker. I could see the barrels stickin' out. For a second, I was scared he'd let off a charge in my direction. But they didn't care about me. It was Eph they wanted. I was yellin', 'Eph, for God's sake, watch out!' Only he come walkin' out the open doors of the hotel, onto the boardwalk . . . right here . . ." Walter pointed to a spot, a few feet away. "That meant he didn't care no more whether he was seen. He was hatless. He said, 'Fellers, I'm not out for trouble.' I saw Ben Tidwell draw his pistol. His

shot missed Eph by a mile but it took out one of the big windows.
I heard Bertha screamin' from somewhere inside, an' then I saw
young Georgie skedaddlin' across the lobby as fast as he could,
draggin' his game leg, tryin' to git outa the line of fire. Bonafacio's
shotgun went off like thunder. The charge blew away a goodly
part of Eph's left shoulder an' staggered him bad, but he managed to draw an' aim. Like I said, he was never fast. He just took
all the time he needed. He shot Ben Tidwell in the bridge of the
nose. Killed him on the spot. Harry Tidwell was firin' by then.
Harry couldn't hit a bull in the ass with a handful of rice, but
one slug, as like as not by accident, caught Eph in the stomach.
Even so, Eph managed to fire one more time, and killed Harry.
Bonafacio was takin' careful aim with the shotgun—he still had
one charge left—an' there was another blast. He went down, too."
Walter was silent for another moment; then he spoke again.
"That's how it ended. Eph died less'n twenty minutes later. All
four men lyin' in the mud an' water, and the rain pourin' down.
And Georgie, in there somewhere, hollerin' for Bertha. An'
poor, fat ol' Herman . . . drunk as a coot, standin' in the open
window of his room up above with a Winchester lever-action. It
was him who got Bonafacio."

"Herman?" Rae looked at the old man with amazement. "He
sided with Ephraim?"

"Eph was his friend," Walter said. "He an' Eph an' Bertha had
grown up together."

"But I would have thought . . ." Rae was still astonished. "But
didn't he know about Ephraim and Bertha?"

"He knew."

"And he still took Ephraim's side?"

"Herman Gutierrez was as straight as a die," Walter said.

"And that's how it ended?"

The old man thought about this. "There was one thing more.
Two years later, when Herman was dyin' with heart trouble, we
was sittin' by his bedside. He said to Bertha, 'I'm sorry about
Georgie. I oughta listened to you about them pigs.' She didn't
have anything to say to that. He said, 'I tried to make it up when
Eph come back.'"

"What did she say then?" Rae asked.

Walter frowned. Finally, he shook his head. "I don't recollect that she said anythin'. I think she just sorta sat there, starin' at him."

"And she died the year after Herman?"

Walter nodded. "That's when she asked me to look after Georgie. An' I did. An' I took good care of Roy, too." He finished what was left of his cigarette. "Seems to me I took care of everybody most of my life . . . but I don't know as anybody ever looked out for me much."

IN THE WEEKS that followed it turned cold, and they spent more time in the cabin. Walter had little more to add to the story . . . his thoughts grew increasingly fragmented, random. His body, if possible, seemed to grow more shrunken, and it was clear that he was failing.

Once, he said, to Rae, "D'you reckon there's a heaven, the way folks claim?"

"I don't know, Walter," she said. "What do you think?"

"It sure would be a surprise if'n there was," he said. "Wouldn't that be somethin'? To see Georgie again . . ."

"Maybe there's something to it," Roy agreed.

"I don't mean the kinda heaven they push at kids in bible class," Walter went on. "Where everybody moseys around on clouds, wearin' white nightshirts an' playin' harps. I wouldn't care for that sorta bullshit."

"Neither would I," Rae said.

"I don't believe there could be a heaven like that," Walter said. "You know why?"

"Why?"

"Ain't nowhere to piss."

"What?"

"The only recourse open to them folks would be to piss off'n the side of a cloud when they had to go. An' they'd have to get mighty close to the edge, 'cause the feller next in line might be barefoot. In all them bible pictures of folks standin' around on clouds, I never saw one outhouse or *excusado* for gents or ladies. Have you?"

"They mightn't ever have to go," Roy said. "Maybe in the afterlife, bothersome things like that don't exist."

Walter thought this over for a minute, frowning. Finally he shook his head and said, "Nope. That don't make no sense. If they never have to go, that means they don't never eat or drink."

"That might be."

"Well, what the goddamn hell kinda heaven is that supposed to be?" he demanded. "Where you never get nothin' to eat or drink? Shit, that ain't no fun."

"Maybe if they're ghosts or disembodied spirits, they don't get hungry," Roy said. "It might work that way."

"If'n I was a ghost I'd sure git hungry, all right," Walter said. "Once in a while I'd like a cup of coffee or a bowl of beans, or some nice barbecued spareribs. An' I wouldn't want no disembodied or ghostly spareribs either . . . I'd want the real McCoy, somethin' I could sink my teeth into, even if I ain't got none."

Rae sat down beside him. "Walter, baby, what would you like, really? I mean, for a hereafter?"

Those rheumy, glazed lizard eyes with their hooded lids stared at her. "Just nothin'," he murmured. "I'm ready for my quiet time. Damn it, I deserve it."

He looked down into his lap for a moment, and then he said, "I'm tired. Can I have some wine? I wanta lie down. Bring me wine."

They put him to bed. Before he fell asleep he drank a glass of red wine and smoked a cigarette, with the two of them sitting on the edge of his bed until he had finished. They were both careful about not letting him smoke alone. The last thing he said was, "Tuck me in, Roy. I'm cold."

THAT NIGHT IT snowed heavily, and the temperature went down to the lower teens. Once Roy got up, slipped on his boots and a jacket, got a flashlight, and made a trip to the outhouse.

The snow had almost stopped by then. On the way back to the cabin there was no breeze, just a few flakes silently drifting down, lit whitely by the lancing beam of the flashlight. Back inside, he stoked the sheepherder with billets of wood and then returned to bed.

He and Rae slept late, until almost nine. When he got up to

put on a pot of water, he saw that Walter was gone. He said, "Oh, my God."

Rae sat up in bed, half asleep: "What is it?"

"He's not here."

"What?"

"Walt's gone."

Outside, in the fall of fresh snow, they saw his prints, barefoot, leading away from the cabin. A single set going away, and none coming back. In the cabin they found a half-gallon bottle of wine that was almost empty. They dressed quickly. Roy said, "He must have gotten up in the night, drank some wine, and then wandered off. Rae, you better wait here."

She knew what was in his mind. For a moment she stared at him, and then she said, "No. I want to come."

They put on their jackets and went out. Roy said, "I got up during the night. I should have checked on him."

"Roy, stop thinking like that."

"He can't have gone far."

The tracks were easy to follow. If Walter had gone out earlier, when it was still snowing hard, they would not have found him until spring. Rae said, "Why would he take off like that?"

"No telling. He might have started for the outhouse and gotten confused and walked off in the wrong direction. He might have had a dream, or his mind might have been somewhere, eighty or ninety years ago. I don't know."

After that they didn't talk for a while. It was cold, and very quiet. They could see where he had fallen in the snow every so often. As old and weak as he was, he'd kept going.

They were on the high, timbered slopes now, far above the town. Roy was puffing, and Rae was out of breath, too. And still the tracks went on, over rotted deadfalls and through thickets of aspen.

The morning was bright and clear, and there were no sounds at all except for the noise they made walking. The boughs of the tall pines were loaded with the fall of snow, and from time to time, in the warmth of the morning sun, one of the boughs would shed itself of the load it had been carrying and bounce upward like a spring that had been released. Somewhere, in the deepest

part of the woods, a couple of crows called back and forth. Rae
said, "What could have made him come up here?"

"I don't know."

They kept on. They were very high now, and it was cold, and
the big snow-laden pines towered around them. Roy said, "You
better go back to the cabin."

"No."

"Rae, I don't think he'll be alive."

"I want to stay with you."

The tracks ended by a rocky outcropping, a promontory of
gray, eroded granite. There had been wind up here, so that the
ground was either bare or else, in the hollows, the snow had
drifted deep. In a few places they lost the tracks altogether but
were able to find them again, farther on.

Walter had gotten all the way up to a little razorback ridge,
and there, as if aware for the first time of where he was, had
crawled into a kind of shallow alcove that was half-filled with
drifting snow. There were animal tracks. Roy said, "You better
wait here," but she shook her head.

One of the old man's hands reached up out of the drift. The
sleeve of the heavy blue sweater they had dressed him in for bed
was visible, and both knees, bent sharply, in his striped cotton
pajamas.

Roy knelt and began brushing away the snow; she helped.

They could see that he was lying on his back. Roy said, "God
damn you. You goddamned old fool. Why didn't you stay put?"
He began to weep. "If you'd just stayed put, things would have
been all right."

The old man had died in a curious position. Almost a boxer's
crouch, with both arms raised, the hands clenched into fists, chin
tucked protectively into the right collarbone. Roy carefully
brushed more snow away. Some small animals had already been
at him, perhaps a fox or a raccoon . . . part of the left ear and
cheek were gone. Roy tried to move the body. It was stiff. Up
here with the wind, it had been much colder. The upraised arms
were frozen solid. His back was frozen to the rock so that Roy
couldn't break him loose . . . then, finally, he did come away
with a small crackling sound. Roy sat there for a minute, resting,

and then he said, "If I'd left him at El Mirador this wouldn't have happened."

"Roy, stop it."

"It's true."

She was weeping, too. They stayed there like that for some time, and then Roy finally stood up. "We better get back. It's a long way."

He put Walter across his shoulder. The old man seemed to weigh no more than a chunk of firewood. His legs faced front, and the thin, bare feet were a whitish-gray.

It took a while for them to get to the cabin. They put Walter in his bed and drew a blanket over his face. Roy said he needed a drink, and she got some wine and glasses, and they sat at the table, drinking and smoking. Finally, Rae said, "Are you going to bury him in the cemetery?"

"Yes. I'll dig the grave later."

"Where?"

"Alongside my father."

Rae nodded. She knew where George Gutierrez's grave was. She and Roy had walked through the cemetery a number of times. She said, "I think that's the right thing to do."

"The two of them belong together."

She nodded again; then she said, "Roy, shouldn't we notify the sheriff or somebody?"

"No."

"Isn't it the law?"

"I'm not notifying anybody."

"But there has to be a death certificate."

"The hell with it," Roy said. "I'm not going to have an autopsy done on him, not for the sake of satisfying some damned medical or governmental statistic that nobody is ever going to look at. It's going to be a ranch burial." He looked at her. "You don't know what that means. In this country, years ago, when a person died, his family took care of burying him. No funeral home, or anything like that. They buried him and asked his friends to be present, that was all. It was a very private thing. That's how I want to do it. I don't care about death certificates, Rae. As far as I'm concerned, he died of exposure and old age."

And that was his mood when they had the funeral the next day. It took Roy most of the rest of that afternoon to dig the grave and nail a crude coffin together out of pine planks he and Rae found in a scrap heap in back of the Imperial Hotel. The planks were almost a century old and they had cured to an iron hardness, so that they were difficult to saw. The ground in the cemetery was rocky and half-frozen. When Roy swung the pick, sparks flew from the flinty rubble. It was like the town didn't want to take the old man back.

THEY ASKED LLOYD Parmalee and Rowdy and Pearl, who drove up in Lloyd's big tandem-wheel flatbed. All of them put the coffin on that and brought it to the cemetery. When the box was lowered into the grave, Pearl Lowdermilk began weeping. Rae was dry-eyed, but she looked terribly pale and drawn.

For the eulogy, Roy spoke a few words: "This old man is Walter Gordon Kelly, a cowboy and a soldier, and a citizen of the Territory of New Mexico. He did his best to take care of those he loved, and who loved him." Then he read a passage from Bertha Gutierrez's old diary. She had kept her entries in one of the hotel's ledgers, not on a daily basis but from time to time, as the mood took her—sometimes there would be a gap of months, and then there would be pages of her thoughts. It was in this ledger that Roy had once found a lock of his father's whitish-blond hair, folded in tissue paper, on which was inscribed: "G. Gutierrez, his hair, age 1." The passage Roy had chosen to read was brief:

August 16th, 1890. Today, Walter won six of the eight horse races at the Jenkins ranch, and we were there to see him. It is an annual affair, and everybody comes from miles around. Walter looked so splendid when he accepted the grand purse. It was a hundred dollars. Everyone said he is the best rider in New Mexico. All the young girls think he would be a catch. Though not tall, he is very handsome and dashing, with thick, black hair and a ready smile, and the merriest eyes.

Lloyd Parmalee stood there with his head bowed.

And Rowdy Roth. Dressed in black Levi's, black highheeled boots, and a leather jacket. Even without the front teeth he looked as much like William Antrim Bonney as Central Casting could have made him. Black Stetson held in one hand, his head bared to the fine drizzle that had started to come down. Eyes straight ahead as he sang in a fine, clear baritone the old prayer-poem, "*Shema Yisrael Adonoi Eh'oth . . .*" "Hear, O Israel, the Lord is our God . . . "

Lloyd had brought extra shovels. The three men began. The box resounded hollowly against the first spadefuls. And then that sound died away and there was just the sound of shoveling.

In the cabin afterward they had a wake with cheese, posole, tortillas, enchiladas, bourbon, wine, and beer. Rae had been up since dawn cooking an enormous pot of spaghetti sauce on the primitive sheepherder stove, and now Pearl was helping her make sandwiches. The cabin grew warm with so many people in it, and Roy opened the door. There was a lot of conversation but it was somehow strained, as if the air had to be filled with words. Everybody helped themselves to paper plates which were heaped with food. They were drinking fast, too.

Pearl was in agreement with Rae about the legalities of a funeral. "Roy, you ought to have notified the county coroner at least," she said. "I mean, that old man ain't officially dead until it's entered in the records."

"No coroner is going to make Walter any deader than he is," Roy said stubbornly. "He's gone, Pearl. That's all."

"But supposing he had heirs someplace?" she insisted.

"He didn't have anybody except me."

"He might have left an insurance policy or something."

"He never had anything like that," Roy said. "I've known everything he owned, for the last forty years. He was just an old man who needed a place to sleep, a few clothes to keep him warm, and some tobacco and liquor."

"It's a shame he didn't make more of his life."

"Well, Pearl, he stayed alive for longer than anybody I've ever known," Roy said. "That ought to count for something."

"But he wasn't doing the Lord's work."

"Just keeping alive was a full-time job for Walter," Roy said. "When he got done with that he probably didn't have any energy left for a sideline. You want to remember, he had no education or skills. He was just a broncbuster and a cowboy. When he got crippled, he couldn't even do that."

"He had a wicked thirst," she said.

"Back then, most people drank a lot," Roy pointed out. "Today, they use grass and coke to make life tolerable. Yes, he was a drunk."

"Well, I hope he's happy."

"I wouldn't know about that, Pearl."

Lloyd and Rowdy were sitting with Rae at the table. Rowdy was drinking straight bourbon and telling Rae how he'd almost hit top prize money at the Calgary Stampede two years earlier, until a big faun-colored Brahma named Deathwish got him down and did a flamenco dance on the small of his back for twenty seconds. "The booger played real music on my vertebraes with his hooves, like they was a marimba," Rowdy told her proudly. "I still got the hoofprints, if you wanta see 'em. The clowns, after they'd pried me out of the dirt, claimed I could always hire out as a doormat when I got enough of rodeoing. You'd make a real good cowgirl. I could teach you easy."

Rae was still looking pale and distraught. She tried to smile, and then shook her head and said, "I'm sorry, Rowdy, what were you saying? I wasn't listening."

Pearl had a whiskey-and-water in one hand and a third plate-ful of Rae's spaghetti in the other. She said, "I need a little something for my stomach. Funerals always do that to a person. Folks don't realize how chopped up they get at an interment. Eating gives 'em something to concentrate on. When my Ben died, the Ladies Auxiliary and I barbecued a whole calf. Seventy people came. We had three barrels of beer, and I baked I don't know how many pies . . . apple, peach, and lemon meringue. Everybody said it was the best funeral they'd been to in ages. Helen Zumwalt and Maudie Dalrymple said they was glad funerals like Ben's didn't come along every day 'cause their girdles wasn't built to stand the strain."

There was the sound of a car pulling up outside the open door. Roy went to see. A woman was getting out of a gray jeep that had a New Mexico State Health Department emblem painted on the doors. Pearl came to the door with her glass, and looked past Roy. "Oh, for God's sake, if it ain't old lard-ass herself."

Maude came toward them. She said, "Roy Aldous Gutierrez, I been looking for you. Pearl, what in heaven's name are you doing way up here?"

"We're having us a wake," Pearl said. "Come on in."

"I heard there'd been a death," Maude said. "That's why I'm here. Where is the late deceased? Not in that cabin, I hope."

"We buried it," Pearl said.

"That's a criminal offense. What'd it die of?" Maudie said. She came inside.

"It died of living too long," Pearl told her. "It was Roy's Uncle Walter."

"Where'd you hear that Walter died?" Roy asked.

"Word gets around," Maude said. She introduced herself to Rae, and then took off her jacket and touched her blond curls. "We'll have to dig him up and do it over proper, Roy."

"We're not digging anybody up," Roy said.

"I can quote you the official state statutes on home burial," Maude insisted. "You have to have a death certificate signed by a doctor or the coroner, and the remains ought to be processed by a mortician." She poured herself a double hooker and eyed the food that had been set out. "There hasn't even been a death announcement in the newspaper. You can't do things like that."

"Well, I did," Roy said.

"Roy, don't get uppity with me," Maude told him. "I know my job."

"Nobody's digging up anybody," Roy said again. He was a little drunk by now. "You don't know where we buried him. Nobody here'll tell you."

"Then they're associates before, during, and after the fact," Maude said.

Pearl said, "Maudie, whyn't you dive into that food over there. Maybe that'll keep your big trap occupied for a spell."

"My, that's dandy-looking spaghetti."

"Get yourself a wheelbarrowful."

Roy had wandered off by himself for a moment, and was sitting on the bunk bed. Suddenly, he was weeping.

Rae came to him. He leaned his head against her shoulder. "There's too many people in here. Get me outside. I think I'm dying." He wept harder.

She and Lloyd each got an arm around him and led him toward the door. As they walked outside, Maude said, "What's the matter with him. Why's he carrying on so?"

"Can't you see he's doing his grieving?" Pearl said. "You old walrus! He's grieving for that no-good Walter Kelly. Now, leave him be. Let him unload it. He'll be all right by and by." But by then she had begun weeping, too.

A WEEK LATER, Rae made up her mind to leave. She had not wept anymore in that time but it was clear that she needed to be by herself—she would go off walking for an entire morning or afternoon. Roy could see that she wanted to think, and he left her alone. In the cabin at mealtimes there was almost no conversation at all. Then one evening after dinner, when they were sitting at the table smoking, she said it simply: "Roy, I'm going."

In a way, it was no surprise. He had sensed that she'd been fighting to resolve something. Even so, her announcement hit him hard. For a moment he didn't say anything, and then he nodded. "You have to do what you want, Rae. But can you tell me why?"

"It's too difficult to explain."

"You haven't been happy?"

She stared at him and shook her head. "You know better than that."

"Then why go?" When she did not reply, he said, "It was Walter, wasn't it? And me?"

"Yes."

"I knew his dying really hit you."

She said, "Yes, but there's more to it. You and I—I mean, what we've had here together." Suddenly, she was close to tears. "I broke my own rules about not getting involved. Oh, Roy . . ."

"When we first met you said no strings," he pointed out. "Haven't I tried to keep it that way?"

"Yes." She bit at her lower lip, thinking about this. "You've been good. You've given me a lot. Not just good times, or seeing a whole different way of life." She thought some more. "What I'm afraid of is that if I don't go now, then I may never."

He lit another cigarette and finally said, "All right. When do you want to leave?"

"Quickly. Tomorrow?"

He nodded, and drank some coffee, thinking, *Walter is dead, and it's my fault. And now this. There'll be no one left.* Aloud, he said, "Well, it's understandable. No woman can be expected to want to live a life like this, not on a long-term basis."

But he was thinking, *you knew it couldn't last. And now it's happened. Even Pearl said it wouldn't last.*

Rae was staring at him again. "What I've had isn't such a bad life for a woman."

He shrugged. "I don't know anything at all about you, except that I've been happy with you. And I never asked . . . not once. I figured if you wanted to talk about yourself you would, when you felt like it."

"You must have wondered."

Roy considered this. Then he said, "We've lived together for almost four months. In all that time, you've never made a telephone call. You've never written a single letter. And you've never talked about your past. I mean, people, friends, family, whatever. You've talked about going to college, and working at jobs and traveling around the country, but not about people. I never pried because I knew that was the way you wanted to keep it. However . . . I've wondered. I guess that's natural."

She nodded. "You find a woman in a gas station. She moves in with you for months, and then all of a sudden she goes away. What kind of woman is that? Roy, I don't want to hurt you! Now is when you need someone, and here I am hurting you more, but I've got to leave. Please don't hate me for being what I am."

"Rae, I could never hate you. You know that."

She wept a little then, shook her head, almost angrily, and said again, more to herself than to him, "What sort of woman is that?"

"I kind of understand," he said. Presently, he continued, "Here's what I think. Years ago, there were men people referred to as drifters. They weren't bums . . . I don't mean that. A drifter was just a man who couldn't stay put in one place for long. In this part of the country, a drifter would move from one town or ranch to another. He'd work as a cowboy or a farmhand or on a railroad gang . . . anything to make wages. My father was a drifter, and so was Uncle Walter. There's a lot of it in me, too." He lit another cigarette. "These days, the way life is, there are women who are drifters, too. That's what I think you are. They go along in life, trying one thing or another, living different lifestyles, maybe with men, maybe not. So, they'll stay a while but when it's time to move on, they leave. Maybe they're sad to have to go, but a part of them has to be free . . . it can't be tied down." He stared at her thoughtfully. "I'd say this, Rae . . . I'd do just about anything in the world to have you stay. But there's nothing I can do. I know that." He paused. "I understand. And I'll miss you."

"I'll miss you, too," she said.

He knew he could not talk any longer without breaking down. He said, "Whenever you're ready, we'll drive down to Capitan, to the bus depot."

Rae looked wretched. She said she would go on up to Albuquerque—the destination she had mentioned months earlier. He offered her traveling money, but she wouldn't take it. They talked little more for the rest of that evening.

The next morning, she packed. They both tried to put on a superficial air of cheerfulness. She said she would write, but he knew she wouldn't. Then she was ready, and they left the cabin.

When the bus rolled in she kissed him once and got on while the driver stored her suitcases in the luggage compartment. Roy stood there in the street for a moment, staring up at the windows, but they were made of dark green tinted glass; no passenger inside was visible. In a few minutes the bus left. A cold wind whipped clouds of dust and a few dead leaves along the street, and Roy went into the Smokey Bear Saloon and drank there for the rest of the day.

Five days later, he knew he could no longer take the life at the cabin. The memories of that long, lazy summer with Walter and Rae were too strong. The only chore he had done during this time was to cast a concrete slab for Walter's grave, and when he had made this he knew he'd have to leave or go crazy. The door of the cabin on the slope above the sawmill was padlocked, and Roy got into the jeep and drove away.

That was when he swore he'd never return.

But of course he had.

For almost three years—first in Mexico, then El Paso—he had been convinced he would never hear from her again. Part of him ached to hear some word, but his practical side told him he was a fool to think such thoughts. This side of him was so absolutely sure that he had never bothered to leave a forwarding address with Pearl Lowdermilk.

But now this: her short, handwritten note.

He would never have believed himself capable of such a powerful rush of feeling. In a few days, she would return.

All that night he thought about having her back, and how it might be for the two of them. The next morning, over coffee, he was still thinking about this, and feeling good.

Then he heard a noise—a faint tapping, far off. He got up and went outside, listening. The sound stopped. Presently, it began again.

It was coming from somewhere in the village—the sound of hammering.

TEN

He drove down, and there, on Main Street, recognized Bill Maldonado's pickup parked in front of Rank's Saloon. Maldonado and a sidekick of his named Jerry Oñate were working on the facade of the saloon with claw hammers and a long prybar. They were taking out lengths of weathered planking. A stack of it was piled on the boardwalk.

Roy got out of the jeep and went up to them. "Billy, what are you up to?"

Maldonado was smiling at him. "*Qué tal*, Roy?"

"*Qué quieres aquí?*" What do you want here?

"We're salvagin' us some wood," Billy-Evil said. He was still smiling sociably. Although it was early in the day, both he and Oñate looked like they'd been doing a little drinking.

Roy said, "What for, Bill?"

"To sell it."

"Who'd want that old wood?"

"Why, you know that fancy new art gallery, over in Ruidoso? They got those oil paintings in the window?"

"Yes."

"They make custom picture frames."

"You mean they want wood like that, to make frames?" Roy said.

"*Sí*. Rich *puta* owns that place," Maldonado said. "She said she'd pay us two hundred dollars a pickup load, for nice weathered wood. Ain't that something? Started talking to us. Wanted to know if we knew where any busted-down ol' barns or sheds was. Didn't want regular new lumber."

Roy was beginning to get mad, but he tried to keep his voice level: "Seems like everything these days has value."

"We contracted to bring in four loads," Billy-Evil said.

"Whyn't you go someplace else? And *pronto*."

"Best place in the whole county, right here," Billy said. He looked around. "Got enough of that antique wood here to make lots of frames."

"Bill, this is private property," Roy said. "You've got better sense than that. You're trespassing."

Maldonado did not reply but those sad eyes of his began to look moody and sullen. Roy went on, "Also, you're destroying property I happen to place value on. You don't just walk onto a man's land and start ripping everything up. That's *loco*."

"You're the one who's crazy-*loco*," Maldonado said. "*Cabrón*, you been *loco* your whole damn life."

"That might be," Roy said. "But you're still on my land." A hot, slow burn was beginning to eat at him. He was in fact furious, and he could feel it from the way his heart and lungs were racing. It had been so long since he had lost his temper that the sensation was strange—almost alarming. Picture frames, of antique, weathered wood. Suddenly, it was like everybody wanted a piece of the old town. Larson's Corporation in New York, Gardiner Potts, and now this. Maldonado. Pushing his luck again, trying to see just how far he could go and still get away with it. Roy said coldly, "Get out of here. Right now. You and Oñate."

Maldonado came down the steps of the boardwalk and walked up to Roy. Billy-Evil was no small man—he stood well over six feet—but alongside Roy he looked short. He said, "We want to, we'll tear this whole damn place down."

"Leave my town alone," Roy said. By now he had trouble getting the words out.

"Fuck you."

A tremendous indignation suddenly gripped Roy. What good was talk with a man like Maldonado? How could one reason with such a person? Even being on the right side of the law counted for nothing.

Roy had no idea of what his father might have done—that foot-loose man, who never in his entire life had raised a hand in violence. What Roy did next was purely instinctual.

He swung once from the hip. The blow was awkward, grace-less—utterly without style. The clumsiest child could have avoided it by simply ducking. What it had going for it was surprise. It certainly astonished Maldonado . . . and Roy, too, for that matter.

It had something else going for it—a certain authority that could not be denied. Roy was a very big man. The fist that caught Maldonado flush on the cheek was, in a word, gigantic.

He went down as though poleaxed, and did not move. For a moment, Roy stared at his clenched right hand. Then, without thinking, he stepped toward Jerry Oñate. Oñate dropped the carpenter's hammer he had been holding, and cried, "Don't hit me!" He dashed around to the far side of Billy-Evil's pickup, putting it between himself and Roy, and said earnestly, "It was Billy's idea, not mine."

Roy looked down at Bill Maldonado lying in the dust of the street. For a moment he felt an awful rush of dread, thinking that Maldonado was dead. His grandfather, Tom Wardner, the black horse-soldier, was reputed to have done that once—killed a man with a single blow—but then he saw Maldonado's chest rising and falling.

"Get him out of here," Roy told Oñate. "Both of you, clear out."

Oñate seemed to have no objection to leaving. In fact, he acted as though he was in a hurry. Roy helped him load his friend into the back of the pickup. Just before Oñate drove off, Roy told him, "Stay off this property. I mean it."

Roy was more upset over what had happened then he first realized. Back at the cabin, he tried to calm down but he was filled with a nervous restlessness that left him moody and troubled.

Finally, he drove down to Pearl's. He felt a great need to talk to someone. Maybe she could help.

But for a while she was too full of her own news to listen. "That Gardiner Potts didn't leave until this morning. We had the grandest time, except for Maudie—couldn't get rid of her for five minutes. We all sat around here and ate and drank, and talked our fool heads off into that recorder of his about old times, and then we sang songs. He's promised to come back down in a month and spend a whole week here with me." She smiled maliciously. "Oh, that Maude was fit to be tied! Gardiner even took me for a ride in that Jaguar. You know, for a mild-mannered sort, he's kind of heavy on the gas. I warned him about that speed trap the police have . . . by that big S-curve, just before you get into Carrizozo? Well, Henry Carrillo, the state cop, claimed his radar clocked us at ninety-six coming out of that curve."

"Pearl, I had some trouble today," Roy said.

"Nothing new about that."

"No, *real* trouble."

He told her everything that had happened. As she listened, her expression grew serious, and when he was done she said, "So. You and Bill finally had yourselves a serious discussion."

"I wouldn't call it that, Pearl."

"It's a wonder somebody didn't get killed or hurt bad," Pearl said. "Some of the most sensible discussions I ever heard of ended up with men in the hospital."

"I didn't start it."

"Nobody said you did," she replied, and then stared at him. "And you laid him out? Really? I wouldn't have minded seeing that." She shook her head, musing. " 'Course, you ain't no fighter. You're a big man, Roy, but you ain't low-down mean. I sure would have liked to have seen that! Well, Billy's had *that* one coming for a long time."

"I don't know how it happened," Roy said.

"What're you going to do if he comes back up there with his pals?"

"I don't know."

"Roy, I think you ought to go talk to Lloyd Parmalee," she said, and her expression again grew serious. "Something like this can lead to guns going off."

"I don't need Lloyd's help."

"Don't talk stupid," she insisted. "Lloyd's a deputy sheriff. If need be, he can go down to the courthouse and slap a peace bond on Bill tomorrow."

"I can't do that."

"Besides which," she continued, "Lloyd could handle this, and he wouldn't even need a badge or a gun. You know, he's as old as God, but in his day Lloyd was something else. And I happen to know he ain't very fond of Billy."

"Pearl, I never heard you talk so highly of Lloyd before," Roy said.

"Oh, I never been down on Parmalee," she replied, and then smiled. "Known him since I was a girl. He was barely out of his teens. Everybody said he'd come to no good. Cocky, you know. Wouldn't take but a wrong word to set him off. People said he was too quick with his fists. He used to come to all the square dances we had back then. All us girls was just wild about him, only he was always getting into fights. And, you know something, he'd win, every single time. I even heard he fought some ten-rounders down in El Paso—there used to be lots of boxing matches down there. Anyway, everybody said he was too mean to ever make a decent husband. I used to dance with him. Who-ever was calling the dance would sing out the turns, and Lloyd would just go clippin' around the floor so fast a girl couldn't keep up." She grew reflective. "He always dressed nice, not the way he does now, in those old work clothes, only I never liked the way he cut his hair . . . right to the bone, with those big jug ears sticking out and only a bit of cowlick on top. To this day, he likes it that way. Alma barbers him, you know. So, with his drinking and fighting, folks said he was no good. Everybody crossed him off. And what hapens? Alma and him end up mar-ried over forty years! She gentled him. Got him to straighten up, and today they got four rental apartments over in Carrizozo that bring steady income, and a bank account that'd choke a whale. She was a plain sort of girl, too. Everybody figured she'd turn out an old maid, and she gets herself the best marriage around. Real shy, and as skinny as a broom, with eyeglasses an inch thick.

She must've had something special, though. Some kind of talent, as they say. Lloyd never once looked at another woman after they got engaged. There ain't many men I'd say that much for. It goes to show you, there's no knowing how people'll turn out."

"I'd just as soon leave him out of this," Roy insisted.

"Billy has heard you got a big offer for Sawmill River, you know," Pearl remarked. And from the way she said it, he wondered if she had—somewhere in past years—heard a rumor that he and Billy might be related. That was something that never failed to surprise him about this country. Its people were by nature closemouthed. To them, gossip was anathema. On the other hand, it was next to impossible to keep a secret, let alone live a day-to-day life without everyone's knowing its smallest details. If a person demanded to know where such knowledge-ability had been acquired, the responses were invariably and maddeningly vague: a shrug of the shoulders; a puzzled look; a *quien sabe?* or an "I reckon I heard it somewhere."

Pearl went on now: "My guess, Roy, is that he'll harangue you just for the fun of it. And, by the way, those Larson people called day before yesterday from New York. Wanted to know when they'd be hearing from you. I had a devil of a time, 'cause poor Gardiner was sitting right here with the world's worst hangover . . . and of course I know how much he despises *that* bunch."

"What'd you tell them?"

"Well, I didn't want to upset Gardiner, so I just made out I was taking a telephone order for some of my cheese," she said, and smiled. "The man talking at the other end kept yelling about a bad connection. And I just kept talking about all the different kinds of cheese I had in stock. After a while, he got disgusted and hung up on me. Gardiner likes my garlic-and-pimento best. I love to see a man eat." She looked at Roy. "Did I do the right thing?"

"You did fine, Pearl. I don't have time to think about them."

"I been thinking about something else," she went on. "Roy, could the Mescaleros help you? It wouldn't hurt to go talk to them."

"No. I haven't been up to the reservation in years."

"Roy, one side of your land *borders* their reservation," she insisted. "And you're quarter-Apache, to boot."

He said, "There's no documentation on me."

"They turn up new records all the time," she said. "It wouldn't hurt to go ask. Roy, those people are real good about looking out for their own. Times have changed. If you could get 'em to adopt you into the tribe, why, I can guarantee you there wouldn't be anyone like Bill Maldonado messing with you, or those Larson people, either. The Mescaleros don't take any lip from anybody nowadays. Go on up there and double-check. It can't hurt."

She had put a thought in his mind, but he was still doubtful. "It would be a waste of my time, Pearl. The tribal center isn't interested in me." He was talking about the Mescalero Reservation's headquarters.

"If you got time on the way back, take Route 47," she insisted. "You'll see how Apaches get along these days."

"Isn't there some kind of motel up that way?"

"The Inn of the Mountain Gods, they call it," she said. "Roy, it'll knock your eyes out! Probably the biggest motel in all New Mexico . . . maybe the whole damn country! And there ain't nothing but Mescaleros running it. They got their own private lake where they rap white people ten bucks a day just to wet a trout line, and they even built their own private hatchery to stock it with. They got the fanciest golf course you ever saw."

"I didn't know Apaches were into golf," he said.

"They ain't, you fool . . . 'cause they're too busy making trips to the bank," she said. "That tribal chairman, Wendall Chino—wasn't he something!—went to Washington and got nineteen million dollars of taxpayers' money to build that place. They got bars and restaurants and cocktail lounges spread all around, and you know what? When the State Liquor Commission said they couldn't sell rotgut without a license, Chino just told 'em to go suck! He said it was reservation land and that the Mescaleros would do doodleydick as they damn pleased! I like Chino for that. He went on the warpath for money, not scalps, and not even the BIA and Congress could buffalo him. Why, that place is so high-class it makes the best of Ruidoso look like a Juarez slum.

Roy, you go look at it, and you'll see what I mean about Indians having good sense!"

HE WENT TO the tribal center first, still feeling depressed but at the same time not entirely without hope. There was one thing he knew. Life for Indians was changing, and they themselves were contributing toward this progress. While still a long way from coming into his own, the native American was frequently somewhat different from the image projected by contemporary films and public-service television documentaries.

Here and there across the land, Indians were standing up for their rights, and getting them—they campaigned for recognition and ethnic autonomy, as well as education. Land grants and treaties over a century old were being dusted off, reexamined, and in many cases successfully appealed and litigated in higher courts. Things were done differently now. The days when the Army and the Department of the Interior had casually and cruelly juggled entire tribes from one part of the country to another were gone forever. Today, even that bastion of white supremacy, the Bureau of Indian Affairs, was able to admit that it was no longer fashionable to regard the Indian as a childlike ward of the government, and to prove that it was not just talking hot air, the Bureau had even gone so far as to appoint a few educated Indians to executive positions within its structure—which in the days of the Third Reich would have been tantamount to an orthodox Jew being assigned a decisionmaking role in Himmler's dreaded *Schutzstaffel.*

So the red man was at last finding an identity. It was this aspect of the ethnic resurgence of Indian self-pride that had always interested Roy most . . . for Indians had gotten very good at the business of keeping records and censuses whereby the accurate tracing of familial lineages could be accomplished. A direct link to a tribe, once established, could have real advantages. Very often, a boy or a girl was found eligible for tribal benefits that might range from a college education to direct monetary participation.

That is, if it could be proved.

Right now, Roy was less interested in benefits than in proving that, quite simply, he *belonged*. He was absolutely sure that, somewhere on the Mescalero Reservation, there were people directly related to him, but even this was secondary. If a link could be established, perhaps the tribe could help him protect his land.

But the answer he got was the same as it had been when he had appealed years earlier. One of the officials he talked with, a short, portly Apache, was sympathetic but firm.

Did he have a birth certificate or baptismal papers? A Social Security card? Had he ever attended a reservation school? Was there a discharge, honorable or otherwise, from any branch of the Armed Services?

He had none of these.

"But how could you work at a job without a Social Security number?"

"I'd just make one up," he said. "I was never interested in getting something from the government—all I was after was wages."

The Apache, whose name was Sandoval, stared at him for a moment and then smiled. "And now you're convinced you're a native American."

"Yes, sir. One-fourth."

Roy knew he didn't look it. Sandoval was still regarding him. "And you don't have any papers to prove it?"

"All I have is this," Roy said. He took out the old wedding picture and showed it to Sandoval. After talking with Pearl, he had driven back up to Sawmill River and gotten it from the footlocker. "See here? On the back? 'Tom and Cora Wardner, 1894, Fort Stanton'? They're my grandparents."

Sandoval put on bifocals and inspected the photograph. "She's Mescalero, all right. And this black man . . . well, back then there were plenty of pair-ups like that." He thought about it, and then said, "I'm sorry but this isn't enough."

"They had children," Roy insisted. "Right here, on the reservation. One of their daughters, Minnie—my mother—was born around 1900."

"I've already checked for you. There are no Wardners in our files," Sandoval said. He stared at the photograph again. "Maybe this man used a different name." He shook his head. "Documentation. I want to do what I can for you, but I need something to work with."

"Yes," Roy said. "I've heard that before."

"This isn't the first time you've asked for a search?"

"I came here about fifteen years ago. Mostly out of curiosity," Roy explained. "They said the same thing. My father brought me here, too, when I was about three or four, and talked to the council. His sidekick told me about it years later. He wanted the council to acknowledge me, but they wouldn't have anything to do with us. That must have been around 1928. I think my father knew that one day Indians would start getting their due, so he applied . . . even then there were pretty good educational benefits for Indian children. I might have gotten a college education."

"Do you know where you were born, Mister Gutierrez?"

"Right here, in a medicine man's lodge."

"You've tried the BIA? County health records? State?"

"Yes. There was nothing," Roy said. "Even so, I happen to know I'm one-quarter Mescalero."

Sandoval was staring at him again. Finally, he said, "I believe you, but I can't do a thing."

"I know."

"I'm sorry."

"That's okay."

He was about to turn and go but Sandoval said, "What would you do, I mean, if you could prove it?"

"I don't know," Roy said. "Maybe I wouldn't do anything." He thought about this. "Maybe I'd just like to belong somewhere." He paused. "I guess there have been times in my life when I felt I didn't exist, felt invisible."

"Brother, a lot of us know that feeling," Sandoval said. "That's a real Indian feeling for sure."

DRIVING AWAY FROM the tribal center, he had a moment of doubt. He wondered if there had actually been a wild young girl named Minnie Wardner. Or, for that matter, a squaw named Cora who had allied herself with his grandfather.

Were they part of the fable his father had told him?

Had there actually lived, nearly a century ago, a Negro man

by the name of Tom Wardner? Perhaps born into slavery and
subsequently freed to wander westward as so many of his race
had, enlisting for a couple of hitches as a buffalo soldier, putting
in his years of service on one military post or another, those universally hated garrisons from Oklahoma to California that were
sunbaked in summer and blizzard-whipped in winter? Had
Wardner perhaps cowboyed on those long cattle drives that came
up out of New Mexico and Texas under the stern edict of the
trail-drive foreman: "Point 'em north—move 'em out!"? Yes, there
were thousands of working black cowhands back in those times,
and they made up one more chapter conveniently omitted from
the history books. Had Tom Wardner lived?

But no. Roy knew.

And, again, the information had come from Uncle Walter. A
story that the old man had told him years ago, when Roy was
still a boy, the words almost forgotten now, but not entirely, not
yet. What Walter'd had to say was this:

"Wardner? Your grandpa? Sure, I recollect him, not that I ever
had anything to do with him.

"No one wanted to fool with that man. Not just 'cause he was
a nigger. He was trouble, see? Everybody, white folks and injuns,
used to make a habit of keepin' outa his way.

"I only saw him a few times, once on the reservation, and then
at other times down at Lincoln or Fort Stanton when it was still
a military post, before they turned it into a tuberculosis hospital.
That was a long time ago but I remember him, an' I remember
his name, Tom Wardner.

"He stayed in a person's mind. Musta been six feet five an'
weighed two fifty easy. People said he was the biggest, meanest
nigger in all Lincoln County. There was truth in that. When he
was drinkin' he just got bigger an' meaner. The Mescaleros hated
him, but not 'cause he married into their tribe—they was so igno-
rant, race or color didn't mean a hoot to them. They hated him
'cause they was scared of him, 'specially when he was drunk.
Then he got a chip on his shoulder, no one knew why. They
respected him, I reckon. Tom Wardner didn't exactly look for
trouble but on the other hand he didn't walk away from it, either.

"Mostly when he come to town in his horse and wagon, people
looked the other way. He wasn't sassy—no one woulda stood for

that sorta behavior—but if he happened to take up a grudge against someone—white, Mexican, or injun—well then, y'know, he might git to drinkin' an' then he'd think on it, an' then, he just might go lookin' for that person. Nobody wanted anything that big an' black an' mean on the prowl after him.

"He had a little piece of land on the reservation, over past Cloudcroft somewhere, no one knew exactly. Most of the time he stayed to himself on that scratch of dirt he bullied outa the Mescaleros. Raised hisself a few crops, most likely. Had him his squaw an' some tobacco an' liquor. That was enough for a man like Wardner. No one ever knew nothin' about him or where he came from, except that he'd been a horse trooper. He never talked much. Folks suspected he had a shady past. Back then, you didn't ask where a man was from or what he'd been doin', or where he was headin'. That could cause trouble. If a man committed a crime in one part of the country he'd just move somewhere else and take up a new name, and nobody was the wiser. So, more'n one figgered Tom Wardner was wanted. Somehow, no one ever got around to asking him about it, though.

"Last time I remember seeing him was around '98 or '99. He was way into his fifties by then. A grayheaded ol' nigger. 'Course, when he come to town to drink, he couldn't walk into a bar. Niggers wasn't allowed, which was only right. There was always a couple of niggers workin' around town, y'know, not enough to git on your nerves, but a few. Some of the bars had a little place out back for 'em, mebbe a shed or a storehouse, with a bench or two. A nigger could always drink his liquor out back with his own kind, which was the best way to do it, 'cause they had their own way of talkin' an' laughin' over things amongst themselves. So there was never no trouble. Come to think of it, niggers had it pretty smooth in this part of the country. Why, I remember places down in Texas where I cowboyed, where a nigger never got a chance to even git off his horse for a drink of water 'fore he was told to move along. That Texas sure can be a hard place if they take a dislike to you.

"There was a story that old Tom Wardner once killed a man in a fistfight, but I never believed any of that. No man with a lick of sense woulda gone up against something like him with bare hands. He was too big. Nobody liked him. He hated whites an' injuns, and they hated him right back, but that don't mean nothin'. It's always been that way.

"As for the man hisself, I couldn't tell you nothin' about what sort he was. Like I said, nobody knew anything about him. He was uncommonly silent even when he was dead drunk in the middle of the street. I wouldn't be surprised if he never even talked much to the other niggers we kept around town. They'd shy away from him too, when he had a bottle under his coat. He mostly stayed off by hisself, with his squaw woman an' a pack of half-breed brats. All things considered, I reckon he knew that he had the world by the ass. Years later, I heard he drunk hisself to death. Now, if you want my opinion, I'd say that was a first-rate life for a shiftless nigger, then or now. Squaw to hoe the corn an' beans, chop firewood, an' fetch water, and at the same time she was pullin' rations an' money from the Indian Agency, which he doubtless traded for drink. Yes, I'd say it was a real sweet life for old Tom. He musta knowed it, 'cause he stayed with that squaw until the day he died. I heard he just got old and big an' fatter.

"A long time later, somebody mentioned that he'd died down there on the reservation. Probably they buried him there. No one ever knew where. Not that it matters."

HE TURNED OFF onto Route 47, as Pearl Lowdermilk had suggested. The road crossed a cattle guard. This was good timber country, and like the ski area it was one of the prettiest parts of the Mescalero Reservation.

Several miles up the winding road, the Inn of the Mountain Gods came into view. It was located on the shore of a jewel of a lake.

Roy knew that native Americans had come a long way but now he was surprised to see how far they'd traveled. There was, indeed, a beautiful golf course. Small sailboats and catamarans were out on the lake's blue waters. He thought that, someplace, there might be a private landing strip for small planes. He said aloud, "For once, Pearl wasn't exaggerating."

The inn itself was simply huge. All done in cedar shakes and dark-tinted glass walls. The grounds were superbly landscaped, with rock terraces and little streams and waterfalls.

Two immense wings stood out on either side of the main complex. There looked to be a thousand rooms for paying customers, every one of them facing on a lakeshore view that he suspected might be as lovely as anything that could be found in the Swiss Alps.

Roy parked the jeep in front and got out to look around before going inside.

The core of the inn was an A-frame, but it had to be the biggest A-frame ever. The supporting girders were painted a subdued brown and they must have been a hundred feet high and weighed twenty tons each.

Inside, there were gift shops and boutiques loaded with Mescalero jewelry and pottery, as well as coffee shops and restaurants.

There wasn't a white desk clerk, or bellhop, or waitress in sight. They were all reservation kids, and they looked simply great—young and healthy, and dressed in neat-as-a-pin uniforms whose colors had been designer-coordinated to match the overall aura of unobtrusive elegance. Roy figured he could have searched the place from one end to the other and not found anyone resembling the kind of reservation old-timer he'd been around years ago, but he was willing to bet that these marvelously handsome young Indian boys and girls were into hair spray and blow-dry combs.

The whole place looked modern, and very expensive. Everything was air-conditioned, and unoffensive mood music came from concealed Muzak loudspeakers.

For a moment, he almost smiled, thinking of Neil Larson's visionary schemes to "re-create" historical environments. Larson wanted a "real" Indian village, full of natives fooling with bows and arrows, and maybe galloping around on pinto ponies after domesticated buffaloes. But there were real Indians living right here on this reservation, and Roy knew that some of them were making fortunes out of timbering, tourism, and mining. Their tribal chairman spent more time in Washington than he did planting corn, and he knew exactly how to talk to federal legislators in a language they could understand. Roy didn't doubt for a minute that there were Indians within ten miles of where he stood who could not tell a bow and arrow from an Australian boomerang but who knew how to read the Dow Jones, and who made a point of seing to it that their kids went to good schools, including Harvard and Princeton.

Suddenly, he felt terribly out of place, in his worn jeans, boots, the patched workshirt, and sweatstained straw Stetson. But he wanted to see more.

In the cocktail lounge, he had a little difficulty getting a drink because there was a convention in full swing. The New Mexico Association of Chiropractors, a placard in the lobby said. The lounge was full of conventioneers and their wives and children, and they all stared at him as if he'd just walked off an old movie-set. At the bar, he managed to get a glass of wine. People gave him plenty of elbow room. He lit a cigarette and thought, *wouldn't it have been something to have brought Uncle Walter to a place like this? He wouldn't have known what to make of it.*

A voice behind his shoulder said, "Is everything satisfactory?" He turned.

A tall, brownskinned, handsome man stood there. He wore black-rimmed spectacles and had on charcoal-gray slacks, a white shirt, a bolo tie that had a piece of turquoise in it as big as an egg, and a black blazer with silver buttons. He said, "I'm Harold Andrews, the assistant manager."

His voice was cultured. Someplace along the line he had gotten rid of that inimitable glottal, singsong intonation almost all bilingual Indians have. Roy said, "Everything's fine."

"I'm glad," Andrews said, but the tone of his voice meant something else.

Roy felt uncomfortably like a saddle tramp who had somehow turned up at a bankers' luncheon. He said, "I just wanted to see this place. I'd heard about it."

"Something else, isn't it? We're very proud of it. Passing through?"

"I had business at the tribal center."

"You're Mescalero?" Andrews asked, staring at him.

"Part."

"I see."

"Soon as I finish my drink, I'll be on my way."

"Take your time," Andrews said. But he didn't mean it. His expression seemed to say, "Mister, we've had our own difficulties . . . it hasn't been easy for us, either."

The expression wasn't exactly unfriendly. Yet a gulf separated the two of them. Andrews wasn't about to reach across it.

But, in a way, the assistant manager seemed to understand the situation. Roy did, too.

For a few moments, they regarded each other, and in that time the message was clear. This sophisticated, swarthy man—other Indians, not without their own sense of humor, would have called him a "red apple," meaning he was red on the outside and white on the inside—had climbed no small distance up the ladder of success. The look in his eyes said, "Yes, we Mescaleros know how to take care of our own." And: "Yes, we have interracials on the reservation . . . but not here. This place is for white men with money to burn . . . what we have here is a big playpen for palefaces to hang out in. We try to give them what they want . . . and what they want is Indians who look like Indians . . . or at least what they imagine Indians ought to look like. Not you, brother. So why don't you finish that drink and leave?" Still staring at Roy, Andrews smiled, and his smile was not at all unkindly; it simply said, "Sorry about that. It's nothing personal, you understand."

Roy was not stupid. He knew how to take a hint.

Some distance down the road leading away from the Inn of the Mountain Gods, he pulled off and parked; there, under the cool shade of some tall elms, he made a sandwich and drank a can of beer.

He had some thoughts of his own, and they went like this: *this Neil Larson is wrong when he tells me that selling Sawmill will bring enough money to change my life. Everything will still be the same. You might as well face up to that. People are people, and nothing changes.*

At best, the money might bring with it an easier and more

comfortable way of living. For however many years he had left. Five? Ten, with luck? Roy didn't see himself getting much past the early sixties.

On that night he first returned, Pearl had been not far off the mark when she'd told him how awful he looked and that he'd come home to do his dying. He knew that his body, after too many years of liquor and smoking and haphazard diets, was wearing out. His mind seemed split in two: one side found pleasure and even joy in being alive . . . but the other part knew he would never last another twenty years.

So, then, what difference did any of it make? A real sum of money would buy comfort and security. Those were not such small things for someone who had not had too much of either.

True, he loved Sawmill River Flats, but so what? When he died, without heirs, the town would eventually become tax-delinquent, and when that happened it would be sold at auction to the highest bidder.

Someone would get the town, sooner or later. No argument there.

The polarities of his situation were evident—his father, George Gutierrez, would have spotted them immediately—and in a way they were almost amusing because they presented both sides of one of the oldest philosophical arguments around:

a) all existence is random, and therefore meaningless. Or,
b) purpose and design are a part of, or are apparent in, nature—a view essentially teleological.

What struck him as amusing was that nobody today had the time or inclination to consider that kind of problem. Philosophy was as out of date as alchemy. What interested people nowadays were things like living, and making love, and acquiring money and security and status, and staying healthy. People worried about the threat of war, buying a house, inflation, being successful, and capturing that elusive will-o'-the-wisp, love. They jogged or rode bicycles or swam, cheated on their taxes and, when they thought they could get away with it, on their spouses, too; they refused to be satisfied with anything less than a full draught from the cup of life.

After all, what was the point in fretting over unsolvable questions? There were too many of them, and, worse still, one question had an irritating way of leading to another, and then another. There was no end to it. All one ever got out of it was a troubled mind. Best leave such things alone. Life was confusing enough, as it was.

THAT EVENING, STILL troubled, he dragged out the old footlocker from underneath the bunk and searched through it.

Near the bottom were a number of his father's journals—ordinary school notebooks with black cardboard covers. He had not looked into them in several years. The entries were in his father's small, crabbed handwriting, and they dealt with whatever had captured George Gutierrez's fancy . . . in short, anything under the sun, often accompanied by rather skillful drawings of flowers, beetles, Indian petroglyphs, or cave drawings, all sorts of scientific trivia, as well as lists of expenditures for gasoline, food, clothing, and "refreshments," the last representing a sizable ongoing investment. The pages were foxed and faded, as were a number of snapshots held in place by black corner mounts, most of them showing Roy at one age or another. Several showed the three of them together: a younger George and a younger Walter, with the boy standing between them, spindlylegged, all of them smiling and frowning and squinting into the bright sun while they posed shyly—beside a primitive gas station, or at the edge of Grand Canyon, or under the long portal of Santa Fe's Palace of the Governors.

Some of the notes were written in pencil but most were in ink, done by an old gold-nibbed Waterman fountain pen that Roy still had. In themselves, the entries were of sufficient interest but even more fascinating was the indication they gave of how this strange man's mind had worked.

July 5th, 1948—Pecos, N.M.
Yesterday we celebrated the adoption of our Declaration of Independence. W. roasted a whole saddle of pork and it tasted so fine that I was reminded of the immortal essay on roast suckling pig. Our anticipation was so great to remove

the roast from its spit that W. dropped it into the embers. He was angry, but I told him not to mind. We scraped off the ashes and it never mattered a bit.

Today, we are resting. In a few days, we may head south.

Recently I have been doing some reading, in the Bible and elsewhere. Atheists ought to read the former, not for the message, which is of no importance, but for the diversity of its contents and the richness of its language. Using it, as well as a few other textbooks I have at hand, I was able to unearth a few intriguing notions. At some point in the future, they may be of use to R.

Vitiligo, or LEUKODERMA—the loss of melanin from the skin. Reason for this condition: unclear. Vitiligo appears as milk-white, irregular patches, seen most commonly on hands, wrists, face, neck, and upper trunk. Afflicted individuals (less than 1% of pop.) are usually in good general health, but vitiligo presents a cosmetic problem that can be serious in dark-skinned individuals. Normal skin color rarely returns. *No known cure.*

Most significant dermatologic disease mentioned in Bible is *"tsaraat,"* which translates as leprosy (ref: Leviticus). Not to be confused with contemporary psoriasis or syphilis. A possibility, however, that certain types of biblical "leprosy" may have been a form of vitiliginous dermatophytosis.

Tsaraat: regarded as a divinely ordained punishment for sin. Considered fatal and incurable. (But isn't *all* life fatal, sooner or later?)

Lepers were banished from normal society.

Purity and Pollution, in relation to religious concepts:

People in "polluted" states are believed to be dangerous not only to others because they may spread their pollution, but they themselves are often thought to be in danger of attack by demons, who are attracted by the defiled person's impurities.

There is a universal belief that bodily functions involve pollution. These include:

Menstruation, sexual intercourse, birth, illness, death, and all bodily excretions and exuviae (urine, feces, saliva, sweat, vomit, blood, menstrual blood, semen, nasal and oral mucus, and hair and nail cuttings). The entire body below the navel, the feet, the hem of the garment, the floor or ground, are viewed as polluted because most bodily excretions derive from the lower part of the body.

Violence is also viewed as a polluting phenomenon (murder, hunting, warfare, quarreling, cursing, etc.).

Anomalies and Pollution. This category includes strange, unusual, or unclassifiable phenomena: certain events of nature (such as comets or lunar or solar eclipses). Also: *unusual births* (twins or other multiple births, breech deliveries, miscarriages, or stillbirths). Also: *physical deformities,* esp. sexual (e.g. monorchids—men having one testicle—hermaphrodites, eunuchs), children who cut their upper teeth before their lower, also all persons not considered fully in control of their faculties (children, drunkards, the insane, or the mentally or physically handicapped, such as cretins); and perversions of social relationships, esp. sexual (e.g., adultery, homosexuality, bestiality, incest, birth of children to unwed parents . . .).

Sacrifices. In Judea, the *hatta't,* or "sin offering," was an important ritual for the expiation of certain defilements. The guilty laid their hands upon the head of the sacrificial animal (an innocent bullock or goat), thereby identifying themselves with the victim, making it their representative (but *not* their substitute!) for their sins. By the shedding of blood, the sin of mankind was wiped out and a new relationship of life—eternal life—was effected between God and man. Like the innocent victim of the *hatta't,* Christ died *for* men—i.e., on the behalf of but not in *place* of them.

Scapegoat (Hebrew *Sa'Irla-'Asa'zel*). A Yom Kippur ritual involving a goat symbolically burdened with the sins of the Jewish people. (again, see Leviticus 16:8–10) This animal was chosen by lot to placate Azazel (a wilderness demon), and then thrown over a precipice outside Jerusalem to rid the nation of its iniquities.

By extension, the term scapegoat has come to mean any group or individual that *innocently* bears the blame of others.

Isaiah, in my estimation, catches the idea of Messiah-pariah-scapegoat perfectly:

> . . . the crowds were appalled on seeing him
> —so disfigured did he look
> that he seemed no longer human. . . .

> Like a sapling he grew up in front of us,
> like a root in arid ground.
> Without beauty, without majesty, we saw him.
> no looks to attract our eyes,
> a thing despised and rejected by men,
> a man of sorrows and familiar with suffering,
> a man to make people screen their faces;
> he was despised, and so we took no account of him.

> And yet ours were the sufferings he bore,
> ours the sorrows he carried.
> But we, we thought of him as someone punished,
> struck by God, and brought low. . . .

> Harshly dealt with, he bore it humbly,
> he never opened his mouth,
> like a lamb that is led to the slaughterhouse,
> like a sheep that is dumb before its shearers,
> never opening its mouth.

George Gutierrez's notebooks were filled with such stuff. He had been like a small boy, burning with curiosity to learn everything there was to know about life.

Roy read on, but nowhere could he find anything that might shed a little light on the questions and troubles that plagued him. It was all very interesting, but none of it led anywhere. He was not necessarily looking for ready answers—none existed, and he knew it. He would have been satisfied with a hint—a clue—but there was nothing.

His father, who had been everything to him for so many years, now was of no help at all.

Still troubled, he finally went to bed. The day had been wasted. But tomorrow—well, that was something to think about.

Rae was to arrive then.

ELEVEN

THE BUS WAS due in from Roswell at 2:15, and Roy was there early, waiting on Capitan's main street. He was dressed in clean Levi's and a fresh blue shirt that had been ironed earlier that morning by Pearl Lowdermilk, and he had brushed his workboots clean and then given them a coating of neat's-foot oil. Waiting in the parked jeep he told himself to be calm but it did no good. He was nervous. Worse, he feared that she had missed the bus connection or perhaps, for some reason, decided not to come at all.

The bus came in finally, with a roar and a stench of exhaust fumes, and stopped in front of the Smokey Bear Motel. A couple of people who looked to be local ranchers or farmers got off, and then a woman with a suitcase came down the bus' steps.

For a moment, he didn't recognize her. And then he did. He got out of the jeep and went over.

"Rae?"

"Hello, Roy."

It was her, all right. Those wise, sad eyes. And the face, still as beautiful as ever.

She'd aged a lot, though. Looked older than the way he remembered her, three years ago. Lines ran down either side of her mouth and crow's-feet crinkled the corners of her eyes when she smiled at him. She was still lovely, and he thought, *she'll always be lovely.*

But something had happened. She looked so thin and poor. The thick fall of hair had real gray in it now. She wore eyeglasses, and had on a white drip-dry shirt, slacks, and loafers.

"Rae, it's good to see you."

"Good to see you, too."

She seemed uncertain about what to do. Just stood there. Then, hesitantly, she set down her suitcases, came up, embraced him, and kissed him on the cheek. For a moment, they held each other tightly, and her hair smelled clean and fresh. He said, "I'm glad you're back."

"So am I. Oh, Roy." When she stepped back from him he saw that there were tears in her eyes.

There was something else besides her appearance that had changed drastically. He could intuitively sense it, and now he thought, *you'd better step softly. She's had a bad time of it.*

Three years ago, she had been many things—intelligent, quick, beautiful, and above all independent. Now, there were still all these sides to her—except for the independence. There was something about her that reminded him of a wounded bird that could not fly.

None of it mattered. She was back. That was what counted.

She had caught his sober expression. She said, "I guess I've changed."

"Nothing's changed," he said. He looked at her and smiled, and then added, quite irrelevantly, "You're safe here now. I'll take care of you."

She smiled, too. "I know."

He picked up her suitcase. As they walked across the street together, he offered her his free hand, and she took it, holding tightly.

DRIVING AWAY IN the jeep, he said, "You must be exhausted."

"A little. It's hot."

"Did you come on the bus all the way from Shrevesport?"

"God, no. I could get flights from there to El Paso, and then up to Roswell." Roswell was sixty miles to the east. Anybody who was going to the small, surrounding towns used the local bus lines.

Roy said, "I could have driven over there to get you."

"That's all right."

"Reach behind you, down on the floorboard," Roy told her. She did, and there was a paper sack containing a chilled half-gallon of white wine, a carton of cigarettes, and a can of mixed nuts. He said, "I was in such a rush to leave, I forgot the cooler. Got the wine at the package store. They keep it nice and cold."

"You remembered my brand," she said, looking at the Marlboros. "Any cups?" He motioned toward the glove compartment and she opened it. That was where they had always kept them. She got them out, opened the wine and the mixed nuts, and they drove on. She said, "Have you been at Sawmill all this time?"

"No, I left. I traveled for a while. Then I took a job. I was only back a week or so when your letter came in."

"We'll have a lot to talk about," Rae said.

"Yes." He thought for a moment. "Do you feel like stopping at Pearl Lowdermilk's to say hello? I'd just as soon skip it for today, but she knows you're coming."

"Not today, if it's all right with you," she said. "I don't want to see anyone else. You want a cigarette?"

"Yes."

She lit one of the Marlboros for him, passed it over, and then lit one for herself, inhaling deeply and letting it out slowly. A warm breeze came in the open windows, whipping at her hair and flattening the white shirt against her chest. Roy said, "We'll skip Pearl, then. Later we can drop by. We'll have to. Her nose gets out of joint if she feels she's being ignored."

"I know. Later." Rae drank some of her wine and looked out the window.

"We'll head straight on up to Sawmill."

"Good. How is the old place?"

"Pretty much the same."

"I can't wait to see it. And the cabin?"

"I've stocked it with plenty of food."

She drank more of her wine. "I thought about Sawmill River a lot."

He nodded. "We had a pretty good summer up there, didn't we?"

"The best."

"I wasn't sure you'd be on the bus."

She looked at him. "I wasn't sure you'd be there to meet it."

"You know better than that."

"Yes." She thought about this. "I was hoping you'd be there. On the bus I was nervous the whole time."

"Why?"

She glanced at him again. "Because of what I did to you before."

"Don't worry about it."

"I just walked away."

"That's in the past."

"And you left, too?"

"Yes. With you and Walter gone, it was lonely."

"Where'd you go?"

"Down to old Mexico. All the way to Merida, in the Yucatan. Then I worked in El Paso for a few years."

"Was it good?"

"Mexico was fine. El Paso was just staying alive. Finally, I got fed up and decided to come back to Sawmill."

"It's where you belong," Rae said. "I mean, in my mind, that's what I associate with you . . . you and that old town, together."

"I've had an offer to sell out."

"Really?"

"Some company back east. They want to develop it."

"Well, I hope you don't."

"They made me a good offer."

"But that town means a lot to you," she said, and then: "Of course, it's yours to do with what you want."

"I haven't made up my mind yet," Roy said. He glanced over at her and then grinned. "It's really good to see you again."

She smiled. "I feel the same about you."

Drinking the wine and smoking and talking, he was beginning to relax. He said, "We'll see how it goes, all right?"

She thought about this. Then she said quietly, "Roy, I can only stay a few days."

It hit him hard, and she could see that it did. Presently, she said, "I have something to take care of. Business. Maybe I can come back after that."

"Important business?"

"Yes. Important to me."

"Are you in trouble?"

"No. I'm not in any kind of trouble at all."

He was still feeling it strongly. To have her come back, and then go away again. He said, "You know I'd take care of you."

"I know that."

He finished his wine and handed her the cup. "Would you pour me some more?" She refilled it, and he said, "But you might be back?"

"I don't know," Rae said. "Maybe. Let's talk, all right?"

"All right."

"Do you know, you're practically the only man I've ever known that I could sit down with and talk to, or listen to, for hours?" she said.

"That's hard to believe."

"It's true," she said. "During that entire summer, we weren't apart more than half a day. That takes some doing. There aren't many people I want to be around for more than a week at most."

"It was a fine summer."

"We'll talk, then," she said. "But not right now. I just want to be with you at Sawmill." She stared out the window again. They were in the high country now. "Roy, I've got to get my head together. Unwind. You know?"

"Sure. Let's not talk."

She nodded, and then smiled. "I want to, though. Only not today." She refilled her own cup. "I hate seeing people get hurt. I didn't mean to hurt you then. That's the truth. And I'm not going to do it now. I just want to be with you."

"And then you'll leave?"

"I have to."

"Rae, I care a lot about you."

"I know. I care about you, too. I mean that. I thought about you. Not just sex, or that you were decent. I put in a lot of time

analyzing what was going on inside my head. I mean feelings."
She paused, and then said, "I've changed."

"You're the same."

She shook her head. "No, I'm different. If I was the same, there would have been no point in my being on that bus today."

"What would you have done if I hadn't been waiting?"

There was no hesitation. "I would have hired someone to drive me up to Sawmill."

"Rae, sometimes you mystify me."

She smiled wryly. "Well, we certainly ought to do something about that."

Not much later, they topped the rise that would bring them down into the old town. Roy parked for a minute, and they had more wine. She said, "You were right. The town is still the same."

Roy said, "You know, when I left last time I swore I'd never come back."

She was silent. Then she said, "Yes. I thought the same thing, that morning you drove me to the bus stop."

AT THE CABIN, she wandered around. Looked out the single window, and then went to the open door. Came back, drank some wine, and inspected the shelves of books. She said finally, "It's good to be back."

He watched as she opened the suitcase and got out a pair of shorts, tube socks, and sneakers. Most of the clothing in the suitcase looked new, and the shorts still had a price tag on the waistband. When she had finished changing, he said, "What'll we do for supper? I can cook a chicken if you like."

"Could we just have sandwiches? Something easy?" she said. "Is there aspirin?"

"Headache?" he asked, getting her the bottle.

"Yes," she said. She shook four into the palm of her hand and, one by one, washed them down with the wine.

Then she asked if she could take the bottle of wine and go for a walk. She had done something very similar on the first day they had brought Uncle Walter home. Gone off by herself.

When she had left, he made up plates of sliced ham and cheese, along with mayonnaise and bread. He brought in a supply of split wood for the night and then opened a fresh bottle of wine for himself and found some quiet music on the transistor. He sat at the table and read. An hour passed, then two. Finally, he went to look for her.

She was at the beaver pond, curled up with her back against a deadfall.

It was the best time of day, when it was very quiet, with the sun low in the west. She had drunk most of the wine she had taken, and on the ground beside her there was a litter of cigarette butts. Roy said, "I brought more wine."

"Sit by me."

He did, and refilled their cups. "How are you feeling?"

"Very tired. Better."

"Headache gone?"

"Almost."

"You need time to rest up," he said, lighting a cigarette. "It's always been the same with me. Whenever I come back up here after having been away for a long time . . . well, at first I can't wait to get here. Then, I'm disappointed, and I start wondering why I've come back. But gradually, everything settles into place. It takes a week or so. For a while, I'm edgy. Then I slow down and start relaxing."

She turned and stared at him. "What do you do here when you're alone?"

He smiled and shrugged. "In a way, I don't do anything. Then again, I'm busy all the time. I don't mean chores. Time passes. Something's always happening. After a few months you get a real feeling of the seasons coming and going."

"I hope you don't sell all this," she said. "Do you feel like talking to me about it?"

He filled her in on everything that had happened. Larson and his dream of a nationwide chain of historic re-creations and whether or not the whole scheme was merely a ruse to cover a land-development racket. The historical society, up in Santa Fe. His visit to the Mescalero Reservation.

She listened, at times asking a question or putting in a brief comment. And again it came to him how good it was simply to be with someone, talking.

It seemed that with the others, like Pearl and Rowdy and

Lloyd, he listened most of the time, and when he did speak it wasn't always easy to know if they'd understood what he was talking about. Rae, though, had that capacity for attentiveness to whatever was being discussed.

Finally, he stopped, lit another cigarette, and smiled. "There's sandwich makings on the table. You've got to be tired."

"Yes. It's a good kind of tiredness," she said.

"Feel like going back? It'll be dark soon."

"All right."

Hand in hand, they walked slowly up the slope to the cabin, carrying their cups and the wine. It was dusk now, and the air was cool. Crickets sounded their monotonous song, and small black shapes of bats flickered and swooped against the twilight sky.

In the cabin they ate by lamplight, with the radio playing quietly. She had not been exaggerating about her exhaustion. Before they had finished eating, she was nodding, and he said, "You'd best get to bed."

"Too much wine and fresh air," she said, and yawned.

When she stood up, he had to guide her toward the bunk bed. He could see that she was almost asleep on her feet.

By the bed, she put her arms around his waist and held him for a moment, with her head resting against his chest. It was something a sleepy child might do—a reassurance that someone else was there. He helped her undress, and she climbed under the blankets still wearing her socks and panties.

She turned once on her side so that she was facing the wall, snuggled down, and presently she was breathing slowly and heavily.

He went back to the table, turned down the lamps, had another drink, and sat there alone for a long time, listening to the sound of her breathing and feeling her presence in the cabin.

During the night she was restless and ground her teeth. Once, she talked in her sleep, but he could not make out what she was saying.

IN THE MORNING, they woke very early, and he began touching her. She came slowly out of a deep slumber, seeming almost drugged at first, and then gradually she was more and more awake, and then aroused, tenderly at first but later with an aching need that grew more and more fierce. He kissed her, and beneath the blankets both her hands touched his hardness, and then her lips and mouth were down there, too, a delicate, leisurely exploration, a wet and tentative touching that was unbearable, and he lay very quietly, not moving at all, letting her do what she wanted, until her own needs grew unendurable, and with a moan she gave her mouth completely. When he could bear it no longer, he pulled her away and then went to enter her but he felt her stiffen with fear. He said, "Do you want me to?"

"Yes," she said, moaning again. "Be careful, though. Please. Be very careful." She guided him with both hands, and he entered her gently, only a little way at first, and then more, until finally she placed her hands on his buttocks and drew him in, filling herself with all of him, crying out sharply and moving her head back and forth. He said, "I didn't mean to hurt." "It doesn't hurt," she said, and she was weeping now. "It doesn't hurt at all." He knew the way she liked it best, the way she had shown him, scarcely moving, not thrusting, but with all of him in her, very deeply, pressing against her, moving just a little in time with her open thighs, and still more gently, the two of them almost motionless now, yet moving, too, for what seemed hours, and then he felt something very deep inside her begin to open, like a flower in the heat of the sun, and she went into a violent spasm, gasping and crying out loudly, and with that he lost control, too, and came, thrusting savagely now—that was when she relished and accepted all his strength and violence, yes, it was then that she could not get enough of him.

Afterward, lying close together and sharing a cigarette, he said, "Why were you afraid?"

She was silent for a moment. Then she said, "It'd been a long time. I didn't know if I could."

"We never had any problem before."

"I know. But that was three years ago."

"Are you sick?"

"No," she said, "but I was." She was quiet again, thinking. Finally, after a long time, she said, "Year before last, I nearly died. That's not an exaggeration. I spent two months in intensive care."

"I didn't even know how to get in touch—that's my fault."

"I was unconscious most of the time, or else delirious," she said. "For a while I was on the critical list. I couldn't have written if I'd known where to."

"What happened?"

"It was a tumor in the uterus," she said. "Benign—there was no malignancy—but the surgeon who did the job was a jerk. He cut or perforated something. By the time they found out, I was running a temperature of a hundred and five. Peritonitis set in and on top of it there was a fever of unspecified origin, what they call an F.U.O. The antibiotics didn't do much. That's when they went back in and really opened me up. Look."

She drew down the blanket. Across the lower part of her stomach there was a long, vicious, crescent-shaped scar. She touched it, and said, "There were half a dozen rubber tubes hanging out of this cut for over a month, draining pus. When I got out of the hospital finally, I weighed exactly one hundred and one pounds, and that's not much for a woman who's five-ten. They sent me to a convalescent home, and after that I had to rest. I'm just now starting to get my health back."

"You know, last night when I undressed you and put you to bed, I saw how thin you were," Roy said. "But what I noticed was that your legs and arms were white—you used to be so suntanned. It must have been a terrible thing to go through."

"It was more than that," she went on. "It broke me completely, mentally. Roy, I was alone, and I knew I was going to die. Even the doctors knew it—I could see it on their faces. Something just cracked inside me—to be thirty-three and to know that you're dying." She paused. "I'd have to say that ever since then I haven't had a lot of faith in the medical profession."

"Anybody can make mistakes, even doctors."

"Not with *my* life they can't," she said bitterly. "They cut out half my insides. I can't have children. I wasn't even sure I could have sex. That's why I was so afraid when you started to go into me. I was scared. I couldn't help it."

"But it was all right?"

She smiled. "Yes. I was too tense at first. You know, for such a long time I hurt so badly, everywhere below the waist. That's what I was scared of before—that you would be in me, and the pain would come back."

"Did it?"

"No. It was in my mind," she said. "The doctors told me I had to be very careful about having sex. What an awful thing to tell someone—just saying something like that can create a block. But there wasn't any kind of problem at all."

They lay there quietly for a while, just being close. He said, "Rae, is there anything more you want to talk about?"

For a moment, she did not reply, and he thought she had dozed off to sleep again. Then she said quietly, "What do you think a woman like me thinks about a man like you?"

He had no answer. He could feel her face against his chest, pressing against the fabric of his shirt. Almost murmuring, she began to talk, and it was like she was telling a story that described someone else. Some other woman, some other man:

"She might, for example, say something to herself like, 'Well, I know this man. He lives by himself up in the mountains, and he has a thing for me. And, actually, I have a thing for him, too, although I'm scared to admit it.'

"Let's say that this happens to be a woman who has been around and who knows how to get by on her own. Like, she's her own person. So, she might say, 'Well, I can go see this man, because I like him a lot. But there's a risk that if I'm with him too long I'll want to make it a forever thing. And do I really want this?' He has some problems, see? Actually, so does she, in her head. She's very objective, you understand, and at the same time strongly attracted to him.

"Maybe she's traveled her own journey, and has taken some hard shots. She's pretty suspicious, of herself more than anyone else, so that it's become hard for her to know if she's capable of any kind of real relationship with somebody.

"She's also lonely, and she has her own needs. The safe bet would be for her to simply use him, like, 'Hi, I'm here, where's the bed, let's fuck, it's been great, see you around sometime.' Only she can't really do that because she cares a lot about this man. Also, quite selfishly, it would leave her with a lot of rotten feelings about herself. And if there's one thing she doesn't need, it's more bad feelings about being a no-good miserable bitch. She's got plenty of guilt and despair as it is.

"Being cautious, her strongest reaction to all this is to stay away. Let's say there are other men she could be involved with. Every time you turn around there's another man. They're all dying to help her, or so they say. That's one of the reasons she's so strongly attracted to this man. He's not interested in domination or ownership or *machismo*. He's just a very nice guy."

She paused to light a cigarette, and when she had it going, puffed, and then passed it to him. "Anyway, she finally decides to go see him again after years. And things are still good. Nothing's changed that much. So, she's left with the same damned problem. Should she maintain a distance? Or else maybe she ought to do something about it."

"Pearl would say that this woman is in a predicament," Roy said.

"That's for sure," she said. "Should she just go on drifting through life? Or should she take the plunge and let someone get close to her again? You know, she tried that before, and it was almost the end of her."

"How does she see this man?" he asked.

"A very special person," she murmured. "He's not rich. He's not handsome at all. In fact, when she was with him before—she has a perverse way of looking at things, you know—she thought of that old fairy tale. The one about beauty and the beast?"

"But no kiss is ever going to change me into a Prince Charming," he said.

"On track," she said, smiling. "In this version, it's the pretty young maiden who's changed. This woman's starting to show her mileage—she isn't the knockout she used to be. That's not important, though. What counts is that this man is the kindest person she's ever known."

"You're as beautiful as ever."

"Roy, you'll never make a liar."

"You said this woman had tried it before."

"That's right." She puffed at the cigarette and then stubbed it in the saucer he had put on the floor by the bed for an ashtray. "I was married. Twice, in fact." She smiled again. "There's nothing like marriage to make a person a drifter for life, if she's not careful. Anyway, those are some of the things that can go through a woman's mind. I hope I've presented her accurately enough—the good and the bad. Some people might call her a bitch. Maybe she is. But I like to think she means well. She really doesn't want to hurt anybody. But at the same time she's afraid of being hurt. That's why she ran away from this man before. Her head is pretty fucked up. Offhand, I'd say she's scared and dubious about life and the future. She's lonely, and maybe depressed, too . . . and selfish. Yes, and vulnerable. She knows what manipulation is. She knows when a man is manipulating her, and she knows when she's doing it to a man. And, lastly, she knows what a cheap racket manipulation always turns out to be."

"Rae, you'll just have to figure out what's best for you," he said.

She grinned, and then began climbing over him. "Right now, I'm going to figure out how to make a dash for the outhouse. If I don't piss, I'll bust."

LATER, THEY GOT dressed and had a quiet morning. It was cloudy and cool, and he built up the fire in the sheepherder and set the coffeepot up front, away from the flue, so that it would simmer without boiling. They sat at the table in their stockinged feet, with cups of coffee in front of them, and talked more. Behind the glasses there were circles under her eyes; he could see that she was still tired but relaxed and easy. He said, "What you were telling me about before . . . I still don't understand why, after so long, you'd want to come back."

"It's clear to me. I thought about it for a long time—not just when I was sick, but later, when I was recuperating. Finally, I made up my mind, so I wrote."

"I never thought I'd hear from you again," he said.

"I was happy here."

He said cautiously, still not wanting to pry, "Sounds like you had a bad time."

She smiled. "What do you want? The usual horror story?"

"I'm sorry. I was wondering, that's all."

"Roy, it's not really all that interesting," she said. "These days, everybody has his or her very own horror story. I got sick and nearly died. I always thought I could handle life hands down, but for once I was in a situation that handled me. It really scared me, and it wasn't my fault. It changed me. Before that, if I was in a bad situation, I figured it was my fault. Like, maybe I should have been reading the people I was around more carefully, and paying more attention to the way things were going. I'd say, 'Rae, you're a bright woman, and this is a bad scene, and you ought to know better.' Who doesn't make mistakes?" She lit a fresh cigarette and went on. "What I always called it was *the bad place*. Everybody has one. I don't care who the person is. We all have something we can be scared of. Do you know what I mean? It's like a bad place inside your mind."

"In a way," he said.

"You do, too," she said, staring at him. "Whether you know it or not, anyplace away from Sawmill River Flats is your bad place. The only thing is, you can't hack it up here by yourself. So, after a while, you go back down to civilization and face the world, and get kicked in the ass." She paused, and then said, "When I was a little kid my mother got divorced, and for a couple of years I lived with my grandmother, north of Sacramento. She had the most beautiful white hair, and she was the neatest, cleanest person I've ever known, and in all the time I was with her she never raised her voice once. Some little old ladies are sweet, but this one wasn't. She was a lapsed fundamentalist and an alcoholic, to boot. Looking back on it now, I can see that she was one hundred percent committable, but I didn't know that then. To save my soul, she punished me, and, to hear her tell it, it was for my own good. Her brain was overdosed with gin and Baptist gibberish. If I didn't eat all my dinner or got dirty playing or came home from school five minutes late, that was it. I spent a lot of time locked in a broom closet under the stairwell, in the dark. One time, she made me stand in a basin of cold water out on the back porch, for three hours, at night. This was one old lady who had some pretty fancy tricks. She told me that when I was twelve, Satan's curse would descend upon me, and everybody would know I was dirty and impure, and, of course, when I started menstruating I thought she was right. And always—*always*—I was going to 'the bad place.' I didn't have any idea of where this place was, except that it was worse than hell, and I was going to go there. Gradually, in my mind, that got to be my bad place. That was where Rae Ehrenson was going to go." She drank some of her coffee. "And I suppose that in a way I did."

He stared at her for a while, and then said, "You've talked a lot this morning. More than you ever did before."

She thought about this and then nodded. "Well, maybe it's time. Before, I could come and go as I pleased—it was different."

"And now?"

She stared at him. "Roy, I swear, I don't know." Then, presently: "That's the truth. I wanted to come see you. That's all I know."

"I'm glad of that."

She shook her head. "Don't ask me for answers. There are no magical answers, not anymore."

"But you're talking—I like that."

"If you once start, it's not so hard," she said. "It gets easier." Suddenly, sitting there, she looked close to tears. "Oh, Roy—I'm no mystery at all—can't you see that?"

"I wish you'd stay."

She set her forearms upon the table between the two of them, hands clasped, fingers interlocked. "Why?"

"I love you. I always have."

"The way I am?"

"Yes."

"But you don't know me."

"It doesn't matter."

"Yes, it does."

"Rae? Could you have gone elsewhere?"

Again the look. "Yes. I could have. I still can."

"But you came here?"

"Yes."

"Then there's no problem. Don't leave. That's all."

"No. I have to do something."

"But why?"

"I thought you might have guessed," she said, and then frowned. "It's something I've done a lot of thinking about. And I've made up my mind."

"What is it?"

"I have a son," she said simply. "His name is Joshua. He's seven years old. I haven't seen him in two and a half years. That's why I can't stay. I'm going to get him. And there isn't a thing in the world that can stop me from doing that."

WHAT SHE HAD to tell after that was simple enough:

"My mother took me back with her and we ended up living in a commune. She was still in her twenties, and very pretty. She wasn't a hippie, really—just looking for something. On the other hand, she wasn't that bright either. The commune was wonderful, and there were lots of kids. We all lived on oatmeal, barley, fresh greens, unpasteurized milk, and food stamps. There was sex, and there were drugs—natural stuff like mescaline, hash, and grass—no synthetic junk. There was a river where we would all bathe naked, and then the grownups would do massages and Rolfing and tactile encounters in the sun. So my mother was very much into this, and by the time I was about seventeen, I was, too, because everything was so natural and free, like sex and loving and grass. Well, I fell for this beautiful boy, and what happened was that he didn't care that much for me. I didn't know how to hack that. I gave him everything of myself, and that went on for a couple of years. There were mirrors in the commune, and I knew how good I looked to men, and it was like I was giving all of myself and he was giving nothing. Finally, we had a fight, and we ended up having a communal wedding. There was no certificate, but as far as I'm concerned it was a real marriage. Three months later he split, just took off on me, with a fifteen-year-old—he liked young girls. By then, I was about twenty. That's kind of old for a man who likes young stuff."

"And then?"

"I left—split." She stared at him. "I put everything into that relationship, I really did. And it didn't work. It took me years to get over that. I kept feeling that it was somehow all my fault, that there was some deficiency in me."

"I see. Go on."

"What do you want—one more horror?" she asked, looking at him again. "I moved around. I took three years of college at UCLA, mostly in biology and chemistry. I got to know different

people. Most of them weren't really so bad, but I'm not so sure
if they were really that good either. Sex, drugs, prostitution,
kinks like SM and home movies—I've known folks who were into
all that. Does it make any difference? I don't think so. Finally, I
met a man and I liked him, and we were good together. This was
in San Diego, and that's where I'm going to get my boy, Joshua.
Josh's father was a handsome man, but he was into all kinds of
things. His family has tons of money. Or at least they claim to—
I've never met anyone in San Diego who admitted being poor.
Actually, they *are* wealthy—they sent money to me while I was
sick. Well, we got married, and this time it was by a rabbi, because the family was Jewish. He used to take it out and wave it
under my nose and say, 'Have a sniff, and find out what real
kosher is like.' Finally, I got pregnant with Josh. When the time
came, I was under anaesthetics for most of it—they told me later
it was a bad delivery. And while I was in there, bleeding my guts
out, he was out, diming around. There's a strip of beach north of
La Jolla where the kids hang out—you know, suntans, blond hair,
surfing, and caps on the teeth. So my husband was parked in his
van at the side of the road with two teenage girls, and they must
have been doing a job, because his trousers were found around
his ankles, and they didn't have much on either when some truck
driver blew a tire and his rig swung into them. Don't ever tell
me that whiplash is an ambulance-chaser's scam. That particular
whiplash took my old man's head almost clean off. He's only
thirty-six, and he's in a respirator. He can blink his eyes and
drool, and he's got an I.Q. that's out of sight, and that was the
second time that I cracked up. Finally, I got a divorce."

"What about your boy?"

"Roy, I hardly know him," she said. "When the grandparents
saw that I couldn't handle it, they offered to take him. They're
very decent people. They made me a proposition. I couldn't help
myself. They said they'd give him the best. I had nothing. What
was I going to do, live off them?"

"Was there a formal transfer of custody?"

"No."

"I don't think you'll have any trouble then, getting him back."

"I've already talked to them," she said. "They understand how
I feel. Roy, they're really good people."

He finished his coffee, and then stared at her and smiled. "I'll be darned."

"What's the matter?"

"You have a son."

"What's so unusual about that?"

"Nothing—nothing at all," Roy said. He shook his head. Still smiling. "I just never figured. So, you have a son. I think I'll have a glass of wine on that."

"Isn't it early?"

He glanced at the transistor radio's clock. "Hell, it must be about seven in the evening, if you happen to be in London." He got a bottle and two glasses. "Rae, what are you going to do with this boy?"

"Raise him."

"How long did you say it's been since you've seen him?"

"Almost three years. When I left—after we buried Walter— that's where I went. Then I went to Louisiana, and after that I got sick." She paused, and added, "I was thinking even then about taking him. But, you know, his grandparents were putting a lot of pressure on me. They love him."

"If he was mine, there wouldn't be anybody pressuring me," Roy said. "No, sir." He poured wine into the glasses. "That's a shame—I mean, you've lost so much time with him, when you could have been watching him grow up, and been having fun with him." He shook his head. "Time passes too fast."

"I'll make it up."

"Why, sure you will." He stared at her. He was feeling good. "What are you going to do after you get him?"

"I don't know," she said.

He was thinking. After a while, he managed to say it: "Do you reckon you might want to bring him back here? I mean, just for a while?"

It was her turn to be quiet. She looked at him, and then, after a long time, she said, "Yes. The thought had crossed my mind."

"You know something, Rae? You sure can go all round the barn before you let out what's on your mind."

"Roy, I can't help that," she said. "Can't you see it from my side? What am I supposed to do, walk back into your life after hurting you and say, 'Here I am, only I happen to have a seven-year-old, and I want to be with you, but if you want that, then you take my boy, too'? That's bullshit—a manipulative trade-off —the oldest hustle in the world. 'Here's my cunt, but if you want it, there's a price tag on it—a seven-year-old boy.' "

"Rae, if you're thinking that way, you should never have stopped here," he said. "You should have gone straight on out to San Diego."

"I know."

"Then why did you?"

She was silent again, stared down at her coffee cup. "I love you, Roy."

For a while, neither could speak. Then he said, "Do you think it would work? Bringing him here?"

"Roy, I don't know. I've only been with him a few months since the day he was born. I don't know anything about being a mother."

"I've scared some kids, you know."

"I don't believe that. You're kind."

"Most of them never hung around long enough to explore that possibility," he said. "I'm worried about something else, though —most kids these days need all kinds of things. A regular life, being with people who know how to raise them right, school. All that. My father raised me the best way he knew how, because he had to. I came along, and he and Walter were stuck with me. Life up here mightn't be so good for this boy."

"It was a good life for you, Roy."

He groped around, foundering. "But his grandparents are wealthy. Or you could get married again. Then he'd have himself a real father."

"What's a real father?"

"A real father is important to a boy," he insisted. "Of course, I want you here—and your boy, he's welcome, too. You ought to know me better than that. Hell—having a kid around? That sure would be something! But, Rae, you've got to face reality. If his grandparents found out about me—I mean, about the person you and your boy were living with—I'd practically guarantee they'd make trouble. You don't want that."

"Where I live and who I live with is not their business," she said.

"I've never been around a kid. Supposing I'm no good at it?"

"You were incredibly wonderful with Walter," she said. "I never saw anything like it. He was a child."

"You could do a lot better than being with me," he pointed out.

She looked at him angrily. "Do you really believe that?"

"I'm only trying to be practical."

"Well, I am, too," she said, and drank a little of her wine. "I'd do this. I'll bring him here. We could give it a try. But only if you want me to."

"Really?"

"Yes," she said. "I'd like that. I've thought about it. I'm going to have this boy with me no matter what. I wanted to tell you everything, and I'll tell it to you again, now. I am selfish, Roy— I love you, and I want to be with you, and I want my son, and I want to raise him up to be a good human being. That's all I really want, and that's an awful lot. I can't help it if I'm a selfish bitch."

He thought about this. Finally, he said, "How long would it take to go get him?"

"A week. Less. His grandparents know I'm coming."

"Do you need money?"

"They sent me money—I have almost three thousand in travelers' checks."

"When would you want to leave?"

"Soon. The quicker the better," she said. "Roy, do you really want us here?"

"You better go fetch him."

"Do you really mean it? I mean, it isn't just because you want me here?"

"Sure I want you here," he said. " 'Course I do."

He grinned, and she said, "You know something, when you smile, you're so homely you're just gorgeous? You really are. What are you so damned pleased about?"

"Nothing," he said. "I was just thinking of what it might be like—having a kid around this old town again."

TWO DAYS LATER, Rae was ready to leave. Now, there was excitement and enthusiasm about the trip, very different from the mood they'd felt when she had left after Walter's funeral. This time she was returning. She promised to be back in a week at most. The plan was for her to catch the shuttle flight at the Roswell airport that would connect with El Paso and then on to California.

On the drive down from Sawmill River, they stopped for a brief visit with Pearl, who shook hands with Rae and said, "Why, sure! I remember you. How've you been? You're just as pretty as ever. My, how the years do fly. You hardly look any older at all. I been wondering when Roy'd bring you by to say hello. How about some coffee and a sandwich?"

"That'd be wonderful," Rae said. "It's good to see you again, Pearl."

"I guess you two been hiding out at Sawmill," Pearl said, setting out cups. "Don't it get horrible lonesome up there?"

"Not really."

"Well, I reckon you got Roy to talk to. Only he never says much. He's one of those silent types."

"He can be a real talker at times," Rae said. She began helping Pearl make sandwiches.

"Really? What's he talk about?"

"Different things."

"Where you been keeping yourself all this time?"

"I've been out of state," Rae said.

"Traveling, I reckon."

"Sort of."

"Must've been fun," Pearl remarked. "I don't know why a woman travels."

"For the same reason a man does, I guess," Rae said.

Pearl gave her a look, and then a bit of a grin. "I suppose that's so. Funny, I never thought of it that way." She was slicing bread. "Well, I hope you're ready to settle down for a while. Roy here needs someone to look out for him."

"It's the other way around," Rae said. "He looks out for me."

"There are folks around here who think well of you and Roy. You want to remember that. That ought to count for something. How about the two of you coming down to dinner on Friday? I'll fix something nice and simple."

"Could we have a raincheck, Pearl?" Rae asked. "I'm leaving today on a trip."

"Where to?"

"California."

Pearl stared at her. "You just *got* here, and you're leaving again?"

"I'll only be gone a week."

"Heavens, you really *do* like traveling, don't you?"

"Not really—I've had enough of it."

"Well, I should hope to say," Pearl agreed. "There're limits to the amount of distance a woman needs to put under her."

"This is more like a business trip," Rae told her.

"Well, I can't help wondering what'd take you all the way out there to an awful place like California," Pearl said, shaking her head.

"It's a secret, Pearl," Rae said. She was smiling.

Pearl stared at her and then frowned. "You're as bad as Roy. 'Muddy waters run deep,' as the saying goes. Talking to him is like listening to the Sphinx. Take care of your business, then— it's none of *my* affair."

"It's sort of a surprise," Roy said.

"Good. I haven't had a real surprise in nearly thirty years."

They sat down and had coffee and something to eat, and Pearl went on, "Roy, you're going to have to put me on salary for handling your affairs—another telegram, and then a letter, came in for you—from that New York crowd. You want me to get them for you?"

"Don't bother," Roy said. "I have a pretty good idea of what's in them. It's too nice a day. Why spoil it with bad news?"

They stayed with Pearl until noon and then left, with plenty of time to catch the afternoon flight at Roswell.

When the time came to say goodbye, he felt an awful wrench of unhappiness, remembering the emptiness he'd felt three years ago. He said, "Rae, I'll miss you."

"I'll miss you, too," she said. She looked wretched. "It won't be for long—I promise."

For a moment, he was filled with dreadful premonitions—plane crashes, another serious illness—anything that would keep her from returning. "I'll worry."

"Don't. That never does any good."

With that, she turned and walked out on the apron to the waiting shuttle plane, without ever looking back once, and he was alone again.

IN ROSWELL, HE stopped at a building-supply store and bought three gallons of white latex interior paint, a quart of blue enamel, and some cheap brushes. Earlier that morning, they had talked about having him clean up the cabin a little. Roy was eager to do this—it would keep his mind occupied until she got back. He had decided to redo the mud-plastered walls and brighten up the place in general—the sheepherder was a good stove, but after several months of constant use it tended to leave a patina of soot and fine ash everywhere. The blue enamel was for the front door and window trim. He also got a gallon of linseed oil for the plank floors and overhead beams.

Something else had happened earlier that same morning besides the plans they talked over. They had made love again, and later Roy—for a short time—walked about the cabin wearing jeans but no shirt. It was the hardest thing he'd ever had to do. Rae must have known how difficult it was for him—during that entire first summer, he'd never quite been able to accede to that request she'd made to see him shirtless—but now she made no remark or comment. She did not stare; neither did she make a point of averting her gaze.

For the next few days he worked at the tasks he had set himself, until it seemed that the cabin looked brand-new. He scrubbed out the chimneys of the kerosene lamps and refilled their reservoirs, and then carefully trimmed the wicks with scissors so that the flames burned bright and evenly. He put in a sizable food order with Pearl, who wanted to know if he was expecting the Dallas Cowboys for houseguests. The pit beneath the outhouse got bucketed down with raw lime until it smelled as clean and fresh as any outhouse ever smells, and then, on impulse, he painted the interior with some leftover latex. Fresh batteries were bought for all the flashlights, the big electric lantern, and the transistor radio—up here, there were no public utilities to pay but batteries were an endless expense. He aired the mattress Uncle Walter had slept on—the boy was to use this —and then fixed a pull-curtain on a wire so that the bed could be hidden from the rest of the cabin. This was the way they had arranged it when Walter was alive. It was not a great deal of privacy, but it would have to do for now. More firewood was cut and stacked, and he reglued the old wooden chairs, which had gotten loose and wobbly.

He went to bed at night tired and lonely and slept fitfully, troubled by an uneasiness that he knew would stay until she was back, and on the fourth night he wakened suddenly, sensing that something was wrong.

It was dark and silent in the cabin, and silent outside, too. He wasn't sure what time it was—sometime after midnight. For several minutes he lay there motionlessly, breathing quietly and listening.

There was no sound. Yet something was not right. Finally, he got up and slipped on his jeans and boots and went out. The night air was chilly, and he drew his shoulders up against the cold. He was still listening, but there was nothing. Even a small noise would carry a long way on such a night.

Then he saw it. Far down past the south end of the old town. Two faint red sparks . . . the twin brake-lights of some car or pickup truck, and then a brief splash of white from the headlights as it turned a curve and went into the woods.

Whoever it was had his motor off. Coasting downhill.

Roy stood there shivering in the chill for several more minutes. He was about to go back in when he saw a flare of bright yellow light, and with that he grabbed a shovel and ran for the jeep. They'd set fire to the town.

TWELVE

It was Schmidt's Mercantile, as well as two other frame buildings. They went quickly. By the time Roy got there flames were leaping twenty and thirty feet into the air, lighting up the night around him. The ancient, weathered wood snapped and crackled, sending clouds of hot, glowing cinders skyward, but it could have been worse. That entire side of Main Street would have burned except that there were big gaps in the row of buildings on either side of Schmidt's and the two adjoining houses.

The fire was too hot to approach. Dismayed, Roy stood back a way, watching helplessly. In half an hour, it burned down, and then he was able to get close enough to begin working with the shovel. He spent the rest of the night this way, pitching dirt onto the glowing embers. By daylight, the fire was under control and he was exhausted. Tendrils of smoke still rose in the quiet morning air. He went back to the cabin and got the five-gallon water cans he used for drinking water, and with these made trips from the beaver pond to the smoking ashes, emptying the cans and refilling them, again and again.

By noon, he judged it was safe to stop. At the cabin, he fixed a sandwich and opened a can of beer. He was too tired to think straight but, even so, behind the fatigue there was a growing anger, and a bitterness, too, for the stupidity of what had been done.

Earlier, he had found the firebomb, just inside what had been the entrance to Schmidt's. A gallon gasoline can, burnt and crushed now but not so unrecognizable that he couldn't tell what it was or what it had held. He'd sniffed at it, and beneath the stench of char and ash, there was the smell of gas. A firebomb, he knew, was easy enough to manufacture. You sprinkled gasoline around and then dribbled a trail across the floor to where it was safe, outside; and then you took a lighted cigarette and folded a book of paper matches over the filter end, and set it on the dribble. That was all. In seven or eight minutes—the time it took for the glowing cigarette to burn down to the matches—there was a fire. Time enough for a leisurely departure, coasting along a downgrade, maybe laughing with whoever was with you and passing a bottle back and forth in celebration of an enormously funny prank.

It had to be Bill Maldonado, and perhaps a friend or two for companionship. Roy was sure of it. Kids out for a summertime shack job might accidentally, or even uncaringly, set a fire, but he doubted that they would go to the trouble of rigging a genuine incendiary device. But Billy-Evil might be capable of such a gesture. Maldonado knew how to hold a grudge, and he had a sense of humor that was, at the kindest, simplistic. Yes, it would be just like him to be sitting around with some of his cronies, half drunk and bored, and say, with a mischievous twinkle, "Whyn't we head on up to Sawmill River and toast a few marshmallows? Build us a real bonfire, *qué no?*"

Roy knew something else, too.

He'd never be able to prove it. Not in a million years. If he'd caught them in the act, that would have been a different story. But he had no case. If he accused Maldonado, he'd get a blank look.

And Billy's pals would back him up. All of them looking innocent. At the same time they'd be laughing at him.

They might even point out—all of them keeping perfectly straight faces—that there was really nothing to get so excited about.

After all, how much harm had been done?

A couple of old, falling-apart buildings? Up in the middle of nowhere? Why make such a fuss over something that wasn't even important?

Why, shucks, those buildings ought to have been bulldozed years ago! It wasn't even safe for a person to go walking around inside them. Someone could get hurt.

Sure 'nuff. Why, you might even say that whoever'd set a match to those old shacks was doing the county a service.

SITTING THERE IN the cabin, he began to brood, and with this his anger deepened. He paced the floor, smoked one cigarette after another, and drank wine. A dark mood gripped him. True, the wanton burning of Schmidt's had been an attack on something he cherished, but there was more to it than that. It demonstrated clearly that the values he'd lived by—a respect for the rights of others, along with a certain amount of patience and honesty— were laughable. Or, at the very least, they were held in low esteem.

And not just by the likes of Bill Maldonado. Neil Larson, too, had no real regard for anything that stood in his way. When that New York businessman wanted something, he went out to get it— he talked persuasively and reasonably, but at heart he had a brigand mentality, and the weapons that never left his side were legal contracts and money.

For the next few hours, Roy worked hard. By now he was as angry as he'd been on the day he'd struck Billy-Evil. There was something else eating at him, too. A curious stubbornness took hold of him, that had its roots in resentment, as well as a kind of resolve not to be pushed at or badgered anymore. And as he worked, he made plans about what he was going to do.

He made up some handpainted signs, using the last of the blue enamel, that said various things, like NO TRESPASSING, PRIVATE PROPERTY, and VIOLATORS WILL BE PROSECUTED, and nailed them to trees bordering the primitive road that led to the village. Years ago, he had put up a few similar signs, but now he had more than a dozen of them posted, so that the message would be clear to any unwelcome visitor. In the ruins of the steam-driven sawmill he found thirty feet of logging chain, terribly rusted but still serviceable, and so heavy that he could barely lift it, and mounted this at a narrow place in the road, between two tall spruces . . . padlocked, that chain would at least slow down visitors when he was not at home.

With a fresh bottle of wine for company, he got out his typewriter and wrote a letter to Gardiner Potts, informing that gentleman that he was always welcome, but that he, Roy, was not interested in deeding his property to the state as an historical site.

Then he wrote another letter, to the Larson Corporation in New York, in which he said that ". . . after giving much thought to the proposed transaction and carefully weighing the pros and cons," he had regretfully come to the conclusion that Sawmill River Flats and its adjacent land was not for sale, lease, or franchise at any price, and that ". . . further exploratory communications of a negotiatory nature would, in essence, result in a waste of time on the part of all parties concerned."

He signed this letter:

Roy A. Gutierrez
Mayor, pro tem
Sawmill River Flats, NM

and then, for good measure, at the lower right-hand corner, he affixed the embossed stamp of his notary of the public seal, that ancient, nickle-plated antique he had found years ago in a Cerrillos junk shop.

After that, he put on a fresh shirt and jeans. Then he dragged the old footlocker out from under the bed and found the old cap-and-ball, .36-caliber Colt, still wrapped in oiled flannel.

In itself, the weight of the antique pistol, inert and heavy in his hand, seemed invested with a special authority. It was really a beautiful weapon, with a long octagonal barrel and walnut grips that had aged to a dark brown, and it had been well cared for. Most of the blueing along the barrel and frame had been worn away years ago, but there was no rusting or pitting anywhere. It was a fine old gun, and now, to make sure it would still work, he stood in the cabin's doorway and fired a test shot toward the beaver pond below, cocking the hammer and then aiming, and then squeezing the trigger gently. The gun went off with a loud bang and bucked sharply against the heel of his hand, and seemingly in the same instant, seen dimly through the haze of white smoke left by the shot, there was a small geyser of water as the slug struck the pond's surface, followed, just as quickly, by two faint slapping reports . . . the beavers, sounding an alarm with their tails. With that, Roy stuck the gun into his belt, took cigarettes and wine, and left.

DRIVING DOWN HE thought, *Roy, don't be a fool. Don't do a thing like this.*

Then he said, half aloud, "You've got no business with a gun. Things like that lead to real trouble. You're thinking to bluff Bill Maldonado. But Billy is dumb. How do you get through to someone like that?"

He thought, *if it really came to a showdown, could you do it? Could you actually take out a gun and shoot someone?*

"You better be practical," he said to himself. "If something like that happened, you'd be looking at a trial and a jail sentence."

And with that, you'd lose Rae, he thought.

He pulled the jeep over to the side of the road, poured another cup of wine, and tried to sort everything out in his mind.

It seemed to him now that if the three of them were happy, well, at least there was a chance they'd go on together. He said, "A chance . . . why, that isn't so bad. How many people are there who ever get that much?"

He thought, *she's all you ever wanted.*

But now this.

Harassment from a stupid man. *If you take it sitting still, why, Bill'll feel obligated to keep on.*

"What does a man do when another man attacks something he loves?" Roy said aloud.

And he thought, *he knows about Rae, too. He knows how much she means.*

Roy wondered how far something like this could ever go.

What would he do, for example, if Maldonado should some

day go after her? Suppose Bill understood that she and the town were all that mattered to him . . . why, then, if one thing didn't work, a fellow might have to try something else, *por qué no?* After all, a man is a man, and he's got a natural right to enjoy whatever he wants, especially if a weaker *hombre* stands by and lets him.

He thought, *unless it's stopped right now, there'll be no end to it. You might as well face it.*

He lit a cigarette, finished his drink, put the jeep into gear, and drove on.

ROY STOPPED AT the Smokey Bear Saloon to ask if anybody had seen Billy-Evil and learned that he was over at Lincoln rehearsing for the pageant, so Roy went there.

It was hot and cloudy, and long before he got to Lincoln, fat, heavy raindrops were spatting down on the highway's hot asphalt, a prelude to one of those torrential gullywashers peculiar to the southwest. When the storm hit, the visibility went down to zero, and he pulled over to the side of the road to wait it out with the windows rolled up and another drink of wine for company. The inside of the windshield quickly fogged up, and he cracked a side window to let fresh air in. The downpour lasted less than twenty minutes, and it passed as quickly as it had come, moving off over the foothills to the north, with loud rumbles of thunder and occasional glimpses of lightning flashing savagely among the low, murky clouds. Sitting there, his indignation grew. In the town, the pageant rehearsal had been called off. Muddy water, three inches deep, was rushing down the main street, carrying with it branches and leaves. The arena where most of the pageant was staged was a morass, and its crude viewstands, knocked together out of rough lumber, were empty.

Bill Maldonado and some of his friends were standing around at one side of the arena. Roy parked the jeep and went over to him. He still had the old .36 stuck in his belt. For a moment, he had considered slipping it into the glove compartment, but then decided not to.

When he got closer, he heard someone in the group say in Spanish, "Here's Gutierrez." Maldonado was drinking a can of beer. In the pageant, he led the posse that pursued Billy Bonney, after the Kid broke jail—it hadn't really happened that way but visitors always enjoyed a good chase scene. He was dressed in an old-time costume—plaid shirt, bandanna, jeans, and "shotgun" chaps—and he looked very good with his big black Stetson tilted far back on his head. He and his friends had evidently sought shelter during the storm. Now he smiled agreeably and said, "*Com' esta,* Roy?"

Roy spoke as directly as he knew how; there was a tightness in his chest that made breathing hard: "You know why I'm here. I'm going to tell you just one thing. If I catch you or anybody else on my property, there'll be real trouble. I mean it."

Maldonado was still smiling. "Where'd you get that gun?"

"It's loaded," Roy said. "And not with blanks."

"That sounds like a threat."

"It's a promise," Roy said. "I'm warning you."

"*Amigo,* I don't know what you're talking about," Maldonado said.

"You're a liar," Roy said, "and I'm saying it to your face."

Maldonado stopped smiling. A couple of his friends eyed the pistol in Roy's belt and looked uneasy, as if they were suddenly wishing they were somewhere else. A loaded gun, and calling someone a liar was not something to fool with. Roy was staring at Maldonado. "Billy, you cross me one more time and, I swear, I'll get you."

Maldonado considered this for a long moment. And then there was a faint shift of expression . . . those sad Spanish eyes that always seemed fixed on distant smoky mountains grew a shade thoughtful, almost reflective . . . and with that there was an almost imperceptible wilting of his posture, a minute slumping of the shoulders. He knew Roy meant it.

Lloyd Parmalee and Rowdy came sloshing over to see what was going on. They looked like flood-disaster victims, Lloyd especially, not the lawman and outlaw they were supposed to be playing. Rowdy didn't have his teeth in, and he hadn't shaved in a week or so; he called out, "Hi, Roy. What you doin' here?"

Roy turned from Billy-Evil. "Hello, Rowdy. Lloyd, how are you?"

"What're you doing with that old cap-and-ball popgun?" Lloyd asked; as a gunsmith, he could identify any gun at a glance. "Come to join the pageant?"

"No, I just had some business," Roy said.

Suddenly, Lloyd became alert. He looked from Roy to Maldonado. "Something going on?"

"It's been taken care of, Lloyd," Roy said.

Maldonado stepped forward. "He's got a loaded gun, Parmalee, and he's been making threats. I've got witnesses who'll back me up on that."

"Roy, what are you doing runnin' around with a loaded pistol?" Lloyd asked.

"Spreading the word, that's all," Roy said.

"What happened?"

Roy told him. "Last night somebody set fire to my town. Three buildings went up. I'm tired of it, Lloyd."

"Do you know who did it?"

"I know," Roy said. "But I can't prove it."

Rowdy Roth said, "I'll give twenty-to-one *I* know." He stared at Maldonado. "Sonuvabitch, I might even go as high as fifty-to-one!"

Lloyd thought about this. Then he said, "Roy, you better give me that gun for the time being." Roy did, reluctantly, and Parmalee went on, "I'm not about to see anybody get hurt."

"I want him arrested," Maldonado said. "I spent all last night in Capitan, and I can prove it."

Lloyd walked up to him, followed by Rowdy. "Don't you be telling me what to do. Who d'you think you're talking to?"

Parmalee stood there, looking like a small, drowned beagle. He had a funny expression on his face, and his eyes had narrowed into slits. A wiry little fellow, inches shorter than the man he was speaking to, but as tough as rawhide. He was water-soaked and bedraggled, and his Stetson looked like a wet pancake; yet at that moment, he was obviously tense and utterly without fear. Roy thought of Pearl's recollection of a much younger Lloyd, a tightly built, small young man who had never backed down from a fight, and never lost. Parmalee said, "Bill, you don't faze me worth shit. I've about had it with you. For years you been braggin' about how hot you are. I been keepin' an eye on you, and

I know what's been going on. I'm telling you straight out—lay off Gutierrez here. Stay away from him and that town of his."

"I never went near the place," Maldonado insisted.

"Piss on you," Lloyd said. "And piss on your friends, too. I wouldn't mind locking all of you up for a spell."

"On what charges?"

"Incurable ugliness," Rowdy chimed in. "We're out to keep America beautiful."

"Billy, you been haranguing Roy for years," Lloyd went on. "It's gone far enough. Whyn't you and your pals haul ass out of here. Move along now."

"How come you're sticking up for him?" Maldonado demanded angrily.

Lloyd said, " 'Cause I like him. And 'cause I don't like you." He turned. "Come on, Roy. We'll walk you back to your jeep."

He and Rowdy and Roy walked away. Rowdy said in cooing tones, "Lloyd, you gotta be something else! Did you see Maldonado? Looked like a rabbit that doesn't know whether to shit or go blind!"

At the jeep they lit cigarettes and passed the wine around. Lloyd returned the pistol and said, "Don't ever let me catch you carrying this thing around again, Roy, not loaded, anyhow. You know better than that."

"He set that fire, Lloyd," Roy said. "I'm sure of it."

Lloyd nodded. "If he comes around again, you let me know. We heard you got that nice young gal staying with you again. You just take care of her, and don't get any more ideas about sidestepping the law. How is she?"

"She had to go on a trip," Roy said. "She ought to be back soon." Suddenly, he saw that his hands were shaking. Lloyd and Rowdy saw, too.

Lloyd stared up at Roy seriously, and then he said, "I'm glad we happened along when we did. A man loses his temper, well, things can get out of control."

STILL A LONG way from being calm, he stopped at Pearl's on the way back to see if any mail had come. The first thing she said was: "You two must have ESP going between you."

"What are you talking about, Pearl?"

"She long-distanced here, not three hours ago."

"Rae?"

"No, you knothead, it was Mary Tyler Moore. 'Course it was her."

"What'd she say?"

"We had a nice chat," Pearl said, doing her cat-and-mouse thing. "They got a terrible smog alert. She said she started to go to the beach but couldn't find it."

"Pearl!"

"She sounded fine," Pearl went on. "It was a real good connection, so we just gabbed away, since she was paying. You know, Roy, that girl ain't half bad. I mean, she really wanted to know how *I* was doing for a change. You ever notice how when most people sit down to chat with you, all they're really waiting for is a chance to leap in and complain about how awful *their* miserable life is? They don't give a tinker's damn about you! Selfishness, that's all friendship ever is! Maudie'll walk into this trailer and dump herself down and say, 'Pearl, I'm worried about you, and I want to hear how things are going.' Along about the time I'm getting ready to open my mouth, she's got her whole face buried to the hilt in a roast chicken, and at the same time she's talking about how awful it is for *her*. You know, I've gone through at least *four* menopauses with her in the last twenty years? I know more about her tangled-up old sewer pipes than I care to. She wolfs down Midol like it was candy. When she ain't complaining, she's bragging about some new crash diet she's found. 'I lost six pounds this week,' she'll say, getting up from my table, which looks like an earthquake hit it. 'Where, Maudie, in your little toe?' I ask her. She wants me to use her special estrogen cream on my face for all these wrinkles. I told her wrinkles come from being old and skinny. Hell, if you're blown up like a blimp, you can be eighty and still have a complexion smoother'n a baby's behind."

"Pearl, what did Rae have to say?"

"We talked about my sciatica."

"You have as much sciatica as I do," Roy told her. "I've watched you split kindling and haul bales of alfalfa for the goats. Don't hand me that."

"I'm failing, Roy. Like the one-horse shay. About ready to fall apart."

"Twenty years from now I'll be hearing the same. Now, come on, tell me, what'd she say?"

"Oh, you're no fun at all," she said. "You can't take any joshing. I always said that about you. No sense of humor." She gave him a sour, complacent smile: "She's coming in tomorrow morning on the ten-o'clock flight, at Roswell. Wants you to be there to meet her. Said she was bringing her friend. Sounded cheerful."

He was flustered. "I wasn't expecting her for another couple of days. Did she say anything else?"

Pearl thought about this, frowning, and then she said, "Everything went fine. That's what she told me to tell you. She said for you to be waiting. If you hadn't of come by, I was going to phone Lloyd Parmalee and ask him to drive up to Sawmill. Say, who's this friend? She said she was sending cartons of stuff by UPS. Coming in light, herself. I reckon you got yourself some company, Roy." She thought again. "Hell, *quien sabe*, maybe it's about time."

"Pearl, can you do me a favor?"

"I never lend money. It's the best way I know of to lose friends."

"Nothing like that. Can I use your shower?"

"Go ahead. What've you been doing, cleaning out a fireplace? You smell awful." Even though he'd changed clothing, the stench of smoke and charred wood was on him. He told her what had happened, omitting the part about having the pistol. When he was done, she said, "Well. So you and Bill Maldonado had it out. And Lloyd and Rowdy got in on it." She shook her head. " 'Course, Maldonado's nine-tenths bluff. Even so, I think you did a smart thing, stringing a chain across the road and posting no-trespassing signs—anybody comes on the property now, they won't have an excuse, if they can read." She stared at Roy for a moment. "You go take a shower. Hand out your stuff and I'll put 'em through the washer and dryer. It won't take long. I can lend you a bathrobe. If you feel like it, stay the night. I'll rustle up some dinner."

"I might take you up on that, Pearl," he said. "It's been a long day."

He took a shower and then sat around the kitchen with her, wearing a bathrobe that stopped far short of his knees, while she ironed his jeans and shirt. They shared a bottle of wine she had set on the counter. "I bleached hell out of everything with ammonia and Clorox," Pearl said. "You ought to buy some new underwear. A woman likes a touch of glamour in a man, not a scarecrow." She glanced at him in the bathrobe. "You got the longest legs I ever seen on a human, and feet, too. What size shoes d'you wear?"

"Sixteen."

"You don't say." She drank some of her wine and then went on with her ironing. "Harold always liked military creases in his shirts . . . I had to make 'em straight as an arrow, or he wouldn't even put one on. Size sixteen, you say." She thought about this. "No wonder your girlfriend's in such a rush to get back. Everybody to her taste, as the saying goes."

The hot shower and the wine had relaxed him, and now he realized how exhausted he was. Supper was on the stove, and it was good to sit there with her for company. He lit a cigarette and then smiled at her. "That's nonsense, Pearl—there's no correlation between size of feet and anything else. Wasn't Harold a short man?"

"Harold was startling," she said, and had some more wine. She grinned to herself. "To be honest, I never saw anything like it in my life. After he'd have his bath, he'd sit in my lap, and I'd dry him. It was something, all right."

"Pearl, was he the love of your life?"

"Oh, shucks, Roy, I wouldn't go that far," she said. "Harold was made to be a loving man, that's all, and he only knew one way of showing it, the devil. Being so small, y'know, he was all vanity. 'Fill the cup to overflowing,' he used to sing. And he could. I used to be thankful when he'd go off to his job. I'd limp back to bed and snatch some shuteye."

"What did he work at?"

"Harold? Oh, he was a professional hairdresser," Pearl said. "Had a beauty salon over in Roswell. He would do the ladies. Hovering like a bee, y'know. And didn't they love it? Oh, women are awful! Big old ranch gals, in for a perm, acting dainty and all uncertain. You ever notice how a woman drops her eyes when she's talking to a man? Well, that ain't modesty . . . in a manner of speaking, she's just evaluating the conditions. He let 'em all have a good look. In the bars over in Roswell, all the men used to tease him about being flapwristed, 'cause he worked with ladies, but Harold didn't mind. He knew."

"Was he a good man for you, Pearl?"

"I wouldn't know about that," she said. "We was married four years before he left."

"Was it good, though?"

She stared at him, and he caught a hint of times past—there was a thoughtful expression about her eyes, hidden now by deep, furrowed wrinkles. She said, "Best ever, honey."

They had a late dinner, and that night he slept badly, troubled by dreams. The next morning, after coffee, he was off. "I'll get that food order first thing," she told him.

At Roswell there was rain, and some flights were late, but by eleven it had cleared. Rae came out of the plane lugging two carry-on suitcases. She looked terribly wan and tired. Behind her was the boy.

Roy ran out to meet them. "I'm glad you're back." She was smiling, and then she set down the suitcases, put both arms around his neck, and kissed him: "Oh, I am, too. You'll never know."

THIRTEEN

HE WAS AN ordinary, garden-variety sort of boy, somewhere between three and four feet tall, with thick wheat-colored hair that
was not particularly neat, and large brown eyes that stared
straight into Roy's. There were scores of freckles across his upper
cheeks and snub nose. He had on hornrimmed eyeglasses, a battered tweed peak-cap, jeans, sneakers, and a blue t-shirt that had
"I'M REAL PEOPLE" emblazoned across the chest.

He was a nice enough looking boy but the thing was that when
he shook hands he let off what had to be the widest grin in the
world—it astonished Roy. The wide smile said simply, *"Hey!"*
Roy grinned back, unable to help himself.

That smile was something else again.

"My name is Roy," he said. "So, you're Josh."

"My real name's Joshua."

"That's a fine name," Roy said. "I looked it up in my dictionary.
Do you know what it means?"

"No."

" 'Jehovah is salvation.' "

"It does?"

Roy was regarding him thoughtfully. Finally, he said, "I think
I'm going to call you Huckleberry, though."

"Is that a name?"

"It's the name of a boy in a book," Roy said. "Huckleberry Finn. I never saw a picture of him, but in my mind I think he must have looked exactly like you when he was little. Lots of freckles, and a big grin. He was always getting into terrible mischief. Also, he hated combing his hair."

"What's the book called?"

"The Adventures of Huckleberry Finn."

"Did he have adventures?"

"He sure did."

"I can read."

"I'll bet you can."

"Is it a kid's book?"

"It's sort of a book for everybody," Roy said.

The boy was staring up at him with interest. He said, "You're big."

"Yes."

"How big are you?"

"Pretty big."

"Is that a real cowboy hat?"

"Sort of," Roy said. "Say, where'd you get *your* hat?"

The boy grinned again. "Found it!"

"You found it?"

"Apparently, it was lying in the gutter," Rae said. "His grandmother told me he even wears it to bed."

Josh pulled the peak down over his forehead, so that he had to tilt his head back to look up at Roy. "Isn't it a great hat?"

"It sure is," Roy said. He picked up the suitcases, and the three of them began walking toward the parking lot. "In fact, it's a super hat."

"Mommy says we're going to stay with you."

"Yes."

"She says we're going camping."

"Kind of. We're going way up in the mountains."

"Will it be fun?"

"I hope so."

"What's up there?"

"All kinds of things. You wait and see."

"Do you like to skate?" Josh asked.

"No, I never learned how."

"I know how. I can skate pretty good."

At the jeep, Rae took the back seat so that the boy could sit up front, and they drove off. Roy said to her, "How was the flight?"

"All right. Tiring—I'm glad it's over. Has anything been happening here?"

"Nothing important."

In the front seat, Josh was eyeing Roy. Suddenly, his eyes got mischievous behind the hornrimmed spectacles, and he flashed that big grin. "Wanta hear a dirty story?"

"I'm not sure," Roy said.

"Pig fell into a mud puddle!" Josh cried, and doubled over giggling.

Roy shook his head. "I never heard that one before. That's what I like about you, Josh—never a dull moment."

"You're sure you know what you're letting yourself in for?" Rae asked.

"No one ever said it was a snap being around a boy," Roy told her. "I guess you just learn as you go along."

She nodded. "I've got a lot of learning of my own to catch up on, now that you mention it."

THEY STOPPED IN Lincoln and bought Josh a soft drink. The pageant's dress rehearsal was in full swing, so they went over by the clapboard arena to watch Lloyd Parmalee and Rowdy practicing to be Pat Garrett and Billy the Kid.

There were maybe twenty or thirty tourists in the grandstands, observing the goings-on.

Down in the arena, Bill Maldonado and his crowd were showing off by performing rope tricks with their mounts: it was not yet time for them to turn into the posse that chased the Kid out of town.

.44's were going off right and left. Booming reports were audible from one end of the village to the other, as various local quick-draw artists practiced this or that shoot-from-the-hip technique. The noise imbued the day with a festive quality.

Lloyd Parmalee was about a foot too short to be Pat Garrett, but in the gunsmoke nobody noticed.

Chester Garcia, who owned the curio shop and played Deputy Bob Olinger, was taking it easy on a bench in the grandstands, drinking an Orange Fanta. There was ketchup smeared all over the front of his shirt to show where Billy had blown away his chest with a charge of buckshot. Chester had his Stetson tilted back on his head, and he was smoking a pipe. One of his little girls was sitting on his lap.

"Roy, are they shooting real bullets?" Josh asked.

"No," Roy said. "They're acting out a kind of story."

"What's the story about?"

"It deals with a young fellow who lived around here a hundred years ago. He was a cowboy and an outlaw, named Billy the Kid."

"Was he a good or a bad outlaw?"

"Depends on who you listen to," Roy said. "Some say he was terrible. Others claim different."

Suddenly, someone had burrowed up alongside Rae like a terrier. It was Rowdy Roth. He beamed at Rae, exposing that awful grin. "*Hi*, Rae! Lloyd an' me spotted you. We come to say hello."

"Hi, Rowdy," she said. "It's good to see you again." She gave him a hug and a kiss.

Lloyd came up and got a kiss, too. Looking abashed, he rubbed at the cheek that had been kissed, and said, "Heard you was back. Howdy, Roy."

Josh stared up at them through the hornrimmed spectacles. Lloyd and Rowdy were in their old-time costumes, and each had twin six-guns strapped to his hips.

"Say, you still want to go rodeoing?" Rowdy asked Rae. "I'm hittin' the circuit next month. Whyn't you and me an' Roy give it a whirl? We'll have us a time." He looked down. "Hey there! What's this you got?"

"This is my son," Rae said.

"I'll be durned! You got a son?"

"That's right."

"You hear that, Lloyd? Rae's got herself a boy." Rowdy bent over. "What's your name, son?"

"Joshua."

"I'm Rowdy Roth." They shook hands. "This here is Lloyd Parmalee. You want to go rodeoing with us?"

"Sure!"

"We'll teach you how to cowboy. How'd you like that?"

"Terrific."

"You going to stay around for a while?"

"I don't know," the boy said. "We're going camping."

"Up at Sawmill, I reckon," Rowdy said. "Well, that ain't so bad." Still smiling, he stared into Josh's eyes, courting him outrageously. "Y'know, me an' your momma an' Roy are old-time friends." He picked Josh up in his arms and set him on the top rung of a corral post. "If you want, we'll teach you how to make *do* around these parts! You like ridin' horses? Me an' Lloyd, we'll show you. You're a real whippersnapper. This here's good country for a kid. There's something goin' on *all* the time! Best life ever! You like guns? Me an' Lloyd, we'll teach you to shoot. Hey? You want to let one off?"

"Let what off?"

"You want to shoot one of my guns?" Rowdy set the boy back down on the ground, and with a wink toward Rae, drew one of his .44's and handed it to Josh. Rae said, "Be careful."

"Don't worry," Rowdy said, placing the big pistol in the boy's two hands. "Point it straight out in front of you." He helped Josh cock the pistol, and the boy, with both eyes squinched shut behind his glasses, pulled the trigger.

The pistol went off with a fearsome blast and a cloud of smoke. The boy opened his eyes and stared up at everybody. He blinked and said, "Wow!"

"That's why Lloyd insists on .44's for the pageant," Rowdy explained. "You can't beat a .44 blank for pure display. Lloyd handloads 'em with a secret combination of fuller's earth and Johnson's Baby Powder."

"I put in eighteen grains of Du Pont 2400 and top it with sealing wax," Lloyd said modestly. "At the muzzle, it'll blow apart a beer can, but out past six feet, it wouldn't hurt a fly."

Roy stood there, listening and enjoying the way the boy was taking it. Josh's expression was serious and attentive, as though he was trying to figure out how much of this was real and how much was pretend.

That in-between mind of the child.

Equally at home with make-believe and reality.

Roy could have pointed out that the real William Bonney had never, according to legend, carried a .44.

The Kid had always been partial to a .41 double-action Colt with bulldog grips. A quick and deadly little belt-gun, a Saturday-night special of that era, easily concealed, but powerful enough to cut down any man at close range.

Why spoil it for the boy? There was, after all, a certain kind of reality about today: guns and noise, and that strange, sweet-acrid taste-smell of smokeless gunpowder that smarted one's nostrils and at the same time filled the mouth with saliva—a strange smell, of violence and power and destruction.

Roy said nothing, merely kept silent, and watched to see what the boy would do next. It happened easily and naturally.

Josh turned to Lloyd. The old roofer-gunsmith, with his laconic style. Saying little, and at that murmuring softly, agonizingly shy in direct conversation with Rae, somehow crippled and ill at ease, as though the niceties of ordinary talk were something that had for his entire life escaped him. Very serious.

Josh, regarding all this through his hornrimmed spectacles, was serious, too, and perhaps even adoring. Squinting upward in the by-now blindingly hot sunlight: "Mister Parmalee? Are you a real cowboy?"

Lloyd thought this over. "I used to cowboy a little. That was long ago."

Rowdy said, "Whyn't you quit braggin' so much?"

The boy said, "You *look* like a cowboy."

Rowdy laughed. "Parmalee's death warmed over, but he's still *numero uno* around here." He glanced at Roy. "Say, feel like a drink?"

"There's wine in the car."

They all walked over to the jeep together and there they shared some Chablis. Josh said to Lloyd, "I bet you're tough."

"He was pretty mean in his time," Rowdy said.

Lloyd looked embarrassed. "Being tough don't mean nothing."

"Will you come see us?"

"I wouldn't mind that," Lloyd said. "When it's convenient."

Josh was staring at the tin badge pinned on Lloyd's deerskin vest. "Is that real?"

Lloyd looked down at it, and then at the boy. "Yes, it's real, son. I'm a deputy."

The boy turned to Rae. "You see? I bet he knows about everything."

"No, I don't," Lloyd told him. "If you're here when you're bigger, I can teach you about working. You'd have to be older. I'll show you roofing. Hardest work there is." He glanced at Rae. "I had three kid brothers. Helped raise 'em. That was some chore." And then, as though this outburst was too much, he added, "Fine boy you got."

"Thank you."

"Hang on to him."

"I intend to."

Lloyd nodded. Then he said something that was meaningless to her. "Don't worry—we'll keep an eye on things. Rowdy an' me."

"Good," she said.

He came as close as he could to blushing. The Adam's apple in his turkey neck bobbled. "It ain't nothing."

Roy and she and the boy left presently. Driving up to Honcho, she said, "What did he mean about him and Rowdy keeping an eye on things?"

"I had some trouble with Bill Maldonado," Roy explained.

She looked at him. "Serious?"

"It could have been. Don't worry about it, though. It's all settled."

Josh began talking about Lloyd and Rowdy and firing that big .44. "They really are cowboys, aren't they?"

Roy glanced over at the boy and smiled. "Why, sure, Josh. Lloyd and Rowdy are among the last, and the best."

THEY STOPPED AT Pearl's to pick up the food order.

She took one look at Josh and said, "Well, now . . . where'd you come from with all them freckles?"

"I come from California," he said, and treated her to that smile.

"This is my son, Josh," Rae explained.

"You don't say!"

"Josh, Mrs. Lowdermilk's a friend of Roy's," Rae said.

"Some people got more secrets than the rotten CIA," Pearl said sourly. She bent over to shake hands with the newcomer. "He's your son, you say?"

"That's right."

"So, this is the surprise you were talking about last week. Come into my kitchen where it's cool." The tall, old woman turned to Josh. "You must be awfully thirsty on a day like this. Are you thirsty?"

"I had a Seven-Up where we were before," Josh told her. "Everybody was shooting guns. I shot one, too."

"You didn't! Really?"

"We stopped down in Lincoln to watch the pageant," Roy explained.

They went into the trailer, and Pearl said to the boy, "You look half starved. Are you hungry?"

"A little."

"I figured so. Later, I'll take you out and show you my goats. You ever seen goats?"

"I think I have. On tv."

"How old are you?"

"Almost seven."

"You ever have a black-and-white?"

"What's that?"

"Oh, it's something that kids like, with vanilla ice cream and chocolate syrup," Pearl said. "You think maybe you could find room for something like that?"

"Sure."

"Well, then, you just get up here on this stool by me and watch."

He flashed that grin at her again, and then climbed onto the bar stool and propped his elbows on the formica counter. She began taking things out of the refrigerator and the freezer compartment. Then she rummaged around in an overhead cupboard until she found a tall, fluted crystal glass of the sort used by old-time drugstores. Rae said, "That looks like real art-deco! It must be fifty years old."

"I got a full set of eight," Pearl said, and, to the boy: "With a black-and-white, you start with vanilla, and build on it."

Roy said, "Pearl, I never knew you had a sweet tooth."

"On occasion, I'll put something else in my stomach besides that wine you live on," she said.

She worked slowly, as she always did in the kitchen, in no hurry at all.

Two scoops of vanilla went into the tall glass. Then chocolate syrup . . . quite a bit of it. Then a huge dollop of whipped cream from a pressurized can. He was growing more and more interested, while she seemed to be in less and less of a hurrying mood. She said, "That's the basic ingredients," and then frowned. "It don't look right yet, though. Does it look right to you?"

"It looks great," the boy said.

"Looks kind of naked, you ask me," Pearl said.

She got out a can of crushed walnuts and sprinkled a couple of spoonfuls over the whipped cream, and then inspected what she'd created. "It's coming along," she said, half to herself, and then went back to the refrigerator. "Maraschino cherries add a nice touch of color, don't you think?" she asked, placing several atop the walnuts. Then she poured some of the cherry syrup from the can. "That about does it."

"Pearl, he's liable to get sick eating that much," Roy said.

"He won't get sick," she said. And, to Josh: "Will you?"

"No," he said. She served him the black-and-white on a saucer and set a long-handled spoon and a paper napkin beside it. He said, "Thank you, Pearl."

"You sure know the way to a boy's heart," Roy said.

"I know all about little boys," Pearl said grumpily. "Just 'cause I never had kids, it don't follow that I don't know about 'em." She turned back to Josh: "D'you like ice cream goopy?"

"Sure."

"So do I. The goopier, the better. It's awful, having to wait so long for it to get soft, though, ain't it?"

"I like it when you can stir it around with a spoon and then drink it," Josh told her. "That's the best."

She nodded. He sat there, waiting for permission to begin, and she watched him expressionlessly. Finally, he said, "Can I start?"

"Oh, I suppose so," Pearl said. She glanced at Rae and said dryly, "I never yet seen 'em wait longer'n five seconds after it was set in front of 'em." She turned back to the boy. "Where'd you get that hat?"

"I found it."

"Well, in my house you take off your hat when you eat," she ordered. The hat came off, and he began working on the black-and-white. "What're you going to do with this boy?" she said to Rae.

"We're going up to Sawmill River."

"Well, whenever you get tired of having him around, I might buy him off you," Pearl said. "I might even go as high as a dollar ninety-five. I bet he'd be real handy to have around. That is, if I could afford to keep him in ice cream." She looked at Roy. "You fixing to spend the rest of the summer up there?"

"We may, Pearl."

"Ought to be fun. He'll keep the two of you busy." She glanced at the boy. "He's bright. No doubt about that. His manners ain't bad either. Whoever's had him been doing a pretty good job of bringing him up."

"He's been living with his grandparents," Rae said.

"Their name Ehrenson?"

"No. His name is Stein. Ehrenson's my maiden name."

"You mean you're married?"

"Divorced."

"Well, that's nice," Pearl said. "So. You were married."

Rae obviously was in a good mood; she was not about to let Pearl turn her day bad. She smiled and said, "Yes, by a rabbi, as a matter of fact."

"You don't say. You don't look Jewish."

"I'm not."

Pearl glanced at the boy. "So, that's why his name is Joshua. Well, it hooks up. I reckon it's the intent that counts. A rabbi presiding over the ceremony has to be pretty near as legal as a Lutheran minister, which is what I always had." She nodded. "Marriage is important. These days, it seems like nobody's got time for it. Everybody wants to be free."

"Lots of people don't want to be tied into a contract," Roy pointed out.

"So I've heard," she said dourly. "But that's small consolation to the man who's just been caught fishing without a license." She thought about this, and then lit a cigarette. "It's awful important for a child to have a real name. There's a reason for doing things right, else nobody would know who in hell was related to who. Look at all these young snotnoses today, ratting around from one end of the country to the other, with guitars and backpacks and nary a worry in the world. Roy, your father was no different. He never had a lick of sense either. You see what it comes to? Here! Let me show you something. It just came in the mail today."

She went out of the kitchen and down the hallway to her bedroom. In a moment she returned, holding a large, plastic coat of arms done in bright colors.

For a moment, Roy stared at it. And then he remembered.

It was from the genealogical outfit in Illinois he had sent off a twenty-five-dollar money order to, over a month ago. Thinking that it would be something that might please the old woman.

"You see this?" Pearl said to them. "This tells me who I am. I don't have any doubt about *that*. Some organization sent it to me as a gift, wasn't that something? Didn't cost a cent. I can't for the life of me figure out how they ever found out where I live. They also sent a chart made out of old paper, with my whole family tree on it. I'm going to have it framed. Why, it analyzes my entire background, and I don't mind admitting, I was awful curious to read what they had to say. Ain't this lovely! You know what? My maiden name—Grüber—goes clean back to Otto the Bald! He was a German king, over a thousand years ago. He ran most of Germany back then. Owned it flat out. 'Course *I* don't own any part of Germany, even if I am a grandniece eighty-seven times removed. I mean, I don't think I could collect on it if I put in a claim. But at least I know who I am and where my folks come from. That's what comes of doing things right and proper." She looked immensely pleased with herself. "I'm going to hang this right on that wall over there. Wait'll old Dalrymple sees it! She'll just be green with envy."

She carefully propped the plaque against her spice shelf, and then turned to the boy. A good part of the black-and-white had disappeared. She said, "It's gotten too goopy. Might as well throw out what's left."

"No, Pearl."

"You mean to say you *like* it that way?"

"Sure."

She reached out and laid one of her large work-roughened and callused hands on his head, tousling the thatch of wheat-colored hair. "Next time you come by, I'll show you how to make a banana split. Think you could live with that?"

"When?"

"Ask your Mom and Roy," she said. "If they forget, you come by anyway. You remind 'em, okay?"

Once again he flashed that big smile. "You're neat."

"Not many think so."

"I like you anyway."

She studied him for a long moment. Then she said, "Why, sweetheart, that's real nice. And I thank you." She got up and went out of the kitchen. They heard her blowing her nose in the bathroom. She came out presently, and said to Rae, "Well. You're lucky to have him."

"I know," Rae said.

Pearl shook her head, and suddenly, for a moment, she looked worn and old and said, "No, you don't . . . you'll never know." Then she pulled herself together. "Roy, your supplies are in the back of the truck."

"I'll get them," he said.

She turned to the boy. "Soon's you finish that, let's you and me feed the goats. We'll get a bucket of feed pellets."

"Okay. Do they bite?"

"They better not," Pearl said. "If they do, we'll just bite 'em right back."

Going up to Sawmill, the boy had a thousand questions. Why did the road twist and turn so? Why wasn't it paved? Where were all the people? Were there bears?

Roy answered as best he could.

At the narrow point in the road, he got out and unhooked the logging chain, explaining to Rae about the burning of Schmidt's Mercantile. "I don't think there'll be any more trouble," he added, and she said, "I hope so."

They drove on, passing the new signs he had posted: NO TRESPASSING. PRIVATE PROPERTY. STAY OUT.

When they reached Sawmill, Roy drove up Main Street so that the boy could see it. Josh said, "It's a whole town . . . with no people in it! Why aren't there people, Roy?"

"They're all gone, Josh," he said. "There's just us."

"Did anybody ever live here?"

"Lots of folks at one time."

"Where'd they go?"

"Some died. Others just went away. It was a long time ago."

"Are there ghosts?"

"Not really."

"I'll bet there are," the boy said. "Are they the scary kind?"

Roy smiled, and shook his head. "No. They're not scary at all."

"Are there kids here to play with?"

"No, Josh. You'll be the only boy in town."

"Were there ever any kids?"

"Yes, a long time ago," Roy said. "Actually, I was the last kid. When I was a little boy, my father used to bring me here."

"Why?"

"It was a good place to visit. We had fun."

"Is your father here now?"

"He's dead."

At the cabin they turned him loose to explore, with instructions to stay nearby. They brought in the cartons of food and the suitcases, and unpacked. Roy showed her the boy's bed, against the wall by the sheepherder stove. "Do you think this'll do?"

"It's fine."

"Lloyd has a little camping trailer at his house. I could have borrowed it but then I thought Josh might get lonesome or scared with nobody close at hand. When I was his age, I used to wake up at night sometimes."

"This'll be great," she said. Then she glanced at him. "What do you think of him?"

"Rae, he's a good boy."

"He likes you."

"I hope so." He thought for a moment. "Was there any trouble with his grandparents?"

"No," she said. "His grandfather cried, but then he said he'd always known I'd come for the boy, sooner or later. He said it wasn't a real surprise, and that he and Josh's grandmother had talked about it. Even so, they took it hard. They gave me some money. I didn't want to take it, but they insisted."

"Did they ask about your plans?"

"Yes," she said, looking at him. "I told them there was a man I cared about and that we were all going to live together on a ranch up in the mountains. That sounded all right to them. I couldn't describe this town or the life, so I called it a ranch. They want me to keep in touch."

"Of course. He means a lot to them."

"Yes."

They made a light supper, and then put the boy to bed early. He complained about this a little, but they could see that he was overtired and already half asleep. After he'd been tucked in, they sat with him for a while. On the pillow beside him was a stuffed toy animal for company—a rabbit. The boy said, "He sleeps with me every night."

"Does he have a name?" Roy asked.

"I call him Jim."

"That's a good name for a rabbit. Did you have fun today?"

"Sure."

Roy said, "Aren't you going to take that hat off?"

The boy thought this over. Finally, he said, "I'd just as soon not."

"All right."

"Roy, what are we going to do tomorrow?"

"Anything you want to."

"Can we go see Pearl again?"

"Maybe in a couple of days."

In a few minutes, he was asleep. Rae said, "Isn't it something, the way they just fall off like that."

"He's had a long day."

The twilight was still hanging on so they took some wine and glasses and went outside to sit in the quiet evening. They stayed there for quite a while together, smoking and talking very little as the valley grew darker. Roy had left the door of the cabin open, and the transistor radio was playing music with the volume turned low. He said, "How do you feel?"

"Tired, but wonderful." In the fading light he could barely make out her face but he could see that she was smiling. She said, "You?"

He nodded. "Great."

"I can't tell you how good it feels to be back."

"I'm glad."

She lit a cigarette, and for a minute the two of them were silent. Then she said, "I'm a little scared."

"About what?"

"Everything."

"Don't be."

"I'm worried about whether I'm doing the right thing. Responsibility . . . it really frightens me."

"I know. You just have to do whatever you think best. For yourself and for him. I have a hunch that's what most parents do . . . play it by ear."

"Roy, I don't want to mess this boy up."

"You won't. I'd bet on that." He thought about this. "You'll be okay with him. And he'll be fine with you."

"You know, I want you to be happy."

In the dark, he smiled. "Rae, I couldn't ask for anything more. That's the truth."

"But what'll happen to us?"

"I don't know. We'll see."

"You're in an odd mood. I can feel it," she said. "You've got something on your mind."

He smiled again. "I suppose so."

"What?"

"Oh, different things," he said. "Pearl today. She was so excited about that coat of arms. I sent for it, you know. It was a mail-order pitch that came in a month ago. So I put her name on it, with a money order. I thought it'd be something she'd get a kick out of. I didn't think she'd take it seriously."

"Well, what about it?"

"Listening to her, something fell into place, that's all. I can't put it into words."

"Was it something good or bad?"

"It was good," he said.

Now it was dark except for the stars, and then it grew brighter again as a nearly full moon rose above the slopes, flooding the valley in a cold, silvery light. Rae yawned and then stretched. "I've had it."

"You better get to bed."

"You coming?"

"Not yet. You go ahead. I want to sit out here for a bit by myself," he said.

"I'll stay with you, if you want."

"No, that's all right."

She got up and came over, bent, and kissed him, one arm draped loosely around his shoulders. "It's getting cool. You want your sweater?"

"I'm all right. I'll come in soon."

"Good night."

" 'Night, Rae."

IT WAS PEACEFUL in the bright moonlight. Time passed. He sat there quietly, smoking and drinking. When a cigarette burned down to the filter, he flipped it between thumb and middle finger, and then, after a while, lit another, the spurt of the paper match sounding loud in the silence.

Except for small night noises it was very quiet. An owl hooted somewhere, and, faintly, he heard the movement of some animal down at the pond, perhaps a deer or an elk come to drink.

He could feel the presence of the sleeping woman and boy in the cabin. It was a sensation, very tangible, and he liked the mood that it built up in him, a mixture of self-satisfaction and contentedness.

He poured another glass of wine and thought again about the whole business of Pearl and her coat of arms. In a way, it was silly, but then again it was something that was important to her.

Then a fleeting echo of drunken Herman Gutierrez came to him. That poor man. All the words that had never been spoken between him and his wife, Bertha. And the empty life they had passed together.

He had done one good thing in his life. He'd given his own

name and had provided a home and an upbringing to Roy's father.

From the way Uncle Walter described him, Roy had an image of an ordinary sort of man who sat alone in his room a great deal with a bottle of whiskey and perhaps a newspaper or a book to read.

What difference did it make, really, if the gunfighter, Ephraim Munger, was Roy's real grandfather?

It made no difference at all.

What counted was Herman Gutierrez never saying a word about what had or had not happened—simply keeping his mouth shut and giving an infant boy a name and a home.

And what counted now was another boy, asleep in the cabin, with a stuffed toy animal for company.

Maybe the memory of Sawmill River Flats—this summer, and, with luck, other summers to come—might stay in this boy's mind for the rest of his life. Memories . . . of a warm and golden time with a man and a woman who cared about him . . . a springtime childlike idyll.

Sweet childhood innocence. What better time to be alive and to be loved? To know that all's well with the world.

Yes. All's well with the world.

SITTING IN THE moonlight, Roy thought of his father. Once again, he couldn't help wondering what had led George Gutierrez to devote so many years of his life to bringing him up in the fashion he had. There were only a few clues to this riddle—a vague hint or two.

One was that despite Uncle Walter's dour opinions, Roy had a strong hunch that his father had gotten a lot of enjoyment out of having a boy around.

It might be, too, that the self-educated naturalist and amateur scientist in him had risen to Roy's presence, as a kind of challenge. He could have asked himself, "How will this child turn out? What will become of him? How best to equip this boy, to arm him against the vicissitudes that will be his lot?"

His father might have been a much better parent if he had not been an alcoholic and a cripple and a footloose wanderer.

But then, if he had been anything else, he would not have been Roy's father at all.

If he had failed to teach Roy to be practical or cunning or even clever, it was because George Gutierrez himself was a stranger to these traits. The most generous thing that could be said of him was that he respected others and at the same time enjoyed appreciating whatever life had to offer him.

How could these qualities be taught or passed on? Once, in Roy's fourteenth year, George Gutierrez had taken him aside and attempted to instruct him in the ways of the world. The better to formulate his thoughts, George wrote an entry in one of the notebooks, and then asked his son to read it. It was the closest he had ever come to what used to be called a "serious" father-and-son talk.

Roy stood up and went into the cabin now, feeling in the dark for the flashlight that stood on the shelf. He found it, turned on the bright beam, and went to the footlocker that contained the past. There he located the notebook he was looking for and, not wanting to take a chance on waking Rae or the boy, tiptoed back outside.

Even with the moonlight he had to use the flash to find the exact page. The script was badly faded, and in places almost impossible to read:

Be your own man [George Gutierrez had written]. *Live by your personal values, not someone else's. Do your best to be honest and upright—no one will ever fault you for trying your best. Meet a man half way, but go no further. Life is short. Have fun and adventures. If something good comes your way, share it. You'll find yourself enjoying it a lot more. Don't be stingy. A tightwad has a poverty of soul. Pay bills on time—the hardest reputation to get rid of is that of being a poor credit risk. Travel all you can. Brush your teeth three times a day. Open your eyes and observe what's happening around you. This is a splendid land. There is nobility in man but it's not easy to find. Watch out for women who swing their hips a lot when they walk. Try to learn something new every day. Keep an eye on people who go out of their way to do you a favor. Nine times out of ten it's them-selves they're helping, at your expense. Before you laugh at people, remember that they may be laughing twice as hard at you. A lie invariably comes back to you in spades. Don't curse prejudice because, like the Democrats, it's here to stay. Prayer is for fools, but don't forget that anyone who gets scared enough is liable to be foolish. Your best critic is yourself. No one else in the world knows you half so well. Think straight. Never be afraid to laugh at yourself because that's a sign of maturity and intelligence—the man who takes himself seriously is in for a shocking disappointment. Don't fret about the hereafter. It will take care of itself. Honor yourself and those you love. In itself, that is no small task.*

He closed the notebook and poured another drink.

In a way, the responsibility of raising a boy might not be so difficult for him. After all, his father had taught him how.

Because of that man, the past would always be with Roy: the great, beautiful southwest, and its people. George Gutierrez had given him all that.

In time, Roy might leave this place again, taking her and the boy. But they would return. It's always easier to leave when you know you have a place to come back to.

HE IS A little drunk now from the wine, and in his mind there is a memory, a faded and ancient recollection that is almost like an old dream—something that might never have happened, really —but he knows that this was never a dream, it *did* happen.

The memory goes so:

IT IS NIGHT. A clear, starry night.

He and his father and Uncle Walter are seated around a small campfire.

They are off somewhere on the high plains, on one of their endless explorations. All about them it is dark. There are no lights, no houses, no town, no sounds except their own, although in one direction, far beyond the edge of the horizon, there is a vast pale glow in the sky from some town or city, perhaps Las Cruces, he cannot remember exactly. It lights up the sky like an awful, distant conflagration.

Supper is long done with, hours before, but still they have not begun getting ready to turn in.

His father and Walter sit by the fire drinking, and he is with them. He and his father have a single, heavy blanket draped across their shoulders, to fend off the night chill at their backs.

His father is feeling very good because he and Walter have been drinking all evening. George Gutierrez is in one of his marvelous moods, good-natured and ready to spoof himself, and feeling at ease with the world.

He is smoking a handmade cigarette, and from time to time he glances up at the night sky, as if curious to see what the great constellations are up to, but the glare of the fire makes them invisible. Occasionally, a piney knot explodes, and then a trail of fiery sparks shoots skyward.

Suddenly, with an expert flick of his finger, he pitches what is left of his cigarette into the flames, and rises.

The blanket slips from Roy's shoulders. George pauses a moment, smiling fondly down at him. He stoops, readjusting the blanket, tucking it around Roy: "Stay warm, darling."

Then, favoring his bad leg, he hobbles into the circle of light cast by the flames and stands very erect, striking a declamatory pose, rather melodramatic, and, fueled by whatever it is that he has been drinking on this evening, recites a poem in the old Middle English language, in the ancient way, straight out of Geoffrey Chaucer, where the vowels and inflections are stressed in different, queer fashions, the way words were spoken in our language many years ago:

> *When that Aprille with his shoures soote*
> *The droghte of Marche hath perced to the rote,*
> *And bathed every veyne in swich licour,*
> *Of which vertu engendered is the ff our.*

When Zephirus eek with his swete breeth
Inspired hath in every holt and heeth
The tendre croppes, and the younge sonne
Hath in the Ram his half course y-ronne,
    And smale fowles maken melodye,
That slepen all the night with open ye.

    So picketh ham nature in hir courage
    Than longen folk to go'n pilgramages.